Dear Reader,

At Harlequin we are proud of our long tradition of supporting causes that are of concern to women. The Harlequin More Than Words program, our primary philanthropic initiative, is dedicated to celebrating and rewarding ordinary women who make extraordinary contributions to their community. Each year we ask our readers to submit nominations for the Harlequin More Than Words award, from which we select five very deserving recipients.

We are pleased to present our five 2008 award recipients to you in this, our annual *More Than Words* anthology. These real-life heroines provide great comfort to those they help. And we hope that by sharing their stories with you, we will give you comfort in knowing that these women are working so hard for those who need it most. With the help of some of our most acclaimed authors—Linda Lael Miller, Sherryl Woods, Curtiss Ann Matlock, Jennifer Archer and Kathleen O'Brien—we are pleased to publish these five inspiring stories. These authors have donated their time and creativity to this project, and all proceeds will be reinvested in the Harlequin More Than Words program, further supporting causes that are of concern to women.

I hope you enjoy this book as much as we enjoy publishing it! The women highlighted in these pages, and the fictional novellas penned by our authors, are truly inspirational.

Please visit www.HarlequinMoreThanWords.com for more information, or to submit a nomination for next year's book.

Sincerely,

Donna Hayes
Publisher and CEO
Harlequin Enterprises

More Than Words
VOLUME 4

LINDA LAEL MILLER

SHERRYL WOODS

CURTISS ANN MATLOCK

JENNIFER ARCHER

KATHLEEN O'BRIEN

HARLEQUIN®

TORONTO • NEW YORK • LONDON
AMSTERDAM • PARIS • SYDNEY • HAMBURG
STOCKHOLM • ATHENS • TOKYO • MILAN • MADRID
PRAGUE • WARSAW • BUDAPEST • AUCKLAND

ISBN-13: 978-0-373-83622-2
ISBN-10: 0-373-83622-8

MORE THAN WORDS

www.eHarlequin.com

Printed in U.S.A.

CONTENTS

~Stories Inspired by Real-Life Heroines~

ment—and a summer camp that siblings can also attend, giving them the opportunity not only to participate, but to witness and experience firsthand their sibling's accomplishments. In addition to riding lessons, there are opportunities to groom horses or help with tack.

Classes—limited to four riders—are held every afternoon and evening and all day Saturday. Stretching exercises are part of the therapy—reaching toward a horse's ears, for example. One mother of a nine-year-old Down syndrome child says just learning to hold the reins was a big challenge for her daughter. "She couldn't do that at first. Now she steers, trots, and posts. She has made gains socially and emotionally, too. It's such a happy place."

Learning letters of the alphabet is often an integral part of the exercise, as well as picture and color recognition ("Stop your horse at red"). An army of volunteers assist—some 150 each week. Usually three people are needed just to help a single child, one leading the horse and the other two walking on each side.

Instruction is adapted to meet individual needs. Jeanne supported an educator, and past executive director, in developing the Achievement Rainbow Program (now distributed to therapeutic riding stables all over the world), a curriculum that allows the children to have fun learning while achieving therapeutic goals associated with the rainbow colors.

SARI would be a remarkable accomplishment by any measure, but Jeanne, now 84, remains a dedicated board member and a fund-raiser who works tirelessly to help raise the nearly $300,000 a year that it costs to operate SARI Therapeutic Riding. Four major fund-raising events are held each year, including a night at the theater in March (Jeanne invariably has all the tickets sold by Christmas, says SARI's executive director), and the popular Bowling for Ponies event. Through Jeanne's extensive contacts, support comes from corporations, associations and community clubs, as well as individuals. "When I phone someone now, sometimes they don't even say hello, just 'What can I do for you?'" she laughs.

Clearly, an enterprise on this scale involves crucial health and safety issues. In the eighties, Jeanne helped form two associate bodies: the Canadian Therapeutic Riding Association (CanTRA), responsible for insurance matters and a certification program for instructors, and the Ontario Therapeutic Riding Association (OnTRA), which provides networking, community education and fund-raising support for SARI and other therapeutic-riding facilities in Ontario.

Jeanne is now so deeply involved with SARI that she can't imagine life without it. "I guess I'll have to turn over the reins at some point," she says, "but it's not easy." Then she adds, in classic understatement, "Not that others couldn't do it, but perhaps they don't have my drive!" Indeed. The mere contemplation of her activities and energy would floor most people half her age. And she's not done yet. She looks forward to SARI's thirtieth-anniversary celebrations in June 2008, by which time, she reveals, the barn is to come down and the arena extended. She is already engaged in a campaign to raise the million dollars these plans will cost.

For Jeanne, the work is energizing—and endlessly rewarding.

She is buoyed by the children's achievements, and the miracles that occasionally occur: One child whose parents were told he would never walk is now walking, after just two years at SARI. And a former student, wheelchair-bound and now in his thirties, told Jeanne he has never forgotten the thrill, when first placed on a horse, of being able to look down at people instead of always seeing them looking down at him. Memories of Sari, and of children like these, Jeanne says, have enriched her life beyond measure.

For more information, visit www.sari.ca or write SARI Therapeutic Riding, 12659 Medway Road, R.R. #1, Arva, Ontario, Canada N0M 1C0.

LINDA LAEL MILLER
⌦ Queen of the Rodeo ⌫

❧—LINDA LAEL MILLER—❧

The daughter of a town marshal, Linda Lael Miller is a *New York Times* bestselling author of more than sixty historical and contemporary novels that reflect her love of the West. Raised in Northport, Washington, the self-confessed "barn goddess" now lives in Spokane, Washington. Her most recent *New York Times* bestsellers include *McKettrick's Luck, McKettrick's Pride, McKettrick's Heart* and *The Man from Stone Creek*. Dedicated to helping others, Linda personally finances her Linda Lael Miller Scholarships for Women, awarded annually to women seeking to improve their lot in life through education. More information about Linda, her novels and her scholarships is available at www.lindalaelmiller.com. She also loves to hear from readers by mail at P.O. Box 19461, Spokane, WA 99219.

CHAPTER
~ONE~

The old horse stepped through a shimmering curtain of angled rain, stately as a unicorn for all its diminutive size, muddy hide, overgrown hooves, tangled mane and too-prominent ribs.

Callie Dorset stood in front of her tilted rural mailbox, one of a row of them jutting from the ground like crooked teeth, a sheaf of bills and flyers clasped in one hand. She stared, momentarily transfixed, heedless of the downpour.

Cherokee?

It couldn't be. Her childhood pony had been sold off years ago, along with most of the family ranch. Taken somewhere far away, in a gleaming horse trailer from an auction house, never to return.

And yet here he was.

Callie stuck the mail back into the box, slogged down one side of the grassy ditch separating her from the horse and up the other, then stood close to the rusty barbed-wire fence, spellbound.

"Cherokee?" she said, aloud this time, the name barely audible over the fire-sound of the relentless spring rain.

He nickered, nuzzled her shoulder.

Callie felt almost faint, stricken with a hopeless joy. Her hand shook as she reached out to caress his soft, pink-spotted nose.

She repeated his name, wonderstruck.

Blinked a couple of times, in case she was seeing things.

Somehow, he had found his way back.

But how?

Behind her, snug in the ancient Blazer, Callie's seven-year-old daughter, Serena, rolled down the passenger-side window. "Mom!" she shouted, in her sometimes slurred, always exuberant voice. "You're getting *wet!*"

Callie turned, drenched with rain and tears, and smiled. Nodded. "Shut the window," she called back. "You'll catch cold."

Serena's round face clouded with concern. Her exotic, slanted eyes widened. "Doesn't that horse have a house to live in?" she asked, scanning the pasture, which was empty except for a few gnarled apple trees, remnants of an orchard planted so long ago that only ghosts could recall it as it had once been, green-leaved and flourishing with fruit. An old claw-footed bathtub served as a water trough, and someone had dumped a bale of hay nearby.

"Serena," Callie said, trying to sound stern and not fooling the child for a moment.

Serena closed the window, but she watched from behind the silvery sheen of steam and water droplets, troubled.

Callie turned back to Cherokee. Stroked his coarse forelock, trying to find it within herself to leave him—again—here in the cold gloom of an ordinary afternoon, and failing utterly.

But she had to do it.

She had to take Serena home. Start supper. Try to figure out how to pay all those bills, lying limp and soggy in the mailbox.

As if he understood her dilemma, Cherokee nudged her once more in the shoulder, then turned and plodded slowly away to stand, distant, hide steaming with moisture, under one of the lonely apple trees.

Callie ran the sleeve of her denim jacket across her face and oriented herself to Serena, her North Star. She retrieved the bills and the flyers from the mailbox, sniffling, and got behind the wheel of the Blazer, cranking up the heat.

"You're *wet*, Mom," Serena reiterated sagely, visibly relaxing now that Callie was back in the car.

Callie tried to smile, wanting to reassure the child, but fell short. She'd seen so much loss in her thirty-one years—her parents, most of the homestead, Denny—and Cherokee. There were times when it was impossible to pretend it didn't matter, all that sorrow, even for Serena's sake.

Callie looked back once more, knowing she shouldn't, and saw her old friend watching her. She bit her lower lip, then shoved the Blazer into gear and made a wide turn in the mud of the road, headed for home.

The house was small, its shingles gray, its porch slanting a little to one side, like the mailbox she'd just left. The roof needed patching, and the yard was overgrown, but the windows glowed with warm welcome, because Callie had left the lights on when she drove to town to pick Serena up after school. It was an extravagance, burning electricity that way, but she was glad she'd done it.

Inside, she tossed the mail onto the antique table beside the front door and peeled off her wet jacket. Though considerably drier than Callie, Serena shook herself like a dog just climbing out of a lake, laughing.

She was such a happy child, in spite of so many things.

"Cocoa!" Serena crowed. "Let's have cocoa, with *marshmallows!*"

"Good idea," Callie agreed, bending to kiss the top of her daughter's head. Serena's hair was chestnut-brown, just like Denny's had been. She had his green eyes, too. "Just let me change."

She helped Serena out of her pink nylon coat, hung it on the peg next to the jean jacket.

Five minutes later, wearing slippers and a bathrobe, her blond, chin-length hair toweled into disarray comical enough to make her daughter point and laugh, Callie met Serena in the tiny kitchen at the back. Serena had already got the milk out of the refrigerator, taken the marshmallows from a pantry shelf and placed two mugs carefully on the table.

"Who does he belong to?" Serena asked.

Callie, busy measuring cocoa powder into a saucepan, stopped, turned to look at her only child, now sitting in her usual chair at the table, legs swinging.

"The horse," Serena clarified.

Callie's throat thickened painfully. "The Martins, I guess," she said. She didn't know her neighbors well; they were renters, according to the local grapevine, and not the sort to mix. When they'd moved in a few months ago, at the tail end of a long, ragged winter, Callie had made a chicken casserole, and she and Serena had gone over to welcome them, wending their way between U-Haul trucks to knock at the front door. No one had answered, and Serena, hoping for a playmate her own age, had been gravely disappointed.

"He's lonesome," Serena said sadly.

Callie's eyes burned. She was standing in a warm kitchen, with her daughter, the person she loved most in all the world, but her heart was still out there in the rain, under the dripping limbs of an apple tree. How had Cherokee come to belong to those people? What hard, winding, convoluted road had led him back, so close, but not-quite-home? He must have arrived recently, or she'd have seen him as she drove to town.

She couldn't speak, so she merely nodded, acknowledging Serena's remark, and went back to her cocoa-making. After the hot chocolate came supper, the beans-and-franks combo Serena loved, and "homework." Serena attended a special education program, with only six other children at the local elementary school. Two, including Serena, had Down syndrome; the others were mildly autistic. Callie was grateful for the program and the people who ran it, underfunded though it was. It gave Serena a place to go, something to be part of, in the larger world, and made it possible for Callie to earn a living.

Not that waiting tables at Happy Dan's Café was much of a living, but it kept the electricity on and the property taxes paid and food in the refrigerator, at least, and all the customers were long-time friends, people she had always known. She had to do a lot of juggling financially, but Callie didn't feel sorry for herself, and neither did anybody else who mattered.

Sure, the roof of the ranch house leaked and the old barn out back looked as though it might fall over at any moment. She had to shuffle the bills like a deck of cards and deal a sparse hand to be paid every month.

But she had Serena, and that made her rich.

She and Serena washed and dried and put away the dishes after supper. Then Serena did her homework, had her bath and put on her favorite flannel pajamas and crawled into bed with her teddy bear. Callie read her a story, listened to her prayers—*"please give the poor horse a house to live in"*—tucked her in and kissed her good-night.

All the while, she thought of Cherokee.

She didn't want to call Luke Banner, but it was all she could think of to do. He was the only veterinarian in the small eastern Washington town of Parable, and if anybody knew anything about the old horse that had turned up, as if by conjuring, in the Martins' pasture, it would be him.

He'd been as much a part of her childhood as Cherokee, Luke had. He'd been Denny's best friend, and hers, too—after Denny, of course. One summer, between their junior and senior years of high school, when Denny was away working on an uncle's wheat farm, Callie and Luke had gone to a dance together, just the two of them, and kissed under a bright moon, and for a while after that, sick with guilt, Callie had believed she was in love with Luke.

Then Denny had come home, good-natured, trusting Denny. Things had returned to normal—on the surface, at least. Deep down, though, something had changed, and Luke withdrew quietly from the circle of three. They graduated, and Luke went away to college. Denny took a part-time job at the sawmill in Parable and signed up for extension classes in computer science. Callie waited tables at Happy Dan's, taught herself to make jewelry and watched helplessly as her widowed father fell slowly away from her, like the outlying regions of the ranch that had been in his family for three generations.

After her dad's death, Callie and Denny were married, and the two of them had tried hard to turn the old house into the home it had never really been.

Denny had done well in his computer classes, and Callie had begun to sell some of her jewelry, a few pieces online but mostly over the counter at Happy Dan's, to tourists and a few generous locals, and they'd sat nights around the kitchen table, drawing up plans.

So many plans.

They'd replace the roof on the house and shore up the barn. Get Callie a horse to ride, because she'd never stopped missing Cherokee, have some kids.

The horse never materialized. Seven long years of hoping had passed before Callie got pregnant; she'd miscarried twice before Serena came along.

Sweet, angelic Serena.

Literally a gift from God.

But in Callie's experience, God gave with one hand and took away with the other. Serena had been barely three months old when Denny was killed in a car accident on his way home from a job interview.

There hadn't been much insurance—just enough to pay Denny's funeral expenses, with a very few dollars left over, and those had quickly gone for groceries and the special needs of a Down syndrome baby.

"Hello?" The voice sounded impatient, jarring Callie out of the sad mental maze she'd drifted into.

She stiffened, clutching the telephone receiver in her hand, pressing it hard against her ear.

"Hello," Luke repeated.

Callie cleared her throat, blushing. "Dr. Banner?"

"Speaking," Luke said.

"This is Callie Dorset."

Silence. Luke had been back in Parable for several months by then and, small as the town was, he and Callie had tacitly avoided each other the whole while. Callie could not have said why, exactly—they'd never had a falling-out or anything like that. It was just—awkward. So many things to say, and no way to put them into words.

"Callie." He said her name gruffly. "What can I do for you?"

Callie closed her eyes, but Luke's image was branded into her mind just the same. Longish blond hair, blue eyes, rangy frame.

Why had she called him? Why not simply knock on the Martins' door again and ask about Cherokee?

Because she'd known they wouldn't answer.

And because something inside her wanted to hear Luke's voice.

"Callie?" Luke prompted.

"There's an old horse," she began, and then couldn't figure out how to go on from there, and so went silent again.

"An old horse," Luke repeated. "What horse? Where?"

Callie swallowed hard. "Next door to my place."

"The Martins," Luke said, and now there was an edge to his tone. "You know them?"

"I *knew* them. They moved out a few weeks ago, Callie—owing a pile of rent to old Mrs. Payton."

"Oh," Callie murmured, at a loss. "Maybe they're coming back for Cherokee, then."

"Doubtful," Luke replied. "They left their dog in my kennel, here at the clinic, along with the four pups she had a couple of days after she arrived. And I don't think there's going to be a happy reunion."

Callie, standing in her kitchen, dragged a chair over near the wall phone and sank into it. "He's over there alone, then," she fretted. If she'd had anyone to stay with Serena, she'd have gone out there into the darkness, rain or no rain, and thrown a halter on Cherokee. Led him home to stand in her own rickety barn. Found a way to buy him some hay and oats, run a hose in to fill the old trough.

"Is he sick?"

"Thin," Callie answered. "I could see his ribs, and his hooves need trimming, too."

Luke was quiet for a few moments, then he said, "I'd better call the animal control people. My barn is full at the moment, or I'd take him myself."

"He could live here," Callie heard herself say. Her heart fluttered in her throat. *He could come home.*

"I'd better have a look at him, just the same," Luke said.

"I can't pay you," Callie said, to get it over with.

"I didn't ask you to," Luke replied.

After that, the conversation faltered and eventually wound down to goodbye.

Callie barely slept that night.

The next morning after breakfast, Callie drove Serena to school and saw Cherokee still standing under his apple tree as they passed. The storm had moved on, but the grass sparkled with moisture and the sunlight was dazzling.

"Poor horse," Serena said, her lower lip jutting out a little.

Callie reached over to pat her arm. "He'll be all right," she said, hoping it was true. She'd already called Happy Dan's and switched shifts with another waitress, so that she could have the day off to get the barn ready for Cherokee, but she wasn't about to raise Serena's hopes until it was a done deal. Too many things might go wrong: the Martins could return for their horse, or they might have sold him to someone, or Luke might change his mind and call in animal control.

After she'd walked Serena into the school building, Callie returned to the Blazer and headed for the feed store, spending a full day's tips on a few bales of hay, a bag of grain, a sturdy new halter and lead rope, a grooming brush and a currycomb.

When she rounded the bend skirting the Martin place, there was Luke's truck and fancy horse trailer, parked alongside the road. She drew up behind and got out to watch as he led Cherokee slowly down the slope of the pasture, toward an open gate.

Luke approached, Cherokee plodding along at his side. He nodded to Callie but didn't smile. "He looks sound," Luke said. "Needs a little fattening up, though." He paused, looked her over. "You're sure about this, Callie? It's not cheap, keeping a horse."

Callie flushed, at least on the inside, and lifted her chin. "I can manage," she said, not knowing how she would.

Luke handed her Cherokee's lead rope and opened the back of the horse trailer, pulled the ramp down. "Don't go getting all insulted," he said. "It's a lot of work and pretty expensive, that's all I meant."

She stroked Cherokee's long neck, and let her pride-stiffened spine soften a little. "He was mine once," she said, though she hadn't meant to. "It's like a miracle that he's back, after all this time."

"I remember," Luke said. He took the lead rope back and led Cherokee up into the trailer, secured him there and muttered a word of encouragement, man to horse. Then he climbed down again, raised the ramp and shut the trailer doors. "There's a question of ownership here, Callie," he said, facing her. He wore jeans, battered boots, a blue work shirt and an old cowboy hat, pushed to the back of his head. "Even though it seems they've abandoned him, the Martins could still press some kind of claim. Don't get too attached."

Callie nodded, looked away. She remembered the day Cherokee had been taken away to the auction, only three days after she'd ridden him in a local parade, reigning as that year's queen of the Parable Rodeo, and wondered if she could bear it if it happened again.

Luke hesitated, then laid a hand on her shoulder. "How are you, Callie?" he asked gruffly. "You're getting by all right?"

Getting by was what Callie was good at.

Coping.

Making do.

Putting a brave face on things.

"I'm fine," she said.

That was when he flashed the old grin, the one she remembered. The one that made the ground tilt under her feet, like some crazy carnival ride about to spin off its base, with her still aboard and scrambling for balance.

"Let's get this horse over to your place," he said.

A few minutes later, Callie was parking the Blazer by her barn, and seeing it the way it must have looked to Luke. The boards were weathered and the roof sagged. The door hung from rusted hinges, and she hadn't had a chance to rake out the stalls or clean and fill the water trough.

Like as not, Luke would say something meant to be polite, then get back in his truck and drive off, without ever unloading Cherokee from the trailer.

She got out of the Blazer and stood waiting for him, shoulders squared, and ran sweat-dampened palms down the thighs of her jeans. Worked up a smile as he swung down out of his truck.

Waited nervously while he assessed the barn.

Inside the trailer, Cherokee stirred impatiently, as if he knew he'd come home, this time for sure, and was anxious to get on with things.

"I guess it's been hard without Denny around to see to the place," Luke said.

"It's been hard," Callie confirmed, but that was all she was willing to give him. She could tolerate a lot of things, but Luke Banner's pity wasn't among them.

She felt relief when he unlatched the doors of the horse trailer, pulled the ramp down again and went inside for Cherokee. In fact, she barely refrained from doing a little victory dance.

When was the last time she'd wanted to do that?

Cherokee nickered and tossed his head once he'd descended from the trailer. Stood looking around, remembering.

Callie put both arms around the animal's neck and hugged him, out of sheer joy, and when she let him go, Luke was getting equipment out of his truck. A metal kit of some kind, and some tools.

Callie opened the back of the Blazer and tugged at one of the hay bales stuffed inside.

"Leave it, Callie," Luke said. "I'll do that."

She knew how stubborn Luke could be, and he was doing her a favor, after all, so she tamped down her pride and gave some ground. "Okay," she replied, and went into the barn to rake out a stall for Cherokee.

Luke brought him inside, looked around. "The old place has held together pretty well," he said, surprising Callie. "Not that it couldn't use a little work."

Callie's cheeks burned, and she went on with her raking. Her barn wasn't fancy, like the one on Luke's ranch on the other side of town. But it had space for an abandoned horse, and it sure beat leaving the animal standing in a lonely pasture, with only an apple tree to shelter him from inclement weather.

They worked in companionable silence for a long time, Callie cleaning up the floor and then swabbing out the water trough in the best stall, Luke clipping Cherokee's hooves and then filing them smooth.

That done, Luke examined the horse again and gave him a shot.

Callie went into the house briefly to put a pot of coffee on to brew.

When she came outside again, Luke was carrying the last of the hay into the barn. Cherokee stood contentedly in his stall, munching on a handful of grain Luke had given him in the bottom of an old bucket.

"There's coffee," Callie said, suddenly shy. She'd have taken the new brush and groomed Cherokee, but she'd have had to pass Luke to do it, since he was blocking the way into the stall, and she wasn't quite brave enough to do that.

"Sounds good," Luke replied, when she'd been hoping he'd say thanks, but he had to get back to work since he had a veterinary practice to run.

She nodded and hurried back inside the house, bringing the coffee outside, in the same mugs she and Serena had used for their cocoa the night before. His black, hers with cream and sugar.

You remembered, his eyes said as he took the first sip of the hot, strong brew. He could smile with those eyes, not even moving his mouth.

"Thank you, Luke," Callie said, to get over the awkwardness of the moment.

"All in a day's work." He lifted his mug in a little toast.

"You must have a lot of animals to look after," she said.

"Here's my hat, what's my hurry?" Luke teased.

Callie relaxed a little. "I have a daughter," she told him, and then wondered why she'd blurted those particular words. Parable was small, and everybody knew about Serena—including Luke Banner.

"I wish I did," Luke said. Rumor had it that he and his elegant wife, Roberta, had divorced soon after he decided to come back to Parable and take over his dad's thriving veterinary practice so his parents could retire. They traveled a lot now.

Luke's tone finally registered; he'd spoken so wistfully that Callie wondered if children had been an issue in the disintegration of his marriage, on top of the unpopular move from Seattle to Podunk, but she didn't know Luke well enough to ask him such a personal question. Not anymore, anyway.

"Serena's the best thing that ever happened to me," Callie said, because it was true, and because she wanted him to know she'd never regretted having her little girl for so much as a moment, even though they'd known about the Down syndrome, she and Denny, early in the pregnancy.

"I've seen her once or twice," Luke said. "You've got every right to be proud."

Callie frowned slightly. If Luke had seen Serena, he'd seen her, too, since she and her daughter were always together except during the day, when Serena was at school. Why hadn't he approached? Said hello, at least?

She didn't realize she'd spoken aloud until Luke answered her.

"Why didn't you?" he countered. And he wasn't smiling, with his mouth or with his eyes.

Flustered, Callie didn't know what to say. She took another sip of coffee and almost choked on the stuff.

Luke emptied his cup and handed it to her. "I'd better get moving," he said. "You wouldn't want a puppy, would you?"

Callie was a moment catching up. "A puppy?"

"I've got four of them to find homes for," he said. "Once they're weaned, of course."

Callie remembered the dog the Martins had left behind; Luke had mentioned it on the phone the night before. What kind of people could just turn their backs and leave like that? "Maybe," Callie said. "Serena would love to have a dog."

Luke nodded. "Animals are good company for kids," he said, opening a back door on his extended-cab pickup truck and setting the kit inside, then the tools he'd used to trim and file Cherokee's hooves. He nodded toward the barn. "Is that horse gentle enough to ride?"

Callie nodded. She meant to give Cherokee a little time to mend and get used to being back home, then saddle him up for some careful exercise.

"I read about a woman up in Canada," Luke said. "Her name's Jeanne Greenberg. She founded an organization called SARI, in memory of her daughter. You might want to look her up online."

"What kind of organization?" Callie asked, realizing that she didn't want Luke to go.

"Therapeutic riding," he answered, climbing into the truck and leaving the door open.

Something quickened inside Callie. She thought of Serena, and her secret dream. She wanted to be a rodeo queen, Serena did, with a sash and a pink cowgirl hat with a gleaming tiara above the brim.

"Like you, Mom," she'd said, looking up from one of the old photo albums she and Callie sometimes went through together.

How long had it been since Serena had mentioned that dream?

"Thanks again," Callie said, waving to Luke.

"I'll be back tomorrow after the clinic closes," Luke called. "To look in on Cherokee."

With that, he shut the truck door and started the engine.

Callie watched as he drove out.

When he was gone, she took their two mugs inside, washed them out at the kitchen sink and set them in the drainer.

That done, she returned to the barn and brushed Cherokee down, silently promising that, this time, he could stay. She'd find a way to make it happen.

At three o'clock, when school let out, she was there waiting, like always, when Serena came out of her classroom.

"I have a surprise for you," Callie said.

Serena's green eyes brightened. "Ice cream?"

"Better."

"We're going to the rodeo?"

Callie chuckled, ruffling her daughter's shiny hair. "The rodeo isn't until July, silly-girl," she answered. "And, anyway, this is even better than *that*."

"What?" Serena insisted.

Callie relented. She knew Serena would never last until they got home—she'd be frantic with curiosity by then. "Do you remember that horse we saw yesterday? The one you said was lonely?"

Serena nodded, clearly puzzled. She clutched her schoolwork in one hand and looked up at Callie solemnly.

"Well, he's in our barn, right this very minute."

Serena's face was instantly luminous. "God gave him a house!"

Callie crouched, so she was at eye level with her daughter. She took both Serena's shoulders in her hands and squeezed gently. "Right now," she said carefully, for her own benefit as well as Serena's, "he's just visiting."

"Can I ride him?" Serena caught her breath. "Can I be a rodeo queen?"

"His feet are sore, and he doesn't feel very well," Callie said. "So it wouldn't be a good idea to ride him. But maybe when he's better. I'll ride him first, and if he's gentle enough, you can try, too."

Serena considered the situation. "If I'm going to be a rodeo queen," she said, "I have to *ride* a horse, Mom."

Callie smiled. "Then I guess we'd better take very good care of him," she replied. "Will you help me?"

Serena wheeled her arms, beaming, her joy uncontrollable. "Yes!" she shouted. "Yes, yes, *yes!*"

CHAPTER
❧ TWO ❧

At home, Callie introduced Serena to Cherokee, stood her on an old milking stool in the stall and showed the child how to brush him. Callie's heart squeezed with love for both the little girl and the old horse, watching as they established an immediate bond.

Later, inside the house, while Callie was cooking supper—macaroni and cheese this time—Serena sat at the table, busily coloring on a sheet of paper. After the meal came the bath, the story, the nightly prayers. *Bless my mom,* Serena had said earnestly, her small hands pressed together and her eyes squinched tight shut, *and bless our new horse. Thank you for giving him a house to live in. And please let me be a rodeo queen.*

Smiling, Callie urged her daughter into bed, tucked her in, kissed her good-night. Usually, Serena fought sleep as long as she could, wanting a glass of water, using the bathroom, padding into the kitchen to solemnly inform Callie there was a monster hiding in her bedroom closet. A monster-routing ritual generally ensued, and sometimes a second story had to be read. That night, the little girl drifted off right away, smiling as she dreamed.

Callie stood awhile in the doorway to Serena's small room, watching her, loving her, and hoping she hadn't set Serena, herself and Cherokee up for a big disappointment by having the horse brought to the ranch.

A long time passed before she finally turned away, went back to the kitchen and logged onto the aging computer in the corner of the room. She'd sold a few more of her necklaces, old-fashioned fragments made from pieces of antique china, and spent the next half hour packaging the orders. The profits were slim, but she'd be able to purchase more supplies and keep going.

Callie's life was all about keeping going.

She was about to log off the Internet, check on Cherokee once more and indulge herself in a long, hot bath, when she remembered Luke's reference to the woman in Canada—the one who'd founded a therapeutic riding program. What was her name?

Jeanne Greenberg.

Using Google, she found www.sari.ca, and quickly became immersed in Mrs. Greenberg's compelling story. Jeanne and her husband, Syd, had had a daughter, Sari. Like Serena, Sari had Down syndrome. The Greenbergs had raised her, with their other children, in a loving household, and horses were very much a part of all their lives. When Sari died suddenly at fifteen, the Greenbergs were of course devastated, but they were determined to help other children like Sari, and other families like their own. They set apart five acres of their farm outside London, Ontario, including the barn, and began a therapeutic riding program.

Callie's heart beat a little faster as she read and reread the information on the SARI Web site. Riding would mean so much to Serena, and to the other kids in her special-ed class at school. There were so many things they *couldn't* do—but here was a way to empower them, bolster their confidence.

Soon, though, Callie's practical side put on the brakes.

Whoa, it said. *It's one thing to let Serena ride Cherokee, with you right there to supervise, but you know* nothing *about therapeutic riding. Or starting an organization like SARI. What about insurance? What about the cost of setting up a nonprofit organization? What about training?*

Callie sighed. The dream was too big. She had her hands full just keeping her little two-person family going as it was—and now she'd added Cherokee to the mix. Horses ate like—well, *horses.* They needed veterinary care, exercise, cleaning up after.

She logged off, shut down the computer.

Set aside the dream.

But it kept sneaking back into her mind.

For the second night in a row, Callie didn't sleep much.

HAPPY DAN'S WAS DOING a brisk late-breakfast business when Callie hurried in the next morning. She and Serena had dressed and eaten early, then gone out to the barn to tend to Cherokee. After that, she'd dropped Serena off at school and rushed to work.

Happy Dan, who owned the place and doubled as head fry cook, didn't look all that happy. But then he never did. He was big, with a hound-dog face drooping from prominent bones and graying black hair pulled back into a long but thin ponytail. He always wore a ratty T-shirt, sweatpants and running shoes that had seen not just better days, but better decades.

"You're late," he snapped.

"Sorry," Callie said, hastily tying on her apron and then washing her hands at the sink behind the counter out front.

"Leave her alone," interceded Hal Malvern, the only lawyer in town. He was a good-natured sort, always grumbling that he ought to move to the city, where people sued each other once in a while. His suits were as old as Happy Dan's running shoes, but he wasn't poor. He just didn't see the need to spend a lot of money on fancy clothes when he never actually had to set foot in a real courtroom. He and Judge Wilkins usually settled any case that came up over coffee right there at Happy Dan's, in a corner booth.

Callie favored Hal with a smile. "What'll it be?" she asked.

"The usual," Hal replied.

Callie relayed the order to Happy Dan, then went for the coffeepot. She was refilling cups all along the counter when the bell over the café's front door jingled and Luke Banner walked in.

For Callie, everything stopped. As far as she knew, Luke hadn't set foot in Happy Dan's since his return to Parable. But here he was.

He smiled at her, hung his cowboy hat on a peg by the door, along with a dozen other hats on a dozen other pegs, and approached the counter. Took the empty stool next to Hal's and reached for a menu—just as if he took his breakfast at Happy Dan's every morning of his life.

"May I help you?" Callie asked.

"Coffee," he said. "I'll get back to you on the rest."

Happy Dan pounded on the little bell on the pass-through, signaling an order was up.

Callie gave Luke a cup of coffee and rushed to pick up two ham-and-egg platters.

"It's bad enough I had to *take* those orders, then cook them," Happy Dan grumbled. "I hope you don't expect me to *deliver* them, too."

"Oh, lighten up, you old coot," Hal told him cheerfully.

"I *said* I was sorry," Callie told her boss, in an undertone.

"Hustle your bustle, Callie," Happy Dan retorted.

Callie hustled, all right. By the time she got back to the counter to take Luke's order, she was breathless.

"What'll you have?" she asked, pencil and pad at the ready.

"Dinner," he replied.

"We're not serving dinner," Callie said. "Breakfast till eleven-thirty, then we switch over to lunch. Dinner isn't served until five o'clock, by which time I'll be out of here."

Luke smiled. "I wasn't ordering dinner, Callie," he told her reasonably. "I was asking you to have dinner with me. Tonight. You and Serena."

Hal wheeled on his stool and spoke in a booming, trial-of-the-century voice, addressing everybody. "Luke wants to take Callie out to dinner!" he announced. "Sounds like a date to me!"

Everybody in the café cheered—except for Happy Dan, who muttered something, and Callie, who blushed.

"Will you, Callie?" Luke asked, still smiling. "Have dinner with me, I mean?"

It was another beans-and-wieners night, due to budget constraints, and Serena would be delighted at the prospect of an outing. Callie was less enthusiastic, though, mainly because Happy Dan's was the only public eatery in Parable, and she already spent most of her day there.

"Yes," she whispered, oddly flustered. "Okay."

Hal spun around to report her answer to the room. "She said yes!"

Another round of applause erupted.

Luke chuckled, shook his head.

"Oh, for heaven's sake," Callie sputtered.

Hal reached across the counter to pat her hand. "Wear something pretty," he told her, in a stage whisper.

"Pancakes and eggs," Luke said.

Callie stared at him, confused.

Luke grinned again, tapped the plastic menu with a finger. "Breakfast?" he drawled.

Callie blushed again and turned in the order, then took great care to fill every coffee cup in the room for the second time. She knew Happy Dan wouldn't fire her—good help was hard to find, especially in a town like Parable, and, anyway, they were friends—but she wanted to keep busy. If she didn't, she'd have to think about Luke Banner, and why his presence in the café and his perfectly harmless dinner invitation had rattled her so much.

Luke ate while she took and served other orders and rang up tickets at the cash register. Before he left, he said he'd be by her place around six, to look in on the horse. They'd go on to dinner from there.

Callie merely nodded.

At three that afternoon, she was waiting when Serena rushed out of her classroom, eager to go home and feed Cherokee. Several of the other kids in the program followed in her wake, staring at her in awe.

The special-ed teacher, Miss Parker, joined Serena and Callie in the corridor, smiling. "Serena caused quite a stir in class today," she said. "She wants to bring her horse to school for show-and-tell."

Callie squeezed her daughter briefly against her side. "It would probably be easier to bring the kids to the horse," she told Miss Parker.

"That's a great idea," Miss Parker replied. "How's next Friday afternoon? I'm sure we could arrange for the school van to bring us out to your farm."

Next Friday afternoon? Callie opened her mouth, closed it again.

Serena gave an exuberant bleat of joy. "Next Friday you can all see our horse!" she told the assembled members of her small class.

"Wait," Callie murmured.

"It's settled, then," Miss Parker said.

Serena was jumping up and down, and so were the other kids.

There was simply no way Callie could throw cold water on the plan—it would be like canceling Christmas.

"It's settled," Callie agreed, trying not to sound reluctant.

Serena talked all the way home, fidgeted in the car seat while Callie retrieved the mail—all flyers this time, but no bills, thank heaven. Serena bolted from the Blazer the instant Callie shut off the engine in the driveway beside the house, and bounded toward the barn, piping, "Cherokee! Cherokee! We're home, and my *whole class* is coming to visit next Friday afternoon!"

At least, that was the gist of what she said. Although Callie knew other people often had difficulty understanding Serena's speech, Callie herself heard her child's meaning when she spoke, rather than her actual words, in that weird alchemy of motherhood.

Callie sighed, but Serena's happiness outweighed her own concerns about cleaning, cookie-baking and taking time off work. Smiling, she followed the little girl.

Cherokee nickered and blew his big horse lips, pleased to see them both.

"You need to walk around a little, buddy," Callie said, opening the stall door to slip his halter on over his head, then clip the lead rope into place. Once, there had been pastures, but they'd been sold off a long time before, so there was nothing left of the property besides the house, the barn and a half acre of high grass, littered here and there with old tires and scraps of rusted metal.

Callie walked Cherokee slowly around the yard, Serena scampering alongside. When Callie let Serena hold the lead rope for a while, the child calmed and her face shone.

After half an hour or so, Callie returned Cherokee to his stall and showed Serena how much hay to put in his feeder.

"Can I brush him again?" Serena asked, already heading for the milk stool, retrieving it from the corner where Callie had stashed it the night before.

"Sure," Callie said.

Cherokee munched on hay and switched his tail slowly as Serena groomed him.

"Rodeo queens," Serena said wisely, "know how to take care of horses."

Callie smiled. "It's part of the job," she agreed.

Standing on the milk stool, the brush in one small hand, Serena looked down at her school dress and pink jacket, now generously decorated with horse hair. "I guess I should have changed my clothes first," she said.

"You'll want to do that, anyway," Callie told her. "We're going out to supper tonight."

Serena's eyes widened with excitement. "We *are?*" A pause. "Can we bring Cherokee with us?"

Callie laughed. "They don't allow horses in restaurants, silly-girl," she said. "Finish up there, so we'll have plenty of time to get ready."

Serena nodded and speeded up the brushing process. "Are we going to Happy Dan's?" she asked.

"Probably," Callie said. She might not have been all that thrilled about returning to the workplace on her off time, but she *was* looking forward to seeing Luke.

Serena climbed down off the milk stool, patted Cherokee in companionable farewell and left the stall. Callie followed, bringing the stool along, putting it away again.

"We're *probably* going to Happy Dan's?" Serena pressed. "Don't you know? Aren't you *driving?*"

Callie ruffled her daughter's hair, chuckled at the question. For all that Serena was only seven and was considered a "special-needs" child by the system, she often talked like an elderly wise woman. "Luke—Dr. Banner—invited us to dinner," she said. "So I suppose *he's* driving."

"Who's he?" Serena asked. Serena wanted to know everything—how to surf the Internet, why stars could still shine long after they'd burned out, if a little kid could ever be president of the United States.

"He's Cherokee's doctor," Callie answered. Then, after the briefest of hesitations, added, "And an old friend of mine. Your dad knew him, too."

They didn't often talk about Denny; Serena had been a baby when he died, and to her, he was just a man in a picture. His parents lived in another state and weren't much interested in their granddaughter. "Dr. Banner brought Cherokee here yesterday, in his horse trailer."

"If he's your friend, how come you call him 'Dr. Banner'?"

They'd reached the back door, and Callie opened it and shooed Serena inside. "I just do," she said.

"No fair," Serena protested. "That's like saying, 'Because I said so, that's why.'"

Callie grinned. "Forget being a rodeo queen when you grow up," she joked. "You ought to be a lawyer instead."

Serena frowned. "I don't want to be a rodeo queen when I grow up," she said seriously. "I want to be one *now*."

Callie felt a stab of pain, thinking of the Greenbergs' daughter, Sari. She'd only lived to be fifteen. A lot of Down syndrome kids died young; they were prey to so many health problems. What if Serena *didn't* grow up?

"Mom?" Serena peered up at Callie, worried by something in her expression.

"Go and change your clothes," Callie said gently.

Serena tarried a few moments, then brightened again and dashed off toward her room, shedding her school clothes as she went.

Callie closed the kitchen door and just stood there, one hand to her heart, breathing through the fear that the thought of losing Serena always aroused in her.

Serena reappeared seconds later, wearing only her underpants. *"Mom,"* she prodded. "Get dressed. You can't go out to dinner looking like *that*."

Callie looked down at her waitress uniform, which was something less than prepossessing even when it was fresh from the clothes dryer, let alone after a full shift at Happy Dan's and the feeding and grooming of a horse.

Heat pinkened Callie's cheeks.

She simply didn't own anything suitable for a—well—a *date*.

But this *wasn't* a date, she reminded herself. It was just supper with an old friend, at a local café. Jeans would do, and a cotton blouse.

"Hurry *up*, Mom," Serena said.

"I'm on it," Callie replied, with a little smile.

She headed for the shower, with a brief pit stop in the bedroom to grab clean clothes. Fifteen minutes later, scrubbed and dressed, she felt—presentable.

"That isn't what you wear on a date," Serena said in a tone of kindly disapproval when Callie joined her in the kitchen to pour a cup of cold coffee leftover from breakfast and zap it in the microwave.

"Fresh out of slinky black cocktail dresses," she answered. She looked perfectly *fine* in her best jeans and sleeveless top, she assured herself.

Luke arrived at five-thirty but headed for the barn instead of the house.

This was reported by Serena, who stood with her face pressed to the glass of the window to the right of the back door. Callie was online—several new orders had come in for her necklaces, exhausting the supply on hand, and she chided herself for going out to supper when she ought to be stringing more beads.

She considered fixing a meal at home and inviting Luke to join her and Serena, but she knew her daughter would be let down. Serena loved going out—loved going *anywhere*.

"Does he have a little girl?" Serena asked, catching Callie's full attention with the tremulous note of hope in her voice.

"No, honey," Callie said softly, leaving the computer to join Serena at the window. "He doesn't." The glass was smudged with nose and handprints. Beyond it, Luke's late-model, mud-splattered truck gleamed in the sunlight.

The expression on Serena's round face was heartrending. "Do you think he wants one?"

Callie stroked Serena's bangs back from her forehead and considered carefully before speaking. "Are you thinking of volunteering for the job?"

Serena's sudden burst of laughter was a profound relief to Callie. "No, silly-mom," she said. "I'm *your* little girl."

"You sure are," Callie confirmed, cupping Serena's face in her hands and planting a noisy kiss on her forehead. "And don't you forget it." Looking up, and still a little unsettled, Callie saw Luke coming out of the barn, moving toward the house.

"Here he comes!" Serena cried. "He's *handsome,* Mom."

Luke *was* handsome, Callie thought, watching his approach. As a boy, he'd been a heartthrob. As a man, he was—more so. And more of everything else, too.

At home in his own skin. Quietly confident. And quite probably the most intelligent man she'd ever known.

Callie swallowed and left the window, intending to open the door.

Serena beat her to it, though, and bounded out onto the small back porch. "Hello!" she shouted. "My name is Serena and I'm seven years old and next Friday my *whole class* is coming to see our horse!"

Luke stopped in the middle of the yard, took off his hat and grinned. "Howdy, Serena," he said. "My name is Luke and I'm thirty-two years old and I think your class is going to be real impressed with old Cherokee."

"Mom says she's fresh out of slinky black cocktail dresses," Serena chimed in merry apology. "So she's just wearing jeans."

Luke chuckled at that and shifted his gaze from Serena to Callie, now standing behind her daughter, and blushing again. "She looks all right to me," Luke said. "*More* than all right, as a matter of fact."

Callie was foolishly pleased by the remark—and troubled by the way it made her feel inside. She was a positive person, and regularly did six impossible things before breakfast, like any single mother, but making too much of an invitation to supper would be a major mistake. Luke had a thriving veterinary practice, she was a waitress and part-time jewelry maker. Best keep things in perspective.

"How's Cherokee doing?" she asked.

"He's fine," Luke replied.

"Are we going to Happy Dan's for supper?" Serena asked.

Luke grinned, advancing toward them again. "No," he said.

"McDonald's?" Serena queried.

"Nope." By then, Luke was standing at the base of the porch steps. He put out a hand to Serena, and they shook. "My place. I thought we could have a barbecue on the patio. But if you'd rather go to McDonald's—"

"No," Serena interjected quickly. "Do you have a horse?"

Callie laid a hand on her daughter's shoulder, squeezed lightly.

"Couple dozen of them, actually," Luke said modestly. "A few dogs, too."

"Maybe I'd better take my own car," Callie interjected, watching the interaction between Luke and Serena and pondering the bittersweet feelings it aroused in her. "Just so you won't have to drive all the way back out here."

Luke's gaze was steady as it rose to Callie's face. "Sure," he said. "Makes sense."

Callie nodded, relieved. Serena, on the other hand, was disappointed.

"If this is a *date*," the child whispered, loudly enough for the neighbors to hear, never mind Luke, "aren't you supposed to ride in *his* car?"

Luke chuckled again, raised his eyebrows a little.

"I'm just being practical," Callie told Serena. And Luke.

Luke led the way to his place, Callie and Serena following in the Blazer, although Callie could have found the gracious old farm in her sleep. Spacious green pastures with white rail fences bordered the road, and the old-fashioned red barn was like something from a glossy calendar page. Beyond, at the end of a long, curving lane, stood the brick ranch house, modest but substantial.

A yellow Lab appeared, galloping down to the base of the driveway to wait for Luke to open the door of his truck and get out. When he did, the dog greeted him with a series of happy yips, and Luke ruffled the animal's ears.

Callie parked behind Luke's truck, shut off the engine.

"Don't be scared," she told Serena. "I'm sure the dog is friendly."

"I'm *not* scared," Serena said indignantly, and before Callie could do more than put the gear shift in Park and shut off the engine, the little girl was out of her seat belt and on her way to join Luke and the Lab.

Callie hurried after her daughter. "Serena——"

"Serena," Luke said, "meet Bodine. Bodine, Serena."

"Bodine?" Callie echoed.

"Bodine Martin," Luke confirmed with a half smile. "She looks more like a 'Betsy' to me, but she answers to Bodine, so that's what I call her."

Bodine sat on her haunches, looked adoringly into Serena's delighted face and licked her cheek.

"Bodine!" Serena whooped. "Bodine Martin!"

Luke chuckled again.

"She likes to repeat things," Callie explained.

"Most kids do," Luke said.

"Have you——have you heard from the Martins?" Callie asked. They'd abandoned Bodine, and Cherokee, too, but that didn't mean they wouldn't be back.

"No," Luke answered. "It's not likely that I will." He turned to

Serena, who was fully occupied with the dog. "How about a tour of the barn before we eat?"

Serena was enthusiastic.

Callie had always admired the Banner ranch—unlike her own place, it exuded sunny grace. The house and barn and other outbuildings, though old, were well maintained, and the fields where oceans of wheat had flourished in Luke's grandfather's time were grassy pastures now.

As Luke, Callie, Serena and Bodine approached the barn, a teenage girl in jeans and a flattering pink T-shirt came through the doors, dusting her hands together.

"Finished for the day, Dr. Banner," she told Luke, after sparing friendly smiles for Callie and Serena and patting Bodine on top of the head. "Unless you want me to do some filing in the office or something."

No introductions were necessary—Kristen Young had lived in Parable all her life, and the previous summer, she'd washed dishes and bussed tables at Happy Dan's. Pretty and intelligent, Kristen was an animal lover and an accomplished horsewoman. In fact, she was already considered a front-runner for that year's rodeo queen title.

"You can go," Luke told the girl. "Thanks, Kris."

Serena stared at Kristen with a fascination heretofore reserved for the dog—or Luke. She and Kristen had gotten to know each other at Happy Dan's, since Serena spent most of her time there with Callie when school was out.

Kristen favored the child with another smile, warm and genuine. Some people, especially younger ones, were uncomfortable around Serena, but that had never been the case with Kristen. "How's it going, kiddo?" she asked.

"We've got a *horse* now," Serena confided. "Next Friday afternoon, my whole entire *class* is coming to our house to see him."

"Wow," Kristen said. "The whole bunch, huh?"

Serena nodded solemnly.

"Awesome," Kristen said. Her sea-blue gaze turned to Callie. "If you need a baby-sitter or anything, I'm available. This whole rodeo-queen thing is costing me a bundle."

"It costs money to be a rodeo queen?" Serena asked, wide-eyed.

"A fortune," Kristen replied.

"Oh," Serena said, looking a little deflated.

"I might need a sitter once in a while," Callie said, mostly to change the subject. When she had to work outside school hours, she took Serena to Happy Dan's with her. "I'll call you."

"Great!" Kristen said. Then she ruffled Serena's hair, said good-bye to Luke and Callie, and headed for her old car, parked next to the barn.

"It costs money to be a rodeo queen?" Serena repeated, looking up at Callie with her heart in her eyes.

"Yes," Callie said gently.

Serena bit her lower lip and looked down at the ground.

At a loss, Callie simply laid a hand on the child's shoulder.

A short silence followed. Bodine nudged Serena with her

muzzle, making her giggle, then started through the barn door and doubled back.

"I think she wants to show you her puppies, Serena," Luke said. "They're just inside the barn door, to the right."

Serena perked right up at the mention of puppies.

Callie, watching Luke's face, felt a mingling of gratitude and good-natured annoyance. Bodine's babies were still too young to be weaned, but the time would come when they needed good homes, and Callie knew he was hoping she and Serena would adopt one.

Serena squealed with delight when she saw the small yellow bundles of fur gamboling in an old playpen, mostly ears and paws, their eyes barely open.

"How come they're in jail?" Serena asked Luke. "Did they do something bad?"

Luke grinned and lowered one of the rails on the side of the playpen, so Bodine could get in. Immediately, she lay down and the puppies nestled close to nurse.

"They're not in jail, honey," Luke said quietly, crouching in front of Serena to look directly into her eyes. "But they're little, and apt to wander off and get themselves in trouble. This way, Bodine can keep them all rounded up in one place."

"Can I touch them?" Serena asked.

"Sure," Luke answered.

Serena's whole countenance glowed with wonder as she reached through the bars of the playpen and gently stroked one of the puppies, then another.

Callie watched, stricken with love for her child. In that moment, she yearned to make the world safe for Serena, to make it kind and just and pure.

All the things she knew it wasn't.

She was a little startled when Luke's hand came to rest on her shoulder. Their gazes met.

"She'll be fine," Luke said.

Callie tried to smile. "Did you learn to read minds while you were away from home?" she asked.

"No," Luke said. "Just eyes. And yours have always been pretty expressive." He paused. "It's good to be back, Callie. It's really good to be back."

Serena, fully engaged with Bodine and the puppies, let out a joyous giggle. "Back," she echoed. "Back, back, back." Then she turned her head and looked up at Callie, then Luke. "Back where?" she asked.

Luke didn't look away from Callie's face. "Home," he answered.

CHAPTER
∽THREE∽

S aturday was a busy blur, spent doing housework and laundry and filling jewelry orders, with Serena's help.

Sunday morning at work, Hal and all the other regulars wanted a report on Callie's Friday night "date" with Luke. Protesting that it hadn't *been* a date, just a very pleasant evening with a good friend, proved fruitless right away, so she gave up and stayed busy serving breakfast specials.

After the puppy fest and the tour of the barn, during which Serena had insisted on being personally introduced to every horse, in every stall, the three of them had gone up to the house. Luke had washed up at the kitchen sink, while Serena and Callie did the same in a nearby powder room, and then they'd shared an ordinary, delicious supper on the backyard patio.

Serena had been particularly taken with one of Luke's horses, a little spotted Shetland pony named Mahjong. She'd begged for a ride all through supper, and after being assured the animal was gentle, Callie gave her permission.

Once the remains of their supper had been cleared away, they'd all gone back to the barn, and Luke had led Mahjong out of his stall, along the breezeway and into a grassy area nearby.

He'd set Serena carefully on Mahjong's back.

Seeing the expression on her daughter's face, Callie had let out her breath. Serena had been luminous, transported. She hadn't even ridden the pony, really, just sat there on its sturdy back, clinging to its mane with both hands and beaming. And she'd talked nonstop about the experience, too, all the way home from Luke's, all through her bath, even in her prayers.

When the little girl finally dropped off to sleep, happily exhausted, Callie went out to check on Cherokee, making sure he had hay and water, and then just keeping company with him for a while. Finally, she returned to the house.

She'd spent the rest of the evening online, searching for a riding program like the one the Greenbergs had started, in memory of their daughter. There were several—but all of them were too far from Parable for Serena to participate on a regular basis.

"What's on your mind, Callie?" a gentle male voice asked, interrupting her thoughts.

Callie realized she'd been woolgathering and brought herself back to the here-and-now—the breakfast/lunch shift at Happy Dan's Café. Hal was smiling at her from his usual stool at the corner.

Business was a little slow that morning, because it was Sunday, and the rush wouldn't start until after the various church services around town let out at noon. Callie had already wiped down all the tables, refilled all the napkin holders and the salt and pepper shakers, taken and served the orders from the few customers.

"How hard is it to start a nonprofit organization, Hal?" Callie asked, refilling his coffee cup.

"Hard enough," Hal said. "Why?"

She told him about the Greenbergs, and Cherokee, and how happy Serena had been, "riding" Mahjong at Luke's the night before.

"First thing you've gotta do," Happy Dan put in, setting a large, empty jar on the counter, next to the cash register, "is raise money. A program like that costs a *pile* to start."

Callie sighed.

Happy Dan scribbled something on the back of a page torn from Callie's order pad and rummaged behind the counter until he came up with a roll of tape.

"What you need," Hal said to Callie, "is a free lawyer."

"Now, where would she find one of those?" Happy Dan asked, giving one of his rare smiles. He'd clearly been eavesdropping, but he was so eager to help that Callie couldn't fault him for it.

Hal straightened the lapels of his outdated suit, fiddled with the knot in his too-wide tie. "Right here," he said.

Happy Dan taped the piece of paper to the jar.

Callie squinted and read what he'd written.

Give. So Kids Like Serena Can Ride Horses.

Her throat tightened. Her boss could be brusque, but deep down, he was kind, always eager to help where possible.

There were only two customers in the café at the moment, besides Hal—a pair of truck drivers passing through. They paid their checks, and each of them dropped a five dollar bill into the jar.

"See?" Dan said when they'd gone. "You've already got ten bucks."

"My problems are solved," Callie joked.

"Where's Serena this morning?" Hal asked.

"Luke came by the house early, with Kristen, and asked if Serena could help out at the clinic for a little while."

Hal and Happy Dan both looked surprised. Callie was still a little surprised herself, actually. Not by Luke's invitation, but by her own willingness to let Serena out of her sight that long.

Happy Dan gave a low whistle of exclamation. "I never thought I'd see the day," he marveled.

"What day?" Callie asked, bristling a little.

"The day when you'd let that kid *be* a kid," Dan replied. "Most of the time, you act like she's made out of eggshells or something."

"They'll be back here by lunchtime," Callie said, peevish.

"Don't get all bent out of shape," Dan said. "Luke wouldn't let anything happen to Serena, and neither would Kristen. It's about time you trusted somebody, that's all I'm saying."

Hal cleared his throat loudly, plopped his briefcase onto the counter and opened it, taking out a yellow legal pad and a pen. "Let's get rolling with this riding program," he said.

Happy Dan wasn't through pontificating. He shook a finger under Callie's nose. "It's about time for another thing, too," he went on. "You're a young woman, Callie. You need a *life*."

"I *have* a life. I have Serena."

"For yourself."

Hal cleared his throat again. "The riding program?" he prompted diplomatically. "By my estimate, we've got about half an hour before the Baptists and the Episcopalians get out, and the Catholics won't be far behind them. The whole bunch will be hungry as bears, and pretty cranky, too, especially if the sermons run long. So why don't we get started?"

"You've gotta have insurance," Happy Dan said.

"We'll start small," Hal decided, and scribbled something on the legal pad.

Callie blinked.

"Volunteers, too," Dan added. "People who know something about kids with special needs—and horses."

Callie blew, and her bangs bounced off her forehead. "Look, maybe this is getting out of hand. I just wanted——"

"Things like this have got to start somewhere," Hal said. "Might as well be right here."

By the time the first Baptists trickled in, Callie was knee-deep in a dream she'd never even considered before Luke told her about Jeanne Greenberg and SARI.

The brunch rush was in full swing when Luke came in with Serena and Kristen. He spotted the jar on the counter right away and tossed Callie a quizzical grin. Serena and Kristen took the last empty booth.

"I fed *three horses,* Mom," Serena informed Callie, when she approached the table where the girls were sitting. "I wanted to ride Mahjong again, but Luke said I couldn't unless I had your permission."

Callie glanced in Luke's direction, saw him drop a bill into the jar Happy Dan had set out earlier. People had been generous all morning, even without fully understanding the cryptic pitch taped to the glass. The jar was a third full already.

With a smile for her daughter, Callie said, "You must be hungry after working that hard."

Serena nodded importantly.

Kristen grinned up at Callie. "She's a great kid."

"She sure is," Callie agreed. "Now, what'll it be? Today, breakfast is on the house."

"I heard that," Happy Dan grumbled from the other side of the pass-through. But then he grinned. "Good thing I'm such a big-hearted guy."

"Waffles, please," Serena said. "With lots of syrup."

"Waffles," Callie repeated, pretending to write the order on her pad. "With fresh strawberries."

"If you're going to be a rodeo queen," Kristen told Serena, "you've got to lay off the sugar, and go easy on fat, too."

"Why?" Serena asked reasonably.

Luke chuckled, shook his head. "Good question," he said.

Kristen's smile was blinding. She was a beautiful girl, and would probably make a wonderful rodeo queen. "Because you don't want to squash the horse, for one thing," she said.

Callie bit back a chuckle.

Serena pondered for a moment. "Okay," she said brightly. "Strawberries instead of syrup."

"Why didn't *I* think of that?" Callie asked. "Kristen? What about you?"

"The same thing Serena's having, please," the girl answered. "And coffee."

Turning to put in the orders and pour a glass of milk for Serena and coffee for Kristen, Callie nearly collided with Luke. His proximity made her heart flutter a little.

"I suppose you want breakfast, too?" she asked. Considering the hour, he might have opted for lunch.

Luke arched an eyebrow. "That was the general idea," he said. "This being a café and all——"

Callie blushed. She hadn't meant to sound abrupt—it was just that Luke made her nervous in a not entirely pleasant sort of way. Momentarily unable to speak, she lifted the pad and tried to look attentive.

Luke chuckled, apparently amused by her discomfort. "Waffles," he said. "With a side of crisp bacon and some coffee."

Callie hurried away.

She brought the two cups of coffee first, then Serena's milk.

Luke was seated beside Serena, and she was wearing his hat, giggling because it covered most of her face.

Except for Happy Dan, Serena's contact with adult males was limited. Watching her with Luke, Callie ached. Every little girl longed for a daddy, and Serena was no exception. Callie tried to be both mother and father to the child, but there were times when she had to admit defeat, at least to herself, and this was one of them.

Callie was too busy to contemplate her shortcomings for very long, though. There was simply too much to do, since the place was filled with hungry churchgoers, and by the time she'd served everybody, Luke, Kristen and Serena had finished their waffles.

Callie watched, while pretending not to, as Luke reclaimed his hat, kissed Serena on top of the head, said goodbye and left, pausing briefly at the counter to speak to Hal, who was still bent over his legal pad, writing industriously. Kristen lingered a few minutes, chatting earnestly with Serena, then she vanished, too.

Serena looked very small and forlorn, sitting alone in that booth, her body language wistful as she stared out the window.

"Hey, kiddo," Callie said, squeezing in beside Serena. On Sundays, she only worked a half day, since Happy Dan liked to close early.

"Hey," Serena responded on cue, turning to look up at Callie and offer a brave smile.

"You've had a busy morning."

Serena nodded. "So have you."

"Ready to go home and see Cherokee?"

Serena brightened, nodded again.

"We have to stop for a few groceries on the way," Callie said, thinking aloud.

"Do your feet hurt?" Serena asked seriously.

Callie often complained of sore feet after a shift at Happy Dan's. Looking at Serena now, she felt guilty for ever complaining about anything. "I feel fine," she said, smiling and leaning to kiss her daughter's forehead.

With that, Callie transferred her tips from her apron pocket to her purse, tossed the apron into the laundry basket in the back room behind the kitchen, and said goodbye to Dan and Hal.

Dan gestured toward the money in the jar on the counter. "Aren't you taking this with you?"

"Put it in the safe," Callie answered.

"Soon as I've drawn up the papers," Hal put in, "we can open a proper bank account."

"Don't you at least want to count it?" Dan pressed.

"I trust you," Callie said, after shaking her head. She was in the café doorway by then, and Serena was tugging impatiently at her hand.

After shopping for groceries, Callie and Serena went straight home.

And found the Carson brothers, Walt and Pete, unloading a truckload of lumber next to the barn.

"There must be some mistake," Callie began, jumping out of the Blazer. "I didn't order any lumber."

She'd known both Walt and Pete since kindergarten—they ran a small construction company part-time and worked the night shift at the mill. Watching her approach, Walt smiled.

"Luke Banner did," he said.

"Why?" Callie countered.

Serena, anxious to look in on Cherokee, dashed past the three grown-ups and into the barn.

Pete pushed back his billed cap and scratched his head. "He said your barn needed work." Pausing, Pete assessed the structure. "He was sure enough right about that."

"Wait one second," Callie protested. "I can't afford—"

"Luke said to put it on his bill," Walt said.

"He's going to help us with the work, too," Pete added helpfully.

"But—"

"We'd better get this lumber unloaded," Walt went on.

Confounded, Callie checked on Serena and Cherokee first, then went into the house, looked up Luke's number and called him.

"Dr. Banner," he said.

"Luke," Callie said, "Pete and Walt Carson are outside, unloading lumber. They told me—"

"I meant to bring this up at the café," Luke said, when Callie fell silent, "but you were pretty busy."

Callie was fairly strangling on her pride. "I don't need charity, Luke," she whispered, although Serena was in the barn and there was no one to hear. "I know the place is run-down, and I'm grateful for your help with Cherokee, but—"

"Callie."

"What?"

"This isn't charity—it's more like a bribe. You've got three extra stalls over there, and I'm in a temporary overflow situation here. Frankly, I'm hoping you'll take Mahjong and a couple of the others until I've got a few more stalls open and sort of—well—foster them. I'll provide the hay and anything else they need, of course. Kristen can stop by and help with the grooming and exercise."

Callie's eyes burned. Luke was being so generous. Why was she having such a hard time allowing that? "Well, you don't have to rebuild the barn, for heaven's sake," she protested, blinking hard and doing her best to maintain her dignity.

"Don't I?" Luke asked practically. "First high wind, it's going to come down. And then there's winter. It's a miracle it hasn't already collapsed."

"Why are you doing this?"

"Lots of reasons, Callie. Because I can. Because it's right. And—" Here, Luke stopped and cleared his throat. "And because one summer I took a girl to a dance and kissed her and I've never forgotten how it felt."

Callie didn't know what to say to that. She remembered the kiss, too; the light warmth of it still tingled on her lips. "We shouldn't have," she said. "Denny—"

"Denny's gone, Callie. And he'd want you and Serena to be happy. It's too soon to say any more, so I'm going to leave it at that. Consider it food for thought, though."

Callie began to cry, silently and for so many reasons she couldn't have listed them all. "Luke——"

"What?"

She drew a deep, quavering breath and let it out slowly. "Thank you."

There was a smile in his voice. "You're welcome," he said. "I have to take another call, so I'd better let you go."

"Goodbye," Callie said, long after Luke had hung up.

She was still standing there in the kitchen, holding the telephone receiver in one hand, when Serena burst through the back door.

"Mom? Are we going to carry the groceries in?"

Callie had forgotten the groceries. "Yes," she said, but she still didn't move.

"Walt and Pete said they'd help, if you want them to."

Callie was about to say, *We'll do it ourselves,* when she stopped. It was a fine thing to be independent, but everybody needed a hand sometimes, and she wanted Serena to be able to receive help as graciously as she gave it. "Sure," she said instead. "That's nice of them."

Serena's eyes shone with joy. "*And* we're getting a new barn!"

And so it was that Walt and Pete carried in all the grocery bags and stayed for a late lunch of bologna sandwiches, pork and beans and cookies.

After they'd gone, Callie cleared the kitchen table, got out her beads and tools and some old pieces of painted china she'd purchased at garage and estate sales and on eBay.

Making jewelry always soothed her nerves.

Serena, meanwhile, helped by sorting beads into color groups and arranging them in necklace shapes on Callie's bead-board. She had a knack for design, even at the tender age of seven.

"What do you want to be when you grow up?" Callie asked, going through various small bits of china, which she'd already trimmed with special snippers. She finally selected an old-fashioned portrait of an Indian maiden rowing a canoe and smiled at her daughter. "*Besides* a rodeo queen."

"Could I be a mommy?"

Callie's heart squeezed. Despite her limitations, Serena could look forward to a fairly normal life, but motherhood might not be an option.

"Well," Callie said carefully, "you'd need a husband first."

"You're my mommy," Serena reasoned, "and *you* don't have a husband."

For some reason, Callie thought of Luke at that moment, not Denny. And she heard Luke's voice in her mind, too. *Because one summer I took a girl to a dance and kissed her and I've never forgotten how it felt.*

"I *did* have, though. Your dad."

Serena frowned, thinking hard. "Kristen's friend Denise had a baby last month, and she doesn't have a husband."

Callie sighed. "Okay, it's *best* to have a husband."

"Maybe you should get another one. Then I'd have a dad."

Oh, Lord, Callie thought. *How did we get from what-do-you-want-to-be-when-you-grow-up to this?* "It's not quite that easy," she said.

Serena beamed, inspired. "You could marry Luke!"

"Hold it," Callie said, setting down the china piece.

"But he's nice!"

"Yes," Callie agreed. "Luke is very nice. He's a good friend. But that's as far as it goes."

Serena sagged a little. "Oh."

Callie leaned in her chair and planted a noisy kiss on the top of Serena's head. "We've always done just fine on our own, haven't we?"

Serena nodded, but she looked patently unconvinced. "I'm the only kid in my class who doesn't have a dad," she reminded Callie quietly.

Callie hugged her. "You do have a dad, Serena. His name was Denny Dorset, and he loved you very much."

"He's in heaven, though," Serena said. "And that's far. Can't he come and visit us or something?"

Callie could barely speak. "We've been over that before, sweetie," she replied, once she could trust her voice. "Heaven *isn't* far—it just seems that way. I know it's hard not being able to see your dad, but I'm sure he watches over us, always."

"But he can't visit. That's against the rules, right?"

Callie swallowed painfully. "Right," she said.

"It's a bad rule," Serena insisted.

"Nothing about heaven is bad, Serena. You know that. It's just that there are a lot of things we don't understand."

Serena sighed, fiddled with the array of green beads she was arranging on what she called the necklace board. Callie considered the design and laid the bit of china at the base, to see how it would look.

"Gorgeous," she said. "Maybe you'll grow up to be a jewelry designer."

Serena's attempt at a smile was heartrending. "Tell me a story, Mom," she said softly, touching the Indian maiden with the tip of one finger. "Tell me about this girl in a boat. Where is she going? What's her name?"

Relieved, but still choked up, Callie considered the china maiden. "Her name is—Tiger Lily," she said, winging it. Fortunately, she'd had a lot of practice at that. "She's on her way to the trading post."

"What's a trading post?"

"A store."

"Like Wal-Mart?"

Callie chuckled and, since Serena was absorbed in Tiger Lily and not looking directly at her, took the opportunity to dry her eyes with the back of one hand. "Sort of."

"What's she going to buy there?"

Callie drew a deep breath, let it out. Straightened her shoulders. "She's been making lovely necklaces with her mom. And she's taking them to the trading post to sell."

"Does she go to school?"

"Of course she does. School is very important. And Tiger Lily wants to have a good job when she grows up."

Serena frowned, studying the nubile Tiger Lily, with her buckskin dress and long, flowing hair. "She looks pretty grown up already."

"Okay," Callie agreed. "She's already grown up. But she's not very old, because she still lives with her mother."

"Where?"

"In a village."

"Does she have a horse, like Cherokee?"

"Absolutely."

Serena smiled, and her eyes were full of earnest hope when she lifted her gaze to Callie's face. "Does she have Down syndrome, like me?"

Oh, God, Callie thought. "Yes," she said. "I think she does."

"Do you think she has a dad?"

"No," Callie said, still improvising. "She did once, of course, but he had to go to heaven. So now it's just Tiger Lily and her mom— Dancing Feather. But they're very happy together. They have lots of friends in their village, and they make beautiful necklaces to sell at the trading post."

"Not on eBay?"

Callie laughed. "Not on eBay," she said.

"Tiger Lily should get a computer," Serena decided. "Then she could sell her necklaces on the Internet."

"She really should," Callie agreed. "She should get a computer."

Serena's smile brightened. "Okay, she has a computer," she said, taking up the threads of the story Callie had invented. This was part of the story game. "And she's really happy. Tiger Lily, I mean. She's happy because her mom is going to get married again, and then she'll have a dad, like everybody else in her class."

"I see," said Callie—and she did, only too well. "Don't you have some homework to do?"

That night, after supper and Serena's bath and the story, Callie tucked her in and kissed her.

"Good night, Dancing Feather," Serena said.

Callie smiled. "Good night, Tiger Lily," she replied.

And she didn't cry until she was out in the hallway, where Serena couldn't see.

Back in the kitchen, she strung the beads Serena had chosen, carefully set the china image in silver and attached a bale. The piece was exquisite, and it would bring a high price—if she'd been willing to sell it.

She knew she couldn't part with Tiger Lily, though. Not after the story she and Serena had spun around her.

Callie set the necklace aside, methodically put away all her tools, the beads and the design board. Then, reaching for her jean jacket, she ducked outside under the spring stars spattered across the sky.

She sat down on the back step, where she and Denny had had so many long, heartfelt talks. Where they'd tried to count the stars, and even laid claim to a few of them. From the barn, Cherokee nickered companionably, perhaps sensing her presence.

Callie wrapped her arms around her knees and sat with her spine straight and her chin high, biting her lower lip. "It's lonely without you, Den," she said very softly.

There was, of course, no answer besides a soft breeze whispering through the leaves of the maple tree nearby. She and Denny had planted that tree together, soon after they'd learned that Callie was expecting Serena. It had been a spindly seedling in those days, but now it was tall and sturdy, with branches that sheltered birds and provided shade in the heat of an eastern Washington summer.

"As soon as our baby's big enough, I'll hang a tire swing from the strongest bough," Denny had said, full of dreams as always.

Callie smiled at the memory and, at the same time, blinked back tears. They'd had so many dreams, she and Denny, and most of them hadn't come true.

They'd sat on this step and wept together after the doctors had told them their child would suffer from Down syndrome. They'd clasped hands, and Callie had rested her head against the side of Denny's shoulder, each of them leaning on the other.

Now, as always, there were many things Callie wished she could say to Denny—that she was doing the best she could, but sometimes her best just didn't seem good enough. That for all the satisfaction and joy of parenthood, it was hard raising a child alone.

There were times when she was terrified.

Times when she was furious—with God, with fate, with Denny for leaving her and Serena when they needed him so much.

Times, like tonight, when all she could do was find a private place to cry.

She looked up, her vision blurred, and searched until she found Denny's favorite star—the one he'd given her as a wedding present. At Christmas, it seemed to perch on the ridgepole of the barn, but now, in spring, it gleamed slightly to the west, a little higher in the sky.

"Luke's back," she told the star. And Denny. "Cherokee, too."

The maple tree rustled its leaves.

The night was chilly, and Callie huddled in her jean jacket.

The star seemed to flicker and wink.

"Did you see Serena yesterday, Denny? Did you see how happy she was, sitting there on Mahjong's back? She *loves* riding—just like you and I used to."

She felt Denny's responding smile in her heart.

He'd seen, all right.

"I loved you so much, Den," Callie said. "And I always will. You know that, don't you?"

He knew, all right.

Callie rose shakily to her feet. "I think I accidentally started a non-profit organization," she went on, smiling a little through her tears. "I barely thought of it, and things started happening, like magic. People contributing money. Hal jumping in to do the legal work. We're even getting a new barn." She paused, searching the sky. "You'll help me watch over our little girl, won't you? Because I can't do it on my own, not all the time, anyway."

He would.

Callie knew he would.

Heaven, just as she'd told Serena earlier, wasn't *really* all that far away. Sometimes, the distance could be covered in a single beat of the heart.

CHAPTER
❧ FOUR ❧

T he coming week passed at what seemed like warp-speed to Callie—Happy Dan's was unusually busy, and the funds in the contribution jar seemed to be reproducing on their own. Callie and Hal went over the legal documents on her coffee breaks, making little tweaks here and there, and the barn was progressing steadily.

Callie saw Luke several times, but always in passing, and she knew without being told that he was giving her space, a chance to process whatever it was that was happening between them.

And something was definitely happening.

Serena had been on overdrive all week, eager for Friday afternoon to come. She was in a frenzy of joy that morning when Callie, who had taken a rare day off, dropped her off at school. At three o'clock sharp, Serena would board the van, with the other kids in her class, and ride home.

Callie spent the morning cleaning the house, baking cookies and arranging a vegetable tray. Walt and Pete were on another job, and the day sparkled with all the promises of spring.

With her work finished and hours to go before the Great School Visit was to occur, Callie went out to the barn, put a halter on Cherokee and led him out into the sunshine. Since his hide was covered in a layer of fine sawdust from the construction project, which he had endured in stalwart good spirits, she brushed him. From time to time, he nudged her with his nose, making her laugh.

"You want to be ridden, don't you?" she asked.

Cherokee tossed his head, as if in affirmation, and Callie laughed again.

"Sure you're up to it?"

He pawed at the ground with one foreleg. Years before, Callie had taught him to count, and she wondered if he was trying to show her that he remembered.

She checked his hooves carefully, in case he might have picked up a stone or even a nail, but his feet looked good. She brought the milking stool out of the barn, set it on the ground and eased herself onto Cherokee's back.

For a moment, she was as exultant as Serena had been, riding Mahjong. Once, she and Cherokee had traveled all over the countryside, and he'd shared her triumph as queen of the Parable Rodeo. But after he'd been hauled away in that auction-house trailer, Callie had ridden only a few times, on friends' horses. Without Cherokee, she hadn't had the heart to ride.

Now, miraculously, he was back.

"We'll just take it easy today," she told him, her eyes burning with happy tears.

They were traveling in a slow, wide circle when Luke drove in, parked and got out of the truck. He shut the motor off and waited until Callie and Cherokee came up in front of him.

Callie noticed, as she got close, that while Luke's mouth was smiling, his eyes were solemn. She was instantly alarmed.

"Is Serena all right?"

Luke nodded, approached to stroke Cherokee's neck and casually inspect his legs and rib cage.

Callie was still tense. She sat stiffly, looking down at Luke, searching his face. "Something's wrong," she said.

Luke returned her gaze. "I did something, Callie," he said. "Maybe you'll like it, and maybe you won't."

"What?"

"The Martins stopped by my clinic an hour ago, asking after Bodine—and their horse."

For an instant, the whole world went dark.

Luke stretched his hands up for Callie, but she didn't want to get down. Not then or ever.

Slowly, Luke lowered his hands to his sides. Then he took a slip of paper from his shirt pocket and extended it to her.

Trembling, Callie took the paper and unfolded it.

Blinked.

A bill of sale.

Callie opened her mouth, closed it again.

"I bought Cherokee," Luke said. "The dogs, too. I'll keep Bodine and the pups, but for right now, anyway, I've got no place to keep this horse."

Callie's throat was so thick, she couldn't say a word. She finally leaned forward, wrapped both her arms around Cherokee's neck, clinging, and wept silently into his mane.

Tentatively, Luke touched her shoulder.

After a while, Callie recovered herself and sat up straight again. As Luke watched, she swung a blue-jeaned leg over the horse's back and jumped to the ground, forcing Luke to step back a little.

Facing him, Callie dried her eyes with one hand. And she said his whole name. Nothing else, just that.

He looked warily down at her.

And Callie flung both arms around his neck, just as she'd done with Cherokee a few minutes before. *"Thank you,"* she said, drawing in the wonderful, sun-dried laundry scent of his skin, his hair, his clothes.

He held her a little away from him, gripping her elbows.

"I couldn't have stood it," Callie told him. "If the Martins or any-body else had come and taken Cherokee away again——I don't know what I would have done. But I'm going to pay you back, Luke. Every cent. For Cherokee, for the barn——"

Luke cupped her chin in his hand. Grinned sheepishly. "You're not mad at me? I mean, I sort of started this whole foundation thing rolling, and then I sent Walt and Pete out here to rebuild the barn without asking you first—"

"I'm not mad, Luke. How could I be?"

"You've got a lot of pride, Callie. I didn't rightly know *what* to expect."

Callie stood on tiptoe then and kissed Luke lightly on the mouth.

He was surprised at first, but then he pulled Callie close again and kissed her back with a sweet ferocity that left her breathless—and groping for words. Luke seemed to be having the same problem, but he was the one who finally broke the electric silence.

"Did you ever tell Denny about that night—at the summer dance?" he asked, his blue eyes dark with pain.

Callie nodded. "I told him," she said.

Luke sighed, thrust a hand through his hair. "I tried," he said. "Before I left for college, I crept up on the subject a couple of times, but when the chips were down, I didn't have the guts. And I've regretted it ever since."

"Denny understood, Luke," Callie replied quietly. "He was hurt at first, sure, but you know how he was. He didn't carry grudges."

Luke reached past Callie to stroke Cherokee's side thoughtfully. "He was a better friend than I deserved," Luke said. "I'd do things differently, if I could have a second chance."

"Me, too," Callie answered, but she wasn't sure it was true. Yes, she'd been ashamed of deceiving Denny, but she still treasured the memory of that magical summer night and that stolen kiss under an enormous silver moon.

Luke turned to Callie again. "I'd still have kissed you," he said, as though he'd been reading her mind. "But I'd have told Denny right off how I felt about you. Been a man about it, instead of a kid."

Callie raised a hand, hesitated, and then touched Luke's cheek. "But you *were* a kid," she reminded him. "We all were."

Luke was quiet for a long time, just watching Callie. Then he said, "You loved him a lot, didn't you?"

Callie swallowed, looked away, looked back. "Yes," she finally answered. "But it was different than before——"

"Before what?"

"Before you."

A muscle bunched in Luke's jaw. He laid his hands on Callie's shoulders and squeezed gently. "If I'd told you how I felt——"

"Luke," Callie broke in, "stop. What happened, happened. It was one dance and an innocent kiss, not a torrid affair. Things were *supposed* to turn out the way they did——I married Denny and you married Roberta. If things had been different, I might not have had Serena, and that's something I can't even imagine."

Luke's smile was soft, thoughtful. "She's a terrific kid, Callie."

"She is," Callie agreed, thinking of the Tiger Lily/Dancing Feather story she and Serena had made up, and feeling her throat tighten again.

"Were you scared? When you found out about the Down syndrome?"

"Yes," Callie said. "So was Denny. And there are times when I'm *still* scared—that she'll get sick, or be in an accident. All the stuff mothers worry about. It's been hard, Luke—there's no denying that. Serena knows she's different from other kids, and there are a lot of things she'll never be able to do, and that hurts. Just last week, she told me she wanted to be a mommy when she grows up. But for all of it, not a day goes by that I don't thank God for her, exactly as she is."

Cherokee broke into the conversation then, butting at Callie again with his head. Luke and Callie both laughed.

Luke made a stirrup of his hands, and Callie got back up on Cherokee's back. As she looked down into Luke's upturned face, saw the sunlight catch in his hair, Callie's heart gave another pinchy flip.

"If I asked you for a second chance, Callie," Luke said, "what would you say?"

"I'd say we'd have to take things slowly," Callie responded honestly. She could still feel Luke's kiss, the ghost of that warm pressure on her mouth, but she wasn't a smitten teenager anymore. She was a grown woman, with a child and a job and bills to pay.

"That's good enough for me," Luke answered.

"You're home for good?"

"For good, Callie."

"You asked me if I loved Denny, and I told you the truth. Now it's my turn. Did you love Roberta, Luke?"

One hand resting on Cherokee's withers, Luke took a few moments to consider the question. "Not the way I should have," he said. "We wanted different things from the first. I wanted a houseful of kids, Roberta wanted to keep her figure. I loved the country, she loved the city. I love animals——" He paused and smiled ruefully "——and she wished she'd married another kind of doctor."

"You'd want children of your own," Callie ventured.

"Definitely," Luke said.

"What if...?" She fell silent.

"What if one of them had Down syndrome?" Luke finished gently. "Like Serena?"

Callie nodded, miserably hopeful.

"I'd consider myself one lucky man," Luke said.

"Really?"

"Really."

Callie believed him. "But we've got lots of time," she said.

"Lots of time," he agreed.

And then his cell phone rang.

Callie stared off into the distance while he took the call, sorting through all the things he'd told her, tucking them away in safe places inside to think about later.

"Gotta go," he told her, after snapping the phone shut. "Sick cow over at Linstrom's Dairy." He started for the truck, stopped and turned back. "Can I come back later, Callie?"

"My turn to cook supper," she replied with a nod. "Bring Bodine."

Luke's grin was as dazzling as dawn. He waved once, got into the truck and drove off.

SERENA WAS THE FIRST ONE out of the van when it arrived, followed by Miss Parker and the rest of the kids.

"I hope you don't mind," Miss Parker said, "but a few of the parents are on the way. Everybody's excited about your riding program."

Callie started to say there *wasn't* a riding program, not yet, anyway, but she stopped herself, because all the kids—most especially Serena—were watching her with eager, hopeful little faces.

"Okay," she said.

Cherokee stood in the yard, his halter rope dangling, and nickered when Serena rushed over to pet him.

"See?" the little girl said, turning to address the rapt children gathered nearby. "He's a *nice* horse."

"Some of the children were concerned that he might bite them," Miss Parker confided to Callie, keeping her voice low. Even then, they huddled at a little distance, watching Serena.

"Can I ride him, Mom?" Serena pleaded. "Please? Like I rode Mahjong?"

Callie hesitated only briefly. She knew Cherokee was gentle, and she'd stay close by, just in case. "Sure," she said. She approached, hoisted Serena onto Cherokee's back and held the lead rope.

"Look at me!" Serena crowed, while the other kids stared in admiration and no little envy. *"I'm riding a horse!"*

Callie smiled, led Cherokee slowly around in a circle.

One little boy, who also had Down syndrome, broke away from

the cluster of children around Miss Parker and approached. "Can Charlie ride, too?" he asked on his own behalf.

Callie's heart melted, but before she could find the words to refuse, a sporty SUV pulled in from the main road.

"That's my dad!" Charlie cried.

"You can't ride without his permission," Serena said importantly. "That's the rule."

A slender man got out of the SUV and walked, smiling, toward the group. Charlie ran to him, and Callie watched as he swept the child up into his arms and spun him around in an exuberant greeting.

"Charlie wants to ride a horse!" the little boy shouted. "Charlie wants to be a cowboy!"

The man carried him over to Callie.

"Jack Berrington," he said, by way of introduction. The Berringtons were new in Parable, although Callie had seen them several times at Happy Dan's, with Charlie and their three older children.

"Callie Dorset," Callie responded, transferring the lead rope to her left hand so she could offer her right one in response to his greeting.

"Charlie can get on with me," Serena announced. "I'll protect him."

Callie and Mr. Berrington exchanged smiles.

"Is it safe?" the man asked, Charlie straining in his arms.

"Cherokee's gentle," Callie confirmed. "But I haven't got insurance yet."

Mr. Berrington nodded.

"Please?" Charlie begged.

Mr. Berrington looked questioningly at Callie.

"Okay," she said, taking a firmer hold on the lead rope.

Charlie's eyes widened when he found himself sitting astride Cherokee, behind Serena. He wrapped his little arms around Serena's waist and hung on tight, his dad standing close, one hand resting lightly against Charlie's back.

In that moment, seeing the look of transcendent delight on Serena's and Charlie's faces, Callie knew she would do whatever it took to make the riding program a reality—raise the money, jump through the legal hoops, recruit volunteers, all of it.

Three other parents showed up within the next half hour. By that time, Serena and Charlie had dismounted, and Callie was demonstrating how she groomed Cherokee, and how she checked his feet before and after every ride. She showed them through the barn, placed the horse in his stall, fed him and filled his water trough.

Serena glowed with pride, though whether she was proud of Callie or the horse was anybody's guess.

Inside the house, Serena helped serve cookies and insisted on showing off the Tiger Lily necklace to everyone. By the time Miss Parker, the children and the parents had gone, she was happily exhausted.

"Did you have fun, sweetie?" Callie asked, clearing away the party debris. Luke was coming for supper, and she didn't have the first idea what to serve, nor had she mentioned the impending visit to Serena. She didn't want to get her all wound up again—or see her disappointed if Luke was delayed for some reason, or couldn't come at all.

Serena, sitting in Callie's rocking chair in the corner of the kitchen, nodded wearily and yawned.

"Why don't you take a little nap before supper?" Callie suggested.

To her surprise, Serena readily agreed and went off to her bedroom.

Smiling, Callie inspected the contents of her pantry and refrigerator, still mulling over the supper quandary. She finally decided on tuna casserole, a mainstay in her modest repertoire, and started the preparations.

As she worked, she hummed softly under her breath.

Although Serena was sound asleep when Callie checked on her a few minutes later, the child apparently had radar. The moment Luke drove in, she was pounding down the hallway and into the kitchen.

Callie, setting three places at the table, smiled as her tousle-haired, sleepy-eyed daughter rushed to the window and immediately began jumping up and down.

"Luke's here!" she cried. "And he brought Bodine!"

Callie chuckled. "Maybe you ought to let them in," she said mildly.

Serena rushed to the back door and flung it open. "I rode Cherokee today!" she shouted. "And so did Charlie!"

Luke appeared in the doorway, and Callie's heart did funny things again when he immediately hoisted Serena up into his arms and gave her a quick hug and a peck on the cheek.

"All by yourself?" he asked, his gaze connecting briefly with Callie's over Serena's head.

Bodine squeezed past them into the kitchen and then sat down politely, as though awaiting instructions.

"Well," Serena admitted, drawing out the word, "for a little while. Charlie was on the horse with me *some* of the time."

Callie kept her face averted, waiting for the sudden heat to fade from her cheeks.

"How come you didn't bring the puppies?" Serena asked Luke.

He set her gently on her feet. "Their manners aren't good enough for visiting," he said seriously.

Serena approached Bodine, patted the dog tenderly on the head. "I don't think we have any dog food," she fretted.

"That's okay," Luke answered, and Callie could feel him watching her, which, of course, only increased the pink throb in her cheeks. "She's already eaten."

With a relieved sigh, Serena pushed the door closed. "She probably wouldn't like tuna casserole, anyway," she said. Then she looked up at Luke. "Do dogs like tuna casserole?"

Luke chuckled. "Dogs like everything," he answered. "But most of the time, people food isn't good for them."

"Serena," Callie said, finally breaking her silence, "go and wash your face and hands and comb your hair. Supper's ready."

Serena paused, tugging at the sleeve of Luke's long-sleeved western shirt. "Are you going to stay?"

"I count three places at the table," Luke assured her. "So I guess I am."

Serena gave a whoop of delight and ran for the bathroom.

"How's the Linstroms' cow?" Callie asked, to get the conversation started.

Luke grinned. "She'll be all right," he said. "But *you* look a little flushed." He walked over to her, laid the back of his hand to her forehead and assumed a comically ponderous expression. "No fever, though."

Callie didn't answer, because she didn't know what to say. So much for getting the conversation started.

Luke leaned in, kissed the tip of her nose. "Relax," he whispered. "It's just supper."

Callie blushed again. Wished she had something more elegant than tuna casserole to serve. "Nothing fancy," she said.

Luke left her to wash his hands at the kitchen sink. "Oh, I don't know," he said. "I think the company is pretty fancy. You look nice, Callie."

She'd switched her jeans and T-shirt for a cotton sundress while the casserole was cooking and Serena was napping, and even applied a little lip gloss and mascara. "Thanks," she answered.

Five seconds later, Serena was back, hair combed, face and hands scrubbed. Unless Callie missed her guess, she'd even brushed her teeth.

"All this beauty," Luke marveled, "is enough to turn a man's head."

Serena beamed. "You'd make a really good dad," she announced.

Callie groaned inwardly.

"And you'd make a really good daughter," Luke answered.

"Everybody sit down," Callie said.

Everybody sat.

Callie set the casserole in the middle of the table, along with a salad and some brown-and-serve rolls. During the meal, Serena did most of the talking, while Luke listened attentively, nodding in the appropriate places.

Callie nibbled at her food and hoped the subject wouldn't turn to fathers and daughters again. Serena's longing for a dad was painfully obvious, and Luke couldn't have helped picking up on it.

Once they'd eaten, Luke insisted on helping Callie clear the table and wash up the dishes. Serena, meanwhile, escorted Bodine on a guided tour of the little house. Every few moments, she chimed something like, "This is my bedroom!"

Luke bumped his shoulder against Callie's. "Hey," he said. "Relax."

"She's—" Callie lowered her head slightly, and a stray tear slipped down one cheek. "She's getting her hopes up."

Luke lifted sudsy hands out of the dishwater, cupped Callie's elbows in them and turned her to face him. "And that's bad?"

Callie blinked as a defense against more tears. She tried to speak, and found she couldn't. She'd never been as tongue-tied around anyone else as she was around Luke.

"It's *okay,* Callie."

Just then, Serena and Bodine returned.

Luke let his hands fall back to his sides.

Callie sniffled once and summoned up a smile.

"Were you guys kissing?" Serena asked.

"No," Callie said.

Luke merely chuckled.

"You'd better get ready for bed," Callie told her daughter. "You've had a big day."

"I had a nap!" Serena protested, arms folded, lower lip protruding. "And I want to show Luke the Tiger Lily necklace."

"Not now," Callie said.

But it was too late. Serena had already pulled open the drawer in the breakfront, where Callie kept her tools and supplies, and brought out the piece they had constructed together.

She carried it proudly to Luke, like a crown on a cushion, and he took a seat at the table to inspect the fine, colorful beadwork.

"This is beautiful," Luke said, and when he raised his eyes to meet Callie's, she saw a tender respect in them. "You and your mom made this?" he asked, turning back to Serena, who was gazing at him in blatant adoration.

Serena nodded, barely able to contain her delight. "I chose the beads all by myself, and Mom strung them just the way I laid them out on the necklace board."

Luke gave a low whistle.

Serena beamed, then turned uncharacteristically shy. "Could I sit on your lap?"

"Sure," Luke said, silently asking Callie's permission, which she granted with a slight nod.

He pushed his chair back a little way, and Serena scrambled up. She pointed at the necklace, now lying on the table in front of them.

"That girl's name is Tiger Lily. She lives with her mom, Dancing Feather, and they make necklaces together."

"Serena," Callie pleaded softly.

Serena ignored her, rushing on, no doubt encouraged by the attentive expression on Luke's face. "They don't have a dad."

"That's a pity," Luke said quietly. "Are they lonesome?"

Serena's smile was beatific. "They have each other," she said. "Most of the time, they're happy."

"Well," Luke responded, "that's good."

"But a dad would be nice," Serena added hurriedly. "And Tiger Lily wants a brother and sister, too."

That was a new one. Serena had never, in Callie's memory, expressed a desire for siblings.

"Serena," Callie said, "say good-night to Dr. Banner and Bodine. It's time for bed."

Callie half expected an all-out rebellion, but Serena only sighed philosophically, stretched to kiss Luke's cheek and slid off his lap to approach Bodine, who remained at her post near the door.

"Good night, Bodine," Serena said. Then, smiling mischievously, she turned to Callie. "Good night, Dancing Feather. You don't have to tuck me in or tell me a story. I'll tell myself a story."

Callie returned Serena's smile, but she felt her lips wobbling, and her throat was all tight again. "Night-night, Tiger Lily," she said.

Once Serena had left the room, Luke stood. "I guess Bodine and I had better go, too. Bodine's got babies to feed, and I've got some rounds to make in the barn and the clinic."

Callie was both relieved and disappointed. She wanted Luke to leave—and she wanted, even more, for him to stay. Unable to voice either of these conflicting desires, she simply stood still, with her back to the sink and her arms folded.

Luke came to her, kissed her lightly on the lips. "Thanks for a great supper and an even better evening," he said.

Callie could only nod.

"Walk me to the truck?"

She nodded again.

Together, they stepped out into the starry night, Bodine following faithfully.

It wasn't far to Luke's truck, and to Callie's way of thinking, they covered the distance much too quickly. Luke opened the door, and Bodine leaped inside and crossed the console to sit in the passenger seat.

"You have a wonderful dog," Callie managed to say. "She didn't beg once, all through supper."

"You have a wonderful daughter," Luke replied.

Callie bit her lower lip. "I'm sorry about the story—it was just something we made up while we were working on the necklace—"

"Now, why would you be sorry, Callie Dorset?"

She swallowed. "It was pretty transparent," she said miserably.

"Serena wants a dad, and she's set her sights on me."

"Yes," Callie said miserably.

Luke curved a finger under Callie's chin and lifted, looking steadily into her eyes. "Kids are honest," he said. "That's one of the nineteen million things I love about them."

Again, Callie was at a loss for words. Sure, there was something happening between her and Luke, something that might be wonderful, but things had a way of going wrong. Nobody knew that better than she did. And Serena would be crushed.

Luke drew her close, held her against him for a long moment. Kissed her on top of the head. Then he lifted her chin again.

"Good night, Dancing Feather," he said.

And then he got into his truck, closed the door, started the engine and drove away.

Callie stood in the yard for a long time after he'd gone, wondering if she dared to dream again.

CHAPTER
∽ FIVE ∽

Three months later...

Posters advertising the annual Parable Rodeo, to be held at the local fairgrounds, had been all over town for weeks. There were six girls competing for the title of Rodeo Queen, all nice, pretty, accomplished young women, but Callie was secretly rooting for Kristen to win.

Rain or shine, no matter what else was going on in her busy life, Kristen had come faithfully to the ranch every day after school and on most weekends to help with chores around the new barn. Now that Mahjong had joined Cherokee, along with two other good-natured ponies Luke had named Tiger Lily and Dancing Feather, there was a lot more to do. Callie had tried to share her tips from

Happy Dan's with Kristen several times, grateful for her patient work with the horses, but the girl always refused. When pressed, she insisted that it was all part of her campaign to reign as that year's queen of the rodeo.

The contest *had* become a lot more sophisticated since Callie's day. She'd won by selling the most raffle tickets—the town had given away a new lawn tractor that year——and the only prizes as queen were fifteen minutes of local fame, a satin sash and a pink western hat banded in rhinestones. These days, there was a hefty scholarship involved, and a year of appearing in parades and at events all over Washington State.

Now the big day had finally come. The pageant was to be held at the high school gymnasium, and excitement was running high all over Parable. Callie was as nervous as if she'd entered the contest herself, and Happy Dan was closing the café early to attend, even though Parable was overflowing with out-of-towners come to watch or participate in the rodeo that weekend.

Serena, who had become quite a competent rider under Kristen's tutelage, as well as Callie's own, was in such a frenzy she could barely eat her supper. Even when Luke joined her and Callie at the corner booth, she didn't settle down.

"What if Kristen doesn't win?" she demanded in a whisper that carried to every corner of the café. She'd insisted on putting on her best dress first thing that morning, and after hanging out at Happy Dan's all day, she looked a little bedraggled.

"Cool it, Tiger Lily," Luke told her quietly. "It won't do any good to worry."

"But she's the *best!*"

"Serena, eat your cheeseburger," Callie said.

"I can't. Anyhow, I want to save it for Bodine."

"Bodine is on a cheeseburger-free diet," Luke put in. "Eat."

Serena nibbled, but presently demanded, for the hundredth time since they'd sat down to supper, "Can we go now?"

Callie sighed.

Luke grinned, took Callie's hand and squeezed it gently. The diamond in her engagement ring bit into her middle finger. "Soon," he said.

"You said that *hours* ago!"

"Days ago," Luke agreed. "Weeks. Months. Decades. *Eons.*"

"What's an e-non?"

Luke looked down at Callie beside him. "About as long as I've been in love with your mother," he answered. He gave her a light, cheeseburger-flavored kiss. A month ago, under a summer moon, he'd asked Callie to marry him, and she'd gladly accepted. After the wedding, which was two weeks away, she and Serena would move to Luke's place, along with the four horses remaining at her place, and she would operate her fledgling therapeutic riding program from there.

"Will you *always* love my mom?" Serena asked. "For e-nons and e-nons?"

"Always," Luke promised. "For e-nons and e-nons."

"All well and good," Happy Dan grumbled, after seeing the last few customers out and turning the Open sign in the door to Closed. "But what am I supposed to do without my best waitress?"

Callie smiled fondly at her boss. Dan had a part-time staff, and she'd been training her permanent replacement, a middle-aged woman named Nellie, for a full week. "I'll stay until Nellie gets the hang of things," she said. "I told you that."

"About a million times," Luke added, making a big deal, for Serena's benefit, of checking his watch. "Well, look at that. Half an hour till the pageant starts. We'd better get over to the gym if we want a decent parking place."

"Save me a seat," Happy Dan said as Luke got out his wallet to pay for the meal. "And put your money away, Doc."

Serena had already bolted for the door.

Luke and Callie slid out of the booth, and Luke paused to lay a hand on Happy Dan's burly shoulder. "Least I can do is pay for supper, after stealing your favorite waitress," he said.

Dan gave one of his rare smiles. "You're not getting off that easy," he said. "I'll expect you to treat my mother's mean little poodle free for the rest of its crabby little life."

"Deal," Luke said.

"Come *on!*" Serena shouted from the door, struggling with the lock.

They rode to the gym behind the high school in Luke's extended-cab truck, Serena in the back seat, straining against her seat belt.

Half the county had turned out for the pageant, it seemed, and the parking lot was practically filled. Luke dropped Callie and Serena off at the front door, parked on the road and sprinted back to join them.

The gym doubled as an auditorium, and the whole place had been festooned with streamers and balloons, prom-style. Folding chairs covered the basketball court, and all but a few were filled. The school band was tuning up, inharmoniously, by the stage. Callie, Serena and Luke found a spot at the back, and Callie put her purse on a fourth chair, to save it for Happy Dan.

"We're too far away!" Serena protested.

"I'll make sure you don't miss anything," Luke told her. "Fifty cents says you can't keep quiet——" He checked his watch again "——until they start the national anthem. That's five whole minutes from now."

"You're on," Serena replied, and pressed her lips together so tightly that Callie had to laugh.

Dan joined them just as the band labored into "The Star-Spangled Banner," and the crowd got to its feet.

Serena, standing on the seat of her chair, stuck out her palm, and Luke soberly dropped two quarters into it, conceding defeat. Callie smiled at his sidelong wink and slipped her arm through his.

The pageant was long.

Each competitor performed a "talent"——singing, tap dancing, piano playing, baton-twirling, the recitation of a long poem. Finally, Kristen's turn came, and she brought her little dog on stage to perform the tricks she'd taught him. The audience applauded enthusiastically for everyone——and no one cheered more loudly than Serena. Perched on one of Luke's shoulders, she clapped and whistled loudly.

After that came the speeches.

It was the usual I-want-to-have-lots-of-babies-and-save-the-world-in-my-spare-time stuff, but Callie found it endearing. All the girls were so young, and so sincere.

Again, Kristen was last.

"I want to be a veterinarian," she said, and sat down.

She certainly deserved the prize for brevity, Callie thought, clapping hard.

The mayor announced that refreshments would be served in the cafeteria after the pageant, and got in a few precampaign plugs for his reelection while the judges deliberated at their table.

Finally, the decision was made.

The town held its collective breath.

Third runner-up—Susan Farley.

Second runner-up—Amanda Sue Gentry.

First runner-up—Dawn Rushmore.

"And the winner—" the mayor boomed, all but drowned out by a drumroll from the band.

Callie crossed her fingers.

"Kristen Young!"

Applause erupted. Band members tooted horns. Confetti drifted, like snow, from the catwalk over the stage.

Callie barely restrained herself from jumping up and down for joy. Serena bounced jubilantly on Luke's shoulder, clapping her hands, and Happy Dan turned to Callie and enfolded her in a crushing bear hug.

Kristen came forward, smiling tearfully, to accept her sash and the traditional pink western hat, gleaming with rhinestones.

The mayor consulted a note handed up to him from the judges' table, waited until the applause subsided a little and cleared his throat.

"Each of these young women had to write an essay," he said, "telling why they wanted to be Queen of the Parable Rodeo. All of them did a fine job, but Kristen's was outstanding. She wrote that she wanted to be queen because it would give her a chance to tell a lot of people about Callie Dorset's therapeutic riding program. As you may know, Kristen is Callie's first volunteer, and she helped set up the Web site to raise funds and draw attention to the program. As a community, we're all proud of Callie's efforts, and we're equally proud of Kristen for stepping up the way she has."

Callie's eyes stung with tears.

Luke returned to her side, set Serena down and put an arm around Callie.

The pageant was over.

People drifted out, in search of refreshments, but there were still a great many waiting to congratulate Kristen and the other girls. Long after Luke and Serena had gone to eat cookies and drink punch, Callie waited.

When her turn came, she hugged Kristen.

Kristen smiled, wiping away tears. "You'll be at the rodeo tomorrow, won't you?" she said. "You'll bring Serena?"

Callie nodded. "We wouldn't miss it," she replied.

THE NEXT DAY, LUKE CAME BY early, pulling a horse trailer behind his truck.

Puzzled, Callie went out to meet him, clad in a bathrobe, her just-washed hair still wrapped in a towel. Serena hadn't even gotten out of bed.

Luke greeted her with a kiss and headed into the barn.

Callie followed. "What are you doing?"

"Taking Mahjong over to my place," he said. "There's a stall open, now that Bill Ryerson's gelding is over his leg surgery. Since nature abhors a vacuum, I thought it would be a good idea to move the pony in before it fills up again."

Callie watched as he opened Mahjong's stall door, put a halter and lead rope on him, and led him outside, toward the trailer. "Right now?" Callie asked. He'd already taken Dancing Feather, Tiger Lily and Cherokee. Couldn't this wait?

Luke opened the door of the trailer and lowered the ramp. "Right now," he said.

"But—"

Luke and Mahjong mounted the ramp together and disappeared into the trailer. "I've already cleared it with Serena," Luke called from inside.

In the next moment, he stood framed in the opening at the back of the trailer, and the sight of him made Callie's heart squeeze.

"Pick you up at ten-thirty, like we planned?" he asked.

"We'll be ready," Callie said. "But I could put coffee on. Rustle up some breakfast—"

"No time," Luke said, descending the ramp, stowing it, and then closing and latching the trailer door. "I've got to unload Mahjong and then check the rodeo stock over at the fairgrounds." He came to her, kissed her again, smartly and on the run. "See you at ten-thirty."

And that was it. He was gone.

Callie turned and went back into the house, wondering at the strange ways of men.

Luke was back promptly at ten-thirty, as promised.

He admired Serena's cowgirl gear, new boots, jeans, a tiny western shirt and a matching hat, bought especially for the occasion. "If I didn't know better," he said, "I'd think *you* were the queen of the rodeo, not Kristen."

"Silly," Serena said, beaming.

Taking in Callie's outfit, jeans and a lacy white top, Luke grinned and shook his head. "You don't look half bad, either," he said.

Callie laughed. "Gee, thanks," she replied.

When they arrived at the fairgrounds, the bleachers were full, and clowns were cavorting in the arena, much to the delight of the crowd. Luke, Callie and Serena had front-row seats, just behind the high fence that protected spectators from bucking broncos and bulls.

Cowboys perched on chute gates, waiting for the first event to begin.

Kristen rode out into the middle of the arena, resplendent in her rodeo queen garb. Her palomino horse, Banjo, pranced proudly beneath her. The rhinestones on her hat dazzled.

And she was leading Mahjong by a long lead rope.

"Ladies and gentlemen!" the announcer boomed over the crackly PA system, "may I present Kristen Young, Queen of the Parable Rodeo!"

"What's Mahjong doing here?" Serena asked.

"I have no idea," Callie answered, trying, and failing, to catch Luke's eye.

Kristen, evidently wearing a wireless mike, addressed the crowd. "Will you please rise for the national anthem?"

Everyone stood.

The soloist from the Baptist church sang.

And when the song ended, Kristen rode directly to the fence, covered the mike with one hand and looked directly at Serena.

"I think I'm going to need some help out here," she whispered earnestly.

Serena's eyes widened. "Me?"

"You," Kristen confirmed.

Luke turned to Callie. "Is it okay?" he asked.

Callie thought a moment—Serena had been riding Mahjong regularly for several months now, and she was good at it, and this was the child's dream—to be a rodeo queen. How could she refuse?

"Okay," she said, a little nervously.

Serena shrieked with delight.

Luke took her by the hand, led her through the nearest gate into the arena, and lifted her into the new saddle on Mahjong's back. Kristen kept a firm hand on the lead rope and mouthed a few words of encouragement to Serena.

And then the two of them rode into the middle of the arena.

The crowd roared with delight.

Serena waved proudly.

And Kristen got down from her horse, walked over to Serena and Mahjong, slipped her sash over her head and put it on Serena.

Callie could barely see, she was crying so hard.

Serena—her sweet, brave little Serena—was, for all practical intents and purposes, queen of the rodeo.

Luke returned to the grandstands, took Callie's hand.

Dreams *did* come true, Callie thought.

The proof was out there in the arena, seated on a little pony named Mahjong—and standing right beside her.

Dear Reader,

It was truly an honor to be asked to contribute a story for Harlequin's wonderful More Than Words project, and when I read about Jeanne Greenberg and her stirring fight to give her daughter Sari the highest possible quality of life, I was deeply moved. Learning of all Jeanne has done, not only for her own child but for many others, I stood in awe once again of the power of a mother's love—and the singular love of a good horse.

I based my tale, *Queen of the Rodeo*, on Jeanne's experience, though of course it's fictional. I offer it to you with a warm and open heart. I hope Callie and Luke, and especially little Serena have touched you, and that they will perhaps also inspire you to take some steps forward—whether as a volunteer, a donor or a fan in the stands. There are so many organizations like SARI that could use your help. Visit www.sari.ca to find out what you can do, or look up a therapeutic riding organization in your area. I'm confident your life will be enriched by the experience.

With love,

Linda Lael Miller

Ruth Renwick
⌐ Inside the Dream ⌐

Imagine you're a seventeen-year-old high school student. You've worked hard, done well and now you're about to graduate. Your classmates are looking forward to the graduation festivities, but for you, the prospects do not look promising. In fact, it's unlikely you will be able to go. There's nothing in your closet remotely suitable to wear for the occasion, and no money to buy what you need.

It may come as a surprise to some to learn how many students face this dilemma. One of the most important occasions in their young lives is looming, and they're actually dreading it because they're probably going to have to miss it. Too many quietly withdraw rather than face the misery and embarrassment of showing up without a dress or tuxedo suitable for the occasion.

Three years ago Ruth Renwick decided to do something about

this. A social worker in the Greater Toronto Area's Peel Region, she was accustomed to helping people in all sorts of troubling situations, so when a fellow worker, Tracey Ciccarelli-Ridsdill, called to ask for help for a single mother whose daughter could not afford to attend her graduation, Ruth went home and ransacked her closets for something suitable. She also provided a corsage, shawl, jewelry and a disposable camera so the girl could take pictures of her graduation.

Helping that girl was the beginning of Inside the Dream, a not-for-profit organization that Ruth set up to assist high school graduates in straitened circumstances. Since that day, she has helped hundreds of young people realize their dreams of graduating alongside their peers.

At a special Boutique Day held once a year in May, the students—who have all been referred by a social worker or counselor—turn up to select gowns (from a minimum of three to five choices for each student, "to give them options"), tuxedos, shoes and accessories. Last year, about one hundred students in the area benefited from this service.

Ruth is touched by their stories. Some of the recipients have such low self-esteem that they're barely able to make eye contact. One girl who was shown a beautiful dress told Ruth, "I don't deserve that dress," and eventually selected the plainest one she could find. Ruth put the beautiful dress in a bag and gave it to her social worker for her. Another girl, verbally abused at home, arrived early at a Boutique Day on her way to her part-time job. "We weren't ready, but she didn't have much time, so we let her come and choose what she needed,"

Ruth says. As she left, the girl told Ruth, "I never had a reason to smile until today." That girl is now at university.

It's students like that—"smart kids in need, kids with great potential"—who inspire Ruth to redouble her efforts. She is constantly on the lookout for people who can help her with donations of clothing and accessories, and isn't the least bit shy about approaching a beautifully dressed woman at a charity event and persuading her to contribute a gown—and to get her friends involved, as well.

As a social worker, Ruth sees all kinds of people in need—so why this particular cause? "I'm a mother," she says simply. "I know what it means to young people to want to celebrate something they have accomplished. It's one of the first big events in your life. I want to help them create memories." And so, with meticulous care, she creates the opportunity for each one of them to be a prince or princess for the day.

Originally from Peru, Ruth had trouble at first believing that there could be such a need in Canada. One mother cried when Ruth took a picture of her with her daughter on graduation day. "She had never had her picture taken with her daughter."

Janace King-Watson, a social worker who has worked closely with Ruth over the past three years, calls her an "incredible blessing" to families. "She makes the young people feel really special and treats them with such dignity," she says. She remembers the beaming face of a boy she had never seen smile, who was transformed by his graduation formal wear. "Something happened that day that made all the difference," she says, noting that many more of the students are now attending their proms as well as graduation, something they were reluctant to do before because they didn't want to embarrass themselves.

The students who come to the Boutique Day are comfortable because they know all their information is confidential. They are each accompanied by a volunteer "godmother" (for girls) or "godfather" (for boys) to help and advise them. The volunteers take tremendous pride in the successful outcomes of the students, Ruth says. "Look what happened to *my* boy…or *my* girl" is a typical reaction.

Volunteers are a big part of the enterprise. They include the hairdresser who styles each girl's hair before her big event, the person who does makeup, a professional photographer, and a seamstress who does the alterations, as well as the many individuals who run errands and donate clothing, and corporate sponsors who provide everything from snacks and dinners to cosmetics and tickets to various events for the students. A school in the area recently held a drive and donated almost three hundred dresses, and boxes of tuxedos were sent from a boutique in New Jersey that was closing. Ruth uses her Web site to solicit donations, but also to provide help and advice to other communities interested in setting up a similar program.

By persistence and persuasion, Ruth is helping to build precious memories for young people who would otherwise be deprived of a pleasure others take for granted. She wants everyone she meets to become involved. "If you can't give me anything yourself," she tells people, "you have friends who might be able to."

It's not just a request for help—it's an invitation to come Inside the Dream.

For more information visit www.insidethedream.org or write to Inside the Dream Formal Attire Program, 3326 Martins Pine Crescent, Mississauga, Ontario L5L lG4 Canada.

SHERRYL WOODS
~ BLACK TIE AND PROMISES ~

ᕇ—SHERRYL WOODS—ᕇ

With her roots firmly planted in the South, Sherryl Woods has written many of her more than 100 books in that distinctive setting, whether in her home state of Virginia, her adopted state, Florida, or her much-adored South Carolina. She's also especially partial to small towns wherever they may be.

A member of Novelists Inc., Sisters in Crime and Romance Writers of America, Sherryl divides her time between her childhood summer home overlooking the Potomac River in Colonial Beach, Virginia, and her oceanfront home in Key Biscayne, Florida, with its lighthouse view. "Wherever I am, if there's no water in sight, I get a little antsy," she says.

CHAPTER
~ ONE ~

J odie Fletcher leaned across her desk and studied the earnest expression on Laurie Winston's face. Though beautiful and popular, Laurie was one of those high school seniors who actually thought more about others than she did about herself. Perhaps it was simply her upbringing, or maybe losing her mother at fifteen had turned Laurie into a more compassionate person. Whatever the explanation, Jodie tended to give more credence to Laurie's heartfelt pleas than she did to those of the teenager's self-absorbed classmates.

Okay, there was more to it than that, Jodie admitted to herself. She paid attention because Laurie was Trent Winston's daughter. A lifetime ago Jodie and Trent had been in a relationship that had been doomed from the start. She'd seen that, even if Trent hadn't.

Trent had ambitions to make it big in high-end residential construction, and he'd needed a woman by his side who could help him make the climb to the top. Jodie hadn't been that woman. She'd had zero self-confidence after years of being the less-than-perfect daughter, the less-than-perfect student, the less-than-perfect younger sister. Back then, she hadn't considered herself an ideal match for anyone, despite Trent's obvious feelings for her.

In what might have been the most unselfish gesture of her life, she'd ended the relationship, setting Trent free to find someone better suited to help him build his empire than a woman still struggling to find herself. He'd fought for her for a while, but in the end he must have seen the wisdom in her decision because he'd finally stopped calling. A couple of years after the breakup, she'd read about his marriage to Megan Davis, the socialite daughter of multimillionaire Warren Davis, a gorgeous, delicate woman with all the right connections. Only then had Jodie truly moved on.

When she'd joined the staff at Rockingham High School last year, she'd been taken aback when she'd gone through the student records and discovered that Laurie Winston was Trent's daughter and that he'd been widowed for two years. Every time she encountered Laurie, she avidly looked for traces of Trent in Laurie's features. Obviously, though, Laurie had inherited her coloring and looks from her mother's side of the family. Jodie did see a tiny hint of Trent in Laurie's persistence and in the way she spoke so passionately when she cared about something, like now.

"There has to be something we can do, Ms. Fletcher," Laurie

repeated. "There just has to be. It's not fair that so many kids miss the prom and all the other graduation activities just because they don't have anything to wear. It happens every year and it's wrong."

Jodie had often thought much the same thing at her old school in a neighboring district, but until this past summer she'd been at a loss as to what could be done. Now she actually had a few ideas, thanks to a friend she'd visited in Canada who was familiar with a program called Inside the Dream that provided clothing, accessories and everything else that was needed to kids who might otherwise have to miss those important senior-year events.

Longtime staff at Rockingham High School told Jodie that as the prom had become more elaborate and expensive, it was no longer within reach for many of the students. More and more young people pretended not to care that they were missing their senior prom. Girls with stars in their eyes, who'd been dreaming of that night ever since they'd started high school, suddenly claimed to have better things to do. The boys, rigid with pride, made their own plans for a guys' night out and swore it was better than any dumb old dance could ever be.

As a counselor, Jodie had seen the same unspoken heartbreak many times at her previous school, but she was curious about what had made Laurie aware of the dilemma faced by many of her class-mates.

"Why is this so important to you?" she asked the teen.

With her pale complexion, there was no mistaking the blush that spread across Laurie's cheeks. She brushed a strand of silky blond hair back from her face. A diamond tennis bracelet winked on her wrist. "Actually it's because of Mike," she admitted. "You know Mike Brentwood, right?"

Since Rockingham High only had a few hundred students, Jodie knew most of them, at least by name. She knew Mike better than most. She nodded. "You and Mike have been dating for a while now, haven't you?"

"Since we were juniors," Laurie said.

"So you know his family?"

Laurie nodded.

"Then you've known for some time that the expense of a big dance might be more than he could handle," Jodie suggested.

Mike was one of four kids being raised in a mostly affluent community by a struggling single mom who earned minimum wage. Money was always tight. Jodie knew more than she intended to share with Laurie. She'd already helped to get Mike's younger sisters and brother free school breakfasts and lunches because they were coming to school hungry too often. Mike had refused any similar help for himself, claiming he got to eat at his after-school job as a busboy at a local restaurant.

"I've known from the beginning that it's tough for his family," Laurie said. "Last year we skipped prom. We talked about doing that again this year, and to be honest, I'd be okay with it, but I can tell Mike feels really, really bad about it, like he's letting me down or something. And then, when we were setting up the organizing committee, I was talking to a couple of girls in my class and they admitted they didn't have the money for dresses and getting their hair done and all that stuff, so I started asking around. There must be at least a dozen girls, probably more, who can't afford to do any of the things that the rest of us can. I didn't ask the boys, but I'll bet there's just as many of them who don't have extra cash. They shouldn't be left out, Ms. Fletcher. Like I said before, it's wrong."

Jodie nodded, impressed by her compassion. "Okay, then, if you've done all this research, I'm sure you have some thoughts about what needs to happen."

Laurie grinned. "Actually, that's why I came to you. You're in the business of fixing things. I only had one idea and basically it sucked."

Jodie laughed at her candid assessment. "What idea was that?"

"To cancel prom and do something different that everyone could afford." Laurie shrugged. "That didn't seem fair, either. In fact, I'd probably get run out of school for even suggesting it."

"You could be right," Jodie agreed. There were some traditions that no one wanted to tamper with. The prom was one of those rites of passage.

"So?" Laurie asked, that earnest expression back on her face. "Do you have any ideas?"

"Actually, I do," Jodie admitted. "But it's only a few months until prom. It would take a lot of work to pull off my plan in time, but I'm willing to give it a try if you'll agree to work with me."

"Tell me," Laurie said eagerly. "I'm sure I can get more people to help if it means everyone will be able to participate this year."

Jodie pulled up the Inside the Dream Web site on her computer and turned the screen so that Laurie could see it. "A friend I was visiting last summer told me about this organization," she explained. "They find donations of dresses, suits, tuxedos, shoes, you name it. Some tuxedo rental businesses donate gift certificates. The organizers get volunteer seamstresses to make alterations. They find hairstylists and makeup artists who can help out."

Laurie's eyes lit up. "That is so awesome. I'll bet we could do that here. A lot of moms give tons of business to the boutiques in the area. I'll bet they could persuade some of them to donate gowns. And there must be a lot of dads who buy or rent tuxedos all the time, too. They might be able to arrange for some rentals or give us their old tuxes."

"Some of your classmates might view getting a free gown or a tuxedo as charity," Jodie cautioned. "They still might not want to go to prom."

"But at least it'll be their choice, then. It won't be because it's impossible."

"What about tickets, Laurie?" Jodie asked. "Have you considered that? The cost of the tickets alone can be prohibitive for some of these students. Unless you're willing to cut costs dramatically and do a smaller event, all of the rest might not matter."

Laurie sat back. "Oh, my gosh, I hadn't even thought about that. We've barely started with all arrangements, but I already know how expensive the hotel and food are going to be. We tried to get good deals, but I don't see any way to cut those costs."

"Unless you did the prom here," Jodie suggested. "That's what lots of high schools do."

Laurie looked skeptical. "I could suggest it, I suppose, but I know the committee would hate it."

"Any other ideas, then?" Jodie asked.

Suddenly Laurie's expression brightened. "I remember some of the moms talking about a fund-raiser they were doing. They found businesses to underwrite a lot of the costs. Do you think we could do that, maybe have a program with ads in it? I'll bet if we explained that this was something kids were going to save and look at again and again and show their parents, too, a lot of stores would see it as good advertising. Then we could cut ticket prices. I think everyone should pay something, though, don't you?"

"I do," Jodie agreed. She had to admire Laurie's enthusiasm and her wisdom. "Okay, then, once you know your hotel and food costs, do a mock-up of the program and figure out possible ad sizes and costs. You could even pitch the hotel to see if they'd give you a bit of a break in return for a full-page ad. I'd suggest you have a separate committee to handle all this, since it's going to be time-consuming."

Laurie started scribbling notes like mad. "We have a committee meeting tomorrow. I'll bring this up then."

"And let's make a list of the donations and volunteers we'll need," Jodie suggested, reaching for her own pad and pen and starting to jot down notes.

"You're the best, Ms. Fletcher. This is going to be the best prom ever."

Not the best, Jodie thought, but if she could make a difference for just a few teens, give them memories she'd never had, it would be worth all the extra time she'd have to put in over the next few months. It would also give her a chance to spend some time with Trent's daughter and get to know her a little better. And maybe find out just what kind of man Trent had become.

TRENT WINSTON SHRUGGED out of his tuxedo jacket, jerked off the annoying bow tie he'd struggled with earlier, and then went to work on the studs in the overly starched shirt.

"I am never, ever going to another black-tie event," he declared to the empty room as he tossed the offending garments onto his king-size bed. To lend emphasis to the statement, he entered his walk-in closet and pulled out two more custom-tailored tuxedos and threw them onto the bed as well.

He looked up to see his daughter in the doorway, staring at him with a bewildered expression.

"What are you doing?" Laurie asked, her gaze on the discarded formal wear.

"I've just made a decision," he announced. "I have attended my last black-tie event."

"Really?"

To his surprise, she didn't seem the least bit upset. For years she'd loved to sit quietly and watch while he and her mother got ready for all of the fancy charity auctions, dinners and dances that Megan insisted they attend if his company was to grow. Megan had considered these extravagant bashes to be an investment in their future. Laurie had always acted as if her parents were leading some elaborate fairy-tale existence—the dark-haired prince taking his blond princess off to the ball.

Since Megan's death, he'd continued to pay the exorbitant prices for these mostly boring functions out of habit, but the reality was that Winston Construction no longer needed the same exposure that it had in its early days. He'd been custom-building luxury homes in the far western suburbs of northern Virginia for more than a dozen years now. His reputation was solid, and word-of-mouth gave him more opportunities than he could ever accept without sacrificing his hands-on approach which included overseeing every detail from framing the house to installing the kitchen cabinets. These days he could just as easily write a check and satisfy the company's commitment to various charities. It would leave his nights free to spend time with his daughter, who was growing up too darn fast.

Tonight she was wearing wrinkled pajamas that to his eye didn't look all that different from the casual pants and tank tops she wore to the mall, though these pants did have some kind of kitty design she probably wouldn't be caught dead wearing out in public. With her face scrubbed clean of makeup, he was able to forget for a moment that she was seventeen, almost an adult. It always caught him off guard when he realized that next year she'd be away at college. Right now, she still looked like his little girl.

"Okay, what's on your mind?" he asked, expecting the lecture Megan would have given him about the importance of networking. In some ways, Laurie was her mother's daughter, savvy about getting ahead. She'd already chosen her college major—investment banking. In other ways, she'd inherited his down-to-earth attitude and total lack of pretensions.

"What are you going to do with those tuxes?" she asked, surprising him.

"Give them to a thrift shop, I suppose. Why?"

"Can I have them?"

He stared at her blankly. "Why would you want three tuxedos?"

She grinned. "Prom's coming up, and yesterday Ms. Fletcher and I came up with this totally awesome idea to make sure that everybody gets to go. Did you know there are kids at school who stay home every year because they can't afford the tickets or the clothes?"

"I had no idea," he said. "And frankly, I'm a little surprised that it matters so much to you."

"Dad, you know why," she said impatiently. "Mike."

The single word was enough to have him grinding his teeth. Mike Brentwood was a good kid. He was polite, hard-working and seemed smart enough, but Trent thought Laurie was way too young to be so serious about a boy. Any boy.

Every time he tried to broach the subject, though, she looked at him as if he'd just arrived from Mars and was speaking some incomprehensible language. Or worse, as if he were some prejudiced jerk who hated the kid for being poor. Trent hadn't always had money. He knew what it was to struggle to make ends meet. He also knew that a serious relationship could be a distraction that a kid like Mike didn't need. He wasn't just thinking of his daughter, he told himself nobly. He was also thinking of Mike and his future.

He decided now was not the time to rehash that particular sore subject.

"If Mike needs to borrow a tuxedo, all you have to do is ask," he told Laurie.

"You're missing the point, Dad. He's not the only one. And Mike would never accept charity from you. He'd be totally humiliated."

Trent could understand that. To be honest, he would have felt the same way at eighteen. Borrowing clothes from his girlfriend's dad would have been too embarrassing. He'd had a tough-enough time swallowing his pride as an adult and letting Megan's father back him when he'd started up his business. Even though the deal had been handled in a totally businesslike fashion and he'd paid back every dime of that money with interest, it had put their relationship on an uneven footing from the beginning. He doubted they'd have had any contact at all now if it weren't for Laurie. Warren Davis adored his granddaughter as he had his own daughter. Trent would never get in the way of that bond, especially with Megan gone.

He sat down on the edge of his bed and patted a place beside him. "Tell me about this plan of yours."

Laurie sat cross-legged beside him and explained that so many kids missed out on activities because they couldn't afford the right clothes or even the tickets. "So, I spoke to Ms. Fletcher and she told me about Inside the Dream, an organization that helps kids get to the prom. We looked at the Web site and decided that even though we only have a few months, we could do the same thing here. The prom committee met today and everyone agreed. In fact, they're really jazzed about the whole idea. I'm in charge of finding clothing donations and accessories. Dave Henderson and Marcy Tennyson said they'd try to get underwriting and sell ads in the program. Sue McNally is contacting hairstylists and manicurists." She rolled her eyes. "With the money she and her mom spend in salons, I'm sure they won't have any trouble guilting people into helping. Ms. Fletcher said she'd try to find a seamstress who could make alterations. And she's in charge of identifying all the kids who might need clothes for that night. I gave her a list, but she'll finalize it. She thinks some are going to be pretty hard to sell on the idea."

"She could be right," Trent warned. He thought of the teenage sons of some of his employees. Their families were struggling to remain in homes they'd had for years and were resentful of the wealthy newcomers who'd moved into the area, even as they accepted that their income was dependent on those same people.

"The boys might have an especially hard time with it. Have you spoken to Mike to see what he thinks?"

She shook her head. "But I'm not worried. I'm leaving that to Ms. Fletcher. She can talk anybody into anything. She's great!"

"Still, it sounds like a lot to be accomplished in a short period of time. It's already January and prom is when? May?"

Laurie nodded.

"Sounds like you have your work cut out for you. What do you need from me besides the clothes off my back?"

Laurie giggled. "Dad, you said yourself you weren't ever going to wear those tuxedos again. If you change your mind, you can buy a new one."

"I won't change my mind," he said adamantly.

Laurie's expression sobered. "It's because of Mom, huh? You don't like going to those parties without her."

"That's part of it," he conceded. "But I never liked going in the first place. Your mom thought they were important for business and she enjoyed them. She'd grown up going to all sorts of fancy events. Me, I feel dressed up if my blue jeans have a crease in them."

Because he didn't want to talk about all the differences between him and Megan, differences that had started to grate before she'd been diagnosed with cancer, he changed the subject. He never wanted to disillusion Laurie with the knowledge that her parents' marriage had been anything but idyllic right up until the end. Her mom was gone. There was no reason to spoil the memories.

"Come on, kiddo, what else can I do to help?"

"After the committee meeting today, Ms. Fletcher and I talked again. We were thinking that it might be fun if we had a big place where all the girls could spend the day together going through the dresses and shoes and stuff, sort of like a real shopping spree. The guys, too. Not in the same room, of course, just the same place, so shopping would be part of the fun. Maybe we could even use the place again on prom night, so the girls could get their hair done, fix their makeup. Did I tell you that Molly Williams is going to ask her mom to see if the department store where she works at Tyson's Corner will donate makeup samples?"

Trent grinned at her enthusiasm. "You're really excited about this, aren't you? It's not all about Mike, either, is it?"

"No, it's not," she said, her expression thoughtful. "I mean, it started that way, but then it got bigger. And when I talked to Ms. Fletcher and she said she thought there was a real need for this, too, then I knew it was something worth doing. Everyone I've spoken to has been willing to pitch in." She wrapped her arms around his neck. "I'm so lucky, Dad. I take way too much stuff for granted, you know. Since Mom died, I guess I've started to realize that things can change in an instant and we should never take anything for granted."

He gave her a hug, this seventeen-going-on-thirty-year-old kid of his. "I'm so proud of you. And I have an idea about that place you want for your shopping extravaganza."

Her eyes lit up. "Really? At first I was thinking about the gym at school, but that's really boring and it mostly smells like sweat, you know what I mean?"

"I do, indeed," Trent said. "Why don't you call your granddad and ask him if he'd let you use the ballroom at Oak Haven? It's been years since he's thrown a party in there, so I'm not sure what shape it's in, but it's certainly big enough."

"And it has that really fabulous chandelier," Laurie said excitedly. "Oh, Dad, it would be perfect. Do you think Granddad would agree?"

"I think he'd like being a part of this project of yours. And I think he would do just about anything for his favorite girl. Heck, if you go back there on prom night to get ready, he might even spring for a few limos to take all of you to the dance." He winked at her. "Just make sure you tell him that was your idea, not mine."

"And it's a great idea!" She bounced off the bed. "I'm going to call him right now."

Trent snagged her hand. "Hold on, kiddo. It's after midnight. You might want to wait till morning."

"Right," she said at once. "I'll call first thing." She started from the room, her arms loaded with the tuxedos he'd tossed aside. When she turned back there was a glint in her eyes that should have been a warning. "There is one thing you could do, Dad."

"Oh?" he asked warily.

"Three tuxedos are a really good start, but we need at least ten. Or gift certificates for rentals."

"I'll make some calls," he promised.

"And one more thing…"

"What?"

"Maybe you could help out with the guys on shopping day and on prom night. Ms. Fletcher's going to be there to coordinate things for the girls. You'd have to come to a couple of committee meetings, probably, but it won't take a lot of time other than that."

"I could do that," he said. "I hope you remember that I'm lousy at tying a bow tie, though."

"Believe me, you're an expert compared to the guys at school."

Again, she started from the room, then paused. "Would you do *one* more thing?"

"If I can."

"Ms. Fletcher has to chaperone at the dance and she always does it alone. There are other teachers there, but mostly couples. I thought maybe you'd come with her. I mean, she's doing all this work, so she deserves to have a good time, too, right?"

Trent's stomach did one of those nosedives it always did when his daughter had just bamboozled him. "Maybe Ms. Fletcher would prefer to get her own date," he suggested mildly.

Laurie shook her head. "She never does, at least not at last year's prom or for Homecoming last fall. I checked. I guess she takes her chaperoning duties seriously. But this time is different. You'll be on the committee, too, so it won't be like a big deal or anything."

"Does she know you're asking me to do this?"

Laurie flushed, a sure sign that there was at least one more surprise in store. "Not exactly. I thought maybe you could ask her yourself, so she won't think it's like some pity thing that I set up." She ran back, dropped the clothes and threw her arms around him. "You'll do it, won't you? Please."

"You just absconded with all my tuxedos," he reminded her.

"I'll give you one back," she offered. "Or you can buy a new one. That'll give you leverage to persuade the store owner to give us some free."

Trent mentally cursed the fact that he'd been blessed with a daughter, rather than a son. A son would never try to manipulate him into something like this. A son wouldn't have him twisted around his finger.

"Can I at least meet Ms. Fletcher first?" he asked, a plaintive note in his voice.

"You'll have plenty of time to get to know her," Laurie promised.

"She's totally awesome, Dad. You're going to love her. Now, promise me you'll do this. No excuses, okay?"

Since Trent had never been able to deny his daughter anything, he nodded reluctantly. "I promise."

But as his daughter's enthusiastic words sank in, Trent finally grasped that this was about a whole lot more than one night and one dance. His daughter—God help him—was matchmaking.

CHAPTER TWO

Mike Brentwood slouched down in the chair across from Jodie, his expression filled with annoyance. Slim and wiry, he was blessed with a quickness that had made him an outstanding receiver on the football team. In addition, he had dimples, wavy brown hair with golden highlights that most girls would envy, and blue eyes that were like chips of ice when filled with the kind of disdain he was obviously feeling now.

"This was Laurie's idea, wasn't it?" he grumbled. "She wants to go to prom and she knows I can't rent a tux, so now she's made this whole big thing out of it. Come on, Ms. Fletcher, give me a break. I don't want to wear some hand-me-down tuxedo that won't even fit right. I'll feel like a jerk."

"Maybe you should think about Laurie's feelings," she suggested.

"She's going to a lot of trouble, not just for you, but for your class-mates. She really wants this night to be special for everyone."

"It's a dance," Mike said disparagingly. "It's not going to bring about world peace. I don't see why it's such a big deal. She didn't raise this much fuss about the Homecoming dance last fall or prom last year."

"I imagine she was trying to spare your feelings," Jodie told him. "Besides, neither of those was the very last dance you'll ever attend in high school."

Mike frowned at her. "Okay, maybe, but I don't see why Laurie didn't just ask me herself, instead of having you get on my case. We talked about this. In fact, she told me just a couple of weeks ago she didn't even care about going to prom this year."

"And I'm sure she meant it at the time, but then she started get-ting involved with the committee and she realized how many kids were feeling left out." She gave him a wry look. "Now she's really ex-cited about making sure everyone gets to go this year. I imagine she didn't want to tell you herself that she'd changed her mind."

"Yeah, well, she should have. I would have told her this whole clothing drive of hers is a dumb idea."

Jodie winced at his depiction of the project. If that's how these kids were looking at it, it was going to be a tough sell.

"I was actually hoping you'd help me to convince some of the other guys that it's an okay thing to do," she said, trying a new tactic. "I need someone the other students respect to pave the way on this. You're a big football star. You're going to college next year on a scholarship. You're the perfect role model for a lot of these young men."

He rolled his eyes at the unabashed flattery. "How many different ways do I have to say I'm not interested?"

"Come on, Mike," she coaxed. "Help me out here."

"Why would I do that?"

"How about because I'm the one who convinced you that you could be accepted by a good college. I'm the one who helped you fill out all those scholarship applications. Let's face it, your future is brighter because of me."

He groaned. "If I'd known I was going to hear about that for the rest of my life, I might not have accepted your help. You didn't say it came with strings."

"It didn't. I was doing my job." She gave him a chagrined look. "I was just hoping you'd be so grateful, you'd want to help. Forget that and think about Laurie. I know it would make her really happy if you agreed to this, not just for her sake, but for yours. She wants you to have this night to remember, too." She watched his face intently. She could tell from his wavering expression that she finally had him. For all of his bluster, Mike didn't really want Laurie to miss out on prom. Jodie sat silently and waited while he weighed the alternatives— a hit to his pride or a miserable, disappointed girlfriend.

"You really don't play fair," he mumbled at last.

She grinned. "But I'm effective, don't you agree?"

"You really think we can convince some of these hard-asses to accept a freebie tux so they can go to a dance?"

Her smile spread. "I convinced you, didn't I? If we work together, who'll be able to resist us?"

TRENT WAS RUNNING a half-hour late when he slipped into the classroom where the latest prom committee meeting was being held. Though there had been others, this was the first he'd been able to attend. Laurie beamed at him as he sat down quickly in the closest seat. One of the other girls was giving a report. Since she had perfectly highlighted blond hair, he had to assume this was Sue McNally, who was in charge of getting volunteer stylists for the big night. Apparently she and her mother—Candace McNally, if he remembered correctly from a few encounters at charity functions—had lined up five hairdressers, two makeup experts, but only one manicurist.

"Don't worry, though," she told the committee confidently. "My mom says once she talks to Henri, all of his manicurists will pitch in. He'll make sure of it."

"Very good, Sue—that's excellent work in just a month," someone behind him said, most likely the awesome Ms. Fletcher.

Oddly, her voice sounded familiar, tugging at a distant memory. A scent, so faint he wasn't sure he hadn't imagined it, teased his memory as well. Trent wanted to shift around for a look, but another student stepped to the front of the room to give a report on corsages.

The whole discussion took him back to his own senior year, when the most important things in life seemed to be prom and graduation festivities. He could recall standing in a florist shop, his palms sweaty, little more than twenty hard-earned bucks in his pocket, trying to decide if three tiny pink rosebuds clustered together with a bit of lace would impress Jean Kerrigan or convince her that he was the biggest loser in the class. The florist—grandmotherly Norma Gates—had apparently sensed his uncertainty and assured him he wouldn't be embarrassed. She'd been right. Jean had been thrilled, right up until he'd jabbed her with a pin while trying to help her put on the corsage without accidentally grazing her breast. Oh, the pitfalls of being an awkward adolescent. He didn't envy his daughter or any of the rest of them the next few months.

He listened to half a dozen enthusiastic reports from those on the committee, impressed with the amount of work they'd accomplished since last month. When asked, he chimed in with his own report on the tuxedos he'd managed to secure. Bottom line, there were already enough dresses and tuxedos for the teens who needed them.

"Do you think we should stop now and be content with our success for this first year?" Ms. Fletcher asked. "You all have done an amazing job, as it is."

Across from him, Laurie shook her head. "I think there are a few more kids we can talk into going if we take another shot at it. I just know they'll regret it later if they say no. Turning us down was, like, some gut instinct. They didn't even think about it."

"I'm not sure I have another argument left in me," Ms. Fletcher responded, sounding weary. "Mike tried, too, with the boys, but some of them were adamant. Neither of us felt we could push any harder."

"They're just being stubborn," Laurie insisted.

"A trait I'm sure you recognize, Laurie," Ms. Fletcher said wryly. "Okay, I'll try one more time."

Trent heard her stand up behind him and watched curiously as she stepped briskly to the front of the room. She was wearing a pair of navy-blue linen slacks, a sweater in a paler shade of blue. Dark brown hair with just enough curl to make it unmanageable sprang into ringlets at the nape of her neck. Her low-heeled shoes made a staccato sound as she walked, but it was the subtle, very feminine sway of her hips that held his attention.

When she reached the front of the room and turned to look at him directly for the first time, it took every bit of his well-developed control not to let his mouth gape. Jodie? Jodie Jameson? Memories flooded through his mind in such a rush that he didn't realize at first that she was speaking to him.

Trying to gather his composure, he stared at her blankly. "What?"

He glanced sideways and saw Laurie regarding him with a confused expression. He forced a smile. "Sorry. I got sidetracked for a second. What did you say, um…" He caught himself just before calling her Jodie and added, "Ms. Fletcher?"

"I asked if you thought it would be possible to round up a few more tuxes?" she said, barely hiding a smile, well aware that she'd completely thrown him and quite pleased with herself about it.

"I'll do my best," he promised.

First, though, he needed to get out of this room and far, far away from the woman who'd walked out of his life twenty years ago with virtually no explanation.

They'd met on a summer job, dated all through college. He'd planned on asking her to marry him right after graduation, but before he could get the carefully rehearsed words out of his mouth, she'd told him she was sorry, but she didn't think they were going to work out, after all. Worse, before he could recover from that stunning announcement, she had whirled around and walked away.

For weeks he'd called and stopped by her apartment, ready to plead for an explanation, but she'd refused to take his calls and pretended she wasn't home. It was as if she'd severed him from her life with one quick, unrepentant slash, leaving behind a wound that simply wouldn't heal.

His heart broken and his self-confidence shattered, he'd been a mess when Megan had literally waltzed into his life at a party one night. He'd been working for a developer of cookie-cutter housing projects and was at the party to network with prospective clients, when Megan had twirled by in another man's arms. Somehow she'd wrangled a switch in partners on the dance floor and that had been that. She was the joy and laughter that had been missing from his life since Jodie's abrupt departure. Her determination to catch him had been a much-needed balm to his bruised ego.

Once again, he dared to meet Jodie's gaze. There was a bit less certainty in her eyes now, as if she understood that this wasn't quite the happy surprise reunion she'd been envisioning. They were two adults in a roomful of impressionable teenagers, including his daughter, so clearly she knew there wouldn't be an explosion of temper, either.

Trent wanted out. Not just out of this room, but out of the whole prom thing. Twenty years ago he'd wanted to confront Jodie and demand answers, but those answers were no longer relevant. *She* was no longer relevant. Life moved on. He hadn't thought about Jodie in years, or if he had, he'd squelched the memory before it could start to nag.

Around him, the meeting began to break up. Suddenly Laurie was beside him, her expression quizzical.

"Dad, are you okay? You look kind of funny, like you've seen a ghost or something."

Yes, that was it, he thought. A ghost. That's all Jodie was. He'd gotten over her years ago. He had a full life, a wonderful daughter. He didn't need to be taking any unexpected strolls down memory lane. He swore to himself it wasn't bitterness he felt when he looked at Jodie. He felt nothing. Less than nothing. She simply didn't matter. He wouldn't allow her to matter ever again, because she couldn't be trusted.

"Sweetie, I have to run. I just remembered an important meeting and I'm late already. We'll talk tonight, okay?"

He gave Laurie a glancing kiss on the cheek and bolted from the room with its scent of chalk and floor polish and lily of the valley, suddenly desperate for fresh air. Lily of the valley, for heaven's sake. How could he have shoved Jodie from his mind for all these years, but still remember her favorite perfume? When Megan had brought home the same scent, probably a more expensive version of it, he'd accidentally-on-purpose broken the bottle the first time she'd worn it. Thankfully, she'd never replaced it.

He filled his lungs with fresh air, then headed for his car. Inside he sat behind the wheel and stared straight ahead, trying to figure out what he was supposed to do now. He supposed he could suck it up and pretend everything was just fine. Or he could come up with an excuse that would get him out of town until prom was over and the "awesome" Ms. Fletcher was no more a factor in Laurie's life than she had been in his for more than twenty years. Personally, he liked option number two, but he knew his daughter. The odds that he could get away with a vanishing act were slim to none.

Besides, as Laurie was bound to remind him, he'd promised to take Ms. Fletcher to the prom, and the one thing Trent had vowed never to do was break a promise to his daughter the way he'd broken so many he'd made to his wife.

"DAD, YOU WERE ACTING really weird today, like something had freaked you out," Laurie said as she dished up spaghetti for their dinner that night.

Ever since Megan's death, Laurie had taken over responsibility for dinner. When she was fourteen, that hadn't amounted to much more than setting the table and warming the meals left by a housekeeper, but for the past year or so, she'd been cooking. She wasn't half bad at it, either.

"Sorry," Trent said. "I just remembered that meeting at the last minute and I got distracted after that." Determined to shift the subject, he asked, "Have you spoken to your grandfather yet?"

Laurie's eyes lit up. "I talked to him a few days ago and then I went by there after school today. I'd forgotten how cool that ballroom is.

It's amazing, Dad. The floor has all this inlaid wood. It must have cost a fortune. And the windows go from the floor all the way up to the ceiling, so there's all this light shining in, or there would be if someone washed them. The ceiling must be fifteen feet high, maybe more. I wish I'd seen it just once when it was filled with people dancing and that amazing chandelier was all lit up."

She frowned. "Of course, it's kind of a mess now. Granddad's been using it for storage. He says he hasn't gone in there since Grandma died. In fact, he says the last time anyone was in there was when Mom dropped off some of our stuff that she wanted out of the attic here. He said if the kids will help clean the place up and if I'll sort through all the old junk and either give it away to charity or decide if I might want it someday, we can use the ballroom for our shopping day. I've already called Mike and he says he can get some of the guys to haul stuff away. A couple of his friends have pickups. And if a bunch of us go after school one day, we can polish the floor and mop up all the dust. Granddad said he'd have a service do the windows and the chandelier, 'cause he doesn't want us climbing on ladders."

"I hadn't realized it was in such bad shape," Trent commented. "Given how little time you all have with planning the prom, studying for finals and so on, maybe it would be better to find someplace that won't require so much work."

"No, please, there's lots of time," Laurie said. "Between Mike and me, we'll find enough kids who'll be willing to help and it won't take that long. It's just a bunch of dusty boxes and some old, broken-down furniture."

Trent winced. "I suspect some of that broken-down furniture, as you call it, could qualify as priceless antiques. Don't go giving any of it away without checking with your grandfather."

"But he said——"

"Trust me," Trent insisted. After growing up in a house filled with furniture from secondhand shops, he had a healthy appreciation for antiques, not just for the value, but for the history. "If he doesn't want those things and you're absolutely certain you'll never want them, then get an appraiser from one of the antique shops to come by and see if they want to take the pieces on consignment."

She gave him an odd look. "Granddad doesn't need the money."

And, truth be told, Warren didn't have a sentimental bone in his body, either, Trent thought, but he hated the idea of carelessly tossing family heirlooms aside. Someday Laurie might come to appreciate them. He should probably go through the boxes Megan had stored there, too, in case there was anything important.

"Why don't you and I do a quick survey before everyone else gets in there to clean?" he suggested. "That way something valuable won't get tossed by mistake."

She shrugged. "Okay, whatever." Her gaze narrowed as she studied him thoughtfully. "So, Dad, what did you think of Ms. Fletcher?"

"She seems okay," he said neutrally.

"That's it? That's the best you can do?"

"Sweetie, we barely spoke."

"Because you took off out of there as if the room was on fire." She regarded him suspiciously. "Did you really have a meeting?"

"Do you think I'd make that up?"

She gave him a knowing grin. "That's what you do whenever you want to get out of something without offending anybody. Besides, I saw you sitting in the parking lot for a whole half hour after you took off."

"You think you're smart, don't you?" he mumbled.

"I *am* smart, and I have the grades to prove it," she responded. "So, what was really going on, Dad? Did you take an instant dislike to Ms. Fletcher or something?"

"Not exactly."

"What then?"

"Nothing. It's not a big deal."

"If it's not a big deal, then it's a little one, but it's still a deal. That means something did happen."

He shook his head. "Your logic astounds me."

"But I'm right," she insisted. "I know I am. Come on, Dad, tell me why seeing Ms. Fletcher freaked you out."

Trent wondered if he could explain his previous relationship with Jodie in a way that would minimize its importance. He had to try. This was no time to start keeping secrets from his daughter, or to let her imagination run wild and magnify things out of all proportion to their importance.

"Okay, here it is in a nutshell. I recognized Ms. Fletcher from a very long time ago. Her name wasn't Fletcher back then, so I had no idea your guidance counselor was someone I actually knew. It just caught me off guard, you know, the way it surprised you that time we ran into one of your school friends when we were on vacation in Maine."

"You know Ms. Fletcher?" Laurie repeated, looking almost as stunned as he'd felt in that classroom this afternoon. "Wow! How cool is that?"

It was so far from cool, it was in another climate zone, Trent thought, but didn't say so. He shrugged, feigning complete indifference. "Like I said, no big deal. It was just unexpected."

Laurie studied him thoughtfully, clearly not convinced. "How long ago?"

"Years," he said. "Way before I met your mother and obviously before Jodie—I mean, Ms. Fletcher—married whoever she was married to. What happened to her husband, by the way? If she needs a date for the prom, then obviously she's no longer married."

"I think he died in an accident a couple of years ago, before she moved here. At least that's the rumor I heard when she came last year." Laurie gave him another of those disconcertingly direct looks. "Were you in college when you knew each other?"

"Around that time, yes."

"Oh, my gosh," she said, her expression filling with excitement. "Mom told me once you had this major thing going with a girl in college, but that it ended before she met you. Was that Ms. Fletcher? Was she like the big love of your life before Mom?"

Her tone scared the daylights out of him. He envisioned her matchmaking escalating to whole new heights. "Laurie, please, don't try to make this into something it isn't. Don't romanticize it. It was years and years ago. We were just a couple of kids."

She stared at him with utter fascination. "Why'd you break up? Did you fall out of love with her or was it because you met Mom?"

Trent was flattered that his daughter thought he must have been the one to break things off. Of course, he wasn't all that eager to disillusion her. In fact, he was pretty tired of the whole topic. He'd rather listen to Laurie spend a half hour discussing the latest fashion trends, a subject that usually sent him into a near-catatonic state of boredom.

"Sweetie, I am not going to discuss any of this with you. It's ancient history and doesn't matter now, but I'm sure you can see why it would be awkward for me to stay on your committee and especially awkward for me to ask Ms. Fletcher to the dance."

"But you just said yourself that what happened wasn't a big deal and it was years and years ago, so why are you backing out now?"

"Please, let it go. Take my word for it. It would be awkward." Make that a disaster, he thought grimly.

"But you promised," Laurie reminded him. "And this makes it even better, because it won't be like two strangers going together. You'll have stuff to talk about. You can reminisce about old times and catch up on everything that's happened since then."

Sure, they could reminisce, Trent thought with an uncharacteristic edge of sarcasm. Jodie could explain why she'd dumped him all those years ago. That was a conversation he could get really excited about.

"Not going to happen, Laurie. Look, your committee is in really good shape. It sounded today as if everything's under control. You don't need me."

"But you made a commitment, Dad, and you always tell me that once you make a commitment, you should never, ever back out of it. Even if it's only something you agreed to do verbally, it's as good as a written contract."

Trent winced at hearing his words thrown back in his face with such earnest faith. He knew when he was beat.

"Okay, fine. I'll stay on the committee and I'll do whatever I can to help."

"And you'll take Ms. Fletcher to the prom," she added as if there were no longer any question about that, either.

"I seriously doubt that Ms. Fletcher will agree to go with me," he hedged.

"But you'll at least ask her, right?"

Once again, Trent wished he'd had a son who never listened to a word he said, much less took it to heart. "Yes, I'll ask," he said grudgingly.

He'd just erect a steel barricade around his heart in case Jodie Fletcher wanted to stomp all over it yet again.

CHAPTER
❧—THREE—❧

Jodie lay awake for half the night. Trent had taken one look at her and fled the classroom practically midsentence. The encounter hadn't gone at all the way she'd anticipated. She'd expected surprise, maybe even a faint touch of dismay, but not the genuine hostility she thought she'd seen just below the polite facade he'd put on in front of the kids.

Sure, she'd dumped him without any warning, but it had been twenty years ago, for heaven's sake. And though their relationship had been heading in a serious direction, they hadn't actually been engaged. They hadn't even discussed marriage, for that matter. She'd broken up with him before things got that far.

She sighed. Okay, she was a big, fat liar. The relationship had been serious. That's why she'd been so scared. That's why she'd called it off. She'd known that sooner or later Trent would see their differences and break up with her, maybe after they'd gotten engaged or even married. There'd been nothing noble about what she'd done. All these years she'd been lying to herself about that. She'd walked away to save herself inevitable heartache.

Still, even though the breakup was all on her shoulders, she'd honestly expected him to have forgiven her by now. They'd both gone on to live happy, fulfilled lives with other people. At least she had. She could only assume Trent had, as well. He'd married a far more suitable woman. He was successful and rich. He had an amazing daughter. She'd never imagined him holding a grudge about something that had happened so long ago, something that had paved the way for everything good in his life that had followed.

She wondered if Laurie had picked up on the tension. She was a smart girl, and Jodie had a hunch she'd involved her father in this project specifically in the hope that he and Jodie would hit it off. She'd seen the anticipatory gleam in Laurie's eyes the second her dad had entered the classroom, almost as if she were expecting sparks to fly. Well, they had, just not in the way Laurie could possibly have been expecting. Jodie, either, for that matter.

Annoyed that Trent's reaction even mattered, she punched her pillow a few times, settled onto her side and tried once again to fall asleep. If she didn't get at least a couple of hours of decent rest, it would be a very long day. She simply wasn't one of those people who bounced out of bed on a few hours of sleep, ready to take on the world.

Unfortunately, even as she tried to count sheep, images of Trent kept appearing. He'd looked good. Really good. His face was a bit weathered from working outdoors, his shoulders thicker, his waist still trim. All the changes had been good ones. Trent was still the most attractive man she'd ever known, pure male, from his thick black hair to his muddy work boots.

"I have to stop this," she muttered, and determinedly resumed counting sheep.

Around the time she counted her five hundredth little lamb, she gave up in disgust. Trent simply wouldn't get out of her head, sheep or no sheep. She concluded that the only thing to do was to call him and face this whole thing head-on. Even if he did harbor some residual and justifiable resentment, surely he could put it aside for a few weeks for the sake of Laurie and the other kids. If he couldn't, he wasn't half the man she remembered.

Come to think of it, she didn't remember a man at all, but a boy, really. As mature as they'd thought themselves at twenty-one, it was only with twenty years' hindsight that she saw how ridiculously idealistic and naive they'd been. For a couple of years they'd convinced themselves that love—okay, passion—was all that mattered. They'd built a future on the quicksand of dreams, not on the rock-solid foundation of reality. She'd just recognized their folly before Trent had. He would have figured it out himself sooner or later, but by then things could have been a whole lot messier.

A glance at the clock told her it was still an hour before dawn, but it was evident she wasn't going to get any sleep. She might as well shower, stop somewhere for a decent breakfast and get to her desk early. She had a couple of tense meetings on today's calendar. Explaining to parents why their children would be attending summer school rather than graduating with their classmates in June was never at the top of her list of favorite things to do. Maybe if she was stuffed with pancakes and plenty of maple syrup, the uncomfortable conversations she was facing would be easier to handle.

And after those were behind her, maybe she could work up the nerve to call Trent and straighten things out, at least enough to make these weeks before prom bearable for both of them. She wasn't hoping to pick up where they'd left off years ago—she was far too realistic for that—but it would be nice to have him back in her life as a friend. That was another sign of maturity, she thought. She'd learned to value friendship.

Unfortunately, something told her it was going to take more than pancakes to work up the arguments necessary to convince Trent of the same thing. In fact, she thought as she sat up and flipped on the harsh light of her bedside lamp, what if she'd misinterpreted his reaction yesterday? What on earth made her think that what happened twenty years ago was so important to him that he might still be angry or hurt about it? He'd probably forgotten all about it and she was the one who'd be dredging up the past for no good reason. She'd wind up looking pathetic. Talk about humiliating.

That thought gave her pause, but she refused to back down. They had to talk, find some way to make peace for the sake of Laurie and this project that mattered so much to her. In person would be better than on the phone, she decided. She could tell from his expression just what he was thinking.

That resolved, she took the time to add a little more mascara to her lashes and a faint hint of blush to her cheeks, something she rarely bothered with. If she was going to make an idiot out of herself with Trent later, then she was going to look darn good doing it.

TRENT HAD BEEN HAVING breakfast at Dinah's Diner every morning for years. It was the local hangout for long-time residents, and he could get a healthy serving of up-to-the-minute gossip along with his meal. He'd met clients for coffee at the red Formica-topped tables, haggled with subcontractors at the counter. Over the years he'd gotten to know the owner, Dinah Lowery, her two white-haired waitresses—Gloria and Hazel—and the steady rotation of kids who held summer jobs and learned responsibility under Dinah's firm tutelage. He might be comfortable enough in places with white linen tablecloths and fancy wine lists, but Dinah's was where he felt totally at ease.

With a set of blueprints under his arm, he waved to Dinah, then headed for a booth in the corner, his regular spot, only to see that it was occupied, and not by just anyone. He'd know that explosion of dark brown curls anywhere. Jodie. Again.

This time the annoyance that zinged through him had as much to do with his booth being taken as it did with the occupant herself. Some habits were hard to break and his morning ritual was one of them.

As he stood there debating with himself, Jodie looked up and a smile broke across her face, then slowly faded at his lack of a responding greeting, verbal or silent.

"Join me," she said, her tone turning the words into a command, not a request.

Trent bristled, but since Dinah had just appeared with his coffee and a questioning look, he opted to sit. If he'd refused the invitation, word of the incident would have been all over town by noon. The interpretations would range from a lover's tiff to outright rudeness on his part.

"I'll be right back with your breakfast," Dinah assured him, then cast a glance at Jodie. "You need more coffee, hon? I'll bring that, too. You look like you need it."

"Thanks," Jodie said as if she'd been promised much-needed salvation. Her tired gaze shifted to meet his. "I'm in your usual spot, aren't I?"

He shrugged as if it were of no consequence.

"Sorry. There wasn't a reserved sign on it," she said, a mocking note in her voice.

"People who come here regularly pretty much know." He skimmed a glance over her. "I haven't seen you in here before. Or anywhere else in town, for that matter."

"Weekdays, I usually eat a banana on the way to work, but I come in here occasionally on the weekends when I have time to splurge on a big breakfast. A couple of my students work here and they recommended the pancakes."

He gave her a pointed look. "It's a weekday."

She shrugged. "I got out of the house earlier than usual." She gestured toward her plate, which was stacked high with pancakes. "This morning I'm on a carb binge."

Trent chuckled despite himself because he recalled exactly what had driven her to such splurges, at least in the past. "You planning to have a bad day? I seem to recall that the number of carbs you required during final exams was extraordinary."

"Oh, yeah," she said between bites of pancakes dripping with syrup. "Two conferences with parents who were expecting their kids to graduate. I have to inform them the diplomas will be delayed till after summer school."

"Sounds grim."

"Not half as grim as the conversation I planned to have after that."

"Oh?"

"I was going to stop by your office to speak to you."

Trent wasn't at all sure how he felt about being on her to-do list, especially in the category of something she was dreading. Then, again, he didn't much look forward to dealing with her, either, even though the past few minutes had been reasonably civilized.

"I don't see we have that much to talk about," he said tightly.

"You made that pretty obvious yesterday," she said. "Seeing me threw you, didn't it?"

He hadn't expected her to be so direct. "Let's just say you had the element of surprise on your side. Seems to me that gave you a pretty unfair advantage."

She studied him, her dark brown eyes filled with some emotion he couldn't quite read. It bothered him, because there'd been a time when he'd known all her moods, when he'd been able to know at a glance what she was thinking.

"Trent, what's this about? Surely you can't still be angry about what happened twenty years ago. People grow apart. It happens. They move on. I did. So did you. We're different people now. Adults. Surely we can spend a little time in each other's company without old news getting in the way."

Trent wanted to explode at her simplistic view of their past. Obviously she wasn't the one who'd had her heart ripped out. Knowing that it had all meant so little to her made him want to break things. If he hadn't had a healthy respect for Dinah, the ceramic mug he was clutching in both hands would have been history.

Then, again, such a move would also have told Jodie way more than he was willing to admit about how much the past ate at him even after all this time. It was a truth he'd only recently discovered—yesterday, in fact—and he was still trying to figure out what to make of it. He'd reacted to seeing her on some gut-deep level that had completely thrown him, even as it had apparently mystified her.

Fortunately, Dinah returned just then with his breakfast—two eggs over easy, bacon, whole-wheat toast. It never varied. Today it might as well have been sawdust. His appetite had fled, along with his good humor.

"Heard about what you're doing for prom," Dinah said to Jodie, while casting glances in his direction as if she was trying to figure out the source of the tension at the table. "It's a great thing. A couple of the kids who work for me weren't going to go, but now it's all they talk about."

Jodie beamed. "That's exactly why we're doing it, so everyone can share in the experience. Thanks for telling me that."

Dinah nudged Trent's shoulder with her hip. "Heard Laurie was behind it. You've raised a real decent girl."

"That was Megan's doing," he said, though he was pleased by the compliment.

"Hey, don't sell yourself short," Dinah scolded. "You've been on your own since Laurie was barely fifteen. These past couple of years are some of the most critical for a girl." She turned to Jodie. "Isn't that right?"

"I've always thought so," Jodie agreed. "I know what a mess I was in my teens."

"Me, too," Dinah concurred. She set the carafe of coffee on the table. "Might as well leave this here. It'll save me running back and forth."

After she was gone, Trent felt Jodie's gaze on him.

"She's right. You have done a wonderful job with Laurie. She's never in trouble, she has a great support system at home—that would be you—so I don't know her as well as I know some of the problem students. Even so, just in the past few weeks of working with her, I've come to realize that she's an amazingly compassionate young woman."

"Thanks."

She leaned forward, her gaze locked with his. "A father who gave his daughter such solid values surely wouldn't let her down by walking out on a project that's so important to her, would he?"

He blinked at her sneaky tactic. "Boy, you really do know how to go straight for a man's Achilles' heel, don't you?"

She grinned and sat back. "The kids think I have a knack for it."

"You don't have to sound so blasted pleased with yourself," he grumbled.

"In my line of work, you develop survival skills early on, or you get out," she said. "Figuring out what makes people tick and how to use that is a survival skill." She stared straight at him. "So, Trent, are you in or are you out for the whole prom thing?"

He didn't know why she bothered asking since they both knew it was a foregone conclusion. "I'm in," he said grudgingly.

"Good. Then you'll line up a few more tuxedos?"

"Once you've gotten a few more boys to agree to go," he challenged.

She sighed dramatically. "I've got to tell you, I'm fresh out of ideas on how to accomplish that. Mike was supposed to help but he's thrown in the towel, too. Frankly, if it weren't for Laurie, I don't think he'd participate at all."

Trent wasn't entirely sure whether to buy her claim that she had no strategy. He had a feeling there was something more behind it. He couldn't resist challenging her. "Really? I never took you for a quitter. Then again, you did walk out on the two of us."

She winced slightly but ignored the jab about the past. "I'm not quitting, I'm regrouping," she insisted.

He ignored the alarms going off in his head, telling him not to get any more involved with this project—or with her—than he already was. "Ever thought about asking for help?"

Her gaze narrowed. "From you?"

"I am a guy," he reminded her.

"Yes, I'm aware of that."

"I do get how the male mind works in a way that might elude you, or even the less-experienced Mike." He pushed aside his plate and tossed his napkin on the table. "Let's start with why they're objecting to going in the first place. Any ideas?"

"They say it's not their thing," she said, then shook her head. "I know that's not it, though. These kids act tough and disinterested, but they want to fit in, maybe even more than most. They're just afraid they'll get it wrong, that they'll look foolish in front of their friends. Some of them simply don't want to admit that they don't have the funds to rent their own tuxes. It's a matter of pride. Young male pride is quite a force."

"How did you convince Mike to go along with this?" he asked. "I'm sure he had the same reservations."

"I mentioned that he needed to think about Laurie's feelings. Believe me, that was the only thing that resonated with him."

Trent grinned. "Exactly. Female power. Are most of these guys dating girls at school?"

He watched as understanding dawned. Her expression brightened.

"You're absolutely right. I can't imagine why I didn't try the same thing with them that I did with Mike. I suppose I know him better than I know the others, and how important Laurie is to him. I'll get right on this as soon as I get to school."

"Hold it," he said, not entirely certain why he was pushing this. Maybe it was because of Laurie. More likely, it was because he wanted to prove something to Jodie. He had no idea what. That he was better at persuasion than she was? How idiotic was that? Or maybe that being around her didn't bother him as much as she probably thought it did? Whatever it was, he couldn't seem to back down. "I'm thinking these guys might be more easily persuaded in a man-to-man conversation."

"You want to handle it?"

Her surprise was unmistakable. In fact, he thought it might be just the tiniest bit excessive. Once again, he had the feeling that she had an agenda. Regarding her suspiciously, he shrugged. "Unless you don't think I'm up to the task."

Suddenly she looked just a little too pleased with herself, confirming his suspicion that this had been her plan from the beginning. She'd reeled him in neatly, the hook firmly embedded in his own stupid ego.

"Fine," she said too cheerfully. "You want the job of persuading these boys to go to the prom, be at school at three o'clock. Most of them will be in detention, I'm sure. It should be quite a conversation."

Trent found her attitude slightly disconcerting. Maybe he'd got it wrong, after all. Maybe it hadn't been about tricking him into doing exactly what she'd wanted him to do all along or maybe she was looking forward to seeing him fail. He wasn't overjoyed by either alternative. Worse, he had a hunch that the mention of detention had been deliberate, a warning that she didn't expect him to make much progress with this particular group of young men.

"I'll be there," he said grimly.

And those boys would go to prom, if he had to bribe them to do it. He reminded himself to stop by the bank for a few twenties on his way to the school.

JODIE HAD THE UNCOMFORTABLE feeling that Laurie knew all about her past with Trent. The teenager had appeared in Jodie's office fifteen minutes ago clutching a pass from her study hall teacher. She claimed she wanted to go over some new developments with their project, but so far the conversation had been pretty rambling and her eyes hadn't left Jodie's face, as if she was trying to learn something from her expression.

"Laurie, I thought you wanted to talk about prom," Jodie said when the scrutiny had gone on a little too long.

Laurie sat up a little straighter. "Sorry, I was just thinking about something else for a minute. I really do need to talk to you about prom." She launched into the arrangements she'd made with her grandfather about using Oak Haven. "We'd probably need eight or ten kids for the cleanup. Should I get the kids on the committee or some of the kids who are going to benefit from all this? Maybe if they helped, they wouldn't feel as if they were getting something for nothing."

"Sort of the way sweat equity works in the Habitat for Humanity program," Jodie said enthusiastically. "I like that. I think the kids will appreciate what's being done for them more if they have to work for it. We won't make it a requirement, because some of them have after-school jobs, but I think most of them can be persuaded to pitch in. When did you want to clean the place up?"

"I think it has to be no later than the last Saturday in March," Laurie said, her expression thoughtful. "We probably need to do the whole shopping thing a week or two later, so there's time for any alterations to be done, and prom is the first weekend in May."

Jodie looked at her calendar. "That makes sense. I'll mark it down." She hesitated, then asked, "Are you counting on your father to be there?"

"I know he wants to go through the place with me ahead of time to make sure there's nothing valuable that should be saved, but we didn't talk about him helping." She gave Jodie an oddly knowing look. "Why? Do you want him to be there?"

"I was just wondering. He didn't mention anything when I ran into him earlier today."

Laurie looked taken aback. "You've seen my dad today?"

"I saw him at the diner." She grinned. "I accidentally sat at *his* table."

Laurie laughed. "I'll bet that got to him. All the regulars at Dinah's have their special tables and heaven help anyone who sits at one of them by mistake. They go all territorial."

"I noticed," Jodie said. "I haven't run into that problem on the few Saturdays I've been in. It's usually packed with families and everyone just fends for themselves. I often wind up at the counter."

"So, did he sit with you or just get huffy?"

"He sat. We talked. Actually, he's going to come by the school this afternoon."

She didn't like the excitement that flashed in Laurie's eyes. She recognized that look. It confirmed her suspicions that Laurie had her own agenda for her father and Jodie.

"Then you two have, like, a date or something?" Laurie asked, clearly struggling to keep her tone neutral, when she looked as if she'd like to leap up and do a little victory dance.

"Hardly. He's coming to talk to some of the holdouts, to see if he can convince them to participate in the whole prom thing."

"Oh," the teenager said, sounding deflated.

"Laurie, did your father mention that he and I knew each other years ago?"

She nodded but revealed nothing about what Trent had said.

Jodie pressed on. "So, you can understand that the two of us working together might be a little awkward."

"Yeah, he said the same thing," Laurie admitted. Her expression turned earnest. "But I don't get why. I mean, I don't know what happened or anything, or if there was some big love affair or whatever, but it was a long, long time ago. You've both been married to other people, so you moved on, right?"

"Right," Jodie agreed. "It just makes things a bit more complicated, that's all, but I'm sure we'll work through it, at least enough to pull off a successful prom night."

"In other words, I shouldn't get my hopes up," Laurie said, then blushed. "About you two becoming friends, I mean."

"No, you shouldn't."

Rather than looking disappointed, Laurie brightened. "You know, Ms. Fletcher, I figured you getting together with my dad was a long shot, but what with this whole thing from the past and the way you're both acting all weird about it, I'm beginning to think this might be the best idea I ever had."

She bounced up before Jodie could think of a single thing to say.

On her way out, Laurie stopped in the doorway. "Oh, since you're seeing my dad this afternoon, maybe you can tell him about what's happening at my granddad's. He might help if you ask him to. Bye, now. I've got to get back to study hall. I still have math homework to do before next period."

And then she was gone, leaving Jodie to wonder how her attempt to caution Laurie about the danger of false hope had gone so dreadfully awry.

CHAPTER
~ FOUR ~

Half-a-dozen sullen young men, a culturally diverse mix of Hispanic, Anglo and African-American, stared at Trent with suspicion. He'd deliberately chosen to come straight from the construction site, dressed in jeans, a T-shirt and work boots that were filthy thanks to a drenching March storm that had turned the site into a sea of mud. He'd expected Jodie to regard him with disapproval for not being more professionally attired, but she smiled slightly as she took in his appearance.

"Smart move, coming here dressed like that," she murmured as she patted his arm. "It's a very man-of-the-people, I'm-one-of-you look. Good luck."

She made a brief introduction, then turned and left, leaving him alone with an obviously hostile audience. Trent had a hunch, though, that she hadn't gone far. She was probably ready to step in the second he lost control.

"Why don't you gentlemen introduce yourselves?" he suggested, sitting on the corner of the desk at the front of the room. "Tell me a little about yourselves, while you're at it."

"What is this? Some kind of afternoon tea party, man?" one boy demanded.

Trent grinned. "Last time I checked, this was detention. Think of it this way, at least talking to me will kill the time." He stared pointedly at the boy who'd challenged him. "Let's start with you. Your name is?"

"Marvin," the boy said grudgingly.

"Anything else you'd like to add, Marvin?"

"Not especially."

"Do you like school, Marvin? Have a girlfriend? A job?"

The boy gave him a hard look. "Whoa! You looking for workers, dude, count me out. I ain't into breaking my back for no man." He turned and high-fived the boy seated next to him, thrilled with his little show of rebellion.

Trent looked him in the eye. "Unless you clean up that grammar, son, back-breaking work may be all you can get," he commented wryly.

The boy gave him a hard stare. "Say what?"

"I think you understood me just fine," Trent responded.

"I know what this is," Marvin's friend said. "You're one of those do-gooder volunteers who's here to motivate us." He drew quotation marks in the air to emphasize *motivate*.

Trent chuckled at the description. "Do you get a lot of those?"

"Man, all the time," Marvin said with disgust. "If that's why you're here, save your breath."

"That's not why I'm here," Trent assured them. "I understand there's a big dance coming up in May, the junior-senior prom."

"Why do you care about that?" Marvin's pal asked.

"What's your name?" Trent asked him.

"Ramon."

"Well, Ramon, to be honest, I'm with you guys. Dressing up in a fancy suit is just about the last thing I'd ever want to do." He gestured toward his own clothes. "Do I look like a guy who'd put on a tuxedo willingly?"

"I hear you, brother," Marvin said, suddenly more congenial.

The other boys murmured agreement.

"There's just one thing," Trent warned. "You boys all have girl-friends, right?"

All but one, a slender kid with thick glasses and a defeated expression, nodded.

"How do they feel about missing prom?"

One of the Hispanic youths, who identified himself as Miguel, gave him a resigned look. "I have heard about nothing else for a week now, ever since Mariana found a way to get a dress to wear."

"So, the dance means a lot to the girls," Trent said.

All of them grunted in the affirmative.

"I've got to tell you, I don't get it," Marvin added. "I take Devonia dancing all the time—you know, to places where you can look like a normal dude."

Trent grinned. "That's the problem. Your high school prom is a special occasion, especially to women. I guarantee if you guys bite the bullet and get into those fancy duds for one night, it will make your women very, very happy, you know what I mean?"

They looked intrigued.

"I still don't understand why this matters," Ramon said.

Miguel nodded. "It's like Marvin said, Mariana and me, we go to parties. We go to clubs. Why is that not enough?"

Trent regarded him with sympathy. "Because this is arguably the biggest event of all your years in high school. Your girlfriends deserve this kind of memory, right? They deserve a night they can discuss with their friends, instead of having to sit on the sidelines while everyone around them talks about the big dance." He looked each of them in the eye. "Sometimes a man has to step up and do something he doesn't want to do just to make the woman in his life happy. It's one night, right? How painful can it be?"

He leaned forward. "You know what I said about hating the whole tux thing? Absolutely true, but for fifteen years I put one on at least once a month, sometimes more often, just because it made my wife happy. That's what men do. They try to please women, to show them they care about their feelings."

All six young men exchanged looks.

"Dude, you're laying it on kinda thick, aren't you?" Marvin asked.

Trent shrugged. "I'm on a mission. I promised a young woman I'd handle this."

"You mean Ms. Fletcher?"

"Her, too, but I was talking mostly about my daughter, Laurie. You all know her, right? Laurie Winston?" He watched as their faces registered surprise. "This whole thing is really important to her. She wants everyone to have a good time at the dance this year, to not feel left out."

"You really think we won't look like total dorks?" the boy with blond hair and huge glasses asked.

"Jason, dude, you gonna look like a dork forever," Marvin taunted. "What's one more night?"

Trent stepped in. "No, I don't think you'll look like dorks. In fact, I think you'll be surprised at how handsome you'll look."

"Jason, dude, why are you so worried?" Marvin asked. "Can you even find a date for this thing? Or am I going to have to do it for you?"

Though Marvin's tone was taunting, there was a hint of compassion in his eyes. Jason gave him a surprisingly cocky smile. "I can get my own date," he retorted. "That was never the problem." He shook his head. "The whole tuxedo thing, though. I just don't know."

"Same here," Marvin agreed.

Trent seized on the tiny opening he thought he heard in Marvin's comment. "Does that mean you're in, Marvin? You'll consider going if we can get you a tuxedo?"

"These tuxedos you're talking about, they're not going to cost us anything?" Marvin inquired worriedly. "I have to give all the money I make to my mom to pay the rent. With her bad back she hasn't been able to work for a couple of months now. I can't be wasting money on some fancy clothes to wear for one night."

"We have quite a few tuxedos that have been donated, and we also have gift certificates for rentals," Trent assured him. "One way or another, none of you will have to pay for the tux you wear that night."

"Either way, they'll be borrowed, which means the sleeves will be too long and the pants will drag on the floor," Jason said, sounding resigned.

"No way," Trent assured him. "You'll get to try them on ahead of time and someone will alter them so they fit perfectly. I'm telling you, you guys won't recognize yourselves when you look in the mirror. Better yet, you'll impress the heck out of your girlfriends." He turned once again to Marvin. "So, are you in?"

For a moment, Marvin looked as if he were struggling with himself. Trent simply waited.

"What about the tickets?" Marvin asked. "Last year they cost as much as I make in a week. I can't blow that kind of money on a dance."

"Laurie has the committee working on that. They're doing a program with advertising to help underwrite the costs of the hotel and the food. That'll bring the ticket prices way down. They won't be free, but I think they'll be within your budget, certainly no more than a night at some club." He looked straight at Marvin. "How about it? Any other roadblocks?"

"I guess not," Marvin conceded grudgingly.

"Then you'll go?"

"Okay, sure. Why not?" The boy gave an exaggerated shrug. "No point in ticking off Devonia if there's a way around it."

One by one the others nodded.

"You're not going to regret this," Trent told them as he stood up to leave.

"Hold it, dude," Marvin commanded.

Trent settled back on the edge of the desk and studied the surprising uncertainty in the boy's eyes. "What is it, Marvin?"

"I just thought of something else. You know there's more to this prom than buying the tickets and getting dressed up in some fancy clothes. The girls usually get flowers. I checked on that once. Those things are expensive."

"It's being handled," Trent assured him. "Once the girls have their dresses picked out, you can tell the florist what color flowers you want."

Jason raised his hand tentatively. "I've never tied a bow tie before."

"Me, neither," Ramon admitted.

Next to him, Marvin rolled his eyes. Before Trent could chastise him, Ramon scowled at him.

"Oh, like you have," he muttered to Marvin.

"Well, I can figure it out," Marvin retorted.

"Not to worry," Trent promised. "I'm no expert, but I'll be there prom night to help any of you who need it." He looked at each of the boys in turn. "Any other questions?"

"I have one," said a boy who'd been silent all afternoon. "Why are you guys doing this for us?"

Trent tried to explain it as he thought Laurie or Jodie would. "Because prom and graduation are really big deals in a person's life.

Skipping them because you don't want to go is one thing, but you shouldn't miss those things just because money's tight in your family. You should be able to have the same experiences and memories of prom that your classmates will have."

He looked each of the boys in the eye. "The fact that some of you work to help out at home, that's a good thing, something you should be proud of. And no one wants you to have to shortchange your family or yourselves to participate in these special senior-year activities. Maybe someday you'll come across a young man or woman in need of a little help. If you do, I hope you'll remember this and do what you can to give them the same opportunity."

A bell rang. "End of detention?" he asked.

All of the boys were instantly on their feet and heading for the door, which was answer enough. Marvin slowed, then came back.

"Thanks, dude. I'm going straight to Devonia's to tell her about this. Maybe she'll stop looking at me like I've let her down."

"Good luck," Trent told him. "And if you ever change your mind about wanting the kind of work I can offer on one of my construction jobs, come to see me. I can always use a responsible young man."

Trent wasn't sure, but he thought Marvin stood a little taller at his words.

"You never know, dude. I'll see you around."

As Marvin left, Jodie stepped into the room. Trent grinned at her.

"Listening at the door?" he teased.

"Of course," she said, a twinkle in her eyes. "I had to be sure you weren't going to bribe them into going, didn't I?"

Trent thought of the fistful of twenties he had in his pocket. "That was my next tactic," he admitted.

"Well, thank goodness you didn't need to resort to that," she said, regarding him with something that looked an awful lot like admiration. "You were good with them, Trent. Something tells me you had to be persuaded to put on your first tux, too. I certainly never saw you in one."

"Megan's doing," he admitted. "And believe me, I fought it just as hard as these boys did. Harder, maybe." He smiled at the memory of the first ill-fitting tux she'd coaxed him into wearing, one of her dad's castoffs, though she hadn't told him that at the time. "Megan had a way of talking me into doing a lot of things I didn't want to do."

"Then it was a good marriage?" Jodie asked, studying him intently.

Trent froze at the question, at the hint of worry behind it. "You looking for absolution, Jodie? You trying to find out if dumping me turned out all right in the end?"

She frowned at him. "What if I am?"

"It's a little late to be worrying about that," he told her. "You made a decision. You refused to discuss it. I just had to live with it, so that's exactly what I did. I lived with it. I met someone. I got married. I had a child. My wife died. Maybe the exact same thing would have happened if you hadn't walked out. Maybe we would have broken up, anyway. Maybe that was just my fate." He knew he sounded harsh, but it was too late to stop. "I have to tell you, at the time, it felt a whole lot like you'd single-handedly grabbed our future and ripped it to shreds right in front of me."

She blanched. "I'm sorry. I thought I was doing the right thing."

"For you or for me?"

"You, damn it. It was all about you."

He stared at her incredulously. "You actually believe that, don't you? You think you did me a favor."

"I did," she said, though she sounded less confident.

"Well, just a piece of advice, Jodie. In the future if you want to do someone a favor, maybe you should ask them what *they* want first."

Because he couldn't stand here and talk about this for one more second, he walked past her and out the door. Unfortunately, leaving her behind was a whole lot easier than leaving behind the anger and the memories. And until this prom was over, it looked as if the past was going to keep right on nagging at him.

JODIE ARRIVED AT Warren Davis's estate on the last Saturday in March filled with trepidation. Trent had been so angry when he'd walked out on her at school and she hadn't seen any sign of him in the past two weeks, even though they'd had a committee meeting. She hadn't been prepared for him to question her motives. Couldn't he see that she'd been hurt as deeply as he had, that doing the right thing had cost her as much as it had him? Obviously not. She wasn't looking forward to round two, now that the gloves were off.

As she parked on the far side of the circular driveway in front of the huge brick Colonial house, she noted there were plenty of cars and pickups ahead of her. At least she wouldn't be alone with Trent, and he certainly wouldn't cause a scene in front of his daughter. Maybe they could get through the day like civilized adults, after all.

When she rang the doorbell, it was Laurie who answered, her face flushed with excitement. "At least twenty kids showed up, Ms. Fletcher. Isn't that fantastic? We've already made a lot of progress. Wait till you see."

She grabbed Jodie's hand and dragged her through a huge foyer filled with priceless art and an antique Chinese vase that probably cost a fortune. Jodie had to stop herself from gawking.

As soon as she walked into the cluttered, dusty ballroom, her gaze immediately landed on Trent. He'd dressed in a pair of well-worn jeans that hugged his backside and a faded T-shirt that was molded to his chest. She had to stop herself from gaping.

"Dad came," Laurie said, stating the obvious. "Even though you forgot to tell him about it."

"I didn't really have a chance," Jodie responded defensively. She wasn't about to mention that Trent had been in no mood to listen to anything she had to say when she'd seen him.

"Hey, Ms. Fletcher." Marvin walked by carrying two huge boxes as if they weighed next to nothing.

Once again, Jodie was left speechless. She hadn't expected to find Marvin here or Ramon or any of the other boys Trent had met with, but every one of them appeared to be working industriously. Was this more evidence of Trent's powers of persuasion? Or had Laurie worked her magic with them as she had with so many others, her dad and Jodie included?

"What do you need me to do?" she asked Laurie.

"Actually, Dad and I didn't get to go through all the boxes. Last night was the first chance we had to come over and there were more boxes than we expected. There are still a couple that need to be checked before we haul them to the dump. Over here," she said, leading the way to the far side of the ballroom. "Could you go through these and put anything that looks important in that empty box next to them? Someone will take the rest of the junk out in a little while."

"How am I supposed to know what's important?" Jodie asked, but Laurie was already gone.

Jodie sat down on the floor and opened the first box. A college yearbook sat on top. From *her* college. From *her* senior year. She glanced in Laurie's direction, suddenly guessing why this particular task had been left to her. Unfortunately she didn't have a clue which of these mementos Trent would want to save.

Still, it wouldn't hurt just to glance through a few things before she turned the task over to Trent. She flipped through the yearbook to the pictures of the senior class. It had been years since she'd seen that awful photo of herself with her hair curling wildly like Little Orphan Annie's. She rolled her eyes, then turned the pages until she came to the *W*'s.

Trent's picture stared back at her, solemn, yet ridiculously masculine. Even then he'd exuded a confidence in his own masculinity, unlike the other male students in their class. Maybe that had fooled her into thinking he wouldn't be affected by the decision she'd made. She told herself that a man as sure of himself as Trent wouldn't be shaken by her walking away from the relationship. Had she misjudged things so badly?

Under the yearbook, there was more college memorabilia, a banner that had been on the wall in Trent's dorm room, his diploma still in its leather binder, matchbooks from campus-area bars, a couple of T-shirts with fraternity insignia.

Beneath these odds and ends was a framed photo, turned upside down. Before flipping it over, Jodie knew instinctively what it was— a picture of the two of them, taken on a windy day at Ocean City. The waves high behind them, their faces tanned by a week at the shore, they looked very much in love. She couldn't seem to tear her gaze away. Seeing herself with Trent like that, she wondered how she'd ever convinced herself to leave.

"Hey, Ms. Fletcher, is that you?" Marvin hunkered down beside her, looking over her shoulder.

Jodie wanted to hide the picture, but it was too late. "Yes," she admitted softly. "It's from a long time ago."

"Who's that with you?" he asked, then whirled around and looked straight at Trent. "Mr. Winston? That's the dude in the picture?"

She nodded, unable to stop the tears that sprang to her eyes. She swiped at them ineffectively, seeing the sudden dismay in Marvin's expression. "Sorry."

"Did the dude break your heart or something? He seems like an okay guy, but I can get down with him, if you need me to."

She smiled at his willingness to fight her battle. "No need, Marvin. It was the other way around."

"You're not gonna sit here and bawl your eyes out, are you?" he asked worriedly.

"No," she said, though a part of her wanted to do just that. "I am most certainly not going to cry."

"You want to blow this scene, I can cover for you," he offered.

"No, I'm fine. Just a little nostalgic, that's all."

He cast a hard look across the room at Trent. "You change your mind, just say the word, okay?"

"Thanks, Marvin. It's very sweet of you to offer." Who knew the kid had a gallant streak in him?

"How about a soda? Can I bring you a soda?"

"Now, that I will accept," she said, forcing a bright smile. "Thank you."

As soon as he'd set off on his mission, she shoved everything back into the box. Not sure why she wanted to torture herself with the memories, she made a hasty decision. Standing up, she glanced around to make sure that Trent wasn't close by, then hurried from the ballroom. She wanted a few private moments at home with these mementos. She carried the box straight to her car and stuffed it in the trunk, vowing to return it before it was missed. When she turned to go back, Trent was standing right behind her.

"Taking off with family treasures?" he inquired mildly.

"Just packing some stuff up for a trip to the dump," she said.

He shook his head. "I don't think so, Jodie. I know exactly what was in that box. I packed it myself twenty years ago."

"And saved it," she reminded him.

His features darkened. "I wasn't the one who said those days didn't matter." The silence built between them, heavy with nostalgia and regrets. "Oh, Jodie," he murmured sorrowfully. "What were you thinking? How could you give up on what we had?"

To her surprise, he tucked a finger under her chin, then leaned down and touched his lips to hers.

Although she sensed his reluctance, he deepened the kiss until her senses were reeling. Knees weak, she clung to his shoulders, then very nearly stumbled when he jerked away.

"Sorry, my mistake," he said. "I guess some feelings aren't quite as far in the past as I'd hoped. Keep the box, Jodie. Maybe it will help you recall what you gave up on."

She didn't need the stupid box or anything in it to do that, Jodie thought as he walked away. She already knew what she'd lost. What she didn't know was whether it was possible to get it back.

CHAPTER
～ FIVE ～

T rent stood in Warren's driveway and watched Jodie drive off. He tried not to think about the hurt he'd seen in her eyes, the pain he'd caused. He told himself she deserved it, that it was nothing compared with the anguish she'd caused him.

Dark clouds rolled across the sun, promising an early spring storm and cooling the air. He shivered and turned to go back inside, only to see Laurie heading his way, her blond hair whipping around her face in the sudden breeze.

"You were out here with Ms. Fletcher, weren't you? And now she's gone." A frown creased her brow. "What did you say to make her leave, Dad?"

"I didn't say anything," he said defensively. "She was already leaving when I came out here."

"I don't think so." Laurie held up a purse. "She left this inside."

Trent winced. Apparently he'd rattled Jodie even more than he'd realized.

Laurie gave him another accusing look. "Marvin said she was really upset and that you had something to do with it."

"Okay, you want to know what happened?" Trent said mildly. "Your little scheme backfired. I know you deliberately gave her that old box of my stuff from college to go through, hoping it would spark some sort of nostalgic reaction."

"So what if I did?" she asked with a touch of defiance. "Somebody needs to push you two back together."

Trent sighed. "Maybe you haven't noticed, but both Ms. Fletcher and I are adults. We're perfectly capable of deciding whether we want to spend time together without any help from you."

Laurie studied him quizzically. "Do you want to spend time with her?"

"Sweetie, I told you before, it's complicated."

"No, Dad," Laurie insisted stubbornly. "It's only complicated if you *make* it complicated. Either you do want to see her or you don't. Which is it?"

"It's a bad idea."

"That's not a no," she said.

"It's not a yes, either," he emphasized. "It's not an opening for you to keep meddling. You need to stay out of this, sweetie. I mean it. Leave it alone."

She didn't try to hide her disappointment, but she clearly wasn't ready to let go of her plan despite his direct order. "But you'll at least take her to the prom, won't you?" she cajoled. "You promised, and you've always said you would never break a promise to me, and you haven't."

Trent winced. She had quite a knack for inducing guilt, this daughter of his. "I might have to this time," he told her. "I'm sorry."

"Dad, no!" she protested. "This is the most important promise you've ever made to me."

Trent was startled by her vehemence. "Why?"

"Just because I said it is."

It was the kind of logic he'd once tried when disciplining her. He wasn't crazy about being on the receiving end of it.

When he remained silent, Laurie pressed him. "Come on, Dad. Have you even talked to her about going to the prom?"

"No."

"No, you won't take her, or no, you haven't asked her yet?"

Trent smiled despite his sour mood. "You are your mother's daughter, you know that, don't you? Once you get an idea in your head, you don't let up."

She grinned unrepentantly. "Granddad says that's a good thing."

"Your grandfather doesn't have to live with you," Trent said wryly.

"You haven't answered me yet, Dad," she reminded him.

"This is really that important to you?" he asked, already resigned to giving in. Maybe part of him even *wanted* to give in, but he wasn't telling Laurie that. Not ever. Who knew what she'd do with the knowledge?

Her expression brightened as she sensed victory. "Really, really important," she told him.

"Okay, fine, but it's one date. You do understand that, don't you? This is just about the prom and the promise I made to you. Nothing more. It is not about me getting together with Ms. Fletcher."

"Whatever," she said, making it clear that she was only humoring him.

"I don't want to hear another word about me and Ms. Fletcher after that night, understood?" He was determined to get her agreement. Otherwise she'd pester him till he found himself watching Jodie walk down the aisle in his direction.

"I said okay, didn't I?" Laurie grumbled.

"No, as a matter of fact, you said 'whatever,' which usually means you're trying to pacify me now but intend to fight again another day."

Rather than answering him, she turned to walk away. "It's starting to rain. I need to get back inside. Are you coming?"

Trent decided against making an issue of her failure to agree to his terms. Better to let her go and prepare his own battle plan for another day. "No, there's something I need to take care of. I'll check in with you in a couple of hours to see if you need more help." Knowing he was opening himself up to more speculation, he added, "Give me Ms. Fletcher's purse. I'll see that she gets it."

Laurie's expression brightened. "Really?" She looked as if she wanted to say more, but apparently thought better of it. "Great. See you later. Love you."

"You, too."

He shook his head as she ran across the driveway and went inside. He'd always grasped the concept that a parent would——and *should*—— do anything possible for a child. He just hadn't expected his daughter to be so adept at turning that to her advantage.

AN HOUR LATER TRENT had tracked down Jodie's address and driven across the county to the town house subdivision where she was living. He told himself he was doing it because he might bear some responsibility for her running off without her purse. He was also going because he'd made a promise to Laurie and there was no point in postponing the inevitable. Deep inside, though, he knew neither of those was the real reason. On some level he felt the need to check on her, to make sure he hadn't wounded her too deeply with his cutting remarks. She might deserve every harsh word, but he was too much of a gentleman to feel good about lashing out at her. In fact, he'd surprised himself with some of the words that had poured out of his mouth. They'd been way too revealing.

The kiss hadn't been such a smart move, either, but he'd been drawn to her in a way he hadn't been able to control. The way her mouth had felt beneath his had stirred all sorts of memories, good ones this time. The kind best left dead and buried.

When he reached the entrance to her development, he had to hold back a sigh of dismay. The developer of Fox Run Estates had leveled the land before building, leaving very few of the old oaks and maples. Each tiny front lawn had been freshly planted with some- thing barely taller than a twig. He doubted the current residents would remain long enough to see those twigs grow into mature trees, assuming they weren't destroyed by the first heavy snowfall.

At least the construction of the town houses looked solid enough, he thought as he wove through the twisting layout of dead-end streets and cul-de-sacs until he found Laurel Lane and Jodie's street number. He pulled into the driveway behind her car.

He didn't allow himself to wonder what the devil he was doing here in a driving rainstorm. He just bolted for the front steps and rang the bell, then rang it again since he doubted Jodie could hear it over the sound of the symphony she had playing on the stereo.

Finally he heard the tap of her shoes as she crossed the entryway— tile from the sound of it—to the door. When the door swung open, she stared at him with surprise, and perhaps just a hint of wariness.

"I came to apologize," he said, hoping that would get him in out of the storm. "And to return this." He held out her purse.

She accepted the purse, then stepped aside and, without a word, gestured toward the living room.

"Maybe I should go drip all over your kitchen floor instead," he said, gazing at her pale beige carpet with concern.

She finally looked directly at him, surveying him from head to toe. "You have a point. It's this way. I'll make a pot of coffee. You look as if you could use something warm." She hesitated. "Or would you rather have something stronger?"

"Coffee's good." He was going to need all his wits about him to negotiate his way through this minefield of his daughter's making.

Jodie paused en route to turn down the volume on the stereo, then went straight to a cupboard and took out coffee beans. Trent sat at the table and watched her brisk, competent movements, looking for even the faintest sign of nervousness, but unlike him she seemed perfectly at ease. For some reason, that annoyed him. He felt as if he'd been off kilter and on the defensive since the day he'd walked into that classroom and discovered that Jodie—*his* Jodie— was Laurie's awesome guidance counselor and the object of her matchmaking scheme.

When she turned around at last and set a cup of steaming, fragrant coffee in front of him, he decided to turn the tables. "My daughter has plans for us, you know," he blurted.

"I suspected as much," she said.

"And that doesn't bother you?"

Her lips quirked up. "Apparently not as much as it bothers you," she told him. "She's a teenager and she has all these romantic notions in her head. That doesn't mean we have to go along with them, especially given our history."

"You can actually look at it that rationally?" he asked, incredulous.

She regarded him with tolerant amusement. "Is there another choice?"

Before Trent could reply, she held up her hand. "Look, I know you and I regard the past very differently. I hurt you back then, even though I thought I was doing the right thing. I was hurt, too, you know. Walking away was a huge sacrifice for me." She met his gaze. "I loved you, Trent, but I did what seemed to make sense at the time.

And since it was my decision, I suppose it makes it easier for me to see you again without quite so many conflicting emotions."

"There you go again, being all calm and rational."

"You say that as if it's a bad thing."

"It is. We were all about heat and passion, Jodie. At least that's how I remember it. You sound as cool and analytical as if you were talking about the price of coffee beans then and now."

She flushed at the accusation. "Maybe I've just grown up," she lashed back. "Maybe I don't put my emotions out there anymore."

"Oh, you mean the way I do? I'm not supposed to be angry about how you threw everything away?"

"Not after twenty years," she retorted. Suddenly she paused and bright patches of color appeared in her cheeks. "Unless... Did you have feelings for me all this time, Trent?"

"Absolutely not," he said, knowing that he was lying. He had, and he'd hated himself for it every single day that those feelings had affected the life he was trying to build with Megan.

Sometimes he'd go for weeks, even months, without thinking of Jodie, but then memories would flood over him and he'd pull away from the woman he'd married. It was little wonder Megan had mentioned ending their marriage on more than one occasion. Her illness had taken that option away from them. He would never have agreed to let her go through cancer treatment alone.

Jodie gave him an odd look. "Tell me about your wife."

"No," he said fiercely. He'd betrayed Megan enough, if only in his thoughts. He wouldn't diminish what they'd had for Jodie's benefit.

"You must miss her," she prodded.

The comment, common enough from friends for months after Megan's death, caught him by surprise now. Or maybe it was his reaction that caught him off guard. For the first time, he acknowledged that he did miss Megan. Saying so wouldn't be just words, the expected reaction of a grieving husband. For so long, through so many heated exchanges, he'd convinced himself that their marriage had no future.

Then she'd fallen ill, and during those long, devastating months, he'd come to see his wife in a whole new way. Time—and the grace with which Megan had handled her illness—had faded all the bad memories of their endless disagreements and left him at last with mostly good ones, plus a ton of admiration for her bravery.

"Yes, I do miss her," he said. He met Jodie's compassionate gaze head-on. "You lost your husband even more recently. How are you coping?"

"After Adam died, it was hard at first. That's why I changed jobs after it happened and moved here a couple years ago. I needed to start fresh. The change has been good for me."

"I didn't have that option," he said. "Because of Laurie. She needed the stability of her home, of her friends, and being close to her grandfather."

"So, you understand something about making sacrifices for someone you love," she said.

Trent knew the point she was trying to make, but he didn't want to acknowledge it, so he looked straight into her eyes. "What are we going to do about prom? Laurie wants me to escort you and I promised I would. It's important to her that you have a date and enjoy yourself."

Jodie flushed, clearly embarrassed. "It's not necessary. I always go alone, and believe it or not, I do enjoy myself."

For some reason, her rejection of the idea made him more determined to accompany her to the dance, and it was no longer all about pleasing Laurie. He was supposedly masterful at charm and persuasion, and he could tell from the stubborn jut of Jodie's chin that he was going to need all of that skill right now. "But you wouldn't want to deprive me of the chance to see how our project turns out, would you? I can hardly go without a date."

Her gaze narrowed. "You actually care about going to a high school prom?"

He started to insist that he did, but doubted he could sound convincing. "Okay, it's mostly about making Laurie happy. Would it be so awful if we went together?"

"Not awful, just awkward," she said. "I'm sure Laurie will understand that it was a bad idea." She stood up. "Thanks for stopping by and bringing my purse, Trent, but perhaps you should go now."

He snagged her hand. "Hold on, Jodie. Nothing's settled."

"Trent, this is crazy. You're still angry with me. You're only asking me because your daughter wants you to. Why put ourselves through an entire night of misery?"

With each rejection, Trent grew more determined. He scrambled for a more persuasive argument.

"I know you heard every word I said to those boys the other day. All that matters when it comes to prom is that a man do whatever he can to make sure his woman is happy."

She immediately bristled. "I am not *your* woman."

His lips twitched. "Who said I was referring to you? Laurie's the only woman in my life these days."

Her cheeks flushed with embarrassment. Trent took pity on her.

"And it is at least a little bit about you," he admitted. "Prom matters to you, Jodie. I've seen it in your eyes when you talk about that night and how important it is that these kids get to participate. You look, I don't know, almost wistful. Something tells me that expression isn't just about making the night special for the kids, either. Maybe if we can find some way to trust each other again, you'll open up and tell me why that is."

He saw instantly that his insight had startled her, and that she immediately wanted to shut down his curiosity. Before she could utter the refusal that was clearly on the tip of her tongue, he added, "Let me start this whole discussion over again. Forget everything I said. Forget that this was my daughter's idea. Would you please do me the honor of letting me escort you to the prom, Jodie?"

Several emotions seemed to be warring inside her. He could see the battle in her eyes. Finally coming to a decision, she tilted her head, her expression thoughtful as she met his gaze.

"Will you bring me a corsage?"

The unexpected request made him laugh. "If that's what it takes to get you to say yes, then you can have any kind of flowers you want."

A smile spread slowly across her face. "I'll think it over and get back to you about the flowers."

"Don't take too long. I understand the florists are going to be especially busy this year."

She looked away, then lifted her coffee cup and took a slow, deliberate sip. When she looked back, her face was composed, betraying none of her earlier emotions. "Trent, do you realize that you never once asked me to dance when we were in college? I always assumed you had two left feet. Or that you thought I might."

"Neither one. As I recall, we had too many other things to do," he responded. "That just makes this night long overdue."

And maybe forgiveness was long overdue as well.

JODIE COULDN'T SEEM TO keep her hands from shaking every time she thought about going on a date—to the prom of all things—with Trent. How many years had she dreamed of the prom night she'd missed during her own senior year in high school and envisioned it turning out differently? How many times had she seen herself on the dance floor, in the arms of the handsomest boy in the senior class? She didn't like thinking about the accident that had robbed her of her special night and so much more.

As a guidance counselor at Rockingham, she'd been nudged into taking on the prom as one of her extracurricular duties and had had to face those regrets all over again. She'd done it stoically, standing on the sidelines at last year's dance, keeping watch over the punch bowl to be sure no one got the bright idea to spike it. She'd envied the other chaperones who danced in the arms of their husbands or wives.

She wasn't bitter, she told herself at least a hundred times during the planning sessions for the big night. She was happy to be part of an event that these young people were bound to remember fondly for the rest of their lives.

Now, with Trent's invitation still echoing in her mind, she knew just how badly she'd lied to herself. Only now, as excitement stirred inside her, along with a healthy dose of nerves, did she truly understand the magic of prom night.

"If you don't set that cup down, all the coffee is going to splash out of it," Carmen Nogales commented as she entered the staff room and regarded her friend with amusement. "What's going on with you, Jodie? You've been jittery for the past couple of weeks. Everyone's commented on it."

Jodie winced. She'd had no idea her nervousness was that obvious. "Just thinking about prom," she said, making the answer evasive enough that the teacher might assume it had to do with the event itself.

"Really? I know for a fact that you could run that dance with both hands tied behind your back and have it turn out perfectly, so what's different about this year? Does it have something to do with this project that you and Laurie Winston are working on? Fill me in on that. I know the basics, but none of the details."

Unwilling to admit to her own personal insecurities, she told Carmen how the committee was making the event accessible to students who normally couldn't afford to go.

Carmen nodded. "It's all I've been hearing about lately. Marvin is in my first-period history class. He's been grumbling about wearing a monkey suit for a couple of weeks now." She grinned. "You know what, though? I think he's really excited about it. And Devonia is absolutely glowing. Whenever he grumbles, she tells him he's going to be the handsomest boy at the prom. I swear he sits up straighter when she says it. This idea of yours and Laurie's is really making a difference for these kids. For once I don't have the feeling that there's a big group of students who feel left out. I think it's going to be a huge boost to their self-image, too."

"That's the goal," Jodie said.

Carmen gave her a more intense survey, then shook her head. "That's not it, though. You're agitated about something else. Tell me." Her expression turned knowing. "It wouldn't have anything to do with the fact that Laurie's dad is escorting you to the dance, would it?"

Jodie stared at her in dismay. "You know about that?"

"Sweetie, the whole school knows about it. Laurie is practically bursting at the seams with excitement. She might be proud of opening the prom up to more kids, but getting you and her dad together seems to be her crowning achievement."

"Oh, no. I was afraid of that," Jodie moaned. "He just asked to be polite."

"Really? Then why are you so flustered?"

"Do you know Trent?"

"I've seen him. He's gorgeous, single and rich. A pretty incredible combination, if you ask me."

"Exactly, and I haven't been on a date in years, not since I met my husband eighteen years ago." She wasn't about to bring up her past history with Trent and how that was contributing to her bad case of nerves. "The man looks as if he was born to wear a tux and I look exactly like the wallflower I am, who's worn the exact same dress to every school dance since I started as a counselor years ago."

"You're worried about a dress?" Carmen asked incredulously.

"And my hair and my makeup and shoes," Jodie told her, overwhelmed by the magnitude of the transformation she needed to keep up with a man like Trent. "I know it sounds ridiculous. I counsel these girls all the time that all that matters is what's on the inside of a person, but suddenly I get why the right clothes are so important."

"Well, stop your worrying right now," Carmen said decisively. "The students have you and Laurie as their fairy godmothers, but trust me, neither of you can hold a candle to me. Be ready tomorrow by nine-thirty. I'm picking you up and we're going shopping."

"I can't do it tomorrow. We're having the shopping day for all the kids."

"Already? It's only the middle of April and prom's not for a few more weeks."

"We need to allow enough time for clothes to be altered," Jodie explained. "And if we have anyone who's hard to fit, we need to find out now so we can scramble for a new dress or tux."

"So, forget tomorrow. We'll go Sunday." Carmen clearly wasn't going to back down. "We can go at noon."

"I can do that." Despite herself, Jodie felt a stirring of very feminine excitement. It was years since she'd gone shopping for something special. Still, she cautioned, "Just remember that my budget doesn't allow me to splurge on a dress I'll wear only once. It needs to be practical."

Carmen rolled her eyes. "Fairy godmothers don't do practical. Don't you know anything?"

"The state of my bank balance," Jodie commented.

"Give me a figure and we'll work with it," Carmen promised. "Bargain-hunting is my favorite hobby. Trust me, Cinderella won't have anything on you."

"Just as long as I don't have to add scrubbing floors to my duties once the clock strikes midnight."

CHAPTER
∞ SIX ∞

T rent drove Laurie over to her grandfather's practically at dawn on Saturday. Her excitement was palpable, but he detected a hint of worry under the enthusiasm.

"What's wrong, kiddo? Something bothering you?"

"Mike's still not into this," she admitted. "I'm not even sure if he'll show up today. He said he had to work, but I think he deliberately asked for extra hours just to avoid coming over to Granddad's."

Trent thought he knew the boy pretty well and that didn't sound like something Mike would do. He was unfailingly considerate, especially of Laurie. "I think you're making too much of this. If his boss asked him to work some overtime, you know he can't afford to turn down extra pay. We can always make arrangements to fit his tux tonight or even tomorrow."

She turned to him, her eyes clouded with dismay. "Dad, I think he might break up with me over all this. He said something to me the other night about having my priorities all messed up and being more worried about a stupid dance than about him."

Trent glanced at her quickly. "Any chance he's right about that?"

"No," she said indignantly. "From the beginning all I wanted was for him to be able to enjoy the prom like everyone else. That's what I wanted for all these kids. I thought Ms. Fletcher made him understand that."

"Maybe you should have explained it yourself. Talk to him, sweetie. Don't let this issue get blown all out of proportion. Mike adores you. He only agreed to this in the first place because of how much he cares about your feelings. Now you need to listen when he tells you what *he's* feeling, okay?"

Laurie sighed. "I'll try."

Rather than the optimism Trent expected from his daughter now that she had a concrete plan of action, he heard dejection. "Is there something more on your mind?"

"A lot, actually." She turned to him, her expression earnest. "What if everyone hates the dresses or the sizes are all wrong and the seamstresses can't fix them in time? And the shoes. Dad, there are, like, a zillion things that could go wrong with the shoes. Do you know how hard it is to get shoes that fit right, especially if you have to keep them on all evening and dance in them?"

"How many pairs of shoes were donated?" he asked, determined not to show even a hint of amusement at what to her were major worries. Her concern about Mike, he understood, but shoes and dress sizes?

"Two dozen, I guess."

"Lots of sizes?"

"Yes."

"And there are a handful of gift certificates for shoes, too, right?"

"Yes."

He recalled an earlier conversation they'd had, though he'd only had half his attention focused on it. "And wasn't one of the requests for the donated shoes that they go with any color of dress, so some girl in purple wouldn't be stuck with red shoes?"

Beside him, Laurie sighed. "Okay, I'm acting a little crazy, huh?"

"Just a little," he conceded. "But one of the things I love about you is how much every detail about today matters to you. You want these kids to have the best experience of their lives, and I think that's fantastic."

"It's just that I know how girls think. Even the ones who don't have much money want to look as fashionable as they possibly can."

"You don't seem nearly as concerned about the boys," he noted.

She shrugged. "There's only so much that can go wrong with a tux and a pair of black shoes."

"Not according to your mom," he said, remembering the many objections Megan had had when he told her to just go pick out anything and he'd wear it. Then, again, these boys were no doubt as clueless as he'd once been. As long as the clothes and shoes fit, they'd be okay.

As soon as Trent parked the car and they'd started up the walk, the front door swung open and Warren Davis stood waiting for them, a smile on his face as Laurie bounded up the steps to give him a hug. Even on a Saturday morning at dawn, he was already shaved, and every silver hair on his head fell neatly into place, thanks to the stylist who came to the house at least once a week to keep his hair trimmed. He was wearing dress slacks and a silk-blend shirt, though he did have the sleeves rolled up and the collar open. Still, there was no mistaking him for anything other than a man of sophistication and wealth.

"Thanks again for doing this, Granddad," Laurie said. "You're the best."

Warren winked at Trent. "Hey, I got that old ballroom cleaned up for free. Seems like a good deal to me. You two want a little breakfast before the hordes descend? I've got the cook on standby to do eggs, waffles or whatever else you'd like. The coffee's made, too. Trent, you look as if you need to be fortified with a little caffeine."

"Absolutely," Trent said.

Laurie had started through the foyer, but at the mention of waffles—her very favorite breakfast treat—her step slowed. "Any blueberries?"

Warren grinned. "Of course."

"Give me two seconds to make sure everything's set up okay and I'll meet you guys in the dining room," she said. "Tell Sarah I'd like one blueberry waffle with blueberry syrup if she has it. And lots of butter." Her order placed, she darted off in the direction of the ballroom.

Warren watched her go, then turned to Trent. "She's an admirable young lady, isn't she? Megan would be proud. I certainly am."

"Me, too," Trent said.

"So, besides that coffee, what can I get you? Eggs? Bacon?"

"Are those on your diet?" Trent asked, concerned. Warren had had a heart scare this past year. Though he hadn't required surgery and had recovered quickly, he'd been told to change his diet and lifestyle. "I thought you were watching your cholesterol."

"I am. I have a bran muffin with my name on it. I was just hoping I could live vicariously by watching you eat."

"Then, by all means, have Sarah fix me a couple of eggs and some bacon," Trent said, settling himself at the massive dining room table that had been set for four.

"Who else are you expecting?" he asked when Warren returned from speaking to his cook.

"I thought maybe that Ms. Fletcher that Laurie's so crazy about would get here early, too." He studied Trent intently. "Pretty woman. Have you noticed that?"

Trent had a feeling that his former father-in-law was playing a cat-and-mouse game with him, that he knew more than he was letting on. "She is attractive," he agreed.

Warren's lips twitched at the bland response. "Hear she's your date for the prom."

"Your granddaughter has a big mouth," Trent commented.

"Laurie seems real happy about it. Are you finally getting serious about somebody new?"

"No," Trent said at once, then sighed. "Look, Jodie's not exactly new in my life. I knew her years ago, back in college. We met again by chance when Laurie started putting this whole prom committee together. Our history wasn't all sweetness and light, but we're trying to get along for Laurie's sake. That's it."

Warren gave him a searching look. "Too bad," he said eventually. "You deserve to find happiness, son. I know you and Megan had some rough patches. . . ."

When Trent would have interrupted, Warren held up his hand. "I'm not blind. I could see you were both unhappy, but I admired the way you stuck by her when she got sick. No one could have been more caring during that awful illness and I will be forever grateful to you for that. Now, though, it's time to move on. You're still a young man. You could start a new family."

"The old one's tricky enough," Trent commented dryly. "Laurie's a handful."

"She's your daughter, but you need a wife," Warren said.

"And you think I should let my daughter handpick the woman to fill that position?"

Warren chuckled. "Her taste can't be all that bad, since you chose the same woman yourself years ago. Look, I know you don't need my blessing, but maybe you'll feel better if you have it. I'm telling you here and now that there's nothing wrong with moving on."

"You never did," Trent pointed out.

"Different situation. Grace was the love of my life. We had a good marriage. I don't harbor one single regret beyond wishing she'd been with me longer. And at my age, what kind of woman can I expect to find? Some gold digger after my fortune?"

"You have better judgment than to let that happen," Trent said.

Warren shrugged. "You know what they say—there's no fool like an old fool. No, Trent, I'm content with the way things are. I have female friends. Widows I've known for years who are good company, play a decent hand of cards and can carry on an intelligent conversation over dinner. I don't need more than that. You, however, are too young to be settling for nothing more than companionship."

Just then the doorbell rang and Warren was on his feet. "Think about what I've said," he advised as he left to answer the door. "Take another look at this Jodie and consider what might be, instead of what was."

Only after Warren had left the room did Trent feel a smile tugging at his lips. Never in a million years had he expected to be getting relationship advice from a tough old man who had an international reputation for chewing up business rivals and spitting them out without the slightest hesitation. Since Warren hadn't steered him too far wrong all those years ago when Trent had been setting up his business, maybe there was some wisdom in what he had to say about Jodie as well.

DEVONIA WAS NEAR TEARS. Jodie saw the expression on the girl's face and rushed over to her.

"What's wrong?" she asked, handing her a tissue.

"None of these dresses are right for me," Devonia said with a resigned sigh. "Either my chest's popping out or they won't even zip up. I'm not going to be able to go to prom after all."

"I don't want to hear that kind of defeatist attitude," Jodie scolded. "Let's take another look. What size do you wear?"

"Fourteen," Devonia said. "All these gowns were made for the rest of these skinny little things."

"Not so," Jodie insisted. "We got a range of sizes. Come with me. Did you try this rack over here?"

Granted, there were only three dresses left hanging on it, but surely one of them would work. She and Laurie had been very careful to make sure that each girl had at least a couple of choices in the right size. They'd wanted to avoid a moment just like this, when someone who wasn't a perfect size six or eight felt humiliated.

Jodie checked the tags and found two size fourteen dresses and one size sixteen.

"I tried those two on," Devonia said, her discouragement plain.

"What was wrong with them?"

"The blue one was cut too low. My mama would never let me out the front door in that. I know I'll be getting dressed here and she won't know, but I just can't wear it."

"And the red?"

"Too tight across my hips."

Jodie nodded. "Did you try on the sixteen?"

Devonia immediately looked insulted. "I am not a size sixteen."

"Of course not," Jodie said hurriedly. "But if you like the dress and it's too big, we can have a seamstress cut it down so that it does fit. Want to give it a try? It's a beautiful dress. I think the color would look amazing on you."

The shimmering copper satin was only a few shades lighter than Devonia's skin. She held the dress up as they stood side by side in front of a mirror. "See what I mean?" Jodie encouraged. "The color's fantastic."

Devonia's expression brightened slightly. "It's not bad, is it?"

"Try it on. Let's see if we can make it work."

A few minutes later Devonia emerged from behind a curtain that cordoned off a dressing room area. Jodie saw the trepidation in her eyes as she walked toward the mirror.

"It's amazing," Jodie reassured her. "Come on, Devonia, see for yourself."

The teenager finally lifted her gaze to the mirror. Her mouth gaped. "Wow!"

Jodie grinned. "I'll say. Marvin is going to swallow his tongue when he sees you. It needs a little nipping and tucking here and there, but it's perfect for you. Don't you think so?"

For the second time, Devonia's eyes swam with tears. "I never…" She swallowed hard. "I never thought I could look like this. I'm almost beautiful."

"Not almost. You *are* beautiful. Shall I get the seamstress over here?"

Devonia couldn't seem to tear her gaze away from the mirror. She merely nodded.

Jodie barely contained a smile as she went off to find someone to make the necessary alterations. The moment Devonia had seen herself as beautiful for the very first time—one of many such moments Jodie had witnessed throughout the day—was what this entire project was about. First thing tomorrow she was going to sit down and e-mail the founder of Inside the Dream and thank her for the inspiration. Because of it, these kids were going to have a whole new image of themselves and the possibilities that stretched out in front of them.

TWO HOURS LATER, the ballroom was deserted except for Jodie, Laurie and, on the other side of the dividing curtain, Trent. Jodie suspected Warren Davis was lurking about somewhere as well. When they'd all grabbed a quick cup of coffee together before the day got started, he'd seemed as excited as she and Laurie. Trent was the only one who'd been oddly subdued.

"This was totally awesome, wasn't it?" Laurie said, her arms filled with the dresses that hadn't been chosen. They'd be packed away for next year, giving the seniors a head start if they chose to continue with the project.

"It couldn't have gone better," Jodie agreed.

"Did you see the way Mariana looked when she tried on that white gown with the gold thread woven through it?" Laurie asked. "She looked like a delicate fairy. It was as if that dress was made for her." Impulsively, she dumped the dresses on a chair and gave Jodie a fierce hug. "Thank you for making this happen."

"You're the one who made it happen, you and the other kids on the committee who worked so hard," Jodie corrected. "The day you came into my office, you started the ball rolling. I hope you know how proud I am of you. Your grandfather and dad must be, too."

Laurie shrugged. "They'd be proud no matter what I did. It's in the job description."

"No, you really earned their admiration this time," Jodie insisted. "I wonder how things went with the boys?"

"Let's get Dad and go out on the patio out back. It should be warm enough. Granddad said he'd have something for us to eat whenever we were ready. I'll let him know we're starving, at least I am."

"Me, too," Jodie admitted. She hadn't noticed missing lunch in the mad rush to get all the girls outfitted, but now she heard her stomach growl.

"If you go through the dining room, there are French doors that lead outside," Laurie told her. "Think you can find your way?"

"Is there a restroom on that route?"

"Just two doors down from here," Laurie directed her. "I'll get Dad and the food and meet you outside."

"Sounds good," Jodie said.

After she'd freshened up, she found her way back to the dining room and then onto the brick patio outside. She was the first one there and sank eagerly onto a comfortable chaise longue in the sun, relieved to be off her feet. The April afternoon was balmy. Enjoying the lingering scent of the last, fading lilacs, she closed her eyes. She couldn't think of the last time she'd felt this kind of exhaustion, one that came from working hard at something so rewarding.

"You sleeping?"

Trent's teasing voice jerked her back from the edge of sleep. She blinked up at him.

"Nope. Just resting my eyes. It's been a long day."

He studied her intently as he sat down beside her. "A good one, though?"

"It was on my side of the curtain. How about yours?"

He handed her a glass of lemonade from a tray. "You know, I expected it to be all grumbling and complaining, but it wasn't like that. It almost felt as if these boys were transformed right in front of my eyes to young men."

Jodie grinned. "Exactly. The same with the girls. It was a good feeling, wasn't it?"

"It was. Just one problem on my side and I'm not sure what to do about it. Mike didn't show up."

Jodie sat up. "Laurie's Mike?"

He nodded. "She was afraid he wouldn't. He told her he had to work, but she thinks he was just making an excuse."

"I don't think so," Jodie said. "That wouldn't be like him at all."

"That's what I told her. And there are tuxedos and one gift certificate left, so he can be fitted whenever he has the time. Now, the question is, do I tell her now or wait?"

"Don't you think she already knows that he wasn't here? I'm sure she was keeping an eye out for him, despite how busy we were. Maybe you should just wait and see if she brings it up."

Trent looked relieved. "Good idea. Now, tell me, did everything go smoothly with the girls?"

"We had one or two crises, but the problems were resolved pretty quickly." She turned to him. "This might sound silly, but I think I'm almost as excited about the prom this year as the girls are."

"Something tells me that doesn't have anything to do with your date with me, either," he commented.

"Sorry if that hurts your ego, but no, it doesn't. It's about these kids. I can't wait till they're all dressed and see themselves for the first time. It'll be like a glimpse of what they can be if they strive for it."

"You're expecting a lot from a fancy dress or a tuxedo," he said.

She sat up straighter. "No, Trent, really, didn't you see how proud they looked when they tried on these clothes? Oh, I'm not saying they're all going to suddenly find a way to go to college and become CEOs. But when people have only seen themselves one way all their lives, struggling just to get by, something like this can show them they can fit into that other world, that the only thing holding them back is their own self-image. They might start to believe they can work hard and accomplish anything, that they're not that different from all those kids who don't need our help."

His gaze warmed. "You must be an incredible guidance counselor. How could any kid not want to reach for the moon with you in his corner?"

Tears stung her eyes. "That may be the nicest thing you've said to me since we first saw each other again. Are you having a change of heart about the kind of person I am?"

"In a way," he replied, glancing over at her. "A very wise man said something to me recently about letting go of the past."

Jodie wasn't sure how she felt about that. "Even the good memories?"

"I don't think he was talking about tossing everything out the window, just the things that keep you from moving on."

"Then he is a wise man," she said, looking straight at him. "You going to take his advice?"

He smiled slowly. "I'm thinking about it."

"Good to know I still have a little influence around here," Warren Davis announced, joining them with a tray loaded down with thick sandwiches and slices of decadent-looking chocolate cake. Laurie was right behind him with a bowl of salad.

Jodie flushed at the realization that he was the one who'd been giving Trent advice, apparently about her. Still, she was grateful to have another person—someone Trent obviously respected—in her corner.

She wasn't sure it was possible to recapture what the two of them once had. There was too much water under the bridge. But maybe they could find something new together. She knew she wanted to try.

Because from the minute she'd laid eyes on Trent in that classroom a couple of months ago, she'd known that she was still very much in love with him. She hadn't been willing to admit it, even to herself, until now. The thought that he might not love her back was too scary.

But if there was a chance—even a very slim one—that she could have him back in her life, she wanted that chance more than she'd wanted anything in a very long time.

CHAPTER
~ SEVEN ~

Trent didn't mean to eavesdrop, but he couldn't help himself when he heard Mike's voice rise in anger. He didn't intend to step in unless things got out of hand, but he wasn't happy hearing anyone speak to Laurie in that tone of voice. Then he listened to the point Mike was trying to make and that his daughter apparently wasn't hearing. It was difficult to stand by and listen to them struggling to reach an understanding on something so complex that many adults couldn't manage it. Both of them had valid viewpoints, and finding the middle ground seemed all but impossible.

"I did not blow off today," Mike told her heatedly. "Come on, Laurie. Don't you know me better than that?"

"I thought I did," Laurie responded just as angrily. "But when you didn't show up at Granddad's today, I felt like it was a slap in the face.

You know how hard I've worked to make this happen and you couldn't even be bothered to be there."

"Because I was *working*," he retorted impatiently. "I told you I had to work. What part of that don't you understand? I need to work as many hours as they'll give me. My family needs every dime I can earn and I have to start putting away some money for college next year. The scholarship won't cover all of my expenses."

"I know that," Laurie said, sounding somewhat apologetic. "But today was really important to me. It should have mattered to you."

Mike sighed heavily. "What's happened to you, Laurie? If things don't go exactly the way you want them to, then I'm disrespecting you? You never used to be like that. You never used to act like a spoiled brat."

Trent heard Laurie's gasp, then silence. He could feel her anguish, but he could also understand Mike's frustration. When Laurie finally spoke, her voice was thick with tears.

"I had no idea you felt that way," she whispered. "Do you want to break up? Is that what this is about?"

"Are you crazy?"

To Trent's relief, Mike sounded incredulous, as if nothing could be further from the truth.

"Laurie, if you and I are going to stay together, we have to be able to work through stuff like this. We come from very different backgrounds, that's just a fact. You take things for granted that are out of reach for me."

"I was just trying to put them within reach," she told him. "Just for prom, not for anything else. You're fine the way you are. In fact, I love who you are. You're smart and you care so much about your family. You work hard and still keep your grades up and find time for sports and for me. You're terrific. Don't you know how much I admire you?"

"I wish you'd said all that a few weeks ago," Mike told her. "I thought you were ashamed of me."

"Never!" she said fiercely.

"You know, if you'd just said that prom was important to you, I would have found some way for us to go," he told her wearily. "You said it didn't matter, and then, all of a sudden, there's this huge production to make sure all the poor kids like me get to go. And to top it off, you got Ms. Fletcher on my case about it. Do you know how that made me feel?"

"I just meant for you to feel included," she whispered.

"Well, I didn't. I felt embarrassed and humiliated, and worse, I got drafted to talk the other guys into it. It's not that I don't appreciate your motives, but did you ever stop to think about how it would make me feel to have to take all this free stuff from somebody? I was brought up to pay my own way, and if I couldn't, then I did without. The only time I've broken that rule is when I asked Ms. Fletcher to help me get free school breakfasts and lunches for my brothers and sister. It about killed me to ask for that. I only did it because my mom was too proud to, and they were going to school hungry."

"I'm sorry. I guess I didn't think this through. Do you think the others feel the same way?"

"No, and if I can shove my pride aside, I get that you're doing a really nice thing. And prom is going to be great this year, because almost everyone will be there. It's just hard, you know, feeling like I can't provide everything you want."

"I just want you," she told him softly. "Just you."

Silence fell then and Trent didn't want to think about any making up that might be going on, so he slipped away and went down the hall into his office. As he sat at his desk, he thought about what Mike had said, that he and Laurie had to work through things, not make assumptions and run off to lick their wounds.

Was that what he had done years ago with Jodie? Had he been so hurt by her decision to break up that he'd failed to fight hard enough for what he believed they had? Oh, sure, he'd made plenty of calls. He'd even gone by her place a few times, but he could have done more and he knew it. He'd been afraid to push too hard for answers because he thought he already knew what they would be—that she'd tired of him, that she no longer loved him. He hadn't wanted to hear those words spelled out any more clearly than they already had been. He'd made assumptions rather than having faith in what he *knew* they had between them.

Before he could change his mind, he picked up the phone and dialed the number he'd written down when he'd looked up her address a few weeks before.

"Hello," she said cheerily, with yet another symphony booming in the background. "Hang on a sec. The music's too loud."

Once it was muted, she came back on the line. "Sorry. I always thought Beethoven was meant to be heard at full volume."

"You never liked classical music when we were together," Trent commented.

"Trent?" She sounded surprised.

"It's me," he said. "When did you develop this fondness for Beethoven and the rest of the classics?"

"When I was married. Adam liked it and I developed an appreciation for it, too, though to be honest my preference is for Mozart's pieces for the flute. What about you? Have your musical tastes changed at all?"

"Sorry, no. I'm still a little bit country, a little bit rock 'n' roll."

She laughed. "Like the Osmonds."

"Pretty much."

"I assume you didn't call to talk about music," she said. "Is there something in particular on your mind?"

"I was sitting here thinking about some things," he began, not entirely sure what to say now that he had her on the phone. He just knew that everything that had happened wasn't entirely her fault, after all.

"The past?" she asked.

"Mostly," he acknowledged. "I owe you an apology."

"Oh?"

"I still don't like what you did all those years ago, the unilateral decision you made that affected our future."

"Yes, you've made that clear enough," she said dryly. "I'm not quite hearing that apology yet."

"Hold on. I'm getting to it." His lips curved slightly, but the smile faded as he formed the rest of his thoughts. "You made that decision, Jodie, but I'm the one who let you get away with it. I should have owned up to my part a long time ago, but it was easier to blame you. I could have fought harder, made you talk to me about why you decided to end it, instead of just running off with my tail between my legs. Maybe if I'd forced things and we'd really sat down and talked it all through, things would have turned out differently."

"Oh, Trent, I don't know about that. I was pretty stubborn and pretty darn certain I was right. I spent my entire childhood being told by my parents that I wasn't as pretty or as smart or as clever as my sister. When I was in that car accident—remember, I told you about that when we first met—things went from bad to worse. Oh, my folks were there for me, but they couldn't seem to help reminding me afterward that I was less than perfect. When I met you, I was still pretty much convinced that I could never measure up. You were going places and I didn't think I could keep up. Even my folks commented one time that I would probably hold you back."

"That's ridiculous," he said heatedly.

She sighed. "I know that now, but I didn't have the kind of self-confidence and strength then that I do today. That comes with maturity and getting away from all that nonstop negativity."

"I wish you'd explained all this back then," he told her. "I could have told you how wrong you were."

"I wouldn't have believed you. After all, the message had been ingrained in me for a very long time, if not with overt criticism then with comparisons in which I always fell just a little short of my sister."

"But I could be awfully persuasive when I set my mind to it, or have you forgotten that?" He chuckled as a memory came to him. "I got you to go parasailing at Ocean City despite your fear of heights, didn't I?"

She groaned. "I have definitely tried to forget that. Maybe that was when I saw we didn't have a real future. I wasn't sure I was prepared for a lifetime of taking outrageous risks. I'd always pictured myself as a sedate schoolteacher, setting a proper example for her students."

"You could have done both," he said.

"I'm not so sure about that."

"Let me prove it to you, starting with prom."

"I've already agreed to go with you," she reminded him.

"I know, but I'm not sure when I asked and you agreed to go that either one of us was doing it for the right reason."

"And what is the right reason?"

"Because I want to hold you in my arms and dance with you," he told her, his voice low and seductive. "I want to start over, Jodie, see what's left of what we once were or maybe find something new altogether. How about it? Just take the first step on the long road toward a future with me."

She was silent for so long, he thought maybe she wasn't anywhere near as ready as he was.

"One step," she agreed at last. "And then we'll see."

"That's all I ask," he said. "Good night, Jodie."

"Good night, Trent."

He held the phone after she'd disconnected, not ready to break that fragile tie with the woman he'd once loved with all his heart… and just might love again.

THE MAY EVENING COULDN'T have been more perfect. The sky was littered with stars, the temperature balmy. Inside Oak Haven, the ballroom quite literally took Jodie's breath away. It looked different than it had when they'd held their shopping spree there a few weeks earlier. The massive chandelier sparkled like diamonds and spilled light over polished oak floors inlaid with elaborate designs. The part of her that had once dreamed impossible dreams could imagine a full orchestra at one end of the huge room, music soaring to the rafters and mingling with excited chatter and high-pitched laughter. That was the world to which Trent was accustomed. She tried not to let that intimidate her. Instead, she focused on the chatter and laughter around her tonight.

A dozen girls were at the center of a beehive of activity, their dresses nipped and tucked one last time until they fit perfectly, their hair in giant rollers as they awaited a turn with one of the four stylists who had volunteered to help. They jockeyed for position in front of the half-dozen full-length mirrors that had been brought in for the occasion, their eyes bright with wonder as they saw themselves transformed. Several moms had come along for the special night and they sat on the sidelines, smiling at the joy on their daughters' faces.

Laurie darted among the girls, her own pastel-pink dress a fairy-tale confection of tulle and silk and glittering rhinestones. She was a never-ending font of helpful tips, of glowing compliments that kept the other girls beaming with pride.

"I had no idea I could ever look like this," Mariana Padrone whispered to Jodie as she stared at the image in the mirror in front of her. In the white dress threaded with gold, she looked like a delicate princess.

A shy girl with decent but not extraordinary grades, Mariana was destined for community college classes that could fit around her work schedule. Tonight was giving her a little bit of the magic that had been missing from her life.

"You look beautiful," Jodie told her. "Miguel is going to be blown away when he sees you."

"I am so grateful to Mr. Winston for talking him into this," Mariana said, glancing toward the portable dividers that separated the girls' dressing area from the boys'. "He is going to look so handsome in his tuxedo. I wish I had a camera to take pictures so we can always remember tonight."

"Done," Jodie said, grinning at her and pulling a disposable camera from a bag filled with two dozen of them. "There's one for each of you. Allow me to take the first picture."

She snapped it, capturing Mariana's beaming smile forever.

Over the next hour, she took dozens of photos of the girls alone in their finery and then of the couples as they prepared to ride in one of the limos that Warren Davis had arranged to take them from his home to the hotel. The drivers would wait and deliver the students to one of several parent-supervised after-prom parties that would last until dawn.

When the final limo rode away, Jodie turned to find Trent behind her. She'd found him attractive enough in his work clothes, but in a tuxedo he was devastatingly handsome. He looked as if he'd been born to wear one. All those years ago, she had known that his life was meant to be like this, from the fancy clothes to the extravagant events.

Then she reminded herself that this was a high school prom they were about to attend, an event from her world, and he looked as if it were as important as any big-dollar charity event.

"Unlike the boys, you look very comfortable in that tux," she commented. "You must have had it specially tailored."

"I had to," he said. "Laurie took all my old ones for this project."

He pulled his hand from behind his back and held out a florist's box. "You never did say what kind of flowers you wanted, so I had to rely on a tip from my daughter." He glanced from her shimmering sheath of cream silk, which Carmen had talked her into paying way too much for, to the ivory camellia resting against delicate lace and waxy, dark green leaves.

Jodi regarded the corsage with amazement. He'd gotten it exactly right, simple and classy, just like Trent himself.

He grinned at her. "Trust me to pin it on, or would you rather do it yourself?"

She had to swallow against the tide of emotion clogging her throat. "You do it, please," she said softly.

When his knuckles grazed bare skin, she trembled, but she kept her gaze level with his, felt the heat stir between them. The once-familiar sensation was exactly the way she'd remembered it. For the second time in her life, she felt as if her prince had come along.

She'd just never expected to have to wait so very long for him to find his way back to her.

TRENT STOOD AT THE EDGE of the dance floor, Jodie beside him, and felt an unexpected swell of pride that his daughter had turned this night into something special for so many people. Sure, some of the students here were having the night they'd anticipated, taken for granted, in fact, but he could pick out those for whom it was an unexpected blessing. There was an air of bemusement about them, a sense of wonder that was lacking in the other kids.

Even Marvin and his oh-so-resistant cohorts were standing taller, gazing with genuine amazement and appreciation at the girls on their arms. And Mike had finally relaxed and let himself enjoy the party. He and Laurie couldn't seem to take their eyes off each other. Trent couldn't help rooting just a little bit for the two of them. He was impressed more and more with Mike's maturity.

Jodie said something he couldn't hear over the music so he leaned closer, breathing in the scent of the camellia that he'd noticed her touching from time to time as if it were a talisman.

"What?" he asked.

"I said I haven't heard Marvin refer to a single person tonight as a dude," she said, grinning. "That alone is miracle enough for me." She glanced across the room. "Laurie and Mike look happy. Did they settle their disagreement or is this just detente?"

"They talked and settled things, I think," Trent said. "At least for now. Who knows what's in store for those two, but I have to say my respect for Mike has increased lately. He's got a good head on his shoulders. Maybe they can make it, after all."

Jodi studied him quizzically. "Will you mind that very much?"

"I never objected to Laurie dating Mike," he said. "At least not for the reason you're thinking. I thought it was too soon, that Mike especially had a tough road ahead of him and shouldn't add a serious relationship to the mix." He glanced at her. "Sounds like the same mistake you made about me, misjudging what I could handle."

"Okay, okay, I get it," she said. "I thought we'd settled the fact that I'd been an idiot and you were, too."

"I don't recall the word *idiot* ever crossing my lips," he commented.

"Implied," she said. "It was definitely implied."

"We're communicating now, though, and that's what counts," he told her. "We'll never make that same mistake again."

"Never," she promised.

Trent looked around the dance floor and chuckled as he saw Marvin trying to do a sedate slow dance with Devonia. He looked as if he wanted to break loose and speed up the beat. Ramon and his girl were wrapped tight in each other's arms. Miguel's gaze on Mariana was bewildered, almost as if he'd never seen her before and didn't know quite what to make of this precious, lovely creature. Even Jason, small for his age, his eyes too big behind his thick glasses, was talking intently to a girl wearing braces and whose hair was as uncontrolled as Jodie's. Even though she was inches taller than Jason, she was gazing at him raptly and seemed to be hanging on the boy's every word.

Trent looked into Jodie's eyes. "You and my daughter did a good thing tonight," he said. "A very good thing."

"Does that mean you'll help us again next year, even if Laurie's away at college?"

"If you need my help, you've got it," he said at once. "On one condition."

"Oh?"

"Dance with me, Jodie. That was part of our deal for tonight, but every time I've asked, you've suddenly found something requiring your attention. Even the most dutiful chaperone doesn't need to check the punch bowl that many times, especially since we've been standing right next to it for most of the night."

She winced. "You noticed that?"

"I notice a lot of things about you," he said, brushing a wayward curl from her cheek. It was a futile exercise, since more sprang free from the delicate, sparkling combs meant to hold her hair in place.

"Name one."

He laughed. "You did it again. You tried to divert me. Come on, Jodie, it's time to pay the piper. I'm claiming this dance."

She backed up a step. "I can't."

He paused, struck by the genuine fear he saw in her eyes. "What do you mean, you can't? Do you really have two left feet, the way you said the other day?"

"I don't know," she confessed.

He was more confused than ever. "How can you not know?"

"The truth is that I never learned to dance."

Trent didn't even try to hide his disbelief. "But the way you got involved with this, the fact that it's so important to you…" He didn't know what to make of any of it.

"I know it must not make sense to you," she said.

"Explain," he pleaded.

Her cheeks turned pink. Carefully avoiding his gaze, she finally blurted, "You remember that when I was just starting my senior year of high school, I was in an accident, a bad one. Broken legs, broken pelvis."

Trent nodded. "You told me about that and you mentioned it again the other day. What does that have to do with you not dancing?"

"I finished the year in rehab and at home. For a while they thought I would never walk again, but I proved them wrong." She met his eyes straight on. "Don't you remember that when we met our junior year I still had a little bit of a limp? I was so self-conscious about it."

He shook his head. "All I noticed was that you were the most beautiful woman I'd ever seen and that your laugh made me happy. Beyond mentioning the accident, you never made a big deal about it. I had no idea it was so serious."

"I didn't want you to feel sorry for me and I was trying to forget what had been a very painful time in my life, not just physically, but emotionally. I was grateful that I could walk. I really was, but I missed so much, things I can never get back."

He regarded her with sudden understanding. "Like your prom."

She nodded.

"But you came to this one," he said. "Did you go to the prom at your old school, too?"

She nodded. "As a chaperone. I've done it for years. I kept hoping it would make up for what I'd missed, but it's not the same. It couldn't possibly be." Again, she touched the camellia fleetingly. "At least until tonight."

Trent's heart turned over in his chest as he tried to imagine how it must have hurt each year to see young people celebrating the end of their high school days, while she had only memories of pain and heartache from hers.

Not only had her revelation given him a deeper insight into this amazing woman, it also reassured him that even if they spent a lifetime together, there would still be new discoveries to make. The prospect excited him.

"You know," he said, "dancing's not that difficult."

"Maybe not for you," she said. "You've had lots of practice."

"Come on," he insisted, tugging her onto the floor and then into his arms. "Just hold on to me, Jodie. Trust me."

Her body swayed into his and he gave her a moment to relax before he began to move. "Listen to the music—feel it," he encouraged her, wishing he could feel it himself over the beating of his heart and the sweet sensation of her body pressed against him.

"Don't even think about dancing," he said. "Look around you. See what you've done for these kids. You gave them magic, Jodie. You gave them memories they'll treasure for a lifetime, rather than living with the regret of missing this night the way you had to."

A smile spread across her face as she looked around. He could tell the precise moment when she forgot about her fears, her awkwardness. Satisfied that he'd accomplished one goal, he went for another and spun her around and around till she was laughing, her feet off the ground. The kids around them stood back and applauded.

Seeing Jodie let go, listening to the laughter that had once brought him such joy, Trent knew he'd captured a little magic tonight, too.

And this time, he wouldn't let it go. He'd do whatever it took to make sure it lasted forever.

Dear Reader,

How many times in your life have you opened your closet door before an evening out and murmured, "I have absolutely nothing to wear," even though the closet is crammed with clothes? It's one thing to face such a dilemma as an adult, but in the fashion-conscious world of teenagers, it's quite another, especially if the lack of appropriate clothes is real. At no time does the absence of something special to wear seem quite as important as it does for all of the activities associated with high school graduation and, most especially, the prom.

Ruth Renwick, a Canadian social worker, encountered that need firsthand when she learned of a girl who was going to miss her high school prom because she simply couldn't afford a dress to wear. The first dress Ruth took by was too big. With time running out, Ruth searched her own closet and found more options and took them to the girl's home. It seemed such a little thing to her at the time, but the delight she saw on the girl's face, the transformation that took place, led Ruth to think about all of the other young girls and young men in similar circumstances. With her huge heart, the glimmer of an idea, and the help of her family and others such as social workers Tracey Ciccarelli-Ridsdill and Janace King-Watson, Ruth began Inside the Dream. You can read much more about the organization on the Web site, www.insidethedream.org. If you're able to help, please do. If there's a need for a similar organization in your community, start one. It only takes one person with a dream and a vision to make a huge difference in someone's life.

With all good wishes for your dreams to come true,

Sherryl Woods

Dr. Ricki Robinson
~Autism Speaks~

Dr. Ricki Robinson often says that if you don't know a family whose life has been touched by autism—you will. As a doctor and founding member of Cure Autism Now, an organization that combined forces with Autism Speaks in 2007, she is well aware of the troubling statistics: autism is the fastest-growing developmental disorder in North America, with the numbers increasing dramatically from one child in 10,000 a mere dozen years ago to one in 150 in 2006.

Autism, which interferes with a child's natural development, is a lifelong disability, and one that is often difficult to detect in very young children or by first-time parents. Indications of it include little or no eye contact, a delay in expressing, understanding and responding to language, a failure to develop social skills, unusual reactions to the way things look, feel, taste, smell or sound, and repetitive behaviors such as saying words or asking questions repeatedly. Sometimes children who have been progressing normally until about age two suddenly stop, and begin to regress. Some children never talk; others do. It all adds to the lack of understanding about what autism is, Dr. Robinson says.

When Dr. Robinson, affectionately known as Dr. Ricki, began working with children affected by autism fifteen years ago, "there was no future for these children," she says. No medical test existed for diagnosis, there was a lack of physician education, and parents who sensed that something was wrong were advised to "wait and see."

As a general pediatric practitioner, she had noticed increasing numbers of children being diagnosed with autism or related disorders, but says she was "frustrated with the lack of therapeutic resources available for developing integrated treatment plans, and appalled at the lack of scientific research." She was also appalled by the tendency to blame mothers for supposed faulty parenting skills. It was not uncommon for the mother to be prescribed therapy rather than the child. "This was preposterous to me," she says. "I knew we needed a grassroots effort to increase awareness, and to raise money for scientific research."

Fifteen years on, though the underlying causes are still not known, "we have lots and lots of clues now," she says. "And there are so many different things we can do." Thanks largely to her own efforts and the work of Autism Speaks, awareness, knowledge and research are increasing.

Providing hope to families is crucial in light of the stark reality that very little government aid or health care coverage is available to mitigate the costs associated with treating the disorder. Educational budgets are inadequate to meet the challenge in schools. Parents are often left exhausted and financially devastated. For these parents, it's a comfort to know there is somewhere they can turn. Autism Speaks has created a network of parents, clinicians and researchers who are bonded by hope and working toward a better quality of life for those who struggle with autism.

The process of identifying and treating autism has always been complicated. Though research confirms a genetic basis, "unlike disorders that have been linked to a single gene, such as cystic fibrosis, there may be twenty or thirty genes involved in autism," says Dr. Ricki. She believes there are also environmental factors involved and advocates for further exploration to determine how such factors may trigger autism. As a physician and advocate, Dr. Ricki is proud of her involvement in Cure Autism Now's (CAN) Clinical Consensus Group. The group built consensus on guidelines for medical evaluation for autism, so that physicians could more effectively identify the disorder. The CAN Clinical Consensus Statement, now used across the United States, provides guidelines for putting a child through a battery of behavioral screenings in order to make an assessment that can be followed by therapeutic interventions tailored to individual needs.

Parents are very much part of that therapy. One of Dr. Ricki's special gifts is helping parents understand how their child is learning, and that coming to expect that child to become "the best they can be" is an attainable goal. As just one example, a child she began working with fifteen years ago is now about to enter university and, although unable to converse because of motor challenges, can type and is "fully literate" in written communication.

The mother of a young man who has been treated by Dr. Ricki for the past eleven years remembers that when she and her husband first brought their son, then three, to her, he had lost his speech, wasn't making eye contact and had stopped playing with other children.

"Dr. Ricki was the first one to give us hope," she says. "She could see possibilities we couldn't." Right from the beginning, the parents were treated as partners in addressing the challenges, learning how therapies, curriculum and tutoring techniques play into the larger picture, and how to break it all down into manageable, achievable goals.

Today, at fourteen, the boy is "calmer, rich in language, with lots of friends." His mother remains in awe of Dr. Ricki's patience and compassion, her skill and diligent research. "I believe she fundamentally rewired his brain," she says. "She is a very special person."

Funding for Autism Speaks comes from individuals, corporate donors and fund-raisers held throughout the year. Funds raised are used mainly in support of research programs and initiatives. One of the most productive programs is the Autism Genetic Resource Exchange (AGRE). Through AGRE, families provide the genetic material and clinical data that enable scientists around the world to study autism immediately, without having to find the families themselves. The resource is available to all qualified researchers willing to share their discoveries, which promotes collaboration and prevents duplication—accelerating the pace and progress in autism research. "There are now some 154 labs around the world using the AGRE sources," says Dr. Ricki.

Dr. Ricki continues to support clinical research designed to develop medical treatments for autism. She has been instrumental in programs such as the Autism Treatment Network (ATN) and Clinical Trials Network (CTN), which connect families to the most current medical approaches available and seek to establish a standard of care for the biomedical treatment of autism. She encourages parents to have their children participate whenever possible, believing that only through family participation and aggressive research can this devastating disorder be conquered.

A frequent speaker at professional conferences, Dr. Ricki now spends as much time volunteering and training more professionals as she does in practicing medicine. Working with these "amazing families and kids with so few people helping them" is compelling, she says. "I have never felt more needed as a physician than I do working with patients and families affected by autism. I feel like my whole life prepared me for this, and now I'm able to teach and prepare others—which is a true gift."

For more information visit www.autismspeaks.org or write to Autism Speaks, 5455 Wilshire Blvd. #2250, Los Angeles, CA 90036.

CURTISS ANN MATLOCK
∽— A Place in This World —∽

∽CURTISS ANN MATLOCK∽

Curtiss Ann Matlock loves to share her experience of Southern living, so she fills her stories with rich local color, basic values and Southern country wisdom. Her books have earned rave reviews, been optioned for film and received numerous awards, among them two Readers' Choice Awards, given by readers from all over the nation. In addition, her books have received three nominations for the Romance Writers of America's prestigious RITA® Award.

She currently divides her time between Oklahoma and Alabama.

PART
~ONE~

T hat August, the kids came and saved me. I had no idea at the
time that I needed saving. And I include Laura Jean as one
of the kids, even if she was not. Really, I suppose we saved
one another, as if we all grabbed hold of the same line stretched out
from heaven.

Henry had been gone two years, three months and four days. All
that time, and I was still keeping track of the days, marking them off
on the calendar first thing in the morning, right after I started the
Mister Coffee. Then I would slip the calendar back in the drawer,
underneath the dish towels. After this I would take my coffee outside and greet the day.

I followed this pattern each and every day. I am very much a creature of habit, and I cling to the early mornings, before everyone else

has come awake and begun to fill the air with chatter and interfere with my thinking. I tend to live in my own world of thoughts. Henry always said I thought too much, but I never could think how I would stop, or even that I wanted to.

On that particular morning of the day the children came, there was a thin humid mist, but the horizon was turning turquoise with the dawn. Oh, the summer scents were strong! I stood marveling for a few minutes, walked to the fence, reached through to fill the water tank for our old gelding, Bob, then went back inside to eat a couple of boiled eggs and get dressed.

My eye happened to fall—my vision, not my eye, which was still in my head; it is my English-teacher training—on the silver filigree earrings lying atop my dresser. I had found them the previous day, when cleaning out some of Henry's old stuff in the attic. My old stuff is mingled with his old stuff, of course. I had thrown his old stuff away but rescued the earrings at the last minute.

I slipped the wires of the earrings through my lobes and gazed at myself in the mirror. I had bought the earrings on a college trip to Galveston Island, just before Henry and I married. He had never much liked them, said they were too large. I had liked them, and it turned out that I still did, which was a little surprising. It is said we come full circle in our lives.

MONTE ARRIVED A LITTLE early, but I was ready, had a fruit cake finished and two cornmeal-and-ham muffins out of the freezer and heated in the microwave.

Food is the main way that I relate to life, and to people. Food is my way of talking, and I knew right away that I may have made something of a mistake with Monte. I had done the same as feeding a puppy—once you feed them they sure are not going to leave. But how could I not feed the man who was working on my roof? I really should have called a roofing contractor, but it all happened so fast. A summer storm took off a few shingles. I was coming down the ladder from the roof when Monte stopped by. The next thing I knew, he showed up with his tools and said he was putting on a new roof.

I guess I'm a little irritated at Monte for taking over a lot of things, just assuming I want him to do them. Of course, I have not told him not to. There is not a food for saying that you don't want a person to do something. And I guess I really do want him to be around, only I'm all confused about it.

Wrapping the warm muffins in a cloth napkin, I grabbed the mug of coffee I had poured for him and stepped out on the porch.

"Well, good mornin', beautiful." Monte was just rounding the front of his pickup.

My insides got jittery with the word *beautiful*. Monte has called me that on occasion for the many years that we have known each other, so I do not know why it should now jangle me. I turned and grabbed my wide-brimmed straw hat off the hook, plopping it on my head and saying, "Good mornin'. Radio says it's gonna be hot. We both better get at it." I pushed out the screen door.

Monte is an old school friend of Henry's and mine. He and I had dated a couple of times in high school before I dated Henry. Then

Henry went off to college, and I followed the next year and ended up marrying him. Monte went off to the navy and around the world. He came home, used the G.I. bill to become a geologist and went all around the world again for oil companies. He has been married twice, but he lost both of his wives. That's how he puts it, but what he means is he got divorced.

Through the years Henry and Monte stayed in touch. Many a Christmas or Fourth of July, when his family had their reunion, Monte would show up at our door. Five years ago he retired and moved back home permanently, and he and Henry became fast friends again. Since Henry's death, Monte has done a number of things that take a man's strength and some knowledge of electronics, such as changing out the well pump when it broke and clearing tree limbs downed in an ice storm.

In the past six months, though, I suppose that he has all but rented billboard space to say that he would like me to take up with him.

I went over and handed him his coffee and napkin sack of muffins.

He looked from me to the food and coffee and back to me, saying, "I came extra early, because I thought I might be in time for a sit-down breakfast."

"I ate a while ago, just boiled eggs and a banana."

"Uh-huh."

Letting go of any further conversation on that score, I went on to the toolshed for baskets and my gardening tools. When I came back past Monte, still standing in the driveway but now nibbling on a muffin—he had set the mug of coffee on the hood of his truck—a look of pure confusion passed over his face, as if he wanted to help me but did not know what to do with the food.

"Mighty good muffins," he said with his mouth full.

It is impossible for a woman to be complimented on her cooking and remain unaffected, but I did my best. I said that I was glad he enjoyed them, and headed on through the gate to the garden.

We—or *I*, as it is now—have a large vegetable garden and a small orchard of apple and peach trees. I sell a good bit of the produce at a stand down at the bottom of our driveway. Since Henry's demise, the garden and the produce stand have been my saving grace. Both give me a lot of time for thinking, and vegetables and fruits do not require you to talk to them, although I like to think they enjoy my singing. The whole of gardening is a place I feel at home, always have, and suddenly I find myself at ease with Monte, who has followed me and is standing at the rail fence, eating his muffin.

"We are gettin' the best tomatoes this year. Just look at this…" I proudly held up a plump Campbell. "Do you want to take some to your mama?" Not only did I like Monte's mother, but I knew she truly appreciated my tomatoes.

"Oh, yeah…I was supposed to ask you for enough for her to make sauce."

"Got a'plenty." Quite quickly I filled several baskets with the prettiest tomatoes—Campbells and Arkansas Travelers, all of them deep red. Why would anyone want one of those varieties of green or orange tomato? I asked this question of Monte as I carried the baskets over to the fence. He wiped his mouth with the napkin and said he didn't know.

Then, as I bent over to set the baskets down, he said, "Don't you ever wear anything besides bib overalls?"

That question sort of stopped me in my tracks. Slowly, still bent over, I twisted and looked up to see him looking down pointedly at my behind. I straightened.

"It might be nice to show yourself as a woman," he added, giving a little grin. "I know *I* would like to see you in a skirt once in a while."

I said what came to mind, which was "I don't suppose I care what you would like to see me in."

He was clearly surprised by that, and I guess I was a little, too.

The next instant I was realizing how blue his eyes were and noticing the angry-hurt expression on his face. I could not stand it. I whipped around about hard enough to jerk my head off and stepped over to the rows of zucchini. I thought: I dress for myself. My overalls are tough, comfortable and have plenty of pockets to carry a pocket knife and Kleenex and garden snips—and a few dollars and a lipstick on the occasions when I run uptown for something or happen to go to early church service. Work clothes on women are not at all strange in our rural area. And it isn't as though I am twenty-five anymore, or even thirty-five. I'm fifty. And I do not look mannish. When was the last time you saw a man wearing a pink, flowered thermal shirt under overalls?

Monte spoke aloud. He said, "Is it lonely in there, Ellie Perabo?"

his voice carrying across to where I crouched at a zucchini plant. I gazed at it as if it was the most fascinating thing in the world.

He said, "Henry is as dead as he'll ever be, Ellie. But you're alive."

I knew not replying was the rudest thing, and I was trying really hard to get words to my tongue, but I could not figure out for the life of me what to say to him. I just crouched there with a zucchini in my hand, having the urge to offer a basketful to him, as silly as that sounds.

Then Monte turned and walked off.

For a few seconds I almost called to him. I watched him get the ladder and set it in place, and I kept thinking I was going to call to him and run over there and try to talk to him. But I did not, and he went on up to the roof.

The moment of opportunity passed, and all the reasons why I could not possibly explain to him took over. The main reason, which I was fairly certain he would not appreciate hearing, was that I had spent a great deal of my marriage struggling to explain myself to Henry. I did not want to make the effort anymore.

All in all, the best course seemed to be to stay there and pick zucchini, while my mind bounced from what went on with Monte to the fact that the zucchini plants were about done in by squash bugs. Henry and I had never used pesticides. Henry had been devoted to organic farming, had done all manner of study about it and worked himself to pieces with all manner of remedies. For me, it was just easiest and wisest to follow Mother Nature's ways and seasons. Let a zucchini be what it was, and when the time was over, let it go on.

THE SIGN NAILED TO the produce stand said Perabo Fruits and Vegetables in fancy, colorful script. I had designed and painted it myself the month after Henry died. The project kept me busy fourteen hours a day for a week. The sign was far more fancy than the old tin produce stand on which it was posted. The stand sat in the shade of a big old elm south of our driveway entry, which is alongside a main state highway leading to the interstate and Little Rock. We even have a long-and-wide sort of lot that the state paved when they resurfaced the highway. Did I mention that Henry had worked for the state road department?

I have established the habit of opening the stand for a few hours each morning and evening during the highest traffic times. I also put in coffee, cappuccino, packaged snacks and cold drinks, and the news and sale papers. Business has grown with quite a few regulars. Frankly, it is amazing the amount of money I'm making. If Henry had known we could make this good, he would have had me down here every day. I have more than once looked up and said, "I told you so, Henry."

When the large old LTD came chugging past, I was sitting on my red-and-white kitchen stool, watching traffic go by out in the bright sun from behind my dark Ray-Bans. The LTD caught my attention not only because it was old but looked new, but because Henry and I had owned one exactly like it years ago. It was a déjà-vu moment. And then I noticed that the car appeared to have engine trouble. It did this sort of chug-chugging as it headed off the road and to the far end of the paved area. It really is such a perfect place for stopping that cars see it and break down with regularity.

My eye lit on the license plate—Texas tag.

The car sat there for some moments. Then doors on both sides opened simultaneously. No further movement for a curious minute, and then a young woman got out from the driver's side and a little girl popped out from the passenger side and went running around to join the woman. Both females wore baggy T-shirts and shorty-shorts and flip-flops. They stood staring at the car, as if watching for it to spontaneously start.

I have to say that a complete picture of their life came to me—married too young, baby too young, living on hope and expectation, and unseen grace when those ran out.

The two gave up trying to start the car with looks, and the woman bent inside for quite a long period. Curious, I came up off my stool a moment, as if that would help me see better. At last the young woman came out dragging a purse and another child, reinforcing my theory as to her life.

The second child looked to be a boy of about three or four. He kicked and screamed in such a way that I had to watch. He definitely did not want to get out of the car. But he was small enough for her to capture both his hands batting at her face and to prop him on her narrow hip. The little girl handed him a toy, apparently a favorite, because he eagerly took hold of it. The woman started toward the produce stand, and the girl raced ahead, alternately skipping and running.

"Hello," the child said, coming directly to where I sat.

"Hello."

"Our car broke down…over there. That is our car." She pointed at the LTD.

"I see that."

We gazed at each other. The way she regarded me made me remember my sunglasses. I slipped them off and smiled at her. She studied me a moment, then her gaze skittered along the shelf of snacks in front of me and on to the vegetables. She was tiny, fine-boned, with dark eyes and a face bright as a new penny. She asked what were those, and those, and those.

"Peanuts and okra and cucumbers," I said. Most children these days do not see food before it is in a can or box.

The young woman came forward through the shade of the big elm. She looked wilted, as would anyone in the growing heat and carrying a little boy, who possessed the most beautiful head of curls made even curlier by sweat. He did not hold on to the young woman and was clearly dead weight.

As they entered the stand, the boy turned his head to look around. I knew he had caught the scent of all the fruits and vegetables. There are certain people who do that, who are drawn by the scent. He had the face of an angel.

"Mama, I want a peach," said the little girl. "I want one of these peaches."

"Okay, honey…"

Just then the little boy about lunged out of her arms, stretching his hand toward the basket of peaches.

"Oh, dang—Cody, wait! I'll get you one…here. Roline, sugar,

get a couple of dollars out of my purse." She dropped her bag off her shoulder for the girl, and went over to put the boy on the only chair next to the wall near my counter.

"Sit on the chair," she said in a particular fashion, holding the peach away from him until he said something to her. "Good boy." She handed him the peach and touched his hair with her cheek in a tender gesture that washed all over me.

Next the girl handed me up a dollar. I waved it away. "Those peaches are at their peak and have to be eaten now. You kids take this basket of 'em."

I went over to the cooler, pulled out two bottles of Lipton iced tea and passed one to the young woman and opened the other for myself. While I waited to see if she would start a conversation, I thought of various things I might say. Thankfully she started everything by telling about how her car had begun to act up several miles back, right after they had stopped at a Wendy's.

I knew the one she meant. It was a nice place, with picnic tables under trees right off its parking lot. Everyone remarked on it. We chatted about the restaurant for a moment, and then I managed to slip in the question as to whether she was traveling far.

She had come from the Texas Panhandle and was heading to her sister's, east of Nashville about fifty miles. From the facts of her traveling alone, just something about her, I suspected that she had parted with her husband, maybe he'd left her, something of that sort. Of course he could have been killed, maybe in the army overseas, but I did not think so.

Then she said, "The car's twenty-three years old, but it only has about fifty-thousand miles on it and is about like new." She rubbed the cold iced tea bottle over her forehead. "The old man who owned it took real good care of it, kept it in his garage all the time."

I said that model was really nice, that I'd had one myself. "Did it set up much? Sometimes settin' up for long periods can get an engine all clogged."

"Well, yeah, I guess it did…he'd been sick the past couple of years." She gazed off at the car for a minute. "Would you know of a garage nearby?"

"There's Red Jordan's up the road about a mile in town. He's a pretty good mechanic. Won't cheat you." I could see, as if her thoughts ran across her forehead like the news ticker on CNN, that she was adding up all the money she did not have.

She asked if it was okay for the kids to sit there out of the heat a minute while she made a phone call. I said of course it was. She pulled a cell phone from her purse, told the girl—Roline—to watch after her brother, and walked out to the edge of the shade of the elm.

I divided my attention between the woman as she walked around with the phone at her ear and the little girl, who chattered away, while the little boy sat there and kept on eating peaches and lifting his face and hand for the girl to wipe off the juice. He enjoyed the peaches—they were the white-flesh variety, none better—but he did not like the juice. She tried mopping him up with napkins from the dispenser, but these would hardly do. I passed her a wad of paper towels. Then I found a package of Wet Ones and gave her the whole pack.

"Peaches are really good with all that juice, but I usually eat one bendin' over the yard or the sink," I said. Seeing the boy take another peach from the basket, his third, I cautioned, "You might want to limit those peaches, now, or he's liable to get a tummy ache."

"Oh!" Her sweet little face looked stricken.

"It's okay…three is fine," I said quickly, "but maybe you should move the basket over there."

She did this instantly.

I gazed at his little face, at the sweat-dampened hair that curled tenderly around his soft ear. He had beautiful long eyelashes. His gaze focused hard and fast on the peach he ate.

"What's goin' on?"

It was Monte, coming through the rear door, bending slightly so as not to hit his head. Our eyes met before either of us had time to think. I saw the softness in his, and knew it was okay between us.

"Hey," I said, and in so many words explained. "Their car has broken down. They're from out in Texas and headin' over to Tennessee."

"Uh-huh. I saw the car from up at the house…thought they might be broke down." He walked over to the cooler to take out a Coke, snatching a handful of peanuts in the shell from the basket.

The girl told him, "My name is Roline. That's our car broke down."

"Nice to meet you, Miss Roline."

"I am not a Miss."

"Oh, what, you married, then?"

"Nooo." She smiled up at him in a flirty manner that came natural to little girls. Even though he had never had any of his own, kids just seem drawn to Monte, probably because he's a big part kid himself.

"Hey, son," he said to the boy, who did not look up from his peach.

"He's my brother, Cody. He won't talk to you."

"Uh-huh." Monte came over to stand by the counter and crack open peanuts, eating them one at a time. The little girl watched him, craning her neck upward—Monte is a tall man—and asked what "those" were. He cracked a peanut for her. We both watched the young woman out in the shade of the elm, saw her smack her cell phone closed and stand there a moment, her shoulders rigid.

Just then little Cody started pitching a hissy fit. He had finished his peach and wanted another. His sister blocked him from the basket, while at the same time attempting to locate the toy that she had dropped on the ground. His mother was pulled out of her despair and hurried over.

"No!" she said firmly. "Cody, stop." She restrained him, and then he sort of went stiff. "Gosh, you sure are sticky, Cody."

"The peaches, Mama…" The girl gave him the toy—a modernized version of the old Magna Doodle—and he clutched it to him. "I had to take them away because he was eating too many…he was just eatin' and—"

"Roline, get my purse, please." The mother hefted the little one to her skinny hip.

"Did you get Daddy, Mama? Is Daddy comin'?" asked the girl, handing up the bulky purse.

"No, sugar. Daddy's too far away to get over here." She looked at me. "I'm goin' to go see if the car will start. Maybe after sittin' there, it will."

I said, "That's a good idea. You know, sometimes cars do that." I felt compelled to believe this for her. Besides, stranger things have happened.

Monte and I followed along after them over to the car, as if we had been asked.

The young woman put the children inside, then slipped behind the steering wheel and turned the key. Things looked hopeful for a second; the engine actually almost turned over. Then it died.

The young woman tried again, and again, grinding the starter, until I finally could stand it no longer and put a hand on her shoulder.

"Hon, you had best stop before the battery runs down. Monte, why don't you have a look at it?"

Monte went to the front and opened the hood. The young woman and I joined him, and little Roline came up beside me on her tiptoes, and we all gazed into the engine.

Monte said, "Yep, that's an engine," being funny, which I found a little annoying, but the young woman grinned weakly.

"That's an engine," the little girl repeated after him, and he reached down and rubbed her head.

As Monte began taking off the breather and handing me the nuts and bolts, I asked him what he thought the trouble could be, and he said it sounded like the engine wasn't getting fuel, maybe a sticky carburetor or clogged fuel line. Having come from a family of three brothers, all vehicle-inclined, I knew what he was talking about.

About that time Roline began hollering that Cody had to go to pee. "He *has* to go *now*, Mama!"

The young woman disappeared around the car, and I heard her say, "It's okay, Cody…here…right here by the car."

I leaned over to see him jerk away from her. My heart went out to him. It had to all be upsetting to him, and so hot in the sun. I said, "Y'all come on up to my house."

"I guess it's too late," the young woman said, straightening and pushing the hair out of her eyes. She seemed to be shrinking.

MONTE OFFERED TO TOW her car a mile up the road to Jordan's garage and save her the towing bill. While Monte went about the business of getting his pickup truck hooked to the front of the LTD, I finally thought to introduce us all. The young woman's name was Laura Jean Luckett. I thought the name suited her. She struck me as the type of woman about which a folk tune might be written.

"Thank you for all your help," Laura Jean said to me through the open window as Monte prepared to start off.

"Bye…bye!" Roline hung out the passenger window. She was a child who begged attention so much that already she was waving at me as if I was her grandmother. Cody watched through the rear window, but not looking at my face.

They should be buckled in, I thought, waving back, even saying, "'Bye, sweethearts."

I watched the LTD go away down the highway, then turned and went back to shut up the produce stand for the morning. I got the money box—had not made much that morning—and cleaned out the overripe fruits and vegetables, rolled shut the doors and padlocked them, got on my garden tractor and drove up the hill to the house.

The air-conditioned kitchen was cool after the heat. I set the money box on the counter and stood there a moment fluffing my hair, picturing Laura Jean Luckett (her name begged to be said all together) and her children stranded at the garage, waiting for Red to figure out the problem with the car, a process that could take a while. Not to fault Red, who is actually a second cousin, but he is not exactly a ball of fire. He moves and talks so slow that sometimes I want to slap the words out of him.

I just had to go get them; I was at least going to make certain they got something good to eat and drink.

When I drove up in front of the garage, I saw the LTD was in the work bay of the garage, with Red underneath it and Monte looking on. Laura Jean and the kids were in the air-conditioned office, drinking Dr Peppers and eating peanut butter crackers and talking to Jimmy, who pumped gas and did tire work. I should say that Laura Jean and Roline were talking to him. The little boy, Cody, was sitting in a chair to the side, playing intently with his Magna Doodle, and he had on, of all things, a helmet.

Laura Jean's expression welcomed me, thankfully. Roline danced right up to me.

"We don't know yet," Laura Jean reported in answer to my question about the LTD. Her face seemed permanently anxious.

Jimmy jumped in to say he would find out, but I told him I would do it, and poked my head into the work bay to ask, "Do we know anything yet?"

It was Monte who responded with "*We* know a lot of things," and grinned at me around the open hood.

Red, still under the vehicle, drawled, "We-e-ell...I'm not quite sure...but we're a'gonna find out here...in just a few minutes."

So I said, "I'm takin' Laura Jean and the kids on up to the house to have some lunch and maybe rest. You can call us there." Seeing Monte's face, I said politely, "Would you like to join us for lunch, Monte?"

"Yeah, I believe I would," he said, all nonchalant, as if he was not just dying to come.

On the drive home, I looked for an opening to ask about the little boy wearing a helmet, but Roline pretty well occupied the time by speaking loudly from the back seat and telling me about herself. I learned in quite a number of different ways that she was about to turn nine years old, would be going into the third grade, and liked peaches, and Flower Fairies, and horses, which she said when she saw old Bob run over to the fence and along it as we came up the drive. Roline lowered the window and leaned out and waved and hollered at him.

In the rearview mirror, I saw Cody in the curious act of knocking his head against the seat.

When we stopped beside the house, I glanced over to see Laura Jean gazing at the house in such a way that caused me to look with fresh eyes, seeing the cool quietness of the screen porch and the thick honeysuckle growing up one end.

For whatever reason, I said, "I've lived here for twenty-five years. My husband died several years ago. There's just me now."

"Oh, Monte isn't…"

"No." I shook my head. "He's an old friend."

We got the children and tote bags out of the car, and Monte was there, holding the screen door and saying, "Welcome, ladies and lad," in a good-natured, gallant manner as we trooped inside. He was putting on the charm. I was glad for it and his extra pair of hands, both of which helped to smooth the way.

I DECIDED ON THE TABLE on the sunporch, shaded then by the two trees. I would not let Laura Jean help with anything, but insisted she get the kids and herself freshened up and just relax. There really was no relaxing for her, as getting the kids freshened up took quite a bit. I put Monte to work slicing the vegetables and setting the table. I confess to getting carried away and having him get the fifties-vintage cherry-print tablecloth and cherry dishes from the sideboard. It had been a long time since I had received company. Ever since Henry's funeral, actually. Even in death, Henry had been the one to instigate a social gathering. He had been a gregarious, outgoing man, enjoying many friendships. He liked nothing better than to play host at dinners and barbecues. I left all that to him and kept myself busy behind the scenes with the food and whatever else was needed.

For our lunch, I served up chicken salad sandwiches made from chicken breasts I had cooked the previous week and frozen. Along with this, I had cucumbers cut up in vinegar and water and cold sliced tomatoes and cantaloupe. I was pleased with how inviting everything looked. It has always been my belief that pleasant surroundings are necessary for surviving trying circumstances.

Laura Jean came out from the bathroom with the children after what seemed like quite some time, all of them freshly washed and shined. Roline had her hair pulled back in a ponytail, and Cody's helmet was gone so that he was once again a little cherub with curls.

"You sure have a lovely home, Miz Perabo," Laura Jean said, then snatched Roline from reaching out for something on the sideboard.

"Thank you...but Miz Perabo would be my mother-in-law. Please call me Ellie—all of you." I included the children.

There was something I noticed in that moment, and it was that Cody did not look at me, appeared not to hear. The possibility of deafness crossed my mind, and then I realized that I could not seem to bring myself to look fully at him, either. I was, however, too busy to analyze what was going on at that moment. The understanding would come later, as understandings often do. Gradually over the next several hours, I would see that there was just something about the child, as if he had up a shield. And there was an understanding within me, for all of my own ways and means.

Monte, who had many nieces and nephews, fashioned a booster seat for Cody from phone books. Before anyone knew it, Monte had picked the boy up and sat him on the books. I saw the boy's eyes widen, and thought: Uh-oh. There was surprise on his mother's face, too, and her instant attention was on her son, as if to catch him. But the boy focused on the plate in front of him and put a finger on the red cherry, tracing around it.

"It is a red cherry, Cody." Laura Jean bent near him.

He rubbed his finger around and around the painted cherry, even while his mother edged some chicken salad onto his plate.

Cody appeared totally uninterested in the chicken salad. It was Roline who told me that he would rather have grilled cheese. She stood beside me at the stove and instructed me in detail as to how he liked it best, lightly toasted and cut in quarters.

"I like grapes," Roline said, seeing them when I opened the refrigerator. "I like grapes a lot."

Laura Jean cautioned the girl about asking, but I said how is a person to get anything, if they don't ask? "And how am I goin' to know, if you don't tell me?" I added, handing the child a plate with a heaping stem of cold grapes that I told her to share with Cody.

"He will not eat grapes," she said in all seriousness. "But he will play with them. He likes round things. He spins them."

This proved to be the case. The boy spun them around, again and again, until his mother took them away and moved him from the table. And as children often do, Roline did not eat many of the grapes, either. She said, "I want you to know that I would like the television on," which I thought was very clever. The television occupied her while Cody lay on the floor, put his thumb in his mouth and stared at the revolving ceiling fan. I wondered if he had actually fallen asleep. This curiosity became so sharp that I was about to ask Laura Jean if the boy slept with his eyes open, as I had a cousin who sometimes did that, but just then the phone rang.

It was Red. Resisting the temptation to question him and relay the information, I passed the cordless phone to Laura Jean, who put it to her ear and ducked her head as she said, "Hello."

I went into the kitchen and returned with the pitcher of cold tea, refilling glasses, while my ear was tuned to Laura Jean saying a lot of uh-huhs and yes, sir, and ending politely with "I'll have to call you back. Thank you."

Laura Jean carefully set the phone on the table, then told us that the LTD needed a new fuel pump. She said that it had taken Red some time to locate a replacement part, since the LTD was so old. He had found a rebuilt one, which he recommended. He estimated that it would take a day or two to get the part and at least a day to install.

"It's goin' to cost six hundred dollars," she said, her voice falling to near a whisper as she passed a hand over her forehead, brushing back her bangs as she looked at what was left of the cantaloupe slices.

I was ready for all of this, however. I did not wait for her to say that she did not have the money, or waste time asking if she might not have some family to help her. Clearly if either had been the case, she would have said so directly. Whoever she had spoken to on the phone earlier that morning knew the situation and obviously could not be counted on for support.

I said, "That is not such a big problem. I'll pay for it."

I looked at Laura Jean, and she looked at me. Her expression of dismay and hope rattled me, so I averted my gaze and took up the phone to call Red back and tell him to get to work. While I spoke, I avoided looking at anyone, especially at Monte for some odd reason.

When I clicked off with Red, Laura Jean said the only sensible thing she could, which was, "I don't know how to thank you. I will pay you back…I will…" She was near tears, of course.

"Well, I'm older and can do things like this and not worry about it." I gave a dismissing wave and rose to my feet to begin clearing the table. It was all horribly uncomfortable.

Instantly Laura Jean popped to her feet and loaded her arms up and down with dishes, carrying them like a juggler into the kitchen—that girl had waited tables, I could tell—and instantly began running water in the sink as she told me firmly that she would repay me.

"I can do it in installments. When I get to my sister's—that's where we're goin'—over to my sister's and mom's. We're gonna live with them, and my mother can help with the kids while I work. I'm a nail technician, and I make good money when I'm workin'."

"Well…good enough." Not that I really expected the money to be returned, and frankly did not even want to talk off in that vein. I did not want to put Laura Jean into a position of promising things that she could not deliver. "Honey…we have a dishwasher. You don't have to do those by hand."

THERE SIMPLY SEEMED NO question but that Laura Jean and the children would stay with me for the next days while the car was repaired, so there I was pretty much taking over their lives and ordering matters around. I vaguely realized that I had more of a head of steam than I had possessed in some time.

What Monte thought of all this, I did not know, nor did I want to know, at least right at first. Later my curiosity did rise, and that was probably what propelled me to walk outside with him when he left. But I certainly never expected him to do what he did, which was to pull five one hundred dollar bills from his wallet and hand them to me. "For the kids. They'll need some extra. You're not the only one who can play Santa Claus, you know."

By kids, I knew he was including Laura Jean.

I gazed at him a long moment. "Thanks. And I'll tell her."

He winced. "Aw, don't go and do that."

"Wait a minute." I ran back inside and returned with a fruit cake all wrapped. He had been eyeing it since he had come in the door. "Here…this certainly won't hurt you with all you have done today."

"Thanks." He grinned like a boy, and do you know, I think for a second there he was going to kiss me, at least on the cheek. I instantly turned and strode up the porch steps.

He called over to me. "You can cook, but I still would like to see you in a dress."

"And I still don't care what you would like," I said, but with warmth and a kick of my foot, as I let the screen door bang and went back into the house.

PART
~ TWO ~

We went to get Laura Jean's belongings. She flung her things out of the LTD, parked dead beside Red's garage, and I caught them and threw them into my Cadillac. Laura Jean appeared to have only one speed, fast, and I was caught up with her, both of us moving at the speed of burglars.

There was a single large suitcase and a nylon gym bag, pink, with Roline's name on it. Everything else was stuffed into blue Wal-Mart sacks and large black trash bags. I have to say that the bags squished nicely to fit into odd spaces, but they seemed, well, trashy.

After we had finished, Laura Jean had to pry Cody out of the back seat of the LTD, where he had crawled despite the heat. I thought: it is his home.

Back at my house, I emptied linens out of the guest dresser and winter clothes from the closet.

"Oh, you don't need to go to any trouble," Laura Jean protested.

"It is no trouble, hon. Just takes a minute, and the three of you will be a lot more comfortable. Now, you go ahead and use these two drawers…and you have all this space in the closet."

Out of the corner of my eye, I saw Cody had crawled into the very middle of the bed and was focused intently on his Magna Doodle. He drew various circles in a definite pattern that I found intriguing in a child so young.

My gaze moved off to all the plastic sacks of belongings. They just upset me. I thought about the number of suitcases I had in the attic. Maybe I would offer her at least two of the medium ones.

I heard Henry in the back of my mind: Why don't you just give them the house?

My word, you are dead as you'll ever be.

For a moment I was surprised by the thought, but then I said to Laura Jean, "You are welcome to use my washer and dryer all you want."

"Thank you," she said, averting her eyes in the manner with which I was becoming familiar. It was an expression that spoke of trying her best not to take up space in the world.

I said, "Well…I appreciate your thanks, but now you've said it enough. You know, it suits me to do this."

Her head came around, and she gave what was the closest I had seen to a smile. Lordy, she was just a child. It is my own observation that most all of us are pretty much children until the age of thirty, take it for what you will.

I went off and got the roll-away from the hall closet, so all three of them could sleep in the same room. Roline was following behind me, and when I pulled out the bed, she asked what it was. I told her, "This is a roll-away…for Roline."

She was definitely taken with the idea. Using her skinny little body, she helped me to push the bed along the hall, repeating in a singsong voice, "A roll-a-way for Ro-line."

Just as we guided the bed through the door of the guest room, Laura Jean came out with, *"Oh, no! Cody!"*

The tone of her voice caused me to come close to rolling the roll-away over Roline in my haste to move it and jump into the bedroom. Expecting to see blood spouting or something of that sort, I was almost relieved to find what it was.

Cody had messed in his pants, gotten out of his little-boy pull-ups, then, apparently fascinated with what he had produced, had smeared it on the bedspread like finger paint.

Laura Jean took him by the arm and shook him. "No, Cody! No! How many times have I told you no? No…*no!*"

His reaction to this was quite naturally to scream, hit at her and pull away. She lost her grip and he fell to the floor, where he then threw himself around. He banged himself like a ball in a pinball machine, against the bed, the wall, the nightstand, back to the bed and the floor, where he beat his head on the carpet. Fortunately, the carpet was expensive and thick.

Of course, for a number of seconds all we could do was stand there and stare. Then Roline cried out, "Cody, *no!*" and threw herself crying across a corner of the bed.

Laura Jean covered her face with her hands and sobbed.

I scrambled around and grabbed her. Cody seemed in that moment to be okay, having landed himself on the carpet, but Laura Jean was completely undone. She kept saying, "I'm so sorry...I'm so sorry," to both Cody and me.

For my part, I said, "Honey, it will wash. It's nothin'." Then— "You know, you have to admire his art."

Her eyes went wide. Her lip trembled and a laugh popped out of her. Then she was both laughing and crying. It was a bit on the hysterical side and could have gone either way, causing me to brace myself.

The young woman got hold of herself, though. Her gaze shifted to Cody, and emotions passed over her face, pain, regret, resignation, as fast as clouds blowing across the sky. She reached for him, somewhat hesitantly. He allowed her to pull him to her and pick him up. She kissed and hugged him.

I led the way to the bathroom, where I intended to get the water started in the tub and set out towels. There was almost another crisis of sorts, when Laura Jean brought Cody in behind me, and he started screaming again.

"The fan..." Laura Jean said, and reached out to turn off the light switch that controlled the fan, too. With a wide window and two skylights, the electric light was not needed.

I had bubble bath. Laura Jean nodded okay, but I worried for a minute as the bubbles grew and Cody stared at them. It turned out that he was mesmerized by them. I scooped a handful of bubbles and blew gently on them, fascinated with watching the child's fascination. Together we watched several large, round bubbles rise in the air, the light from the skylight hitting them and making them glimmer with color. His little cherub face regarded them with wonder. I gently stretched out a finger to catch one as it came down. I felt like a queen in command of bubbles. Laura Jean joined in, scooped up more bubbles, and Cody's attention turned to her. The two began to play.

Satisfied the crisis was over, I left mother and son enjoying the bubbles and bathing, returning to the bedroom to clean up. I found Roline had gotten the roll-away in place all by herself. She was pleased and cute as could be, sitting on the narrow bed.

I made a big to-do over the feat. "You're a right smart girl," I told her, enjoying her giggling response and the way she said, "Yes, I am a right smart girl."

"Miss Ellie?" she said

"Yes, sweetie-pie."

"Do you have any kids?"

"No…no, I don't."

"Did you ever have any kids?"

"No, sweetie, I never did." I glanced over to see her tilting her head, regarding me with curiosity.

"You seem like you know about kids," she said, most seriously.

"Maybe I never grew up," I said, and tossed her a sack of clothing from the bed that seemed to have her clothes in it. She fell over with it, laughing. Her laughter seemed frenzied, as if she thought she was expected to laugh. Surely the little family was under a great strain.

I put her to work folding clothes into the dresser drawers, while I cleared the bed and carefully remove the soiled spread. Two books slid out of one of the sacks. My eye caught the titles: first one, *Autism Spectrum Disorders*, and then the other, *Behavioral Intervention*.

Well. My fingers seemed drawn like a magnet, and I touched the top book, tracing beneath the title. Much was explained.

"IT'S TIME FOR ME TO OPEN the produce stand for the evenin' traffic. Help yourself to anything in the refrigerator...just make yourself at home. I'll be back up about six-thirty."

I tossed all that over my shoulder as I went out the door, pretty much fleeing the house and their presence. My last glimpse of Laura Jean's face told me she picked up on this.

As I grabbed a basket off the porch, Henry's voice in my head said, "You've gone and done it now."

Oh, shut up!

I strode around to the fig trees on the far side of the house. There were a few freshly ripe fruits. As I picked them, I could still hear Henry's voice in my head: "Don't get carried away, Ellie."

He had so often said that to me. Henry had always seemed to be possessed of the opinion that I was going to do something that was too much—mostly spend too much money, but also maybe choose a wall color that was too bright, dress in something too daring, decorate too elaborately, make a trip too long.

I can't for the life of me figure out the why of his attitude, because I never did any of those things. I have always been conservative. I am not certain that this has been my true nature, though, and perhaps Henry had sensed this. My shy and retiring nature hid a very active inner life, where I have dreamed great dreams. I never could seem to dare to bring them out, though. As unfair as it sounds, I partly blamed Henry for stomping on them before they could be too much.

All that is to say that it was exceedingly doubtful that I would have helped Laura Jean in much of any way had Henry been there. I would not have risked his disapproval; I had been a feather in the wind of Henry's disapproval.

Let me just say that six hundred dollars for a stranger's car repair and bringing a stranger, with two children, one of whom appeared to not talk and be afraid of certain noises, into our home to stay for a few days would definitely have incurred Henry's disapproval. It would have fallen into the category of too much. He would have, well, died at the thought.

Feeling instantly disloyal, I stopped picking figs and looked over at the outbuildings and on to the house and then down to the produce stand. Henry had built it all, much of it with his own two hands. There it stood, so comfortable, well kept, affluent. All because of Henry being so very careful and hardworking. A responsible man. I had to admit that fact, and it was good for me to do so.

Yet, the largest realization was that I had been by his side the entire time. I had built it, too, and was now, as the term goes, a woman of substance. Furthermore, while everyone took my withdrawal as lengthy grieving, what it was in actuality was my acclimating to life on my own. It came to me at that moment that I had left the grieving and begun accepting responsibility of carrying on by myself. And the truth of the matter was that sometime in the two years since Henry's demise, I had grown to like my single state. I liked it so much that it was a little embarrassing.

"Oh, Henry," I said as I turned, unseeing, to put my hand on the fig tree, a fig tree Henry had planted just for me. "I did love you, sweetheart. I did. And I am grateful beyond measure for all you have given me…but I would not bring you back for the world. You couldn't stand me now."

My vision swam with tears as I walked down the hill to the produce stand.

EVENINGS WERE ORDINARILY much more busy than mornings at the produce stand. People were not in such a hurry to get to work on time. This evening I sold all of the cantaloupes and all but one of the watermelons, and most of the green peppers. Between customers I diligently culled the produce of the overripe pieces and put them into, what else, used Wal-Mart sacks, to take up to the mulch pile. While going about this task, I also put a couple of Twinkies and chocolate bars from the snack case into a bag to carry to the children. The extent to which this pleased me made me chuckle out loud and throw in a Twinkie cake for myself.

I was starting to close the doors five minutes early when Patsy's Chrysler 300 pulled up. She stopped with her hood only half a foot from the stand, as was her habit. Patsy never walked an inch more than required. She's my best friend since kindergarten, and is Henry's cousin, so our lives are well intertwined.

"Hey, girl." Patsy came over to give me a hug.

"Hi, hon…how goes it at school?" I guessed that she had heard about Laura Jean and come to see what was going on. The reason I thought this was because it was unusual for Patsy to come by at this time of evening. She had started back to work after a month of summer vacation—Patsy was the L. L. Madison Elementary School vice principal—and liked to go home at the end of the day, get a diet Coke, throw herself into her recliner and watch a movie on the Lifetime channel, something nerve-tingling, with a lot of sex and without a lot of children. She wanted something far removed from her real life.

She said now, "We don't have students yet, and I'm exhausted. I should never have said I would take vice principal again. I'm retirin' for sure in May. I am. Stu and I are goin' to do that Go RVing thing just like Tom Selleck says in that commercial."

"Are you sure that's Tom Selleck?"

"Well, if it isn't, it is someone with his voice…and I just remembered—we *really* need you to come back to substitute this year. Mrs. Reed moved to Florida, thank goodness, because I was goin' to have to tell her that she could no longer sub. She has just gotten too old, and she started pinchin'."

"Really?"

"I thought I told you. She pinched two third-graders and a fifth-grader last year. And today June Deleo called up to announce that she is goin' to have twins and won't be available. We really need you, Ellie."

"Oh, I don't know. I've got the stand goin' pretty good."

"You loved it when you used to substitute. Remember? You said it was perfect because you got use out of that degree you worked so hard for but didn't have to follow all the establishment rules. It will get you out of the house, out with people, Ellie," she added pointedly.

I gazed at her. "I am out with people here every day."

"You are not goin' to keep the produce stand open all winter, are you?" Patsy's left eyebrow went up in the manner that all Henry's side of the family could employ.

"Well, no...but probably through Halloween. I have a good crop of pumpkins, and the Millers want me to sell theirs, too."

"Look, why don't I just have you put on the call list. You can always say no, but maybe sometime—like later in the winter, when everything is shut up—you will want to."

"Okay, I guess," I said, caught between feeling hesitant and yet a little glad. I had enjoyed it when I substituted. I also had the idle thought to wonder what I would wear should I take on the classroom again. I started to inquire about being allowed to wear overalls, but then Patsy got to what she had come for in the first place and asked about Laura Jean.

"What's this I hear about you takin' in a homeless woman and her kids?"

"She isn't homeless. She's on her way to her sister's over in Tennessee, and her car broke down. How did you hear about it?"

"That sounds a little homeless to me," she said. "I just got gas down at Jordan's, and Jimmy said that a strange woman's car broke down here, and that you took in her and her two kids. He said you are payin' to have her car repaired. Six hundred dollars." There went that eyebrow again, reminding me of Henry.

"Monte is payin' for more than half," I said flatly, and foolishly relieved to do so, too. Had it not been true, I might have made it up. Then I reminded myself that I was not married to Patsy. "Do you want these? Cook 'em tonight, and they'll be good." I held out a bag of overripe tomatoes.

"Oh, thanks. Stu will cook them." She looked in the bag, saying, "Well, it is a lot of money. You all should have called the church. We have a fund for things like that. It's part of the mission ministry, you know. It might be a good idea to call Pastor Gene. The church can at least chip in to help."

"Maybe I'll do that…but really, it's all taken care of now." I was not going to call the church. I should have just said so straight out.

"Well, there's not only the emergency fund, but there's the prophet's chamber at the church. It's got a microwave and refrigerator. It's mostly for traveling evangelists, but they've used it for this sort of thing, too. Charlotte Jones's niece used it when she had to get away from her husband because he was beatin' the tar out of her."

"They are all settled in here now." I handed her a bag of cucumbers. I guess I was somehow trying to shut her up with vegetables. It did not work.

"I just don't think it is a good idea for you to get in the habit of takin' in someone right off the highway, Ellie." Just like Henry. Boy, blood is thick.

"One time is not a habit."

"Well, I've worried a lot with you here right on the highway. Anyone could watch and catch you alone and rob you. And I'm just sayin' that I know you are kindhearted, but you don't know what sort of person she is. Anything could happen. She could get in your jewelry, or your purse and get all your personal information."

I was a little surprised at not having thought of any of that, and that Patsy did. I thought of all those movies she watched on Lifetime.

Getting the produce stand doors closed, I turned to bid her goodbye.

"I'll just drive you up," she said, heading for the driver's side of her car. "That way I can meet this girl."

I stopped where I was and said, "I don't think that is a good idea."

"Why not?"

"Honey, I know you mean to be friendly, but Laura Jean and the kids are worn out. They've been up since the early hours and have just had so much stress. They do not need to have to deal with another stranger and be poked into."

"I am not going to poke into them." She put a hand on her hip. "I just thought it would be nice to say hello. That is a friendly thing."

"Not tonight," I said firmly, then gave her a hug and a goodbye, as if she was not stiff as a board and looking at me as if she did not know what had gotten into me. I had never refused her access to my house, even if I might have wanted to a time or two.

She said, "Okay…if you *feel* that way. I could have just driven you up," she called after me.

I waved and headed on in firm strides. I was aware of her car sitting there some moments, her eyes boring a hole in my back.

Laura Jean was at the stove. "I hope you don't mind. You said to make myself at home.…"

Bless her tender heart, she began to look uncertain and to duck her head, as if expecting scolding. I said quickly, "My word, this is so nice." I heaped praise on her, saying that I had not had anyone make me a meal in a very long time. I did not think I could give her too much praise. I imagined she had been starved for it her whole life.

And that girl was enterprising. She had opened jars of my home-made spaghetti sauce and had water ready and waiting for the noodles. She had set the round oak table in the kitchen, complete with tablecloth, as I had done at lunch. There were even small bowls of salad for both of us.

I went back to my bedroom to freshen up and catch my breath. When I returned to the kitchen, Laura Jean would not let me help, but told me to sit. I did, and watched her put the food on the table.

It was fascinating. She went from the stove to the table and back again, and each time, without any glance down, she would step over Cody, who lay on the floor, his thumb in his mouth, gazing upward, unblinking, at the ceiling fan. She had obviously had a lot of practice stepping over him.

Roline was called from in front of the television, and Cody was picked up and sat again on the phone-book booster. Laura Jean had the children join hands for grace. I put my hand in hers and in Roline's on the other side. I peeked up to see a beam of western evening sunlight slanting through the window and across the room, illuminating dust motes in the air. I saw Cody looking at the dust particles, too.

So many people never see things like that...but the boy and I did.

Roline said, "Miss Ellie, do you have a computer?"

"Well, yes, honey, but it's broken, I'm afraid."

"Why are you afraid?"

Why indeed? "It is a figure of speech, and a poor one at that. My computer broke, and I am sorry to disappoint you."

"Oh, that's okay. Our computer broke, too...but Mama took us to the library to use theirs. Do you have a library?"

I thought for a moment. "I don't have one, but there is one in town."

"That's what I meant. Could we go there when we finish eatin'?"

"I'm a...the library is not open in the evenin'. I'm sorry."

"Could we go tomorrow? We could use the computer, and maybe check out a movie."

"Roline, quit pesterin' Miss Ellie," said Laura Jean.

"What is pesterin'?"

"Askin' too many questions."

"What are too many?" The girl looked at me.

"Five," I said, and grinned at her. She rewarded me with a giggle.

Then she reached for her glass of milk and tipped the glass. The milk spread across the table.

I threw my napkin on it, and Laura Jean reached for a dish cloth, telling Roline, who sat with her chin nearly on her chest, that it was okay. Some of the milk had gone near Cody's plate. Rather than eating, he had been twirling his spaghetti in a circle with his finger. He took the same finger and twirled it around in the puddle of milk, and when his mother wiped it away, he threw a fit.

"There is a reason that children are given to the young," I said as I took the wet napkins to the counter.

FOR THAT NIGHT, I TOOK a flashlight and several candles into the guest bathroom, so that the light-fan switch would not be needed while Laura Jean readied the children for bed. Roline begged to take her bath by candlelight, and seeing her enjoyment prompted me to do the same in my own bathroom.

Now that my attention had been called to it, the noise of the exhaust fan annoyed me beyond measure. I actually considered calling Monte on the telephone and requesting step-by-step instructions on how to disconnect the darn thing. Good sense prevailed. I lit candles.

I leaned in close to the mirror after my bath. Mirrors were kind in candlelight. I turned my head, gave myself a good study. What did Monte see?

Leaving this disturbing question unanswered, I slipped into a pair of cotton-and-lace pajamas, soft knit robe and cushiony slippers. *I do not always wear overalls,* I mentally told Monte, imagining his surprise and appreciation as I turned down the bedcovers, then placed there the current book I was reading—the third in the Ladies' Detective Agency books. It was not much of a mystery but a delightful story. It was my habit each evening to enjoy a cup of tea in my best blue Wedgwood china and read for several hours in bed. I very much looked forward to the ritual this evening and, in fact, as I headed for the kitchen, was very glad for the split plan of our house, the master suite on one side, and the other two bedrooms clear on the opposite end. I was actually just about tiptoeing, reluctant to have any further contact with my guests that evening.

Instead, however, I found Laura Jean sitting at the kitchen table, obviously waiting for me. She stood, revealing a nightshirt imprinted with the image of a woman's body in a bikini. I thought that she was far too pretty for such a tasteless shirt, whatever that says about me, who wears overalls day after day.

"I thought, if you would want me to, I could give you a manicure," she said. "I'd like to do something for you, after all you have done for us."

"Oh. That sounds quite nice." I did not want to disappoint her, she seemed so eager to please.

She suggested the table on the sunporch and went off with her bright purple case to get set up, while I made us both tea. I brought the pot and cups and sugar bowl in on a tray. Then she put out her hand, and I gave mine to her.

As Laura Jean went to work with a nail file and studious frown, she began to talk. She chatted on about the lava lamp on top of the bureau in the guest room, how she had had one once, and of Cody's fascination with it. "I think it might help him to go to sleep."

I had forgotten about the lamp, a gift from years ago that had never gone with anything in the house. I said this and added, "Most people do seem to like it. It's a lot like a candle, isn't it? Hypnotic."

"Well…you may have already noticed, but Cody isn't exactly like most people." She paused and looked at me. "I don't like to talk about him when he can hear—" her eyes darted instinctively in the direction of the bedrooms "—so I couldn't explain earlier. But I need to tell you, since we're goin' to be here a few days. Cody has some problems. You see, Cody is autistic."

Her eyes flitted intently over my face, and when I said that I had seen the books in her room, I detected a certain relief pass over her. Secrets come out in the open.

She bent her head again over my fingernails and began to chat more easily. I suddenly knew the full reason why she had suggested giving me a manicure, and I had accepted. It gave us both, comparative strangers and private-natured women, an opportunity to talk deeply without seeming to need to do so.

"It is sometimes called Pervasive Developmental Disorder," Laura Jean said, her tone as if she were reading from the book, as she explained about her son's condition. "It is a neurological disorder, but the cause is not known. Cody cannot help it."

"I understand that," I said plainly. I told her that I was vaguely familiar with autism. "I was a teacher. It was a long time ago, though, and I really do not know much."

"Well, the doctor said it is like Cody's brain misfires, and this produces a wide range of difficulties for him, and these produce a wide range of behaviors. Cody's autism is moderate to severe."

"And aren't we all?" I said.

She looked up at me with a blank expression.

"Moderate to severe in behavior, I mean."

It was a small attempt at some truthful humor, but there was no humor in her. She simply nodded blankly, then said, "Some people act like he's crazy or a brat, or like what he has is catching. Just a couple weeks ago, I was talkin' to these other mothers while I was waitin' for Roline to get out of school. I was explaining that Cody went to a special preschool class where he got occupational therapy. One of them asked about this, and I went to tellin' about it, and the next thing I knew, those women were just gone. They pretty much ran off. Then the other day somebody asked me why he didn't answer when they spoke to him, and I said he was deaf." She ducked her head in that manner of hers. "It just came out. I felt so ashamed, but it's just easier."

"I thought maybe he did have a hearing problem at first," I admitted.

"Well, we all did, too." She went on to tell of when she had first begun to suspect a problem. "I took him to the doctor to have his hearing checked. It seemed okay. I knew there was something wrong, though, but the doctor did not believe me. He said that children develop differently and that maybe Cody was slow and to give him time.

"And Billy—that's my husband—said I spoiled him. When you have two people tellin' you this, well, it's hard not to believe it. But you know, in my heart I *knew*." She pressed her hand and nail file to her chest.

I nodded in understanding. Not that I was a mother, but I was a woman, and there are just things we know, and right that minute I could have provided a list of such things the length of the table.

She said, in a defensive manner, "Cody did not have a problem at birth. He's one who started talkin' early and he was the happiest baby, just smilin', and he would reach for things, too. He said Dada and Mama.

"But then that just faded. He would point to things, so we just didn't notice at first. But then he got where he just howled when Billy picked him up, and he would not let the doctor touch him. They had to hold him down for any kind of examination. And it got so I could not take him in the Wal-Mart because he would have these awful meltdowns. He even beat his head on things. Well, you saw him today."

"Is that why he had the helmet on this afternoon?" I asked.

"Uh-huh. Sometimes he will just hit his head so hard. But right off I knew it was not that he was bein' contrary. It was like he hurt somewhere." She reached for my other hand. "Just relax…let me have your fingers."

I did my best. I was made aware of how hard it was for me to do something new. "What did the doctor say about it then?" I asked.

"He *said* that maybe it was somethin' I had done, like neglectin' Cody and lettin' him watch too much television or somethin'. Our television didn't even work half the time. By then I had read up, and I knew somethin' was not right. I found a pediatrician over in Amarillo. Billy did not want to take him over there, because our HMO would not cover it. But I insisted, so he took me, and well, that pediatrician said it right off after he looked at Cody for a few minutes—'Your boy seems to have autistic disorder.'"

She paused in her filing, sat back and breathed deeply.

I said a few encouraging things about how Cody was a beautiful child and seemed quite bright, things of that nature that every mother wants to hear and which were all true, too.

Laura Jean responded, "Oh, yes, he really is bright about a lot of things. Things you wouldn't expect. Like he can work the television remote to get just what he wants. I can hardly do that. It's his sensory ability that is out of whack, and his communication. He just can't get his thoughts out."

She explained that he could talk on occasion, although he did so only to her and Roline, and the occupational therapist.

"A lot of times when he speaks, it is what they call echolalia. He repeats what is said. He has good rote memory. Right hemisphere in his brain, the doctor says. But strangers and strange places upset him badly…and noise and commotion. It's like he can feel noise. I knew this trip would upset him, but there wasn't anything I could do about it, except try to drive it straight on through."

"Do you think you could do that?" I found the idea a little alarming.

"Well, no, but I could pull over and sleep a few hours in the car. That's what I did at that Wendy's where we stopped for breakfast."

"What about your husband?" I asked, apparently all sense of prying having evaporated. That happens when you put your hands in someone else's hands.

"Billy? Well, it all just got too much for him," she said. "Cody and the bills from the specialist…and me not bein' able to work because I have to be there with Cody. It's really sad. Billy loved Cody so much when he was born. My gosh, he loved him. He could not stand to think there was anything wrong with him."

I refrained from pointing out that such an attitude was more ownership and pride than love. I looked at her face, with the dark circles of fatigue and the reflection of earnest devotion to her children. I wanted to tell her to go look in the mirror to see the face of love.

She went on to say that the previous week Billy had called to tell her that he was not coming home and for her to look in his sock drawer for all the money he had saved. He told her to take the money and go home to her sister and mother.

"My sister said I could come. Mama is well enough to take care of the kids durin' the day, while I get set in a shop and build up clientele. And Billy will send money when he can. He's good about that sort of thing."

She spoke totally without resentment. Perhaps she did not have time or energy left for resentment, but in any case, I was quite impressed with her.

"What color would you like?" she asked, indicating a row of nail polish bottles.

The colors were all too loud for me. I chose clear. Then I allowed her to do a French polish, as she called it. I did like it.

I WAS JUST CLOSING MY NOVEL and was about to snuggle into the sheets when the phone rang. Patsy's number shone on the caller ID. Catching sight of my fingernails, I was so fascinated for a moment that the phone rang again before I answered.

Patsy said, "I thought I'd call to find out how everythin' is goin'."

"What if I'd been asleep?"

"If everything is fine, you are reading."

"I was." I closed my mouth about mentioning having finished early from exhaustion. I did not want to give Patsy encouragement.

"Well, I just want you to know that you can call us anytime you might need us, Ellie. I hope you know that. We would have been glad to help you out with this girl…and if there's any problem, we can be there in five minutes."

I started to say: How would I call if I had been stabbed in my sleep, but I did not think I needed to egg Patsy on. "Thank you, hon. I know you are always there for me. I will call you in the mornin', just to let you know I'm all right."

To this she replied, "Not too early. I don't have to be to school until ten tomorrow."

People's thought processes really are interesting.

THE FOLLOWING MORNING I awoke before God and with a level of enthusiasm I had not experienced since Henry's untimely demise. Had I looked closely at myself—and of course I did not, probably because I did not want to find any reason to be practical—I would have seen that my attitude revealed that I was feeling a little like God. I was determined to give Laura Jean some help that I felt she really needed in the way of mothering and living, no matter not asked for. The least I could do was give a good example of eating nutritious food and provide moral support at every turn. That was the least I could do, and I was quite thrilled to be doing it.

I got dressed directly out of bed, mentally planning an elaborate breakfast of bacon, eggs, cinnamon toast, cantaloupe and fried tomatoes, too, which were a favorite of Monte's. I had decided to include Monte for breakfast, since I intended to ask him to disconnect the fans in both bathrooms. I did something surprising, too. I spritzed on Chanel. When I realized what I had done, I refused to think of it.

With early light still thin, I went out to the garden with my baskets and got myself knee-deep in bushes and vines and the sweet, pungent scent of the moist earth. The gelding, Bob, aging but still a pretty horse, came along to gaze over the fence at me, hoping for watermelon as a little boy does a cookie. When none was forthcoming, he wandered on to the water tank.

A few minutes later, I looked over at the horse to see him stretching his neck over the fence. I could not see his nose, but I heard him snort.

Curious, I edged forward, craning my neck.

It was Cody on the other side of the fence.

Ohmygoodness. My first reaction was a little panic. I started to run over and scoop him up. But then good sense spoke up. The boy was in no danger.

He walked along the fence, in pajamas and bare feet. He was focused on his toy, the Magna Doodle. He was not working it, as he held it with both hands. He came toward the gate to the garden, and Bob followed along on his side but had to stop at the garden fence. Cody continued on past the garden gate, along the fence, and then he turned and retraced his steps. He did not appear to see where he was going, but he must have, because he avoided a bucket and a coiled hose. He reached the fence where Bob was again, and the two walked along together. Bob stretched over and blew, fluttering Cody's hair.

Cody kept focused on his toy and walking.

I stood there watching, while mosquitos buzzed and bit where I could not get them, but I was reluctant to go swatting and scratching and possibly disturb what was going on. I was uncertain of what was going on, but something seemed to be.

"Cody…Co-dyyy!" It was Laura Jean. Bare legs long and lean, she came flying out the screen door and down the steps, frantic as any madwoman. Her yell, in fact, caused me to jump, not to mention Bob, who jerked upward, snorted and pranced back several yards as Laura Jean raced across the driveway to scoop up Cody, who did not seem to even hear her. "What are you doin' out here? Oh, Cody… I've looked all over."

Cody did yell then and squirmed to be put down.

"He's all right, hon," I said, hurrying forward through the garden gate. "I was watchin' him."

She pushed her hair from her face. "He wanders sometime. At home I had to put fasteners on the doors."

"I think he was just gettin' acquainted with our Bob," I said, reaching out to stroke the gelding, once more sticking his head over the fence.

"He was?" Laura Jean looked from the horse to her son, who now sat on the very edge of the bottom step and appeared to be totally absorbed in drawing on his toy.

Oddly enough, the horse seemed to be looking at the boy, as focused on him as the boy was on his toy.

I had an idea. I went into the garden, retrieved a ripe watermelon, came back and cracked it open on the top rail of the fence. I fed a chunk to Bob, saying, "Cody…come feed the horse."

He did not even look up, of course. I suggested Laura Jean get him. She brought him, squirming and having a hissy fit about her taking his Magna Doodle away.

"Cody...look at me feed the horse."

The boy looked at the horse. Juice ran out of Bob's mouth. Laura Jean let Cody go, and he turned away but moved ever closer to the fence until he was walking alongside of it. Bob followed him. Cody stopped, although he still didn't look at the horse. The horse extended his nose through the fence rail to sniff the boy.

I stepped over and went to my knees beside Cody and in front of Bob. "Cody...Bob likes you. Bob likes watermelon, too. See." I pushed a large chunk beneath the bottom rail. Bob sniffed it as he had sniffed Cody, then went to eating the sweet red flesh. The chomping and slurping was loud in the morning stillness. I turned to see Cody's reaction and saw him gazing at the horse, right into Bob's round, glossy black eye, which was almost level with his own.

Then, Cody's eyes, with their long silky lashes, came round to mine.

"Here..." I said. "You can feed him."

I put a chunk of watermelon on the ground just this side of the bottom fence rail, where Bob had to strain to reach it with his lips. Cody squatted and pushed the watermelon several inches, where Bob got it. Then the boy stood, peering intently into the horse's eye, which was watching the boy as intently as the boy watched him.

Then Cody looked at me again, as if surprisingly pleased with himself.

I sat right down on the ground and the two of us fed Bob the rest of that watermelon.

I SAW MONTE'S TRUCK STOP in the driveway, and I stepped out on the porch. "Come on in. I made breakfast."

I saw his eyebrows go up and his mouth open, but I turned from the sight of him and went back inside to dish everything up. Silly as it was, I could hardly look at Monte the entire meal, although I did see his pure boyish grin when I served up the fried tomatoes.

"I'm awful glad you all showed up," he said to Laura Jean and the children. "You got me a darn good meal."

Men are really foolish about food, I thought. And I included Cody with the thought. Since feeding the gelding, Cody at least tried watermelon.

I LEFT MONTE DISABLING the fans in the bathrooms and Laura Jean cleaning the kitchen, and headed out to the garden to gather fresh produce for the stand. I was running late and hurrying.

As I was getting on my garden tractor, Roline came hollering after me.

"Miss Ellie…can I come, too?" She regarded me earnestly. The golden rays of sunlight slanting through a few clouds shone on her dark hair. "Mama says I can, if you say I can. I will help and not bother you."

"Of course you will…you will be no bother, and I could use the help." With this the child smiled, revealing the gap where a new tooth was growing in.

She crawled up beside me on the garden tractor and off we went, the speed of the machine causing a breeze on our faces. I looked down at Roline, and she grinned up at me.

I thought of the entire morning. I had not had so much fun in a long time.

"THIS IS ROLINE. SHE'S MY helper today." Again and again I introduced her to regular customers. Both the child and I were foolishly delighted.

As I watched Roline fill bags and sweep the concrete floor and arrange the tomatoes and zucchini just so to suit her, I thought how it was the first time anyone besides Henry had worked with me at the stand. Oh, people had visited, but not actually worked in the way Roline was doing, which was watching everything I did and following along behind.

There I was sitting on a stool and chatting with an eight-year-old child on another stool, discussing the prospect of closing up for the morning, when a siren sounded. I saw a police car approaching down the highway, lights flashing. Such interruptions were not unexpected on occasion, being as we were alongside the highway. I didn't think much of it.

But to my growing amazement, rather than pass, the police car turned in front of the produce stand and headed right into my own driveway, with siren blaring and lights flashing.

I hopped from my stool. "*Ohmyheaven,* it turned up our drive," I said, as if the child had not just seen that. "I hope Monte didn't fall off the roof!" Heart in my throat, I sprinted to look out the rear of the stand, with Roline right on my heels.

There was Monte, standing on the roof, watching the police car approach.

I took off running up the drive, not even thinking about using the tractor. I'm a little ashamed to say that I clean forgot Roline, too. About halfway along, when I had to slow down because I gave out of breath and leg, I had presence of mind to look back after her, and here came the child, doing her best to run with the cash box, which was large and heavy for her skinny little arms.

I had forgotten more than the child.

HERE IS WHAT HAPPENED.

Cody had called 9-1-1. The best we could all piece together was that he had been upset by the noise of Monte's hammering on the roof. Laura Jean had thought she had him calmed. She had played with him, doing a flash-card game, on the sunporch, which was an addition with separate roof, so the hammering noise was muted. After a little bit, she had left Cody with his Magna Doodle and gone on busily washing their laundry and cleaning the kitchen. She remembered the phone ringing several times, but she had not answered. "It isn't my phone, and I thought it best to let the answering machine pick up." The phone ringing may have upset Cody, too; at least it must have drawn his attention.

"I was watchin' the door, not the phone," Laura Jean said, thoroughly upset and embarrassed, bless her heart.

The next thing she knew, the siren was wailing outside, and before she got to the door, a police officer came bursting through it. The officer, Teddy Corbett, had not bothered to knock. I have known Teddy since childhood; I substituted in his grade-school classes, he attends our church, and he came to many of Henry's barbecues at our house.

On coming through the door and encountering Laura Jean, he had said, "Who are you?" in such a way as to frighten her.

"I was surprised to see a stranger," Teddy explained. "I know Miz Perabo lives here alone now."

His remark and tone on top of Patsy's attitude from the previous day made me begin to wonder how everyone saw me. The way they spoke, it seemed I was considered some helpless old lady.

"Well, I do not think a thief would have an armload of laundry," Laura Jean pointed out.

"You would if you were emptyin' the house," Teddy countered. "Thieves in rural areas have emptied entire houses by throwing everything into pillowcases."

Standing beside Teddy, the second officer, whom I did not know and who had yet to say a word, nodded.

Laura Jean, hand to her hip, frowned at both officers in such a way that they had to look away from her.

Then Teddy gathered his bravery and said, "I'm real sorry, ma'am. It was not my intention to frighten any of you."

"Anyone want somethin' to drink?" asked Monte, who was reaching into the refrigerator, bringing himself out a Coke. Without waiting for a reply, he handed me one, too. His eyes twinkled with a certain understanding, as if he saw right into my mind. At that moment I was quite pleased that he, at least, did not regard me at all like an old woman.

WHILE MONTE WENT BACK UP on the roof to finish the last bit of his reroofing job, Laura Jean and the children walked with me back down to the stand to get it closed up properly. I put up a sign: Closed for the Afternoon.

After that, I led the children along the fence row. I was not in any hurry to take the children back to the house. Monte's hammer strikes still rang out, and finding something to distract us all seemed a good plan.

I had the idea that the children did not spend enough time outside in the fresh air and with nature. I placed the blame of Cody's calling 9-1-1 on his having spent the better part of the past two days in a vehicle or confined in a gas station or a strange house. Of course this led to impatient and wild behavior. I was of the mind, and even said so, that Cody had been quite enterprising to get himself free of that annoying hammering over his head.

As we walked along, I pointed out birds and cloud formations. I picked seeded dandelions and blew on them, sending their seeds whirling in the air. Roline enjoyed doing this immensely, and Laura Jean enjoyed it so much, she laughed like a girl with her daughter.

I held one of the seeded dandelion flowers in front of Cody. "Blow." I formed my mouth in illustration.

He did! And his eyes followed the seeds into the air.

Then we walked beneath the buckeye tree, and I found a few of the hard seed-nuts from the previous year deep in the grass along the fence row. I explained about how the tree put them out in pods each fall. "This entire tree grows from a seed just like this." I gave them a mini-gardening lesson. Roline quickly found a young buckeye growing farther along the fence.

I had begun to see that Cody paid attention to me very often out of the corner of his eyes. I would shift my eyes to him, and he would look away.

Now he put his head down and went along the fence, searching and finding more buckeye seeds down in the grass. He brought them up with his small fingers and took them to his mother. To hold more than one, he had to give her his Magna Doodle, which he had insisted on carrying along with him. Picking up seeds won out.

"Cody loves round things," Roline explained. "Here, Cody, you can have this one, too." Each one she found, she handed to him. He could not hold them all.

"Here, sweetie…put them in your pocket." I dared to take hold and pull open his pants pocket. But I did not look him in the eye. Somehow I sensed a wall up toward me.

Quite soon Bob, always curious, came along the fence. He sniffed at Cody, and Cody stood a moment, staring at him. The gelding's eye reminded me of a buckeye seed. Could that have been the boy's thought? I wondered.

"Can I ride the horse, Miss Ellie? Pleeease?"

That had been inevitable. "After lunch. We'll have a picnic in the backyard."

Telling Laura Jean to keep the children outside, I went to the kitchen to throw together everything I thought everyone might like.

In the middle of my whirlwind of activity, it came to me with a suddenness that I had so missed taking care of someone. Henry had needed my care. He had, in fact, so wanted me to look after him that he had encouraged me to quit teaching and make him a full-time job. Say what you will about that, it had made me happy until the day he died. I was such a woman that needed to take care of others. Why the Good Lord had not given me children, I have no idea.

Once Patsy had said to me, "Ellie, nothing is stopping you from adopting."

Why had I not? Henry. Henry had been against the idea. And I had not gone against him. It was not something I could tell anyone.

And somehow you go along and think: tomorrow…there's plenty of time yet…tomorrow maybe I'll have my own child…tomorrow I'll see about adopting…tomorrow maybe I'll go back to teaching. Only then tomorrow becomes today and it is too late, your time of children passes, your husband dies and there you are, looking back with regrets of paths not taken. That is life.

I found two bags of frozen strawberries to make a dessert. And thought of a Ziploc bag for Cody's buckeye seeds.

Monte came through the door.

"Wash your hands and help me carry this out. We're havin' a picnic."

I EXPLAINED THAT BOB had been a barrel-racing horse. "Even though he is old now, he can still be feisty," I told Roline. "We will have to let Monte see if he can settle him down before you get on him. Monte was a rodeo cowboy."

This impressed mother and child, as I knew it would. Their eyes shifted to him, and he tried to look modest while feeling proud. A few minutes later, Roline had Monte by the hand as they walked toward the corral to get the horse. Laura Jean started off after them with Cody, who cried out and pulled away to come back to the table.

I knew what he wanted and held out to him the bag of buckeye seeds. He took the bag from my hand without looking at me. I gazed after him as he went back to his mother.

MONTE RODE BOB OUT ACROSS the pasture and back, and then hauled Roline up in front of him and rode her out around the pasture and back. The child was in heaven.

"Hi…hi!" Roline called, and waved as she went riding past, secure within Monte's arms.

Laura Jean, Cody and I watched from the shade at the rear of the barn. Thankfully clouds were beginning to gather, blocking the hot afternoon sun. I hauled out a hay bale for us to sit on. I watched as Laura Jean guided Cody to sit.

"Does Cody want to ride the horse?" Laura Jean asked him.

He gave no indication of an answer. His eyes looked at the horse and riders, then back down at his bag of buckeye seeds.

When Monte returned for the third time, he alighted and handed me the reins, saying with a grin, "Your turn."

I held the reins loosely, and Bob's head turned toward Cody. I crouched to Cody's level; the horse's head and mine were side by side. We both looked at Cody.

Cody's eyes came up. He looked at Bob, and then his gaze slid to me. I smiled, rubbed the gelding's nose and said, "Bob likes you, Cody."

I raised an eyebrow to Laura Jean, and, each of us taking a deep breath, she told Roline to slip back as she lifted Cody to put him in the saddle.

Cody screamed in a way that could curdle blood, and his legs kicked frantically in midair. Laura Jean got hit in the head; I grabbed him from the other side. Then he was in the saddle, with Roline's arms around him, and I took off at a trot, leading Bob by the reins, with Laura Jean jogging along beside. The minute the horse started to move, Cody shut up.

We jogged to the edge of the pasture. The only time Cody started to get upset was when we stopped, which I had to do to catch my breath. I showed him and Roline how to make the horse go themselves by making the kissing sound at him. This sound proved to be something that Cody could do. I watched the look on his face when he made the sound and Bob moved. I could almost see a connection in his brain, as he connected something he did with moving the big animal.

Some fifteen minutes later in the kitchen, where we ran to escape the downpour, leaving Monte to care for the horse, Laura Jean made an exaggerated sound upon kissing Cody lightly on the cheek. He repeated this back to her. And then we were all doing it to one another and laughing. It was the first time that I saw Cody really and truly laugh.

As Laura Jean took the children off to wash up and get on clean, dry clothes, I opened the refrigerator, intent on assembling a snack, of course.

Then I paused with the door open and cocked my ear, listening to the sounds of voices and bodies moving through the house. A house that had been quiet for a very long time, even when Henry had been there. A rush of feeling came over me that I did not understand, only knew as change.

THE RAIN CAME DOWN outside. Nevertheless, when Monte learned of Roline's keen desire for computer access, he sprinted out to his pickup truck to retrieve his laptop. He got it set up for her at the desk in the kitchen, using his cell phone for Internet access, no less (what an age we live in!), then threw himself into Henry's old recliner. I brought him a glass of sweet tea and several cookies. Not ten minutes later, I had to remove the glass of tea from his hand, as he had fallen asleep.

I sent Laura Jean for a hot soak, while I watched the children and prepared supper. Roline shortly abandoned the computer and fell asleep on the floor in the sunporch, in front of the television. Cody came to the kitchen with his Magna Doodle, and I gave him his bag of buckeye seeds, which I had retrieved from the grass where he had dropped them earlier. He went off to the sunporch and sat playing beside sleeping Roline. I brought him a bowl of grapes and watermelon cut up and sat myself down with him on the floor. He gave no indication of being aware of me.

I watched him select grapes and line them up on the floor, then line buckeye seeds beside them. Taking up his Magna Doodle, I saw a horse figure drawn there. I drew the figure of a boy on top of it. Then I drew buckeye seeds. I displayed this to him. I saw him look with a sideways glance of his eyes.

Next, and somewhat to my surprise, he handed me a buckeye seed. For whatever reason, I chuckled, and his face came up. He smiled, his eyes meeting mine fully. It was all I could do not to hug him, but I was afraid that might startle him.

For supper, I served ham slices, cheese-topped new potatoes, fresh green onions and green beans, and sliced cold tomatoes. Cody, and Monte, too, especially enjoyed the dessert of sliced peaches I found in the freezer and which I topped with real whipped cream.

Shortly after, Laura Jean took the children off to get bathed, and I walked Monte outside to his pickup truck. Impulsively I stretched up to give him a kiss on the cheek. "That's for all you did for me— for the kids, too—today."

He touched the spot and grinned slowly.

"You're welcome. I should say, though, that if it is goin' to take that much effort to get favor from you, I'm gonna have to give it up."

I do not know what got into me, but I replied saucily with "You come back tomorrow and find out."

"You're usin' me, woman." And he had kissed my lips before I knew what he was about.

I got all flustered and went to step backward, but he held me.

His blue eyes became intent. "You remember, Ellie, that Laura Jean and the kids are only passin' through."

"I remember." What did he think of me?

He got into his pickup, slammed the door.

I took hold of the open window. "You know, we all are just passin' through, Monte. All the more reason to enjoy and do all that we can for one another."

He nodded. "I just don't want to see you get hurt when they leave in a couple of days."

"I'm fine."

He backed his pickup truck, turned and waved as he drove away.

Standing there watching after him, I felt my lips tingle where he had kissed me. And then as Monte's truck passed out of sight, I saw Patsy's Chrysler 300 coming. I blinked, and thought with great relief that Patsy could not have seen the interchange between me and Monte.

The Chrysler approached up the drive. I stood waiting, and saw Stu was at the wheel. The car came to a stop, and Patsy got out of the passenger side. I leaned down and called a greeting to Stu through the open window.

"Hey," he said back, with a wave.

"We hear you had a bit of excitement up here today," Patsy said. "We were just over at the café and ran into Teddy."

"Just a bit." News in this town traveled faster than greased lightning. Teddy was a distant nephew of Stu's.

"Teddy said Monte was here then, too. He's been here a lot lately, hasn't he?"

"He put a new roof on the house. That takes a few days for one man."

"Well, I'm glad today turned out not to be anything serious. I brought something for your friend." She thrust a couple of papers at me.

I took the papers with surprise.

"Teddy told me about the boy. We've got three autistic boys this year, just finished IEP on each of them."

"Really?"

I looked at the papers—one from the state about individual education programs, and another a brochure for an organization called Autism Speaks.

Patsy said, "We've got a new special education coordinator this year, who had this information. There's a real push on for more public education. I know things could be different over in your friend's school district, but I have plenty of this info…shows what is available to her."

"Thanks…I know Laura Jean will appreciate it."

Patsy regarded me expectantly.

I threw my arm around her shoulders. "Come on in and give them to her yourself," I said, thrusting the papers back into her hands.

Patsy would really be disappointed if Laura Jean left without Patsy getting to lay eyes on her. And Patsy was my best friend; I wanted her to know that.

"THAT WAS NICE OF your friend—Patsy—to bring this information for me," said Laura Jean.

"Yes, she's a sweetheart…but she really wanted to get a look at you. She's likes to know what's going on."

We were at the kitchen table, I in a chair, and Laura Jean on a small stool at my feet, giving me a pedicure, the first professional one ever in my life. When Laura Jean had heard this fact, she had said, "You sit right down here. It is not natural for a woman not to ever have a pedicure." She insisted on painting my toenails a bright red, and I let her. My toenails were far enough away from my eyes so that the bright color did not seem so loud.

While she worked over my feet, I read the information Patsy had brought and flipped through the two books on autism belonging to Laura Jean. "Did you say that Cody had been in occupational therapy?" I was trying to remember the bit about this I had learned in college.

"Uh-huh. We were just gettin' started with it—it was through the school."

While I perused the book, she talked about Cody's various

ailments. He seemed to have digestion difficulties and to catch just about everything that came along. Most of the therapies, even a lot of the medical care for autism, weren't covered under their HMO plan. She had gotten some help through state programs. It had taken her months to get him enrolled in the early special education class.

"Now we'll have to go through it all again where my sister lives."

"Yes, but now you'll have experience with the system. And maybe Patsy's information will prove helpful."

She breathed deeply as she recapped the polish. "Sometimes it's all just so much to learn. I just don't…well, I can't seem to keep up. And it's not fair to Roline. Everything I have goes to Cody, and she gets lost in it."

"Of course it is all so much," I said. "Life is so much, for any of us sometimes. But, honey, you are doin' a great job. You have two beautiful children, and thus far you have managed to keep them fed and clothed, and to get the best care possible. You have to go on believin' in yourself. You have to believe, because you are all those two have."

She gazed at me in a way that made me wonder if she'd heard, then gestured at my feet. "What do you think?"

I wiggled my toes. "Oh, my…I like it." Me, with bright crimson toenails. Henry would have died.

A short while later, just before we parted for our beds, I impulsively hugged Laura Jean and said, "You know, the LTD breakin' down has really given you a break from all the struggle. While you're here, you just forget everything and rest. A little rest works wonders."

Later, in my own bed, I found myself worrying about Laura Jean and the kids and their future, as if somehow I had taken over the job for her. I wondered about her sister and mother with whom she was intending to live. I don't know why, but I had formed a picture in my mind of slovenly, uncaring women. This was simply silly. I knew nothing about them. But somehow I felt that if they had been all that helpful, they would have already been over here to get her and take her home. Patsy would have done that for me, and she was not my own blood kin. At least one of my brothers would have done it.

It was within me to ask her about her sister and mother. I thought of discreet and maneuvering ways to go about this. I also imagined asking her to stay with me. But something held me back from that. I thought that Laura Jean would not want it. She was a very independent woman. *Distant* was perhaps a better word.

And maybe I was distant in my own way, too.

What I would be taking on flashed before my eyes and caused me to shake my head.

With a large sigh, I took up one of the books on autism and read long into the night.

PART
THREE

Laura Jean and the children remained with me for another day and a half. Laura Jean seemed to take my advice and to relax and enjoy herself, and to enjoy time with her children. Monte came each day, too. The first day he just came, but that evening he said, "Do you want me to come tomorrow?" and I replied, "Have I not been feeding you?"

I left the produce stand closed, did not even miss going. Although apparently the open stand was missed, as two customers stopped and blew their horns until Monte went down, and three neighbors actually telephoned to make certain I was okay, and came over to get things right out of the garden.

Voices rang out, the screen door banged. Laura Jean cautioned Roline to close the door because of the air-conditioning, and I told her not to worry, I liked the fresh air. I made every one of my special quick-and-easy food dishes. I was delighted to see Monte's appreciative eating, and hopeful to put some weight on Laura Jean.

The children fed Bob watermelon and rode him again. This time they rode in the corral, each by themselves, with Monte holding a guide rope. Cody got pretty good at making the kissing sound to make the horse go. Then Roline used the kissing sound when she took Cody by the hand, and he in turn used it when he took his mother's hand. I used it to move Monte in playing, and pretty soon we were all using the kissing sound for one thing or another.

Cody seemed drawn to Monte, going over to the pump house to wander around while Monte worked on the water well. We next discovered that Monte had given Cody two large bolts with nuts that he repeatedly screwed and unscrewed. I was a little concerned about Cody possibly putting the nuts into his mouth, and of course he did, so I would not leave him while he was occupied with the nuts and bolts. Then Laura Jean hauled out his case of toys and succeeded in getting him involved with playing Lego.

From the kitchen, leaving the door wide open, I watched mother and son, and Roline, too, playing on the porch floor. It was as if I were pasting their image in the photo album of my mind.

Laura Jean and the children helped me pick green beans. Then we girls sat on the porch and snapped them, while Cody made shapes with them and his buckeye seeds. I watched this with some amazement. I went down to the porch floor and began to turn green beans into alphabet letters, spelling Cody's name.

"C...O...D...Y," I said, pointing to each letter. "Cody."

"Co-dy," he said, much to my amazement, and, I think, to his own delight.

With Roline's help, Laura Jean and I used Monte's little computer to check out the Autism Speaks Web site, from the brochure that Patsy had brought. This site provided a wealth of information and links to other sites that told about various therapies and support groups for autistic children and their parents. There was information about a special diet, about play therapies, about speech therapies, about using animals and music. There was information on research studies and breakthroughs and how to get help.

"Look at this...look at this!" we said to one another.

We read all that we could until our eyes were bleary. Laura Jean took notes. I saw the energy seeming to seep back into her, straightening her spine and filling her eyes with hope.

LATE THE FOLLOWING morning, Red brought the repaired LTD.

I was mentally engaged in planning what I could serve for lunch that would follow the special diet we had read about. This would require no wheat and no milk, the staples of Cody's diet, but I was determined to cook up something nutritious that the boy would eat. This was a challenge that thrilled me.

All of a sudden, I heard a car honking. I stepped out on the porch and saw the LTD coming up the drive. My heart fell to my toes. I had never expected Red to be early. Laura Jean had called him the previous evening to check on the progress with the LTD, and Red had told her that it would be tonight at the earliest. I had convinced myself that he would not have the car ready until Monday.

If I could have caught him before anyone knew, I would have told him to go away and come back on the morrow. But Laura Jean heard the horn, too, and came running.

I suggested strongly that Laura Jean consider waiting to leave until the following morning. "You'll be fresh then."

But, where she had seemed to follow my every word before, this time she was adamant about getting on with her trip. She straight away began throwing things into her suitcase and plastic bags. "I can easily reach my sister's house before dark."

It came out of me then. "You can stay here awhile. Just because the car is fixed doesn't mean you have to run off."

She shook her head. "I have to get the kids enrolled in school. That could take a while for Cody. I need to get started."

"You could stay here," I said.

She looked at me. I gazed at her.

Then, "I can't. Back there we'll be with family." She looked away, shaking her head. "And all Billy's family is there. He may come home."

"Oh," I said. *Of course...of course. This was how it was supposed to be.*

I watched her, saw the renewed energy and purpose in her arms and legs. Here with me she had gotten her second wind. I told myself that I was glad.

Turning, I went to the attic and brought down two suitcases— the hunter-green tweed ones. They just looked like Laura Jean, as if they had been sitting up there all this time, waiting for her.

"You've already given me too much. No." She held up a hand and turned resolutely away.

"Honey, these are just rotting up there in the attic, not doin' anybody any good." I helped her to pack.

CODY SAW THE PACKING and got upset. He began looking for certain belongings, which we were not quick enough to supply, so he threw an enormous hissy fit. My heart went out to him. He was as reluctant to get back into the car as he had been to get out of it on the day he came here.

Roline cried quietly and said, "Oh, Miss Ellie, I will miss you."

I hugged her and told her that we would see them again.

"When?" she said, in her factual manner.

"When your mother gets time to bring you back someday. Or when Monte and I come to see you." I included Monte without question.

Laura Jean and I hurried through goodbyes. She had one foot in the car.

I held on to the door and said, "You take care of yourself." I had the compulsion to pack up encouragement in a Ziploc bag for her to take with her, since I would not be there to oversee her life. In far more words than necessary, I said things like "You are a good mother, and your children are doin' just fine. You must believe in yourself. Do not lose confidence in yourself, because that is the only way you can get through."

Finally, at the last, I bent to the window and said directly and straight, "There will always be room for you and the children here."

She nodded, bit her bottom lip, shifted into gear and started off.

I stood beside Monte and waved as the LTD headed down the drive, until, all of a sudden, hardly aware of my actions, I turned and strode to the garden, grabbing a hoe from the fence as I passed. I tore into hoeing a row of green beans. The thought that went through my mind was: *Well, that's that…that's that.*

I saw Monte's shoes first. I looked up at him.

He said, a little uncertainly, "You makin' lunch?"

Struck deeply by what I perceived as his infinite care and patience, I nodded and said, "Yes. Come on in."

I had hamburgers frying and was slicing tomatoes when Monte came over and drew me against his chest and patted my back. I almost cried, but instead said, "Well, that's that…do you want cheese on your hamburger?"

LAURA JEAN CALLED THAT evening to say that they had safely reached her sister's house. She said it had been an easy drive. Then, "Roline wants to say hey."

"Miss Ellie?"

"Yes, honey. So you are there with your aunt and gramma."

"Yep. They have a swimmin' pool and a computer."

"Very good!"

"And a dog, but he's old and barks a lot."

I could hear the yipping in the background. "It might take him a little while to get used to you."

"Yeah…oh…here's my mama…I love you, Miss Ellie."

"I love you, too, honey." I thought my throat would close.

"It's me again. Well, just wanted you to know we're here. And to thank you for all you did. I will be sending money soon to pay you back."

I closed my eyes at that, then said, "Could I say somethin' to Cody?"

"I don't know. Let me see." I heard her call him to her, heard her instructing him. "Go ahead."

"Cody? Hi. It's Miss Ellie." I waited, not really expecting a response, wondering if he knew my voice. I recalled that he surely knew how to use the telephone; he had called 9-1-1.

There came a sound. I grinned. It was the kissing sound. And next I heard him say what sounded like Bob, and Cody, and maybe repeating what I could hear his mother say to him, which was, "Hi, Miss Ellie."

"Hi, Cody."

Then Laura Jean was back on the line. I said, "Thanks for callin'. I'm glad you got there safe. You take care now."

I clicked off the receiver and gathered my frayed self, because Monte was still there and watching me.

One really nice thing about Monte was that he never once tried to remind me that all along the children had just been passing through.

I HAD FORGOTTEN TO RETURN to Laura Jean her books on autism. I found them that night on my bedside table, when I took my cup of tea to bed. I would need to get her address, as there was going to be a small box of articles to send to her. I had found some of the children's clothes in the dryer and a shoe underneath the dresser.

Settling myself in the bed with my accustomed nightly tea, I opened one of the books to where I had left off the night before. I read the words but did not comprehend. I found myself staring into space, scenes from the past three days playing across my mind. I listened to the empty silence, and yet it was a different silence than it had been before Laura Jean and the children had come. Now the silence seemed to hold echoes of their presence.

I knew that somehow we were all different. We had touched one another's lives. I did not know how this difference would play out, but I knew that it would. I fell asleep thinking a lot of thoughts about this.

The next morning, before sunrise, I went to the kitchen to begin the day. When I reached in the drawer for a dish towel, I remembered the calendar. I slowly brought it out, realizing that I had not thought about it since the day Laura Jean and the children had come.

For long seconds I gazed at the X marks on the squares, and the empty squares where I had stopped marking.

With suddenness, I shoved the drawer closed and tossed the calendar in the trash. And that's when I finally cried.

Even as the sun came up, the birds began singing, cicadas chirped in the bushes just outside the porch, and I turned on the radio, the house seemed to echo with silence. *You were alone before, and you knew you would be alone again*, I told myself impatiently.

I tried to pull strength from within myself and did not answer the phone when it rang and I saw it was Monte. Somehow seeing him would make the situation worse. With every intention of going to the produce stand, I ended up getting in my car and going to church. Despite my normal preference for solitude, I was drawn to people. I actually attended service in my overalls, with no makeup except lipstick.

It had not occurred to me that people would ask about Laura Jean, but the instant I saw Patsy, I was reminded. I had to explain to her about them leaving. Then Pastor Gene made a big point of telling me that the very next time I have anybody in need stop on the highway to be sure to call the church. "Here's my card. You just call when you know anyone in need. That's what we're here for."

I told him that I would, but that I just did not think such a thing was going to be any sort of regular occurrence. It seemed to me that he was a little bereft of people to help and he was drumming up business.

"I'll bet your house is really empty now," Patsy said.

"They were only there barely three days." I downplayed it, uncomfortable for anyone to see into my heart.

But Patsy came back with "Well, honey, Jesus was in the grave for just three days, and everything was changed."

I had no reply for that.

The singing had already started when Monte came slipping into the pew beside me. That blew all talk about the girl and children I had taken in out of the water, and people then shifted to speculating about me and Monte.

PATSY WAS RIGHT. THREE DAYS could make a lot of difference. I had set out to help three people who I thought needed it, but I now saw that I had been helped far more. I had been as closed into my world as Cody was in his. Laura Jean and the children had succeeded in bringing me out. I could see this change playing out in my life.

Yes, I was out now, but not especially happy about it. Change is hard. I felt I was moving along in life, but I had no idea of where I was going.

I thought all of that as I drove home from church that day and found myself turning into the cemetery. I stood looking at Henry's grave, then bent to pull some weeds. I listened to hear his familiar voice inside of me. It did not come. I was a little sad, but more accepting, and even a little glad. When it is time to let something go, it is a relief.

I was walking back to my car when Monte drove up. "You followin' me?"

"Nope," he said. "I was drivin' home and saw your car. You wanna go for a burger?"

"Are you payin'?"

"You bet."

While we were having lunch, Monte said, "You look real good in those overalls, Ellie." He was such a little boy in his efforts to lift my spirits. I'm sure it would have surprised him to know that it was this sweet fact of him, and not losing Laura Jean and the children, that almost made me cry.

I reached out and took his hand. Monte had been beside me a long time. "I'm sure glad you're still here," I said, and saw the surprise on his face.

I'M SURE IT WAS NOT A coincidence that Wednesday morning I awoke with a surge of energy and clear idea of where I was going in the second half of my life. It was the third day since Laura Jean and the children had left.

At the post office, I mailed the books and items Laura Jean had left, then walked in the sunshine down the block to the library, where I checked out every book they had on autism and occupational and behavioral therapy. There were only four. The library was small.

I began to read while at the produce stand, during lunch and at bedtime. I had Monte go and pick me out a new computer and install it for me in the office that I had barely entered in years. I spent long hours on the Internet researching and learning about autism and other neurological disorders. The garden suffered neglect, and Monte, of course, began to take care of it, along with everything else around the place. In exchange, I continued to cook and feed him, more lavishly than ever. Some evenings we sat a bit on the porch and I would tell him all I was learning, while he listened or dozed.

By the next week, I called Patsy and asked if there would be a position for me as a special education assistant. I was not yet qualified to be a full teacher in the field, and I was not certain exactly what I was going to pursue, but I was ready to begin.

Patsy said, in so loud a voice I had to hold the phone from my ear, "Oh my gosh! I cannot believe that you called right now! Look how things always work out. Miranda Sykes just up and quit. She left her husband and has gone to Memphis. You start the first day of school."

We arranged to go to the mall the following day. I needed to get a wardrobe. During our drive to the city, I dared to say, "I think I want to go back to school to get a special education teaching certificate. How will I do this?"

"Well, you will start right over at the junior college. And the school district may pick up some of the tab." Patsy went on about the various degrees, so many new since I had been in school. She kept saying, "And then you can...and after that..." She mapped out my life and made it sound so good and promising that I let her go on with it. My future, which had been a blank, was now being drawn in full color.

That evening, when Monte came for supper, I met him wearing a flowing, flowery rayon dress. He gave me a long whistle and made a great to-do of looking me over. Then he cast a puzzled frown. "I still can't see your legs."

The dress fell near my ankles. I picked up its skirt and gave a little kick.

He threw his head back and laughed, then the next thing he swept me up and whirled me around.

"Put me down, and do not get ideas. I bought the dress for myself, and for the first time in my life I did not look at the price."

"You did not buy that dress just for yourself."

"Okay…maybe not."

THE END OF AUGUST SLIPPED into September. The heat of summer lingered, but brilliant fall edged on.

Monte took over working the produce stand the two morning hours. Sometimes I helped him for a little bit, after which I would drive to school, where I worked four days a week with the special needs children. One day a week I went to school for my special education certificate.

After never having much liked the profession of teaching, I was amazed at how much I enjoyed working with these special children. They had many gifts, and I saw that I had the gift to help them bring out theirs. I would hear again and again all day, "Miss Ellie…Miss Ellie."

And there was something else that I found I could give, and that was support and encouragement to the parents. More and more I was sought out on a private level to provide advice for this matter and that regarding the home life of a child. Once I was even telephoned at home by a harried mother at the end of her rope.

This incident had the result of propelling me to locate the local support group, only to discover that it was small and relatively ineffective. I, the normally demure introvert, swung into action——

or perhaps I was pushed, because Patsy said, "So, if there is no group, you start one."

Luckily the new school special needs counselor, a very go-getter type of woman, swung with me. Together we began a support group using the resources from Autism Speaks. At our first meeting, we had a noted pediatrician from Little Rock come to speak. This woman so roused the parents that quite a number got all fired up, and our industrious group began distributing information throughout the county. We even had a dietician come to educate the school cafeteria personnel for special needs diets.

As a direct result of our efforts, our special needs class grew by three more precious children, and a county social worker located two more young toddlers not yet school age who needed early intervention. I saw children and parents blossoming right before my eyes. It was amazing what simple hope and confidence could do.

One afternoon in early December, a mother caught me after class and said, "Miss Ellie…I brought you a kicking and screaming creature, and you have given me a sweet little boy. Even at home. Well…just, thank you."

I responded to her as best I could in my overwhelmed state.

For some reason, that mother and her son brought Cody strongly to mind. I drove home thinking about him, and then, as if brought by my very thoughts, I found a letter from Laura Jean in my mailbox. It would contain a check, I knew. At least twice a month, she was faithful to her promise to send money to repay me.

During those first weeks after she had left, Laura Jean would telephone and we would have long conversations. She told me all about their lives, and I told her about mine. We had much in common, of course. Then Laura Jean went to work, the calls became fewer, and the notes started arriving twice a month. I did telephone her several times, but she seemed rushed and distant, so I settled for sending her notes by e-mail.

One night out of the blue, she telephoned in something of a panic to say that her husband, Billy, had returned. He wanted to get back together with her. She wanted my advice. Knowing full well the risky business of giving such advice, I did my best to remain an objective sounding board. She never did tell me if she had gone back with him. I did not deem it polite to ask.

Now I opened the envelope, and the usual check fluttered to the kitchen table. I sat to read, and their voices came swarming around me.

Hello, Miss Ellie. How are you? We are fine. I know you have said not to worry about repaying you, but I want to. I have a full clientele now, so my income is pretty good. Roline is getting straight As. Cody has adjusted pretty well to his new class. He has learned sign language really fast, and talks a little. It is hard to keep him on the diet. My mother gives him Oreos and milk. Well, I have to go to work. Love, Laura Jean.

This time there was a PS in a childish hand. "I am doing good in school. I still do not like Gramma Jean's dog. Love, Roline. Cody says hi."

I could tell Cody had written the "hi."

Monte came through the back door. I got up and hugged and kissed him hello. Our relationship had progressed to that. "From Laura Jean." I passed him the card, then moved to get an apron and make vegetables to go with the roast I had in the slow cooker.

"Did you see the front of this card?" Monte said, displaying it for me.

I had not paid attention to it and saw for the first time that it read: Normal is a setting on the washing machine.

"That's a truth," I said, and we both chuckled. For myself, I had my own avoidance of social contact and varying degrees of verbal resistance that enabled me to relate to Cody and other autistic children. When I once mentioned this to Monte, he said, "Oh, yeah."

He read the inside of the card. "They sound okay."

"Yes," I said. And then, "I always kind of hoped they would come back. I even left the drawers and closet of the guest room empty." I could not look at him as I said this.

"I know," he said in a tender tone. "They still might."

"No. I don't think so anymore. Too much time has passed."

I saw clearly in that moment that my efforts to learn about autism had been motivated by a bid to enter Laura Jean and the children's world. A way to draw them back to me. To love them and to be loved in return.

It seemed, though, that life had a different path. Laura Jean and the children were doing fine, and I had been propelled out into the world and into something that suited me perfectly. It had worked out differently than I had imagined, but it was working out.

That evening, after Monte left, I went to my office desk, but instead of sending Laura Jean an e-mail, as I normally did to acknowledge the check's arrival, I took out stationery. I sat for a long time trying to figure out what to say.

Dear Laura Jean, the check arrived today. I want you to know I appreciate it. Monte and I enjoy hearing about you and the children. We thought we might come your way in the spring. Come this way if you get a chance. The door is always open. Love, Ellie.

It was saying nothing. I did not know why I wrote it, but I sealed the envelope and applied a stamp.

On my way past the guest room, I paused and gazed in for a long moment. Then I quietly closed the door.

An episode of my life was over. It was time to get on with a new chapter.

THEN, AS IN THE PECULIAR and unexpected way of life, the following Saturday evening, when I was stacking the firewood that Monte was splitting, I looked down the drive to see a car turning off the highway. Familiarity struck me, but the setting sun glared in my eyes. I put my hand up as a shield to the light.

It *was* the LTD.

"Monte! They've come!"

I dropped the firewood and hurried toward the driveway. Bob

came running from the rear pasture. The LTD came up the drive with the horse chasing along the fence and Roline waving out the window and crying, "Hello, Bob!"

And there was Cody's arm waving, too.

The car stopped. The passenger door opened, and Roline popped out and raced toward me.

"Miss Ellie…Miss Ellie! We're here!"

"I see that." I hugged the child to me for a moment, savoring the precious thin arms around my neck. And then she was running away to greet Monte and Bob at the fence.

Straightening, I watched the familiar long legs, now in jeans, sticking out of the car. Laura Jean appeared with Cody, helping him down. My, how he had grown! He stood at Laura Jean's legs, his gaze focused to the side, but my now educated eye noticed the difference in him. He was paying attention.

I bent in front of him. I saw his gaze shift to my chin.

"Hi, Cody. I'm glad to see you." I waited.

His gaze flickered up to mine. He smiled. Then Roline came to eagerly take his hand and lead him to the fence and the horse. I watched them a moment, amazed at my gladness.

Then I looked at Laura Jean. There was something about her that held me back from hugging her. I watched her rake back her bangs and momentarily avoid my eyes in a manner quite like her son's. I waited, a little uncertain.

"We can't stay over there with my sister and mom anymore. They…" She rolled her eyes as if explanation was impossible. "It just isn't workin' out…and I got your letter yesterday. So we're here." I could see her seeking for more words, but I cut her off by putting my arm around her shoulders.

"Honey, I am just so glad you came. Are you all hungry?"

At that she laughed out loud.

THAT EVENING, WE ALL SAT around the oak kitchen table like one big happy family, telling one another everything we could think of. I brought out canned peaches for Cody and nondairy topping; I was very pleased to use a bit of sign language with him, and he was pleased to speak a few words. Roline displayed her longer hair and how her feet almost hit the floor in the chair. Monte did a lot of indulgent smiling, quite like a man who had orchestrated everything.

At one point when I got up to go to the sink, my gaze went to the window. It had grown dark outside, making the window glass a mirror, reflecting everyone around the table in the warm glow of the light from above.

I stared at the image.

"Miss Ellie…" Roline called.

"I'm comin', sweetheart."

Turning from the reflection in the night-black glass, I went to take my place with the others in the full light at the table.

∽— EPILOGUE —∽

I wanted them to stay forever, wanted to add on to the house. Laura Jean argued about this and was adamant about getting her own place. Three months after she moved in, we were both made happy, more or less, when the house next door, on the other side of my pasture, came up for sale. It was old but sound. I bought it, Monte updated it, and she pays rent. The children can go back and forth between our houses in a few minutes' walk.

Laura Jean married police officer Teddy. Remember him? He came around as soon as he heard about Laura Jean's return, stayed for dinner and never left. While I live here alone again, my house is continually full. Most nights during the week, except for those when Monte takes me out so that we can have time for just the two of us, my supper table is full. There are Roline's and Cody's friends, and very often one of my students and a parent in need of boosting, or one of our autism group. They all seem to entertain one another, while I do as I have always done, tend and serve from the background, as suits me.

From the outset, Cody and Roline and I would head out to school each morning together, and we still do. Cody was in my class for the first couple of years, and then he improved so much that he was mainstreamed. Only a practiced eye and ear would pick out any difficulties. He shows amazing artistic ability.

Roline was diagnosed with ADHD, and has the creative mind that goes along with it. She already knows that she wants to be a doctor.

Monte is over here from morning until bedtime. We thought about getting married, but we decided that if it is not broke, don't fix it. He prefers to go home each night to his own place, and I prefer him to do so. I like to share my bed with books. And sometimes a child. At the age of fifty, I received the miracle of having my life filled with very special children. Five years of teaching, and so many children have come and gone, yet they all remain in my heart...and all because of three people who stopped in need.

Dear Reader,

During the writing of this story, I was blessed to meet so many dedicated and thoroughly creative parents. One of these, a mother of an autistic child, who also fosters an autistic teen, summed up what they live with daily when she said, "When you find out, you have to grieve the loss of the child you thought you had. And you feel so alone a lot. But we've got to believe in ourselves and not give up."

Thanks to people like Dr. Ricki Robinson, organizations such as Autism Speaks, and thousands of determined parents who continue to believe and to seek answers, there is so much hope and many and varied therapies for autism disorder. What works for one person may not work for another, but there is help for all. And there is one single, vital and indispensable thing that helps everyone—loving support.

Caring for a child or adult with autism is a 24/7 proposition. An understanding smile, a listening ear, a normal conversation is something we can all give. Simple acts of kindness that can make all the difference. Look around you, and you will likely find that you know more than one family affected by the broad spectrum that is autism. The disorder is showing itself at an alarming rate, sometimes figured to be as high as one in 166 children. It does seem to run in families.

So put this book down now, go to your computer and visit

www.autismspeaks.org to educate yourself and find out how you can help. The ones you help may turn out to be members of your own family.

Do it now. You'll be glad you did.

Curtiss Ann Matlock

Aviva Presser
∽— Bears Without Borders —∽

Bringing warmth and joy to some of the most troubled and impoverished regions of the world sounds like a Herculean task. It's also a particularly poignant one, given that so many of the afflicted are children who have known nothing but deprivation. For a disadvantaged and desperately ill child who has never been given a toy in his life, a hug from a teddy bear can be a small miracle.

Making the world a happier place for children living on the front lines of a global health crisis, such as the catastrophic AIDS epidemic in Africa, has become not just a mission, but also a passion with Aviva Presser. Through Bears Without Borders, an organization she started just over two years ago with Erez Lieberman, her husband, that mission has taken root and is spreading.

The project launched at their wedding, in September 2005. "We were so happy we were getting married, we wanted to make others happy, too," says Aviva. The couple wanted their wedding ceremony to be not just about their commitment to each other, but also a public declaration of their joint commitment to a troubled and needy world.

Aviva has always loved teddy bears, so they decided to make them part of the festivities. Wedding guests were invited to design costumes or bring materials for dressing two hundred bears donated by Build-a-Bear Workshop—a company that provides the materials, everything from stuffing to ribbons to a birth certificate for the finished product, for teddy bear enthusiasts wishing to make their own creation. The dressed bears were sent to victims of Hurricane Katrina and to AIDS victims in South Africa. "The guests also got cards they could include to write a note to the children," Aviva says.

A doctor at a hospital in KwaZulu-Natal, South Africa, described the joy occasioned by the arrival of a shipment of bears at the children's ward. "There were cheers from the adults and ward staff. The children were shy at first—confused about actually being given a teddy bear. Smiles were slow to come, but that changed once they had their arms around their teddy bears."

Developing efficient ways to get the shipments to their destinations was just one of the challenges Aviva faced. Complex customs regulations can make the movement of goods in the developing world a nightmare. But despite her already impressive workload, Aviva, a Harvard graduate student working on unraveling the codes that form the human genome, put her organizational skills to work and gradually amassed a network of volunteers to make, decorate, donate, oversee, distribute and deliver the bears to needy children. Erez, also a graduate student, says he is continually amazed that Aviva comes home at night after a long day's work and starts searching eBay for bear stuffing on one computer while designing a new logo on another.

Harvard was a key ally in getting the Bear Exchange program under way. A collaboration was forged between Bears Without Borders and the Massachusetts General Hospital/Harvard Hospitals Global Health Rotation program, which proved enormously helpful in circumventing many of the distribution problems. With the support of volunteers, exchange residents sent abroad by MGH to its many satellite global health-training programs each carry with them a delegation of bears. In this way, bears arrive in impoverished areas in many parts of the world, bringing comfort to their small, helpless and often desperately ill recipients.

Aviva has learned to rely on the kindness of strangers. "It's so encouraging to see how many people are willing to help," she says. "People we know and people we don't know." She sometimes receives photographs of the children she helps but has never met. Some of the pictures are heartrending, she says. "They make me cry. But they also make me want to do something. The more I see, the more I feel the need." She remembers being touched by a picture of a little boy in South Africa. "He was so sick, but he had a little smile as he hugged his teddy bear." Another little girl with TB and HIV was photographed proudly carrying her teddy bear like a baby on her back. "She may not live to be a mom," Aviva says, "but for a little while at least, she can be a mom, and hopefully, with proper care, her chances will improve."

Since its inception, Bears Without Borders has expanded enormously, reaching countries as diverse as Venezuela, Thailand, South Africa, Haiti, Rwanda, India, Israel and, most recently, Cambodia, where five clinics with several hundred needy children are now receiving bears. "When the children are so desperately sick, it's wonderful to be able to give them a gift that's consoling," Aviva says. They also have new programs in Bolivia and Peru.

Donations for Bears Without Borders come from many sources, including the Internet: two sites the couple find especially effective are the Hunger Site and the Child Health Site, as well as their own Web site at www.bearswithoutborders.org. They are also developing a university network with a Web site that would enable fund-raising events to be held on campuses across the country. Donations of money and materials also come from companies such as Build-a-Bear Workshop and from individuals. Erez says people sometimes show up with "a carload of bears."

Word is spreading, and requests are now coming in from all over the world, mainly from medical clinics, but also occasionally from orphanages. Each request receives a response from Aviva, and she develops a plan for each one, however exotic or distant the locale, or how tiny the population. Because of Bears Without Borders' medical connections, Aviva and Erez have created a sister organization to provide services and medical equipment—such as the mammography unit they, in collaboration with the Greater Good Network, will soon be providing to a South African hospital—to developing countries.

The couple's commitment to helping needy children has grown along with their expanding outreach. As Erez puts it, "Bears Without Borders has become a part of who we are to each other."

Aviva's bears have truly become global ambassadors, bringing hope and healing to a troubled world. And they've only just begun.

For more information visit www.bearswithoutborders.org or write to Bears Without Borders, 270 Windsor Street, #4, Cambridge, MA 02139.

JENNIFER ARCHER
❧ Hannah's Hugs ❧

~ JENNIFER ARCHER ~

Publishers Weekly calls Jennifer Archer a writer who "captures the voices and vulnerabilities of her characters with precision." Jennifer was a 2006 finalist for Romance Writers of America's prestigious RITA® Award with her novel *The Me I Used To Be,* and her novel *Sandwiched* was a 2006 nominee for a *Romantic Times BOOKreviews* Reviewer's Choice Award.

Jennifer holds a bachelor of business administration degree from West Texas A&M University. A frequent speaker at writing workshops, women's events and creative writing classes, she enjoys inspiring others to set goals and pursue dreams. She is the mother of two grown sons and resides in Texas with her husband and two dogs—Marge, a proud mutt, and Harry, a miniature dachshund. Jennifer can be contacted through her Web site, www.jenniferarcher.net.

❧ PROLOGUE ❧

T erri Roxton tapped her fingernail against the face of her watch but the second hand failed to start ticking again. "That's weird," she murmured.

"What, Mommy?" Hannah asked, twisting in her folding chair to look up at Terri, a red ribbon trailing from her hand.

"My new watch just stopped," Terri answered, surprised her daughter had heard her over the chatter and giggling of the eleven other first-grade girls in the school cafeteria. Hannah's Girl Scout Brownie troop had gathered here for their meeting. Three months ago, when Hannah started school and signed up to be a Brownie, Terri volunteered to assist with several of the after-school get-togethers. Today, with Thanksgiving behind them and the Christmas holidays fast approaching, the girls were dressing and decorating stuffed bears to donate to an organization that would send them overseas to sick and orphaned children. Hannah's troop leader, Jana Adams, had set up the Christmas project and Terri was thrilled to be helping out, though she was feeling especially pressed for time right now.

Terri shook her wrist and glanced at the watch again. Still no luck. She turned to look at the clock mounted on the wall at the far end of the large room. Five-fifteen. The meeting was running late. Her mother-in-law, Marilyn, was coming for dinner tonight. It was Marilyn's birthday, and Terri needed to pick up a few things at the store that she had forgotten—namely a cake and candles.

"Maybe Santa will bring you a new watch," Hannah said as she struggled to tie the ribbon into a bow around the plush bear's neck.

"I think I'll see if this one can be fixed before I ask him for a new one. It's extra special to me."

"Because I gave it to you?"

"That's right, ma'am." Terri cupped a hand around her mouth, leaned closer to Hannah and whispered, "Don't tell Daddy, but it was my favorite birthday present."

Hannah giggled. "Daddy let me pick it out. He should'a let me pick out the present he bought for you, too." Holding the bear up for Terri's inspection, she asked, "Is this good?" The red bow was loosely looped, one side twice as big as the other.

"That's close to perfect!" Terri exclaimed. "Let me tighten it just a little."

After evening up the sides and securing the knot, Terri sat the bear next to an identical one with a green bow that Hannah had tied earlier. Each girl in the troop had two bears to dress; one to donate and one to keep for herself—a link to the child across the ocean whose spirit they hoped to lighten with their gift.

"Now all you need to do is dress those two cuties and we'll go home and fix Grandma's birthday dinner," Terri said, wanting to hurry her daughter along.

Hannah reached toward one of the grab bags at the center of the long table. The leader and several of the moms had sent assorted decorating materials and old doll clothes for the girls to use to adorn the bears. She dug through it and pulled out a white ruffled dress.

In the chair next to her, Hannah's best friend, McKenzie, said, "Ooh…I like that one. It's pretty."

Hannah frowned. "But what if they give my bear to a boy? Boys don't want ruffles."

"Good point," Terri said. "I'm sure you can find something else in one of the bags. There's plenty to choose from."

Hannah pulled out a brown doll coat, a tiny denim jacket, a filmy striped blouse and pink elastic-waist pants. She laid them all out on the table in front of her, studied each outfit, chose the striped blouse, then debated with McKenzie and changed her mind.

"Hannah…" Terri started to say "hurry," but then Hannah giggled over something McKenzie said and the sound of her laughter stopped Terri short.

Outside, shadows crept into the neighborhood. Those shadows, though, couldn't touch them inside the glowing cafeteria. The gathering dusk only made the room seem brighter, warmer, safe, set apart from the uncertain world beyond the long line of windows.

Terri sat back and watched the organized chaos around her, watched the twelve bright-eyed girls dressing and undressing their bears. They hummed and talked while they worked, squirmed and danced in front of their chairs. The innocent voices and laughter spread through her, warm and sweet as the hot chocolate they had sipped from paper cups at the start of the meeting. It seemed to Terri her watch wasn't the only thing that had stopped; time had, too. Something told her that this was one of those moments her mother had mentioned when Terri became a mother herself, one of those simple, perfect moments she should not rush through, but savor. Her mother had said that, later, when Hannah was grown and off on her own, these were the memories Terri would cherish most.

"Oh, look!" Hannah pulled two more coats from a grab bag, one red and one green, identical in every way except for their color. Arching one brow in a perfect imitation of her father, Kyle, she said, *"Mah-ve-lous,"* and managed to *sound* like Kyle, too. Though the coats were too small for the bears, Hannah tugged them onto the animals, zipped the zippers, then asked her mother's opinion.

"I think I know a couple of bears who've been eating ice cream with their berries." Terri poked a finger into one stuffed animal's pudgy stomach.

"Mo-om." Giggling, Hannah settled a fist on one hip and tilted her head to the side. "Bears don't eat ice cream."

"Oh, really? And how do you know this, *madame?*"

Hannah gave an exaggerated roll of her eyes. "They don't have bowls or spoons."

"Which bear are you keeping?" Terri asked with a laugh.

"Hmmm." Hannah looked from one animal to the other. "The red bear, I think. I'll give this one away." She picked up the bear in the green coat and hugged it. "Make some kid happy!" she told the stuffed animal.

Smiling and humming "Santa Claus Is Coming to Town," Terri began to clean up the work area.

Ten minutes later in the school's parking lot, she put the key into her car ignition and glanced into the rearview mirror. "You buckled up back there?"

In her car seat, Hannah grabbed for the seat belt and pulled it across her lap. "Oops, I almost forgot."

Terri started the engine and drove away from the school, waving to several other mothers as she passed. Traffic was heavy with weary workers making their way home and shoppers eager for a head start on the holiday rush.

"Look, Hannah," Terri said as they approached the red light at the last intersection before the grocery store. Fat, slushy drops fell onto the windshield. She switched on the wipers. "It's starting to snow."

"Does it snow in that place where they're sending the bears?" Hannah asked.

"Rwanda," Terri said, slowing for the stoplight ahead. "I don't think so. It's tropical there...hot and rainy. They have mountains, though. Maybe they get a little snow up there."

"I wouldn't like not having much snow. Snow's magical, isn't it, Mom? Daddy told me that."

"Daddy's right. It is magical." And cold, Terri thought with a shiver as she reached to turn up the heat. Though she'd lived in the Texas Panhandle all of her life, she still wasn't used to the often bitter-cold winters. Truth be told, she wouldn't mind if it never snowed again.

Before Terri reached the stoplight, it changed to green and she pressed down the accelerator and continued on. Glancing into the rearview mirror again, she asked, "What kind of cake do you want for Grandma's—"

The blare of a horn drowned out the rest of her sentence, and Terri's heart lurched. In the time it took to blink, she turned and saw the truck.

The shadows found them, grabbed hold, then swallowed the car whole.

CHAPTER
ONE

One Year Later

Kyle took the mail from the box then unlocked the door and stepped into the entry hall. The silence slammed into him. After four months of living alone, he still wasn't used to it. Flipping on the light switch, he shouldered the door shut behind him and started into the house. The living room and kitchen looked as bleak and cold as the weather outside. Funny, he'd never thought so before he and Terri separated. When she left to move in with her parents forty miles away in her small hometown, it was as if she took all the color and warmth in the house along with her.

These days, Kyle preferred his twenty-four-hour shifts at the firehouse to his off time at home. He'd become a firefighter just before Hannah was born. The guys at Station Number 2 were his family; he had worked and lived alongside them for the past seven years. At least while on duty, he wasn't alone. He always had someone with whom to talk and share meals. And he heard laughter from time to time, though seldom his own. Kyle wasn't looking forward to the four days off that stretched ahead.

He tossed the mail on the coffee table, then shrugged out of his jacket. Laying the leather garment over the back of the couch, he sat down and sorted through bills and promotional flyers. The envelope at the bottom of the pile shot a chill straight through him, one having nothing to do with the freezing rain that had just begun to strike the windowpanes. Harold McKay Attorney at Law. Kyle hesitated, drew a long breath and blew it out before ripping open the seal.

As he skimmed the divorce papers, he told himself he should be angry at fate or God or whatever force had stolen Hannah's life and his along with it. But Kyle had stopped cursing the heavens months ago; now he only blamed himself. Over the course of his firefighting career, he had saved more than one stranger's life, but he couldn't even save his own daughter.

Lowering the papers to his lap, Kyle leaned back and closed his eyes, remembering that terrible night of the car wreck and the phone call that changed everything. Terri's injuries were minor, but the truck that ran the intersection had hit the rear passenger side of the car where Hannah sat. Over the phone, the emergency room nurse told him his daughter had sustained multiple injuries, the worst being a clipped femoral artery that required immediate repair. Hannah was already being prepped for surgery.

The next day, the doctors said Hannah was recuperating nicely, that she would be fine, and Kyle had believed them. Why wouldn't he? His beautiful blue-eyed little girl was pale but alert. Talking. Even smiling. But on the third day, she contracted an infection that weakened the artery and they were told she would need another operation to strengthen it. Two weeks later, with the infection under control, Hannah was airlifted to Dallas so a specialist there could perform the second surgery.

Opening his eyes, Kyle scrubbed a hand across his face. He felt almost as weary as he had on that morning in Dallas as he and Terri waited for the big-shot doctor to come out and say Hannah had breezed through the second surgery, as she had the first one. But the news the doctor brought wasn't good; it was a nightmare come true. During the operation her artery had burst. Hannah had died on the table.

Kyle left the couch and went to the bathroom to splash cold water on his face. What could he have done differently? He asked that question of himself every day. Every minute of every long, dark night. *Something.* He should've done something. He was Hannah's father. Terri had been beside herself with worry. It was *his* duty to be the strong one, to protect their child. Maybe… Kyle glanced up, stared at himself in the mirror. There were dozens of "maybes"… thousands. But none of them mattered anymore. Hannah was gone. And now Terri was, too. He couldn't hold on to either of them.

Kyle left the bathroom and started down the hallway. He paused beside Hannah's bedroom door and longing ripped through him, jagged as a serrated knife. How many times had he stood here after coming home past Hannah's bedtime and looked in just for a glimpse of her? He imagined doing so now, pushing the door in quietly, seeing blond hair splayed across the pillow, her innocent features softened by sleep and the night-light's glow. He reached for the doorknob, hesitated, then lowered his hand. The room would look the same, but Hannah would not be in it.

In the months after she died, he had encouraged Terri to put their daughter's things away, told her they could do it together, thinking it would be easier for them both to have fewer reminders around of all they had lost. Terri refused, again and again. Now Kyle sorely regretted pushing her. After she moved out, he tried himself to pack up Hannah's toys and bedding, to take down the posters covering her walls, and found he couldn't do it, either.

He returned to the living room by way of the kitchen, where he found a pen in a drawer full of grocery store coupons and loose rubber bands. Lifting the divorce papers from the coffee table, he flipped to the back page, stared at the signature line. After a moment, he glanced up at the framed wedding photo on the bookcase across the room, one of him and Terri when their future looked bright. *Tomorrow.* He would sign the papers tomorrow, Kyle decided. He took them and the rest of the mail to the small desk in the corner where Terri used to sit when she paid bills.

With the papers and mail shoved aside, he reached for the phone and punched in his best buddy's number. He and T. J. Boone shared the same shifts at work and the same time off. The two men were closer than brothers and knew each other's minds so well they sometimes finished each other's sentences. Kyle could be the worst of company, and T. J. would be there, sitting silently beside him while he rode out his misery.

"Hey," Kyle said, when T. J. answered. "Is Marge still out of town?"

"Yeah, and this place is a wreck."

"You want to meet me at Smokey's for some barbecue? I don't feel like sitting home alone tonight."

"I just ate half a bag of potato chips and I'm not hungry."

"Me, neither. I could use a beer, though." Kyle sensed concern in T. J.'s short hesitation and feared his friend heard the troubled tone of his voice. He didn't want tonight to turn into a pity party. Just the thought of that happening made him cringe. He only wanted some company. "So? How about it?" he asked.

"Okay," T. J. said. "See you in ten."

A CHRISTMAS TREE COVERED with twinkling white lights filled one corner of the bar. The restaurant noise was a welcome relief to Kyle. Televisions droned from every corner of the ceiling. Happy Hour laughter trickled through the room. Glasses clinked and silverware clattered.

Kyle sat back and watched T. J. finish off a plate of ribs. Apparently, the aroma of barbecue sauce had revived his appetite.

"You're in a mood," T. J. noted, halfway through beer number two, his bald head gleaming beneath the hanging light above him. "Something bothering you?"

"Maybe." Kyle picked up his beer, avoiding his buddy's stare.

"Wanna talk about it?"

Kyle told him about the divorce papers.

T. J. set down his longneck. "You're gonna fight for her, right?"

Kyle thought about that a few seconds. "When Terri left, she said our marriage doesn't mean anything anymore. That it doesn't have a purpose without Hannah." He shrugged, irritated with himself for getting into this, for revealing too much. "I don't want the split. But, the truth is, I guess I feel the same way." T. J. frowned, and Kyle added, "You know how we were. Our lives revolved around Hannah. And now…"

What else could he say? The truth was obvious. The joy of raising their child had been the glue that held his marriage together. He and Terri married young after only four months of dating. Terri was three months pregnant when they stood in front of the preacher. They had never really been a couple; they'd always been a three-some—he, Terri and Hannah.

T. J. averted his attention to the bartender, took another drink of beer, then met Kyle's gaze. "You said you don't want the split." He lifted a bushy brow. "You still love her?"

Heat suffused Kyle's face. Nodding, he looked away.

"The two of you have been to hell. Maybe you ought to give your-selves some time to find your way back out again before you do some-thing so final."

"I don't know." Kyle shook his head and shoved his bottle across the table. "I'm not sure I could stand to keep watching her torture herself."

He'd never felt more helpless than he had in the months after Hannah's death. Helpless to rescue Terri from the whirlpool of despair that sucked her deeper and deeper into its vortex with each passing day. In the beginning, he had focused on handling the practicalities of their life that she was too despondent to face, convincing himself that's what she needed most. But his recent visit with the grief counselor the firehouse captain had ordered him to see made him realize Terri had needed a whole lot more from him. Still... "You saw how she got," Kyle said to T.J., desperate to keep his voice steady, since he was trembling inside. "It was killing me, watching her like that."

While he had desperately searched for relief from the clutch of his grief, Terri had clung to hers, combing through albums filled with photos of Hannah, endlessly watching home videos, asking anyone who'd listen all those questions that had no answers. *Why our daughter? What did we do wrong? Why couldn't we save her?*

Why hadn't *he* saved their little girl? That's what Kyle felt Terri had meant.

He and T.J. finished their beers, paid the tab, then walked out into the parking lot. The sleet had stopped falling, but the accumulation crunched beneath their boots as they made their way to their pickup trucks, which were parked side by side.

"You got anything going on tomorrow?" T.J. asked, his shoulders hunched against the chilling wind, hands crammed into the pockets of his coat.

"No. You?" Kyle opened the door to his truck, too numb to be bothered by the cold.

"Just watching the Cowboys play. Why don't you come over? Margie won't be home from her conference for a couple of days, so we'll have to settle for pizza."

Kyle nodded, grateful for T. J.'s friendship but feeling a keen sense of loneliness nonetheless. "Maybe I'll stop by."

CHAPTER
✑ TWO ✑

T
erri shivered as she stepped onto her parents' front porch.
She turned to face her best friend since first grade. "Thanks
for humoring me and walking to the diner, Donna. I needed
the fresh air."

"Fresh? More like frigid." The porch light illuminated Donna's red
cheeks and nose. With gloved hands, she tugged the edges of her
stocking hat down farther on her head. "You used to hate winter as
much as I do. What happened?" Before Terri could respond, Donna
stomped her feet and grumbled, "You owe me. I can't even feel my
toes."

"It was only five blocks. When you think about it, it's crazy
people drive anywhere in a town this size."

Donna and her husband, Jack, had bought the house next door to

Terri's parents two years ago when Donna's widowed mother died. It was Donna's childhood home, just as the house they now stood outside of was Terri's. The women had grown up only steps away from each other in the small town of Prairieview. During their childhood, they had walked to school together daily and often gossiped on the phone for hours at night while looking across at each other from their bedroom windows.

"What are you doing tomorrow?" Donna asked.

"Looking for a job. I can't keep taking advantage of Mom and Dad by living here without even helping pay the bills."

"I'm sure they don't think you're taking advantage."

The neighbors across the street had strung red-and-green Christmas lights along their roofline. The peaceful glow seemed to mock Terri's emotional turmoil. "I hear the elementary school's looking for a teacher's aide. I might have to give it a try. It's either that or move back home."

She wasn't ready for that. Everything in Amarillo reminded her of what she had lost: the public pool where she and Hannah swam every summer; the grocery store where they had shopped together; the mothers of Hannah's classmates, whom she seemed to run into wherever she went. But each time Terri pictured the alternative— being surrounded by children day in, day out as a teacher's aide here, her heart raced, and if she wasn't sitting, she had to hold on to something to keep from succumbing to dizziness. Still, jobs weren't easy to come by in a town with a population of just over twenty-five thousand. She couldn't afford to be picky. Terri had worked as a teacher before Hannah was born. And she had known Prairieview's elementary school principal all her life. No doubt, the job would be hers if she only asked for it.

"Want to know how you can pay me back for freezing my butt off tonight?" Donna asked.

"How?"

"Come to work for me at the bakery."

"I don't want you to offer me a job because you feel sorry for me."

Donna scowled. "I'm offering you a job because I feel sorry for *me*. Christmas is right around the corner. It's my busiest time of year. Last December, I almost ran my feet off trying to fill all the party orders and everything else."

And still, Donna had been there for her. Hannah died in December, and throughout the remainder of the month, as well as January, Donna had either driven the forty miles to see her every day, or at the very least called.

Terri loved Donna's bakery: the warmth, the scents drifting on the air, the cheerful jingle of the bell over the door when customers came in. Whenever she stopped by, almost every face was familiar from another time in her life—a carefree time when she was too young and thrilled by the prospect of her future to consider that it might not turn out to be perfect. Working at Donna's Oven would be a comfort, and being with her friend every day a bonus.

"Are you sure?" Terri asked, still certain Donna's offer was made more out of friendship than need—and loving her all the more because of it.

"I'd be thrilled to have you there. It would be temporary, though. Just through the season."

"That's fine. It would give me some time to decide what to do."

"I can't pay a lot, either. Minimum wage."

"That's okay, too. At least for now." Her needs weren't much. Not anymore.

"So, it's a deal?"

Terri offered her hand and they shook. She couldn't recall the last time she'd smiled, and when she did now for Donna's sake, her face felt awkward and phony, as if her cheeks might crack. "When do I start?"

"How about tomorrow?"

"I'll be there."

Donna turned to step off the shelter of the porch, then paused and looked back. "I know it's none of my business, but are *you* sure? About divorcing Kyle, I mean? It's only been a year."

Terri crossed her arms and hugged herself. She stared across at the neighbor's Christmas lights and sighed. "I've tried to talk myself out of it, but I don't see how it can work anymore. I don't know what Kyle and I *are* without Hannah. What's our purpose for being together?" Terri met Donna's gaze again. "I don't even know what *my* purpose is, why I'm even on this earth. I love Kyle, but maybe love isn't enough."

Donna placed a hand on Terri's arm, her face contorting with emotion. "But you and Kyle...I wish—"

"I know," Terri said softly, and hugged her. "After Hannah died, on the nights I couldn't stop crying, Kyle always held me until I fell asleep."

Donna stepped back, frowning. "Then I don't understand why you're leaving him."

"I never saw him shed another tear after the funeral, Donna. Not one. He wanted to box up Hannah's things, to make her bedroom a guest room. He wouldn't cry with me or talk about what happened. He would barely even mention her name. I felt...I don't know... betrayed, I guess. I still do. It's like he could just bury Hannah and go on." Her voice broke and she flattened a palm to her chest. "How can he even breathe?"

Whenever Terri had pressed Kyle to talk about Hannah's death, he'd said they would never feel like living again if they didn't allow grief to loosen the intensity of its grip on them. But Terri didn't want grief to let go, not even a little. Grief connected her to Hannah. In her mind, to let it ease would be to abandon her daughter. To forget her. How could she ever do that? How could Kyle?

"Maybe he just needs some time," Donna said.

Terri huffed and shook her head. "Firefighters pride themselves on keeping their cool during a crisis. It's a job requirement if you're going to last. Call a fireman 'calm' and you've given him the ultimate compliment." Hearing the bitterness that had crept into her voice, Terri looked down at her boots. "Hannah was his *child*. I'm sorry, I just can't admire that depth of calmness."

They hugged again, then Donna left and Terri went inside. She didn't feel like reading or watching television. She couldn't face the concern that seemed a permanent wrinkle in her parents' expressions these days. Though it was early, Terri told them good-night and closed herself in her girlhood room.

Curled up in bed under a pile of blankets, she fell asleep thinking about the Brownie meeting in the school cafeteria before the wreck, the fun of dressing the bears, that beautiful frozen moment of pure happiness. Terri had laughed a lot that evening.

She had not laughed since.

AFTER ARRIVING HOME FROM the bar, Kyle entered the house and tossed his truck keys on the desk alongside the mail. The phone rang as he headed for the couch to watch television. Kyle returned to the desk to answer it.

"Hi," a woman's voice said on the other end of the line. "This is Mary Padilla. I'm calling for Mr. or Mrs. Roxton?"

Kyle wasn't sure why the woman's young voice caused his heartbeat to kick up its pace, why the familiar sound of it filled him with dread. "This is Kyle Roxton."

"You may not remember me...." She paused before adding softly, "I'm one of the nurses who took care of Hannah before she was airlifted to Dallas."

At once, he *did* remember. Hers was the voice that had broken the news about Hannah's fever. Kyle had slept at the hospital with his wife and daughter that night. He woke in the recliner during the wee hours of the morning and saw the young nurse with the kind dark eyes standing beside Hannah's bed, checking her vital signs.

When he had stirred, Mary Padilla had shifted those eyes his direction, and in that instant, he'd seen something more in them than kindness—a level of concern that troubled him. That's when she told him Hannah's temperature had spiked.

Kyle remembered, too, the nurse's gentle way with people, how she had comforted Terri and brought frequent smiles to his little girl's face, even when Hannah was too weak to lift her head. He swallowed hard. "Of course I remember you."

"I've been thinking a lot about you and your wife with Christmas ahead. How are you?"

"Getting by." He didn't see any reason to sugarcoat the truth or to tell her about the divorce, for that matter.

"Hannah was such a sweet little girl. I'll never forget her."

"Thank you." Kyle's throat knotted tighter. Surely Mary Padilla had lost a few patients over the course of her career. The fact that she would remember Hannah and call him as the anniversary of her death drew near both stunned and touched him.

"I'm sorry to bother you," she continued, "but I received a call today from the foster mother of a little boy who was admitted toward the end of Hannah's stay. Her name is Rachel DePaul. She asked me for Hannah's parents' names and wanted to know how to get in touch with you. Of course, I wouldn't give her that information without your and Mrs. Roxton's approval, but I told her I'd give you *her* information."

"Do you know what she wants?"

"Yes." The nurse paused before adding, "I think you should call her and let her tell you."

Baffled, Kyle lifted his gaze to a picture of Hannah above the desk. "Okay." He opened the center desk drawer, took out a pen and a small pad of paper. "What's her number?"

She gave him the DePauls' contact information. "I hope you'll call them. Mrs. DePaul and her husband have something to tell you that I know you and your wife will want to hear."

"I'll call," Kyle said. "And thank you."

"Have a good Christmas. Please tell your wife hello for me."

"Sure," Kyle said. "I will."

He hung up and stared at the number he'd scribbled on the pad. Then he punched it in, but ended the call before the connection went through. He would contact the woman tomorrow. Whatever the DePauls had to say, if it involved Hannah, he couldn't bear hearing it tonight. The divorce papers had unsettled him more than he'd admitted to T.J. or even to himself. But as he put down the phone with a shaking hand, he couldn't deny the level of his distress any longer. His emotions were walking a tightrope. Kyle feared the DePauls' story might be the push that made him lose balance, sending him tumbling into a black hole with no end.

CHAPTER
⚬~THREE~⚬

Kyle stood at the DePauls' front door the following night. He drew a deep breath that, when exhaled, formed a tiny white cloud against the cold blue twilight. Another breath, and then he rang the bell.

While he waited, he drummed his fingertips against his thigh, shifted from foot to foot. When he'd talked on the phone this afternoon to Rachel DePaul, she had asked him over for dinner. The prospect of sharing a meal with strangers whose agenda he wasn't sure of made him wary.

"If you don't mind, could we just talk on the phone?" he'd asked.

"I'd really like you to meet my foster son, Shawn," she had explained. "He and your daughter struck up a friendship last year in the hospital. If you're not comfortable having dinner, how about dessert?" When he didn't answer right away, she added, "I don't mean to be so mysterious, but I'd like to tell you in person what he told me. Don't worry. It's all good."

Kyle had agreed to dessert. Right now, shivering on the DePauls' porch, he almost wished he hadn't. His heart thumped too fast, and the fist that had lodged in his chest on the day of Hannah's death clenched him even tighter than usual. What could the DePauls' foster son have told them about Hannah that he needed to hear? He didn't remember her having a friend in the hospital. His daughter was dead, and he was trying to move forward with his life. The DePauls must have no idea how painful it was to lose a child or they wouldn't put him through this. Why couldn't some people understand how much it cost him to talk about what happened to Hannah? Even Terri didn't understand.

The door finally opened, and Kyle glanced down at a thin little boy with brown burred hair, wire-framed glasses and a gap-toothed smile. Kyle felt a pinprick of pain, as he always did when he came face-to-face with a child. "Hi," the boy said shyly, shifting the stuffed animal he held under one arm until it was in front of him.

A trickle of familiarity ran through Kyle. The toy bear looked exactly like one of Hannah's, right down to the red coat buttoned tightly around it.

"Mr. Roxton?"

Startled, Kyle glanced up. A woman now stood behind the boy. He guessed her to be in her forties. She wore her brown hair short in a sleek, smooth style. Though her dark slacks and pale blouse were casual, something about them said "money"; they were as crisp as her voice, as neat and manicured as the house, the entire tree-lined neighborhood, in fact.

The woman smiled at him, and Kyle managed a small smile in return. "I'm Rachel DePaul," she said, and shook his hand. "We're glad you could make it, aren't we, Shawn?" She touched the little boy's shoulder.

Kyle followed them across polished wood floors into a den with a fire crackling in the hearth. A silver-haired man lowered his newspaper and stood when they entered the room.

"Louis," Rachel DePaul said to the man, "this is Kyle Roxton. Kyle, my husband, Louis."

Louis DePaul. The name rang a bell. The two men shook hands, then Kyle sat on the couch in front of a coffee table and made small talk with Louis DePaul and Shawn while Rachel disappeared into the next room. Minutes later, she returned with a tray of cherry pie and coffee. By then, Kyle had learned that DePaul owned one of the biggest insurance companies in town. That's why his name had been familiar.

"Shawn wasn't living with us yet when his cancer was diagnosed and he entered the hospital," Louis told him as Rachel passed around dessert, then sat in a second chair facing the couch.

Squeezed in close to his foster dad, the boy added matter-of-factly, "I lived in a group home with some other kids." Shawn wrinkled his nose. "I like it here better."

The DePauls glanced at each other. "Shawn's cancer is in remission now." The boy's foster mother delivered this news in an upbeat tone. "He's been home with us for three months."

"Congratulations, Shawn." Kyle set his plate on the coffee table. The pie was delicious, but after only one bite, his nervous stomach wouldn't allow him to eat more of it. He motioned toward the bear the boy still clutched. "Hannah…my little girl…she had a bear exactly like that."

Shawn nodded. "I know. She gave it to me."

Kyle stared at the bear and the fist in his chest opened, became wide wings that flapped wildly. All at once, he couldn't breathe. *Hannah. Oh, God.* What were these people going to tell him about her? For a year, he'd kept his composure in check, but he felt it slipping now. He shifted and reached for his coffee cup, lifted it and was horrified to realize his hand was shaking.

"Well…" Louis DePaul stood abruptly and said, "It's your bed-time, Shawn." Kyle recognized compassion in his tone. "Tell Mr. Roxton good-night."

The boy scowled. "Do I have to?"

"It's eight o'clock," his foster mother said. "You have school in the morning."

"Okay," Shawn grumbled. "'Night, Mr. Roxton."

"Good night, Shawn," Kyle said tightly. "It's nice to meet you."

As the man led Shawn from the room, Kyle avoided Rachel DePaul's eyes and attempted to bring the cup to his mouth again despite his jittery hand. He took a sip and somehow didn't spill any coffee before returning the cup to the table. All the while, Kyle felt the woman's gaze on him and sensed her pity.

"The bear is the reason I wanted you and your wife to come," she said quietly.

"Terri's out of town. At her parents." He looked at Mrs. DePaul and added, "We're separated," then wondered why he'd let that information slip out, why he even thought for a moment it would matter to this woman. She was a stranger. He could kick himself for allowing her to coax him here to talk about something so personal.

"I'm sorry to hear that." She fell silent for what seemed like minutes. Then she cleared her throat and said, "Just before Shawn became ill, he lost his mother in an accident. He didn't have any other family. Louis and I became his foster parents toward the end of his hospital stay. We're sorry we never had the chance to meet your daughter."

Kyle nodded, and the wings in his chest flapped again, so quick and hard his rib cage ached and he felt dizzy. Why was this woman torturing him? Why?

As if she heard his silent question, Mrs. DePaul continued, "Ever since we brought Shawn home, he refuses to go anywhere without that bear. Last week, he misplaced it and became so upset that I finally decided to contact one of the nurses on the pediatric intensive care unit to see if she might shed some light on his obsession with it."

"Mary Padilla," Kyle murmured.

"Yes. She recalled that a little girl had given it to Shawn during a Christmas party some volunteers had for the kids last year. She wouldn't give me Hannah's name, but she said she remembered because she'd been so amazed by your daughter's maturity and kindness. The nurse meant to tell you and your wife about the incident, but things apparently got crazy on the floor after that and she let it slip by."

Kyle remembered the party. It had taken place the day before Hannah flew to Dallas. With her infection cured, she had renewed energy. He and Terri had not known about the party in advance and they showed up late, toward the end. When they had left Hannah earlier, she'd been asleep. It was the one time Kyle had coaxed Terri to leave Hannah's side and get something to eat with him in the cafeteria. They were only gone a half hour at the most.

"Anyway," Mrs. DePaul continued, "later I asked Shawn about the girl who gave him the bear, and he told me about Hannah. During the party, she asked him where his parents were and he told her he didn't have a mom or a dad." Rachel DePaul paused, blinking back sudden tears that made her eyes glisten. "Hannah told Shawn she wanted him to have someone to hug and gave him her bear."

The wings fluttered up to Kyle's throat, wrapped around it, formed a fist again and squeezed. His eyes burned. His body trembled. He turned his head. *Hannah*. His beautiful, smart, compassionate baby. How he missed her. She couldn't be gone. How would he ever accept it?

"I know I don't have to tell you how very special your daughter was. But my husband and I...we were so touched by what she did. We wanted you to know."

Kyle propped his elbows on his knees and leaned his face into his hands. When his shoulders began to heave and his body shook so hard he couldn't stop the sobs that emerged, Rachel DePaul came to sit beside him and placed her arm around him. Tears dampened Kyle's palms. The first tears he'd shed since Hannah's funeral. He didn't try to stop them.

"TERRI?"

At the sound of her mother's voice on the other side of the bedroom door, Terri stirred and rolled over. "Come in." Yawning, she sat up and switched on the nightstand lamp. The digital clock read 10:00 p.m. She had been asleep for an hour.

The door squeaked open and her mother looked in. She wore a robe and slippers and her pink face looked freshly scrubbed. "Kyle's on the phone for you."

Terri drew a deep breath, then blew it out in a noisy rush. "Okay, Mom. Thanks." Her mother closed the door as Terri reached for the phone beside the lamp. She was surprised she hadn't heard it ring. That's how exhausted she was, how deep in sleep she'd been. Lifting the receiver to her ear, Terri said, "Hi." She braced herself for what Kyle had to say. More than likely, he had received the divorce papers by now. She hoped she wasn't in for an argument.

"Terri?" The voice at the other end of the line didn't resemble Kyle's. This man sounded emotional, vulnerable, not at all like her strong, rugged, confident husband. "Were you asleep? I'm sorry, I— I need to talk to you."

Wide awake now, Terri sat straight up in bed. "What's wrong? Are you okay?"

"I'm fine. I just—it's Hannah."

"Hannah?" A wave of panic struck Terri, and she decided she must be having a nightmare. But when she blinked, nothing changed in the room; she didn't wake up. "What are you talking about?"

"Tonight I found out something she did. You won't believe it. No, you *will* believe it, because it was just like her." His voice wavered and he added, "She always cared so much for other people."

"What is it? You're scaring me."

"No, Terri, it's amazing. Just like she was. Our little girl..."

Stunned to hear Kyle sobbing, Terri pushed the blanket aside. Her husband was crying. *Crying.* And he wanted to talk about Hannah. A wave of emotion rose in her, too. How many times had she hoped for this? Prayed for it? "Tell me," she whispered, pressing the phone receiver tighter against her ear.

"I had a call yesterday...."

By the time Kyle finished telling her about meeting the DePauls and Shawn, about the story they had told him, Terri was wiping tears from her cheeks. "Hannah made that bear the night of the wreck— right before it happened," she explained, then told him about the Brownie Christmas project.

"Where were the other bears donated? The ones the girls didn't keep?" Kyle asked, a spark of curiosity in his voice that Terri hadn't heard for far too long.

"I can't remember the details. Jana Adams coordinated the whole thing. She was Hannah's troop leader, remember? She lives a couple of streets over. Her daughter is Madeline. The little redhead."

"Yeah, I think I do remember her." Awkward silence stretched between them. Just when Terri thought she couldn't stand it anymore, Kyle said, "Well, I thought you'd want to know about Shawn. I felt better after I left the DePauls'; I'm not sure why. They didn't tell me anything about Hannah I didn't already know. Not really."

"I know what you mean. She always did have a big heart." Terri drew her lower lip between her teeth, amazed by the sudden change in Kyle, his openness with her. Most of all, his need to talk about Hannah—something she had given up on ever happening.

"I hope hearing about Shawn helps you, too," he said.

Terri wasn't sure anything could ever do that. But still, the story of Hannah's generosity with Shawn did feel like a sort of gift, another beautiful memory she'd cherish forever. "Kyle…thank you."

"Sure." The sound of his sigh rushed across the line. "I got the divorce papers."

"I wondered…."

"I haven't signed them yet." He was quiet for a moment before adding, "I will soon, though. I promise. If that's what you want."

Squeezing her eyes shut, Terri leaned back against the pillow, unable to respond.

"Ever since you left," Kyle continued hesitantly, "I haven't been able to concentrate much. Not even at work. The captain…he…" Kyle cleared his throat. "He suggested I talk to a grief counselor.

Ordered me to, really. And, well, I went. Only once," he hastened to add.

Terri swiped a tear from her cheek with the back of one hand. "I think that's great. I hope it made things better for you."

"Maybe. I don't know. One of the things the lady talked about was that people mourn in different ways." After another clearing of his throat, Kyle said, "I didn't let you grieve like you needed to. I'm sorry about that. Really sorry."

Terri knew how difficult the admission must be for her proud, private husband, how tough this entire conversation must be for him. She pictured Kyle alone in their empty house, broken and hurting, and her heart went out across the miles to him. "It's okay," she said just above a whisper.

"No, it isn't. I shouldn't have pushed you like I did. I should have talked about everything with you. It's just—I couldn't stand watching you fall apart. The counselor…she said a lot of men turn their grief inward and I guess that's what I did. I wanted to be strong for you."

"You don't have to tell me any of this."

"I want to." Kyle's voice broke. "I feel like I failed you. Hannah, too."

"Hannah?" Stunned by his admission, Terri said quickly, "You didn't. Why would you think something like that?"

"Maybe she wouldn't have gotten an infection if I'd insisted they take her to Dallas on the night of the wreck. She could've had the first surgery at a bigger hospital…a better one."

"Hannah got good treatment in Amarillo. She had good doctors—"

"Maybe if I'd quizzed them more about the second operation before they went through with it. You know, weighed the risks."

"There wasn't a choice, Kyle. Besides, I didn't do any of that, either."

"You were by her side every second. I should've been the one to take care of the rest. I should've been smarter about handling things. I wanted to be a rock for you and Hannah."

"Oh, Kyle…" Sick inside, Terri pressed her fingers against her lips. Had she played a part in making him feel so inadequate? So guilty? "You *were* our rock. You always have been. You did the only thing you could by putting your faith in the doctors. We both did. And they did all they could, but they aren't miracle workers. What happened to Hannah was no one's fault."

"But—"

"Afterward, you took care of all the things I couldn't. The funeral. Everything."

"You needed more than that. I was too busy trying to find a way to make you happy again when it wasn't time."

Terri cried quietly for a while, then said, "I'm sorry, too. I thought you were being insensitive, when you were only trying to be strong for me."

"I miss you. I wish you'd come home and—"

"Don't. Please, Kyle. I can't." Terri turned off the lamp and curled up beneath the blankets again, watching the moonlight stream through the window. She ached to comfort Kyle, to hold him and feel his strong arms around her, to look into his dark eyes and let him see how much she still loved him. But after the comforting ended, what would be left for them? "I'm starting a new job here tomorrow. I'll be working at the bakery for Donna through the holidays."

"Why?" he asked quietly, and she knew he wasn't asking about the job, but about her reluctance to try to make their marriage work.

She didn't have the answer he needed. She didn't have any answers. Terri only knew that she couldn't go back. Things would never be the same for them. "Too much has happened. We—" She struggled to find her voice. "We aren't whole without her. We'll never be whole."

The sorrow in Kyle's sigh traveled across the line. "I don't know, Terri. Maybe you're right."

CHAPTER
∽ FOUR ∽

"You awake over there?"

Kyle turned away from the firehouse's meeting-room window. "Hey, Cap," he said to the station's captain, Bill Riemer. "Yeah, I'm awake. Why?"

"It's eight-fifteen," the older man answered in his usual gruff manner. "You think you got special privileges or somethin'? The others are already on the treadmill. What's your excuse?"

"Just catching the morning news before I get started," Kyle fibbed. Though the television was indeed on, he had not been listening. He'd been staring at the bustling street outside, trying to see a future without Terri in it. What he saw was a big, chaotic world that left him feeling empty and lost.

Cap nodded toward the television, his mustache twitching. "Sorry to break it to you, but I don't think you got the legs to pull that off."

Kyle followed his gaze to the program on the screen, where a female fashion model strutted down a runway wearing a skimpy skirt and heels. He reached for the remote control and turned off the TV. "Guess I wasn't paying attention."

"You've been doing that a lot lately." Squinting and chewing on a toothpick, the burly, middle-aged captain tilted his head and studied Kyle. "Did you see that shrink?"

"Yeah," Kyle answered, with a slight defensive lift of his chin.

"And?"

He shrugged. "We talked."

"When's the next appointment?"

"Haven't scheduled it yet."

"Here." Cap tossed something toward him. "Use my phone."

Kyle caught the cell before it could hit him in the forehead, then tossed it back. "I don't need to see her again."

"So you're all straightened out now, huh? That's how come you're watching fashion shows and not hearing half of what's said around here?" He pointed his toothpick at Kyle. "You either keep seeing the shrink or take some time off. I should've seen to one or the other a long time ago. You're an accident waiting to happen."

"I'll call later."

"When?"

"Tomorrow."

Cap glared at him.

"Okay, this afternoon. After the school visit." He and T.J. would be leaving in a couple of hours to teach three classrooms of first-graders the old stop, drop and roll.

"Get outta here." Cap jerked his head toward a hallway that led to the small firehouse gym. "You gotta keep your girlish figure for the latest spring fashions."

Sending a smirk Cap's way, Kyle started off to join the others, but only made it halfway down the hall toward the gym before the alarm sounded. Once, twice, three times. Three alarms meant they had more than a house fire in store. Kyle heard a scuffling of feet and, within seconds, saw T.J. and the rest of the team rushing toward him. Turning, he ran ahead of them back through the meeting room and on toward the lockers for his turnout gear.

TERRI PLACED A TRAY of cookies into the oven as Donna pushed through the bakery's kitchen doors. "Nelda Jansen says hi."

Closing the oven, Terri turned and lifted a brow. "What else did she say?"

Donna headed to the work station and the bowl of dough she had deserted earlier in order to wait on the minister's wife. "You really want to know?"

"No, but tell me, anyway."

"She said you and Kyle should have another baby."

"Figures. That woman never could mind her own business."

"She means well."

"I guess."

Though it was ten in the morning, thanks to the weather Mrs. Jansen was their first customer of the day. The temperature remained in the teens and icicles hung from the tree branches like crystal tears. A beautiful, magical sight, when viewed from a window while tucked away, warm and cozy, inside.

Donna began humming "Dance of the Sugar Plum Fairy."

"The *Nutcracker* ballet starts this week. Jack has business in Amarillo tomorrow. He's going to buy tickets while he's there. You want to go with us?"

"I don't think so, but thanks."

Terri imagined all the mothers and daughters that would fill the audience and envy twisted her stomach into a knot. Hannah had loved the ballet. It had been a Christmas tradition she and Terri shared exclusively since the year Hannah turned three. Kyle was "not a ballet kind of guy." That's what he'd told her when Terri tried that first time to coax him to go. She hadn't minded. She had explained to Hannah that it would be their special "girl-thing." Each year, they'd made a Saturday afternoon event of it: dressing to the nines, going to lunch beforehand, then out for a warm gooey dessert afterward. Last year, they had attended the ballet for the final time on the Saturday before the wreck.

"Oh, come on," Donna coaxed. "You've always enjoyed it. It'll be fun."

Terri trained her gaze on her hands as she used a cookie cutter to make more cookies in the shape of Santa. "It wouldn't seem right."

Donna stopped pounding the bread dough on the butcher-block table and glanced up. "Enjoying it, you mean?"

Terri nodded. She didn't have to add, *without Hannah*. She knew her friend understood what she'd meant.

"You're allowed to enjoy your life," Donna said. "There's no shame in that."

Since working here the past few days, Terri felt as if she was receiving free counseling sessions. She wasn't complaining. Donna had never shied away from mentioning Hannah, and Terri appreciated that. It helped her to talk about her feelings with someone who loved her, someone who had loved her daughter, too. And Donna was always honest with her without being pushy; Terri needed honesty, a gentle "talking to" from time to time, as her dad called it. "I'd feel guilty," she admitted as her face flushed with heat.

"You know," Donna said after a couple of minutes, "there are better ways to keep Hannah's memory alive than clinging to your grief. Ways that would honor her."

Terri went still, rocked by her friend's words, the truth in them. "The college tuition your parents paid for those three hours of Psychology 101 was money well spent."

Donna smiled. "Yeah, I missed my calling. Or maybe I'm just as big of a buttinsky as Nelda Jansen."

"No." Terri shook her head. "You always tell me what I need to hear, whether I like it or not. That's one of the things I love most about you."

Donna blushed. "Aw, shucks."

After filling the large cookie sheet, Terri started on another, switching to the bell cookie cutter this time. *Was* there another way to keep Hannah's memory alive? A way that would honor her daughter's life and allow Terri to heal and find peace?

The timer sounded. She paused to take the baked cookies out. Warmth and the scent of cinnamon wafted over her when she opened the oven. "Kyle called the other night," she told Donna, careful not to let her voice reveal the conflicting emotions colliding inside her.

"Oh? How is he?"

Terri told her about the phone call, about Kyle's meeting with Shawn and the DePauls. About his tears and the regrets he'd expressed. When she finished, she looked up at her friend, and the hope she saw in Donna's eyes made her feel more conflicted than ever.

"That's beautiful…what Hannah did. You should be so proud of her. I am."

"Yes," Terri agreed. And in that instant, a certainty swept through her like a balmy summer breeze on this coldest of mornings. The answer she sought, the way to heal while honoring her daughter's life and memory, was tied to Hannah's loving act toward Shawn. Tied, somehow, to the bear she gave a little boy in need to bring him comfort, though she was frightened and hurting, too.

THE APARTMENT BUILDING was old and small: ten wood-frame units, five upstairs and five below. It was still standing after the fire was out, though the smoke damage was so extensive, Kyle thought it would have to be demolished and rebuilt, anyway, if the landlord planned to continue renting the place out.

Grimy and hot in his yellow turnout gear despite the bitter cold, Kyle lowered his mask, took off his helmet and accepted the cup of water someone handed him. He could still smell the choking stench, feel the heat on his face and back, heat so brutal in its intensity it had penetrated his gear. A small crowd had gathered on the street and their thrill over the excitement of the fire still buzzed in the smoky air as they watched the ambulances and speculated about the victims—two apartment occupants who had been trapped on the upper floor when the truck arrived on the scene. One was an elderly man confined to a wheelchair in 206, while the other in 207 was a sleeping young mother-to-be who worked nights. Cap had brought the old man down, and Kyle, the woman, while T.J., Mosely and Jimmy manned the hoses and extinguished the fire.

A man a few years younger than Kyle pushed through the gathered group of onlookers and rushed toward him, his eyes wild and his blanched face twitching with panic. "My ex-wife—" His hand shook when he pointed to the second floor of the complex. "She lives up there." The man's voice rose an octave as he added, "She's pregnant."

"We got her out," Kyle hastened to assure him. He gestured to the nearest ambulance. "They're about to take off for the hospital so a doc can check her over."

"Is she okay?"

"She seemed to be. Just shaken up."

"What about the baby?"

"I'm not sure. If you hurry, you can catch the paramedics. They can tell you more than I can."

The young man turned and ran toward the ambulance.

My ex-wife, he had said, yet the fear and love Kyle had seen on the guy's face had seemed to be as much for her as for the baby she carried. Kyle watched him go, watched him climb into the back of the ambulance, and he wondered what happened to people. Why did couples who still cared for each other let go so easily when life got tough? When they needed most to hold on to each other?

Kyle couldn't erase that question from his mind on the ride back to the station. It continued to gnaw at him while he showered. By early evening, after he'd rescheduled the elementary school visit and kept his promise to Cap by making a second appointment with the grief counselor, the question had struck a nerve and made him angry. Angry at himself.

Kyle sat back and flipped to *A* in the phone book. Ever since he'd met with the DePauls, then talked to Terri the other night, something else had preyed on his mind—the bears Hannah and her Brownie troop made. Kyle felt a real nudge to *do* something, but what? The only thing he knew for certain was that the nudge came from Hannah, and that it was a push in a positive direction. Now he wondered if that direction might lead him to a solution regarding his marriage. Lead him to that place he had been desperate to go since Hannah's death. That elusive place where he and Terri might find joy in living again, joy in each other. Where he would see her smile and feel like smiling, too. Where he might hear her laughter—a sound he missed every single day.

Kyle knew he not only had to do something, but had to do it soon. The young divorced couple at the fire had brought him to his senses. Terri was slipping away from him, and he wasn't willing to let her go. Not if there was a chance he could hold on, a chance he might find a way to pull them back together. He had to at least try.

He scanned down the list of Adamses in the book until he came to a Carl Adams on Persimmon, a street in his neighborhood. He wasn't sure what he had in mind, but for some reason, talking to Hannah's Brownie leader seemed like a place to start. He'd go from there. He punched in the number and, when Jana Adams answered, introduced himself.

"Yes, Kyle. How are you? It's been a long time."

He heard a familiar note of apprehension tinged with pity in her voice. Even after a year, acquaintances who knew about Hannah's death were wary of talking to him and Terri. No one knew what to say. He understood. Countless times in the past when faced with someone else's loss, he'd experienced the same uncertainty. "I'm doing okay," Kyle said. "I was hoping you could give me some information. Terri reminded me that you were Hannah's Brownie leader." He asked about the charity project the troop participated in last year.

"The stuffed animals the girls made were donated to a charity called Bears Without Borders," Jana told him. "It's an organization out of Boston. They deliver the bears and other toys to orphanages and children's hospitals all over the world."

"Do you happen to know where they sent the bears Hannah's troop made?"

"To a hospital in Rwanda." She paused before asking, "Is something wrong?"

"No." *For the first time in a long time, something's right,* he thought, feeling Hannah's gentle nudge again. "I'm just curious. I guess because the project was the last thing Hannah did before the accident."

"Check out their Web site. It might answer your questions. Do a search for Bears Without Borders and it should pop right up."

"Thanks, Jana, I'll do that." He started to tell her goodbye, then hesitated and said, "Terri told me that making those bears meant a lot to Hannah. And the one she kept..." In the past, Kyle never would have shared something so personal with a virtual stranger, but his instincts told him to do so now, and for once, he didn't fight them. He told Jana about Shawn and his meeting with the DePauls.

"Hannah was always such a sweet girl. She was a good friend to Madeline. Madeline misses her. So do I."

"Thank you. Me, too," Kyle murmured.

"How's Terri? I can't remember the last time I saw her."

"She's living in Prairieview with her parents." Kyle took a deep breath, blew it out. "We're separated."

The woman sighed. "I don't know what to say."

"It's okay. The separation…it's only temporary."

He ended the call, surprised by what he had just told Jana Adams, clinging to the hope that it was true. And determined to make it so.

CHAPTER
❧ FIVE ❧

Adrenaline hummed through Kyle as he punched in his in-laws' number on the phone; he hadn't felt such a sense of anticipation in a very long time. His mother was cooking him dinner tonight and he had to leave soon to go to her house.

But first he needed to talk to Terri. Two days ago, after playing phone tag half the morning, he had finally reached a woman named Aviva Presser at Bears Without Borders. They'd had an informative conversation and had talked again this evening when Kyle had called with more questions. Ms. Presser had been nice enough to answer all he asked without asking *him* about the source of his curiosity. Good thing, because he wasn't sure why, lately, stuffed bears seemed to consume his thoughts day and night. He had told her about

Hannah; Kyle assumed she understood that his sudden obsession was somehow connected to his daughter.

Only an hour ago, after they'd hung up, Kyle had suddenly figured out why he was so focused on the organization and its work—an idea had been taking shape in his subconscious. It was fully formed now, and he couldn't wait to share it with Terri.

After a short, somewhat awkward back-and-forth with his mother-in-law, Terri got on the phone and Kyle told her about his calls to Bears Without Borders.

"That's funny," she said. "I've been thinking a lot about Hannah's bear project, too. Why did you call them?"

He looked out the back window at the swing set he'd yet to take down, and a thread of sorrow wove through him. The empty swings hung limp in the still, frigid air. "This is going to sound crazy, but ever since I met Shawn and found out about that bear, I've felt like I need to do something. Something related to what *she* did."

"That doesn't sound crazy, at all. I've been thinking the same thing."

Kyle hoped he wasn't imagining what he heard in her voice— a renewed sense of hope as fragile yet as pure as what he felt in his own heart.

"What did you find out?" she asked.

"The organization is only a few years old, but thanks to word of mouth and some good publicity, it's really taken off. At first they had to search out places to send the toys, but now they're getting requests from all over."

"How do they get the toys where they need to go?"

"Early on, they teamed up with Massachusetts General Hospital. Some of the resident medical students go through something called a Global Health rotation, where they spend time working in other countries. They delivered the toys for them."

"They don't anymore?"

"Yes, but the organization has outgrown the resident program as their only shipping method, so they're trying to find more ways to get the toys delivered."

"Sounds like a huge undertaking."

"With some pretty high hurdles along the way, what with Customs regulations in developing countries and a lot of other red tape. But they haven't turned down a request yet. With Aviva Presser's level of enthusiasm, I'm sure she'll find a way to keep up with the growth."

"Where are you headed with this?" Terri asked, a surprising hint of playful distrust coloring her voice.

"Why do you ask that?"

She made a huffing sound. "I know that tone. You're preparing me for something."

"*Man.* I never could fool you." At that moment, Kyle physically ached to close the distance between them. He imagined the squint of her sky-blue eyes, the tilt of her head, golden hair draping over her shoulder. He wanted to tease her face-to-face like he used to, wanted to touch the little crease that always formed between her brows whenever she was suspicious. Taking a breath, he said,

"Ms. Presser…the woman I spoke with…she said they've had a couple of people volunteer to make overseas deliveries for them."

"And?"

"I was thinking I might offer."

"To deliver stuffed bears to some developing country? Are you kidding? How? What about work? And the expense? Will they pay for the trip?"

"I don't know if they'd pay or not. But if I offer to do this, I'd want it to be my gift. They need all the help they can get, financially and otherwise."

"But——"

"Cap's been hinting I should take a leave of absence. I only missed a few days of work after Hannah's death, and he thinks I need it. You know, to get my head straight again. And we still have the money we saved for Hannah's college. If you're okay with it, I could use my part to finance the trip." His chest tightened as he added, "I'd make the delivery in honor of Hannah."

"Oh my gosh," Terri murmured. "That's perfect. I've been wondering for days how I could keep her memory alive and honor her." She sighed, then asked him, "When would you go?"

"I don't know yet. I didn't even come up with the idea until less than an hour ago. I'll have to call Bears Without Borders again tomorrow and see what they think." He paused, then asked quietly, "What do *you* think?"

"I think it would be a beautiful tribute to Hannah. Use all the money in the account, Kyle. My part, too. She would've wanted it to help other kids." Terri's voice wavered. "You'd be reaching out to comfort someone in need, like she did. She never lost sight of what was important. Even when she was going through such a tough time."

"No," Kyle murmured. But they had—he and Terri; he sensed she was thinking the same thing. Living life to the fullest was important. Their marriage was important. They had let grief overshadow those realities. At six years of age, their daughter had possessed more wisdom and strength than either of them.

"That little boy's comfort meant more to Hannah than her own," Terri said.

Too emotional to speak, Kyle trained his focus on the swing set outside. When he could talk again he said, "I think giving Shawn that bear *did* comfort Hannah."

"I wish I had half her courage. I wish—"

"Come with me." Before she could say no, he continued, "Hannah sent us a message through Shawn and that bear. I want you along if I get to make this trip. But with or without you, it's something I have to try to make happen." *For Hannah,* Kyle thought. *For us.* "If the organization is okay with it, will you go?"

"I need some time—"

"Think it over. I'll e-mail you the link to the Bears Without Borders Web site. Take a look at it. I'll call you back after I talk to them." A flutter of white at the window caught Kyle's attention. "It's snowing here again," he said.

"Here, too," Terri murmured.

"I bet you're tired of it. I know how much you hate snow."

"I don't so much anymore." Her voice sounded so far away, and again Kyle wished her into the room. "It reminds me of her," Terri said. "Such a miracle...so magical."

"I said that to her once. That snow was magical."

"I know. She told me. Hannah loved you like crazy, Kyle. You were a good father. The best."

"I hope so. I loved her, too. So much." *And you,* he thought. *I still do.* But he couldn't manage to squeeze the words from his throat.

Though Kyle didn't speak for a long stretch of time, *couldn't* speak, Terri remained on the line, the soft sound of her breathing a comfort as he watched lacy flakes drift down around the swaying swings outside their living room window.

AFTER DINNER, TERRI EXCUSED herself, then went to her parents' home office and logged onto the computer. She pulled up her e-mail account, and as she expected, Kyle had already sent her the link to the Bears Without Borders Web site. She clicked on it, and a little of the same energy and anticipation she had heard in Kyle's voice skimmed beneath her skin. Anticipation and hope. Hope for a future she'd thought was lost to her. A future in which she might embrace life again, even while missing Hannah.

If she and Kyle followed through with his idea, they would carry forward in Hannah's memory the act of comfort and caring she had started with Shawn. At the thought, a drop of pure happiness squeezed through a place inside her that Terri believed she had sealed off tight. The drop trickled through her, startling her as the Web site appeared on the monitor. She sat back to catch her breath, stunned by the tiny unexpected spread of warmth that filled her body like sunshine. Real happiness had not been present in her world since that moment after Hannah's first surgery when she'd been told her child would recover.

Terri mentally plugged the leak in her heart so no more drops could fall. How could she feel any happiness, any joy at all, when her daughter was dead? She didn't deserve to. Not when Hannah would never experience such an emotion again.

Tense with guilt and shame, Terri sat forward and moved the mouse to the top of the screen with a shaking hand. The words "Bringing toys and smiles to children who need them…" were printed above another link for a photo slide show. She clicked on it, and the wide, dark eyes of a child gazed into hers. A child at a hospital in KwaZulu-Natal, South Africa. The girl seemed to look straight into Terri's soul and see the raw wound there. Something shifted inside of Terri. The slide changed, and then there were more sick children, a group of them, all holding a bear, all smiling, some more weakly than others.

The dam inside Terri broke and peace spilled out, drowning her tension and shame, her guilt, as the water moved faster, grew wider. She stared at one child, then another, and heard Hannah's laughter deep within her core, felt it race through her, carried along by the rippling stream, cleansing her, releasing her. And she sensed that her daughter would not want her to shut off happiness or try to hold it at bay; Hannah would be thrilled that her mother's heart was beating a little faster, that Terri's brain was swirling with possibilities. If only she could find a way to move forward.

"Such magnificent eyes," Terri murmured through tears that felt like fresh rain on her face. *Someone gave you something to hug. What could be more important?*

She drank in the sight of each child, quenching her thirsty soul, adding more water to the stream, turning it into a river.

"DON'T FORGET TO CALL Donna to tell her I won't be in today," Terri reminded her mom and dad at sunrise. The three of them stood in the entry hall, her parents in their pajamas, Terri dressed, with her purse slung over one shoulder.

"Take my cell phone and you can call her," Terri's dad grumbled. "I still don't know why you gave yours up." He turned and headed for the kitchen to get it.

Terri didn't make any explanations. She had told him numerous times that the cell phone seemed too extravagant an expense after she and Kyle split. Though Kyle tried to send her money all the time, she refused it. She was pinching pennies these days.

"I wish you'd let Daddy take you." Pulling her robe sash tighter, Terri's mother frowned. "The roads are icy."

"I called DPS about the highway. They said it's clear. It's supposed to get above freezing this morning and stay that way through the evening."

"Why do you need to leave so early?"

Because I couldn't sleep...I'm too wound up and excited, Terri thought, but didn't say so. She hadn't experienced excitement in so long, she was almost afraid to admit to the feeling, afraid someone would tell her she was mistaken, that something else caused her pulse to race—too much sugar or caffeine, not enough exercise.

She placed a hand on her mom's arm, hoping to reassure her, understanding all too well the misery of worrying about your child. Terri reminded herself that even though she was an adult, she would always be her parents' little girl. "I promise I won't take any chances, Mom. I'll drive slowly. It's only forty miles."

"Try to start home before dark," her dad said as he reappeared in the entry hall and handed her his cell phone.

"I'll try." She opened the door and cold air rushed in.

"Tell Kyle hello," her mom called as Terri stepped onto the porch. "Call us when you get there."

"You kids try and work things out." A hint of flustered embarrassment tinted her father's words.

"You two belong together," her mother added hesitantly.

Terri paused and glanced back at her parents in the doorway, and just for an instant, she imagined that they were she and Kyle, the way they might've been twenty years from now, seeing Hannah off with words of advice on a snowy day, if life had taken a different turn. She hadn't explained to her mom and dad what she wanted to talk to Kyle about. Of course they would assume it had to do with the divorce. Maybe they thought that she was going to see him to reconcile. Terri hated to mislead them, even by her silence. But she didn't want to take the time now, nor did she have the heart, to tell them they were wrong. She still wasn't sure if any future for her would include Kyle. They had married only because she was pregnant with Hannah. Hannah had been their purpose, the foundation of their life together. Maybe they each needed a new life now—apart from each other—before they could truly move on.

"Dad…" Terri struck a pose, placing a fist on one hip and narrowing her eyes. "Are you trying to get rid of me?" she teased.

His scowl deepened, and he sputtered, "Yes, and no." He winked at her, and she winked back—their longtime father-daughter tradition.

Fifteen minutes later, she called her parents from the road to let them know that the highway was indeed clear. Then she called Donna. Her friend didn't pry about why it was so urgent that she see Kyle. Donna just sounded pleased by the plan. "Why don't you spend the night?"

"Because there's no reason to."

"I can think of one very good one."

"Donna…" Terri sighed and rolled her eyes. "Kyle has to start another twenty-four-hour shift in the morning, anyway. He'll want to go to bed early."

"Like I said…"

The flutter that Donna's insinuation stirred in Terri's stomach felt as strange to her as the happiness she'd felt last night. "We're just going to talk."

"About something good, I hope."

"It's good. But it's probably not what you think. I'll tell you about everything when I get home."

They hung up, then Terri considered calling Kyle to let him know she was coming. But, in the end, she decided against it. She had some things to think through, some things she wanted to be sure of before she spoke to him. And until Terri rang their doorbell, it would not be too late for her to back out.

DRESSED IN A SWEATSHIRT and old jeans, Kyle sat on the couch in front of the morning news while having a breakfast of black coffee and cereal. He tried to ignore the emptiness he sensed in the house. Now that he had a mission, he felt better, but even that didn't fill the silence whenever he was home. Nothing drove away the chill or brightened the drab rooms.

When the doorbell rang, the sound gave him a start and dread clutched his gut. It was too early for visitors. He set his bowl on the coffee table and left the couch, telling himself not to be so paranoid. Any number of people might be outside his door: the paperboy wanting to collect, an overly eager door-to-door salesman, a neighbor needing to borrow something. Still, his heart continued to beat at a thunderous pace. Ever since Hannah's death, he braced himself for bad news whenever the phone or doorbell rang at odd hours; he couldn't seem to reason himself out of it.

Kyle was as surprised to find Terri on the porch as he would've been if an entire crew from Reader's Digest Sweepstakes had been standing there with a million-dollar check made out in his name.

"Hi...come in. It's freezing out there." He stepped back to let her through, and his heart continued to bang like a drum. "Don't you have your key?"

"Yes, but I didn't want to barge in." She hesitated before brushing past him.

Kyle closed the door. "It's your house. You wouldn't be barging."

Terri didn't argue. She unbuttoned her coat, removed it, hung it on the hall tree, then hesitated a second before heading for the living room. "Sorry to show up at this hour. I know I should've called first." She turned to him, and they locked gazes briefly before she glanced away. "I couldn't sleep so I thought I might as well get an early start."

"I've been up awhile. No problem." Terri sat in her old favorite chair, the chintz one that she always complained needed to be reupholstered. The one Kyle navigated to sometimes in the middle of the night when he missed her so much that he couldn't sleep. How many times had he sat there in the dark, breathing deeply, hoping desperately to catch a hint of Terri's scent on the threadbare fabric? Kyle tried to steady his heart and thoughts as he settled on the couch, facing her. "What's up?" He held his breath, warned himself not to hope, but hoped, anyway. *Say you want to come home. That you miss me. That we can make this work.*

She sat straight and stiff as a pencil as her eyes scanned the room, touching on everything in it except him. "Have you called yet about making that overseas delivery?"

"No. I'll call later this morning. Why? Did you look at the Web site?"

"Yes." She brushed lint off the chair's arm, then looked at him, her eyes clear, a little anxious, and so beautiful Kyle almost couldn't breathe. "If they agree, I want to go with you," she said.

It wasn't what he had hoped to hear, but still Kyle was pleased; he wanted to share the experience with Terri. He felt sure the trip he envisioned would benefit not only the children at the other end of the line, but the two of them, as well; it was a start. "Good," he said cautiously, afraid one wrong word might change her mind. Leaning toward the coffee table, he picked up his bowl. "How about some cereal?"

Terri relaxed her posture a little and looked smug as she glanced at the bowl, then back at him. "Sugarcoated, no doubt."

He shrugged, trying his best not to let his expression reveal how much he wanted to cross to her chair and put his arms around her. "Is there any other kind?"

She drew her lower lip between her teeth, released it. "You have any eggs in the fridge?"

"I think so."

Terri stood. "What do you say I make us a *real* breakfast?"

Kyle caught her gaze and, this time, didn't let go. For several seconds they simply looked at each other. Then he stood, too, and said, "I'll help you." This was what he'd missed the most—the small daily intimacies of marriage. The two of them making a meal together, making plans for the day, teasing each other.

Kyle followed her and, when they entered the kitchen, noticed at once that the room no longer looked so bleak or felt so cold with her in it. To Kyle it seemed as if Terri had brought him an early Christmas present. She had made the house feel like home again.

CHAPTER
∼ SIX ∼

Three Weeks Later

Terri ordered tacos, and when the waitress left the table, sat back and took a sip of iced tea. Their plane back from Boston had landed a half hour ago, and she and Kyle were grabbing a quick bite of lunch before Terri made the return drive to Prairieview.

They had determined it might be a good idea to meet face-to-face with Aviva Presser and her husband, Erez Lieberman, the founders of Bears Without Borders, before finalizing plans for a trip to Cambodia, where they would deliver bears to an orphanage outside of Phnom Penh. Faith in each other was crucial; Aviva and Erez needed complete confidence that Terri and Kyle would represent them well as "Bear Ambassadors," and in turn, Terri and Kyle needed to trust them to make certain arrangements with the orphanage before their arrival. While at the meeting in Boston, the four of them had discussed details—what to pack, what shots were required, Cambodia's safety issues and the climate. Terri and Kyle saw photos the orphanage director, Ms. Fremont, had sent, and learned the facility was less than a year old and still testing its legs, so to speak. Toys weren't the only need, not by a long shot; the orphanage was also in short supply of clothing and food, school and medical supplies. They talked about places to stay and eat that the director had recommended, the length of the overseas flight...and the cost of all that.

Kyle and Terri came to the conclusion they should discuss things over a couple of days before letting Aviva and Erez know one way or the other if they would go. Then they did a little sightseeing, spent the night at a quaint hotel and left Boston this morning.

"I won't go," Terri told Kyle now, and took another drink of her tea.

"You have to. I want you to. We'll figure something out." Kyle reached into the bowl at the center of the table and took out a tortilla chip. He dipped it into the salsa and said, "I guess I should've realized a weeklong trip for two to Cambodia on top of this jaunt we just took to Boston was going to cost more than what we have saved in Hannah's account. I'm sorry."

"It isn't your fault. I didn't think it would cost so much, either. But one of us should go, and I'm not sure I'd be comfortable traveling there alone."

"We're both going." A note of finality rang in Kyle's tone. "Like I said, we'll figure something out."

Across the busy restaurant, someone called Kyle's name, and Terri followed her husband's gaze to an attractive middle-aged couple and a small boy wearing glasses. They approached with smiles on their faces.

Kyle stood as the family paused beside the table. "Mr. and Mrs. DePaul, it's great to see you." He looked down at the boy. "You, too, Shawn." Kyle introduced them to Terri.

Terri turned her attention to Rachel DePaul after the introductions. "I've wanted to pick up the phone and call you so many times."

"I've wanted to do the same thing." The woman's eyes brimmed with compassion and understanding.

Terri shifted to Shawn. "I'm Hannah's mom," she said, and had the strongest yearning to hug him. "You met her in the hospital, remember?"

He drew closer to the DePauls and nodded.

"I'm so glad she had you for a friend." Terri noticed he wasn't carrying the bear anymore, and hoped that meant he was getting better emotionally as well as physically; Shawn certainly looked like a healthy child. "Did you have a good Christmas and New Year's?" she asked.

He gave another shy nod.

"How about you two?" Rachel asked Terri and Kyle.

They glanced at each other, then Terri said, "Christmas was low-key, but good." She had spent it with her parents, while Kyle had gone to his mom's. Terri had missed him more than she ever imagined. He still had not signed the divorce papers. At least, she hadn't heard from her attorney that they had arrived in the office. Kyle never brought up the subject. Neither did she. Terri wasn't sure why and wasn't ready to analyze the reasons she hadn't pressured him to get it over with.

"Since I last saw you," Kyle told the DePauls, "some good things have been in the works." He told them about contacting Bears Without Borders, the trip to Boston, the financial snag holding up their plans to visit Cambodia and his certainty they would find a solution.

"Keep us posted," Louis DePaul said, looking thoughtful. "I'd like to hear how the trip goes."

"Yes," Rachel agreed. "I think what you're trying to do is fantastic." She pulled her foster son closer to her. "We have some exciting news, too, don't we, Shawn?"

Shawn blinked up at her, then said, "I'm getting adopted." He looked from Mrs. DePaul to her husband. "I'm going to be their kid forever."

Terri wasn't sure how she could be happy for these people and still experience such a hard tug of envy. But both emotions battled inside of her as she and Kyle congratulated the new family.

After the DePauls said goodbye and left the restaurant, Kyle and Terri ate, then headed for the house. Terri had parked her car in the garage, and she planned to get it and drive back to Prairieview immediately. She had accepted the teacher's aide job at the school there on a temporary basis and would start the day after tomorrow.

Halfway home, Kyle's cell phone rang and he picked up. Terri tuned out his conversation. She was disappointed that the trip to Cambodia might not work out, at least not for her. But more than that, she was dreading leaving Kyle. The past two days she had spent with him had made her realize just how much she'd missed him in her life. They had had separate hotel rooms in Boston, but more than once during the night, she had been tempted to knock on his door and tell him she wanted him to tear up the divorce papers, that she wanted to move home. She wasn't sure what held her back. Uncertainty, perhaps. Fear that she had been right. That, without Hannah, they would discover their marriage was incomplete and always would be. That they had no purpose together without their daughter to raise.

"Terri," Kyle said, and she turned to see that he was no longer on the phone. He lifted his brows. "You'll never guess who that was."

"Who?"

"Louis DePaul. He wants to help us finance part of the trip."

CHAPTER
SEVEN

Two Months Later

Terri made her way down the narrow aisle until she reached 16A and 16B, then turned to face Kyle. "This is it. Do you want the window seat?"

"It doesn't matter to me."

With Kyle's assistance, she lifted her bag into the overhead compartment, then slid into her seat and buckled the belt.

Kyle settled in beside her and smiled. "Here we go."

"Cambodia." Terri sighed. "I can't believe it. Are you nervous?"

"No, I'm excited."

"I'm both," she admitted. "And ready."

"You and the fifty stuffed bears in the luggage hold."

The past two months had been a blur of preparation, anticipation and anxiety. Though she and Kyle continued to live apart, they had pulled together in a way they never had in the past. Both had been determined to make this journey a reality. After Bears Without Borders approved everything, there had been personal airline transportation for Terri and Kyle to coordinate, schedules at work for them both to rearrange, applications to complete and photos to take for their passports, hepatitis and typhoid shots to endure, and her parents' misgivings to soothe. Not to mention a myriad of red tape to wade through. But as the plane lifted off the runway and Terri's heart lifted along with it, she knew without a doubt that all the chaos had been well worth it.

Kyle offered his hand to her, and Terri took it, linking fingers with him. "I feel her here with us," he said quietly.

"So do I." Terri rested her head on his shoulder.

"We have a long flight. You should try to get some sleep."

"I'm not sure I'll be able to. I'm too wound up. Think about what we're doing, Kyle. We're parents who have lost their child and we'll be making a connection with children who've lost their parents. That seems meant to be, don't you think?"

"Yeah, I do."

"I can't wait to meet them. I only wish we could do more to help."

"I bet the bears will mean a lot to them. Every kid needs a toy. I get the impression some of these children have never even had one to call their own." His thumb stroked the side of her hand. "I think connecting with them is going to do as much good for us as for the kids. Maybe even more."

"It already has." Terri lifted her head and looked into his eyes. "I've been thinking about a way we might continue to help each other." Recalling what she'd read on the Bears Without Borders Web site, she added, "A way we can bring smiles to kids who need them."

"And hugs?" Kyle's eyes softened.

"Yes, and hugs," she said, and thought of Hannah hugging the bear that evening in the school cafeteria. Her daughter's sweet voice rang clear as a crystal bell in Terri's mind. *Make some kid happy!*

"What do you have in mind?" Kyle asked.

"Rachel DePaul told me there are a lot of children in the foster system right here in the States that don't have anyone to celebrate birthdays or holidays with them, or to visit them while they're in the hospital. That got me to thinking about how I'd like to continue Hannah's legacy after this trip."

He nodded, encouraging her to continue.

"I really loved working at Donna's bakery. And I'm good at it."

"I've missed your baking."

"I could make cookies and other goodies for the foster kids and put them in gift baskets for special occasions and hospital stays." Hearing her idea spoken aloud built Terri's enthusiasm. "I don't have the details worked out in my mind, and I'd have to get in touch with the people in charge of foster services to find out if anything official would have to be done. Do you think I'd need a food license?"

"I don't know for sure, but I doubt it. Either way, it's a great idea. You should follow through on it."

"I'd start out locally, but I hope it might grow into a real organization that serves other areas of the state, too. Maybe even other states." Terri watched Kyle's face, anxious for his reaction. "I thought I'd call it Hannah's Hugs."

"Hannah's Hugs," Kyle murmured and the warmth in his eyes wrapped around Terri. "That's perfect," he said.

THEY STEPPED OUTSIDE of the airport into a drizzling glaze of rain and warm, sticky air. People swarmed around them—families waiting to take loved ones home, police officers, drivers offering rides. Terri had to raise her voice in order for Kyle to hear her over the cacophony of the street. Moped horns tooted and engines revved. People chattered and called out to one another in a language as foreign to Terri as their faces.

Kyle and an airport baggage handler maneuvered the wheeled carts holding their boxes to a spot by the curb and stopped. The boxes contained the bears and some other supplies the DePauls had donated. Terri pulled the suitcases up alongside them. Through the orphanage director, Bears Without Borders had arranged for a driver to meet them and take them to the hotel. Terri scanned the crowd for a man holding a sign with their name on it.

"Over there," Kyle yelled, then pointed. Several yards away, a white sign with black letters that spelled "Roxton" bobbed above the dark sea of heads.

"I see it," Terri yelled back, and she, Kyle and the baggage handler eased their way toward it, weaving through the throng of people.

In broken English, their driver told them his name was Sim Chun. He directed them to an odd vehicle he called a "tuk-tuk." It appeared to have a motorcycle's steering apparatus and tank, with a covered open-air cabin attached to the rear fork. The cabin's interior contained two long bench seats on either side that, together, could seat six or more people. Since Terri and Kyle were the only passengers, they had plenty of room for their two pieces of luggage, Terri's overnight bag, and the boxes containing the bears and supplies. They stacked them on the empty seating area, as well as on the floor.

Once they left the airport and headed into the heart of Phnom Penh, the rain subsided. Terri held Kyle's hand and soaked in the sights. Neither spoke much, and she guessed that he was as awestruck as she by the surreal scenery—the silhouette of a templelike structure in the distance, barefoot children selling books and newspapers from baskets that hung about their necks, an orange sunset that cast a shimmering glow over the busy city's dirty, congested streets.

Bicycles, mopeds and tuk-tuks seemed the transportation of choice; few cars traveled the roads. Police officers directed traffic as Sim Chun maneuvered their tuk-tuk past open-fronted shops that spilled more noise into the twilight: voices and laughter, blaring Asian music, television programs.

Terri gazed down a wet, puddle-dotted side street lined with rickety, torn umbrellas meant to protect an open-air market from the weather. Shopkeepers closing for the day packed up unsold vegetables in one shop, bolts of cloth in another, and an assortment of other merchandise she couldn't identify as they whizzed past. Rotting garbage overwhelmed her senses one second, followed by the sweet, delicate fragrance of jasmine and something like frying bananas the next.

A short while later, the tuk-tuk turned onto the hotel grounds and Terri gasped. A long paved road led them toward a sprawling white building topped by a red roof. The front entrance rose like a temple above the rest of the structure. "I wasn't expecting it to be this nice," she told Kyle as they pulled up in front.

"Me, neither. Not for the price we paid."

Two hotel staffers came out to help with the boxes and luggage, then Sim Chun told Terri and Kyle he would return at eight the next morning to take them to the orphanage.

After they had settled into their separate rooms, Terri and Kyle met in the hotel restaurant, where they ate crab scampi and orange beef on white tablecloths. Terri was exhausted and fatigue dulled Kyle's eyes. Still, they couldn't stop talking about all they'd already seen, or wondering aloud what tomorrow would bring.

This was what she wished they could recapture forever, Terri thought, as they chattered nonstop across the table. The way they had been once upon a time when they had looked forward to a future filled with endless hopes and possibilities.

CHAPTER
~EIGHT~

S im Chun arrived right on schedule the next morning, this time in a minivan instead of the tuk-tuk. The sun blazed bright in the sky, with no rain falling as it had the previous evening. The van's air-conditioning vents blew tepid air that did little to assuage the stifling city heat. Even with the windows closed, Kyle smelled the dust rising up from the paved potholed street. Behind him in the rear seat, Terri waved a paper fan that she'd bought in the gift shop earlier.

Soon they left the city limits and the pace slowed as the paved road became a dirt track. The flat landscape looked like a patchwork quilt made of squares in varying lush shades of green, the smooth expanse of it interrupted only by an occasional clump of trees and a small winding stream.

"I feel like we've stepped back in time," Kyle told Terri as they passed a water buffalo cooling off in the muddy water and a farmer canoeing around his field. On the road's opposite side, a small herd of emaciated cattle grazed alongside a mud hut.

The driver maneuvered the van around an oxen-pulled cart, and as they passed a scattering of tin shacks, he began to answer Kyle's and Terri's questions. Most of Cambodia's people, he told them, lived in the rural parts of the country, much as they had lived for hundreds of years. Many earned only dollars a day. Countless children had lost parents to HIV, as well as land mines, millions of which still existed unexploded, left behind after the Vietnam War and the bloody Khmer Rouge regime. Sim Chun went on to confirm that the orphanage they would be visiting had only been in existence a year, and that it housed forty-three children and had many needs.

Kyle was glad he'd already relayed that fact to the DePauls. Louis and Rachel had reached even deeper into their pockets and hearts to send clothing and school supplies that Terri and Kyle would deliver along with the bears.

The van turned off the road onto a drive that led to a cluster of wooden buildings in a field where children played. When the children saw the van approaching, many of them ran to stand outside the nearest building, while several adult women gathered the others. They lifted their arms and waved, calling out in excited greeting to Kyle, Terri and the driver.

"Oh, Kyle," Terri murmured, and he reached back between the seats to take her hand. "Look at them."

The black-haired children wore clean, mismatched clothing; some were barefoot, many wore sandals. As the van pulled into the circular dirt drive, big dark eyes in beautiful, scrubbed brown faces peered into the windows, some wary, others eager and curious. "I never imagined we'd have such a welcoming committee." Touched, Kyle rolled down his window and called "Hello!" to the ever-growing group outside.

"Hi!" Terri called out to them in a cheerful voice. Kyle glanced back at her as she leaned out her window, waving vigorously.

When the van stopped and they climbed out, a tall, thin woman with gray hair stepped forward to greet them. "Welcome! I'm Sally Fremont." She shook their hands in greeting. "So you're the Bear Ambassadors. We've all been eager for your arrival. The children, especially, as you can see."

Kyle took one child's hand after another as they drew closer to him and Terri and reached up to mimic Ms. Fremont's handshake. "We've been eager to get here, too," he said. "Believe me..." He gestured at the giggling, chattering crowd of youngsters. "This makes the long flight worthwhile."

Ms. Fremont instructed some of the older children to bring the boxes, then led everyone toward the largest thatched-roof structure. The children seemed to carry Kyle and Terri along like an ocean wave as they all made their way across the patchy grass.

"I can hardly believe we're here," Terri said loudly to be heard over the singsong voices around them. "This is like a dream."

When they stepped inside, Kyle saw that the structure contained only one room with a floor made of wide polished wooden planks. Curtains had been pulled aside at the large open windows to let the air in. The entire space was cheerful, clean and breezy. Rattan cradles hung suspended from the ceiling by rope, and babies slept inside of them. On the other side of the room, small hammocks created napping places for the older toddlers.

A few teenage girls and three women presided over the infants, and they looked up when everyone came in. They took some of the infants who weren't sleeping from their cribs and drew nearer.

A boy about seven or eight tugged on the hem of Kyle's cargo shorts. Kyle stooped to talk to him, and the boy began reciting the ABCs. Kyle shot a quick glance around the room to find Terri, and saw that she was with a group of girls who were repeating English words they had learned for the visit today.

"Baby!" one tiny girl said in a chirpy tone, pointing to one of the rattan cribs. "Go sleep."

"Pretty," said a taller girl with a melodious voice. Then she reached up and touched Terri's face.

When the little boy with Kyle reached the letter *Z*, Kyle ruffled his hair and said, "Good job, bud." The boy made a silly face, then started over at *A* again.

Minutes later, with all the boxes in the building and opened, Terri and Kyle began handing out the bears while the adults in the room clapped and cheered. And as big eyes lit up and smiles slowly spread on even the shyest of faces, for the first time in more than a year, Kyle actually *wanted* to smile, too, and did. Not the dutiful smile he'd forced whenever necessary since Hannah's death, but a genuine smile that reached all the way to his soul.

Startled by a beautiful sound, one he had thought was lost to him forever, he turned to see Terri crouched down next to a girl about Hannah's age, her head thrown back in laughter. The little girl had one arm looped around Terri's neck, while clutching a bear with the other.

Kyle caught Terri's gaze and held it. Though tears streaked down her cheeks, her joyous smile warmed his heart and made his own smile spread wider. *So this is it,* Kyle thought. *The place I've been looking for.*

THAT NIGHT AT THEIR HOTEL, Terri stood outside the door to Kyle's room in her robe. She drew a deep breath, then knocked.

"Who is it?" he called.

"It's me."

The door opened and Kyle looked out, still dressed in the clothes he'd worn all day. "Is everything okay?"

"Yes." She swallowed hard, trying to dislodge the stone in her throat, and took another breath to steady her nervousness. "May I come in?"

"Sure." He opened the door wider.

Terri walked in and stood at the window. Though it was dark, she could just make out the view of the Mekong River far below. "I couldn't sleep."

"Me, neither," Kyle said. "I haven't even tried. My mind is so packed with all that happened today I'm not sleepy."

She faced him. "It was wonderful, wasn't it?"

"It was great. Those kids are something else. That was some concert they put on."

"Their voices were beautiful."

Kyle lifted a brow. "Most of them."

"Kyle…" Terri scowled at his teasing. "Ms. Fremont said they practiced two weeks to get ready for us."

He winced as he stuck a finger in his ear and wiggled it. "That guy front row and center could've used a couple more *months*." Terri's scowl quickly transformed into laughter, and Kyle, laughing, too, said, "It might've been the best concert I've ever attended."

It thrilled her to see this side of her husband again, this teasing, fun-loving side. "I'd like to go back for another visit before we leave."

"We'll plan on it."

"Kids are the same everywhere, aren't they?" She sobered and added, "It made me sad, though. From some of their reactions, I got the feeling many of them have never been given a gift before."

"They probably haven't." Kyle sat at the edge of the bed and turned to face her. He started to say something else, then dipped his chin and, blinking, looked down at his lap.

He was as apprehensive as she, Terri realized, and a sudden rush of love almost knocked her to her knees. He was the same man she'd always loved, with the same dark, mischievous eyes, broad shoulders and strong hands. Hands capable of carrying a full-grown man out of a burning building, or touching her with the utmost tenderness. But he'd been changed by the events of the past year, just as she had. And many of those changes, she suspected, would stay with him forever. He was quieter than he'd been before, but more open and sensitive when he did talk. She sensed his underlying sorrow even when he joked with her, even when he had laughed with the children today. A certain doubtfulness existed in him that hadn't been there before Hannah's accident. Doubt about life. About himself. About the future of their marriage. She intended to erase those last two.

Terri stepped closer to the bed, her heart racing as fast as Phnom Penh's traffic. "I felt Hannah there today at the orphanage, just like I did on the plane." Kyle glanced up at her then, and she continued, "At the school on the evening of the wreck, my watch stopped. The one Hannah gave me. I haven't had it repaired since, but I think maybe it's time I did."

He watched her with eyes so darkened by sadness that she almost had to look away. But she didn't; Terri looked into those eyes that had once provided her relief and comfort, a soft place to hide away from the stresses life tossed her way.

"Terri…" His quiet utterance of her name was a whispered plea.

"Hannah hugged one of the bears she decorated that night and told it to make some kid happy. That's what I felt today…Hannah hugging me and telling me to make some kid happy. But I think she was also telling *us* to be happy, Kyle, that it's okay to live again."

He held her gaze. "Are you? Happy again?"

"I was today."

"What about now? And tomorrow and the next day and the day after that?"

"I think I could be, if—" The fearful hope in his expression squeezed Terri's heart.

"If what?"

"Why haven't you signed the divorce papers, Kyle?"

He flinched, and she knew he'd misunderstood her question. "I guess I was hoping you'd change your mind and tell me to tear them up. But if a divorce is what will finally make you happy..." He turned his back to her, his shoulders slumped.

Terri rounded the bed until she stood in front of him. "Tear them up."

Slowly, he looked up at her. "I didn't hear you."

"Tear them up," she said, louder this time.

Kyle watched her for several moments, then shook his head. "No."

Terri's heart dropped. "You won't?"

"I want *you* to tear them up. And I want to watch."

Relief made her knees weak. Terri sat down beside him and they clung to each other, finally finding the comfort that had eluded them both for so long. How had she ever thought she could give up on what they shared? He held too many of her most precious memories in his soul and her heart in the palm of his hand. There had been something more substantial than mere attraction between them during their brief courtship so many years ago. Who could say if it would've grown into love had Hannah not been conceived? But the fact remained that Hannah *had* come into their lives, and they had fallen in love not only with their daughter, but with each other. That love still existed.

"Do you have any idea how much you just scared me?" Terri asked, easing away to look at him.

Kyle lifted one hand to the back of her neck, slid it up to her scalp, threading her hair through his fingers and drawing her face close to his. "Not half as much as those papers scared me. I love you, Terri. I want you in my life. Always."

"I love you, too," she murmured. "I'm so sorry I pushed you away."

"It wasn't only you…We both made mistakes."

Their lips touched then, and Terri wasn't sure if the tears she tasted were hers or his. She only knew that she couldn't stop kissing him, holding him, afraid if she let go she'd wake up and realize this was a dream.

"We have a lot of work to do when we get home," Terri said minutes later, between the kisses he brushed across her mouth.

"Work?" Kyle leaned back to look into her eyes.

"I need a partner to help me get Hannah's Hugs going."

"I'm your man." His smile warmed her as he lowered her back against the pillows and leaned over her. "But first things first. Just let me look at you." Propped on one elbow, he scanned her face as if starved for the sight of her, skimmed his fingertips gently over her lips, her cheeks, her chin and throat as if she were a delicate, precious piece of china. "God, I've missed you," Kyle breathed, and closed his eyes.

Terri wrapped her arms around him. An ocean separated her from Texas, yet she was home again. Finally. With a future full of promise. One Hannah's love would always touch. One she would share with the man she loved.

Dear Reader,

I hope you enjoyed reading about the Roxtons' journey toward healing and were as impressed as I am by the work done by Bears Without Borders. In *Hannah's Hugs,* Terri and Kyle visited the Bears Without Borders Web site and were inspired to reach out and get involved. If you would also like to know more about this real-life organization's efforts and see for yourself the beautiful, smiling faces of the children served, go to www.bearswithoutborders.org. There you can read about the work of Aviva Presser and her husband, Erez Lieberman, the organization's energetic and enthusiastic founders. This young couple's dedication and willingness to tackle any obstacle that stands in the way of their service to needy children is truly amazing. If possible, please donate to this worthy cause. You, too, can supply "toys and smiles to children in need all over the world."

    Thank you,

Jennifer Archer

Sally Hanna-Schaefer
✑—Mother/Child Residential Program—✑

It happens all too frequently: a woman is abandoned by her partner, left to cope alone with raising the children, struggling just to keep a roof over their heads and food on the table. Sadly, many of these mothers have no means of support, little education and no knowledge of where to turn for help.

Sally Hanna-Shaefer, founder of Mother/Child Residential Program, a not-for-profit charitable corporation that provides shelters and services such as counseling and educational opportunities to homeless women and children in the southern New Jersey area, knows all about how it feels to be in this situation—in the early seventies she was left with three small children, the youngest only three months. Yet this woman, who over the past twenty-five years has helped scores of families, and who likes to joke that she's helping to "change the world, one baby at a time," not only survived, but also became stronger and more resourceful and ultimately a treasure to her community.

For the first few years after her husband's abandonment, Sally provided for her family by taking care of children in her home during the day while their mothers were at work. Once her own children were in school full-time, she cleaned houses, something she continued doing to support her family even after she began work with Mother/Child. She was also a foster parent for a while, but although she says this was a natural role for her—she loves children and always wanted a large family—she worried that too often the children were not getting the individual counseling and care they required because information on their backgrounds was not provided to foster parents. Still, the experience made her realize that she had a contribution to make in helping other families. "I felt that someone should be taking care of the parents, as well as the children," she says.

Sally has always had strong ties with her church, serving for many years as a Sunday school teacher and taking part in a weekly Bible-study group. A friend who was her pastoral counselor following the breakup of her marriage and who also worked as a counselor for the Mother/Child shelter for several years was a member of that group. She remembers Sally getting the Bible-study group involved in helping young, pregnant women and women abandoned with small children, counseling and supporting them through prayer, and offering practical help and advice. Out of this grew the realization that safe houses were crucial in keeping families together.

With financial help from the West Jersey Presbytery, they were able to rent the bottom floor of a small house—"We had just enough for the security deposit and one month's rent," Sally says, "but luckily, the landlord trusted us." They operated a counseling center on the first floor, until they were able to rent the upstairs apartment in 1981. Then they started sheltering three women and their children. A really big breakthrough came in 1987, when after a long application process, they received a five-year Housing and Urban Development grant, which enabled them to buy the property, expand it with a three-story addition, and begin to operate it.

Everyone who knows Sally says this kind of effort is typical of her. A colleague who uses words like *true grit* to describe her says, "Sally will make lemonade out of any lemon you hand her. We just shake our heads—there she goes again!" Dedicated and persistent, she won't give up. She will always find a way.

In the twenty-five years since Mother/Child's modest beginning, the enterprise has grown, so that now twenty-eight families can be helped at one time, in several buildings. The women—who must be over eighteen and able to live independently—come from a variety of backgrounds, where some of the most common problems have been domestic violence, abandonment, drug and alcohol abuse. All are homeless, and pregnant or coping as a single parent. Often there is a history of rootlessness, a lack of a sense of place and direction in life. Many have embarked on destructive paths in the quest to get their needs met.

The women receive counseling and—since an important aspect of the program is the prevention of child abuse—parenting courses to help them understand what to expect of children at different ages. It is important for the families to learn how to care for one another, and respect one another. They must all learn how to change the way they have made choices in the past. They are also taught health and nutrition, shopping and meal preparation, job search and computer skills, and how to apply for housing vouchers.

In 2005, Sally merged her agency with the Center for Family Services to ensure the continuance of Mother/Child and some of its special services. Two such causes are the Mother's Arms Infant Care, which provides child care so that mothers can complete their education or get job training, and the GodMother's Blessing Shop, where program participants and community members can shop for gently used clothing and shoes, toys, strollers, housewares and other items donated by the caring members of the community.

Sally always wanted a large family, and most of her life has been spent building one. The many families she has helped, and people who have helped her along the way in achieving her dream, are truly her family. She values the appreciation expressed by so many of the young women she has helped, but most of all she rejoices in their success, especially when they, in turn, use it to help others. "One young mother, homeless with a two-year-old when she first came to us, went with a church delegation last year to help build houses in Louisiana after Hurricane Katrina," Sally says. It is stories like this that make her profoundly happy.

Sally readily acknowledges the help she has received from her own and other churches in her area, as well as from many other individuals and organizations: schools, the local Scouts and other volunteers, including her own children and grandchildren. Two of Sally's children now work with her full-time, one as her program supervisor, the other as her administrative assistant. But her biggest support is her faith. She believes that God enables people in the humblest circumstances to do great works. "You trust Him, and He empowers you—and sure enough, you find that you *can* do it!"

For more information visit www.centerffs.org or write to Mother/Child Residential Program, 682 North Broad Street, Woodbury, NJ 08096.

KATHLEEN O'BRIEN
⚬—Step by Step—⚬

⁓ KATHLEEN O'BRIEN ⁓

Kathleen wrote her first book in grade one. It was a shamelessly derivative story about Dick and Jane, and was at least seven pages long. Her mother loved it. Her first-grade teacher, Sister Anna Mary, loved it. But it would be almost three decades before Kathleen attempted another novel.

In the meantime, though, she never stopped writing. She wrote some poetry in high school, then took a newspaper job after college. She eventually worked her way up to the position of television critic before throwing it all over to follow her heart, and her husband—a fellow journalist—to make a home in Miami.

When her first child was born, Kathleen decided she had to go back to writing. As a born sentimentalist and a great believer in romance, she decided to try to write for Harlequin Books. The decision was a good one—to date Kathleen has penned more than thirty novels and is a five-time RITA® Award finalist.

Today, Kathleen lives in Florida, is still married to the same extraordinary man, and has two children she adores, though they no longer qualify as children anywhere except in her heart.

CHAPTER
～ ONE ～

I t was after midnight, and Beth Dunnett was worn out. She'd
spent the past fifteen hours moving furniture, boxes and
crates into her new apartment, and every square inch of her
body was begging for rest.

She should go to bed. Daniel almost always slept through the
night now, thank goodness, but he'd be up at dawn, bellowing with
a five-month-old's absolute certainty that his needs were the most
important thing on earth.

And they were, at least to her. Her whole world revolved around
meeting Daniel's demands for shelter, for food, for love. He was her
mission, her reason for living a life that had almost stopped feeling
worthwhile.

So she should sleep, to be ready for him when he called.

But though it had been an exhausting day, it had also been terrifying. Someday this apartment, built above the three-car garage of a large Elmhaven Acres estate, would feel safe to her. Like home.

But not yet. She'd spent the past week visiting, first with Tilly and then alone, for longer and longer periods of times. She'd walked the rooms, planning where to put furniture, carefully getting used to the place, doing all the cognitive-therapy work she'd learned.

It had helped. So did the sight of Daniel, peacefully sleeping, like a blessing on the house. Still, it wasn't one of her safe spots yet, and her heart raced slightly at the thought of getting into her own bed.

Instead, she remained curled up on the window seat in the spare bedroom, which during this hectic day had somehow been transformed into a nursery, and watched the snow fall in the moonlight, transforming the landscaped backyard of the main house.

She'd never seen anything as lovely as this house. Made of pale gray stone, the same as the garage, it wasn't quite a mansion, but it was large. Three stories with a tower at the north end and large, arched windows. All around it the snowflakes sprinkled like glitter onto the branches of the fir trees and turned the little rounded shrubs to sparkling snowballs.

Elmhaven. It was one of the most elegant suburbs in Middlefield, New Jersey, an address she couldn't ever have afforded if it hadn't been for the generosity of the man who owned the house. According to Tilly Argent, who ran the shelter where Beth had been living, Middlefield businessman Scott Mulvaney owed her a favor. Tilly had done a little arm-twisting, and he'd agreed to lower the rent and give one homeless mother a chance.

So far, Beth had seen her landlord just once. This morning, as she'd been lugging the crib up the stairs, double-teaming it with Tilly, who always found time to help her "graduates" move into their new homes, she'd seen him across the yard, climbing into his car.

A brief glimpse, no time for more. She'd had to focus on the tricky steps, or she might have tripped and broken the crib to bits, not to mention her own skull.

But he'd looked like a nice man. Tall, fit, brown hair, easy smile as he waved hello and goodbye together, then zoomed off, probably on his way to work. Beth had been conflicted. She wanted to thank him, but the idea of approaching a complete stranger was enough to send a shiver through her, from head to toe.

Almost one in the morning now. She shut her eyes and tried to feel sleepy. From up here, it seemed as if the whole world was sound asleep, completely at peace. No roaring traffic, no drunken arguments, no sirens close enough to make your heart race.

Nothing but the whisper of fairy-dust snow. The silence was beautiful—and yet, at the same time, so unfamiliar it was disturbing.

The truth was, she couldn't remember a single truly silent night in her whole life.

Not when she was a child, when her mother had kept the television going to drown out her father's tempers, brought on by liquor madness. Not when she was with Tony, who would laugh with his friends into the small hours, then stumble back to their bedroom and shake her awake, just to accuse her of cheating on him.

And not even when she was at Loving Life, the shelter she'd lived in for the past year. It had been heaven, compared with the rest. But she'd shared her quarters with three other mothers and their children, and someone was always awake, colicky or feverish or crying. Mourning a lost dream, or an absent daddy.

Tonight, the only sound in the entire world was the occasional breathy sigh as Daniel wriggled against the teddy-bear-printed sheets and settled back down into his dreams.

She slipped off her shoes, then went over to the crib and reached in to adjust his blue blanket. It was so soft beneath her fingertips, almost as soft as Daniel's velvety cheek. She had a blanket just like it in her own room. And the amazing thing was, she'd made them both herself. Mary Michaelson, who taught knitting to the mothers at Loving Life, had refused to listen when Beth protested that she was all thumbs.

She'd picked up Beth's hands and held them to the light. "Nope," she said. "Just as I thought. Perfectly normal. So turn off the self-destructive tape you're playing in your head, sweetheart. Pick out a color and let's get started."

Knowing Daniel was a sound sleeper, Beth allowed herself the luxury of brushing her fingertip against his cheek. His full pink lips pursed once, dreamily obeying the instinct to nurse, and then relaxed.

"We'll be okay here, duckie," she whispered. "Somehow, we'll make this work."

Finally, she yawned. Surely she could sleep now. She turned on the baby monitor, repeating *Mrs. Akers* in her head as she flipped the switch. She'd done that all day, with everything she placed in the apartment. She'd said the name of the person who had donated it to her, so that she wouldn't ever take it for granted. So that she wouldn't ever forget that, no matter how cruel or violent some people could be, there were many, many others who were gentle and generous, tolerant and kind.

Starting with her landlord, Mr. Scott Mulvaney.

She was halfway out the door when she heard an odd sound. She turned, glancing toward the crib. Had Daniel cried out in his sleep?

But the baby was as peaceful as ever.

Her skin prickled. She listened, unmoving.

She hadn't imagined that sound.

There it was again. A muffled cry. Not in the apartment...but not too far away, either.

Heart pounding, she walked into the kitchen quietly, slid open the drawer next to the sink and extracted a steak knife. *Mrs. Breadlow,* she thought instinctively. A very nice woman who had taught cooking at the shelter.

She returned to the nursery and tugged the night-light from the outlet, plunging the room into complete darkness. Then she returned to the window and peered out into the snow-covered yard, holding the knife at her side.

Mrs. Breadlow might think she was foolish. Danger wasn't supposed to intrude on any place as safe and orderly as Elmhaven Acres. Beth knew better. Danger wasn't supposed to intrude on a little girl's bedroom, in the form of her own drunken father, either.

But sometimes it did.

She scanned the moonlit snow, which seemed as pristine and undisturbed as ever. But after a few seconds she heard the sound again, louder this time.

It sounded like someone crying for help.

Finally her searching gaze found the right spot. Maybe twenty yards from the big house, at the bottom of a sloping stretch of grass, a dark, tangled form pushed the snow into lumps of moonlight and shadow. It looked like a man. A large man, lying in an odd position, as if he'd been knocked down.

She reached up to twist the window lock, then inched open the glass. She shivered as snowflakes landed on her fingers.

"Hello?" The man lifted his face to call out again. "Can anyone hear me?"

The moonlight caught his features for an instant.

It was Scott Mulvaney.

"I'm here," she called tentatively. She leaned her head as far out the window as she could, hoping that she could be heard by the man in the snow, but not by her son, sleeping behind her. Even a sound sleeper might be disturbed by the sound of Mommy yelling.

"I'm Beth. Beth, your tenant."

The form writhed, seemed to half rise but fell back onto the drifts. A groan, and then a heartfelt curse rang out across the snowy air.

"Thank God." His voice was tight, straining. "I need help, Beth, my tenant. I think my leg's broken."

Beth gripped the windowsill, ignoring the cold air that snaked up the long sleeves of her pajamas.

"I'll call 9-1-1," she said.

"Yes. But I need to get inside. *Right now.* I'm freezing. Can you help me?"

She felt herself go numb. It sounded like a reasonable request. After all he'd done for her, surely this was not much to ask in return. Anyone would do it. Anyone would help a man in pain. No one would even think twice.

But Scott Mulvaney was asking the wrong woman. Leaving the shelter of this apartment right now…going out into a strange night to help a strange man…

That was the one thing Beth Dunnett would find almost impossible to do.

CHAPTER
~TWO~

B eth knew she probably looked like the abominable snow-
man as she picked her way across the lawn. In her hurry,
she'd thrown her puffy, hooded coat straight over her flannel pajamas. She'd stuffed the portable baby monitor in one pocket
and a flashlight in the other. She'd even grabbed her blue blanket at
the last minute, in case he needed warmth.

But at least she'd found the courage to come. He probably wouldn't
ever understand how hard it had been to leave the apartment. Tilly
might have told him Beth was an agoraphobic, but unless you'd lived
with the pounding heart, the weak knees, the tingling hands, you
couldn't imagine the struggle. He probably thought "agoraphobia"
just meant she was shy.

A stiff breeze had picked up, and the snowflakes, so gentle before, now circled frantically in the air and dashed themselves against her face. Within two minutes, she was cold to the bone. If he'd been out here long, he must be miserable.

One look at his face confirmed that. The genial good looks she'd seen this morning had vanished, replaced by a tight, grim, pale face with icy eyelashes and blue lips.

"Thanks for coming," he said. He was leaning back on his elbows, with his legs stretched out in front of him. "God only knows how long it'll take an ambulance to get here in this weather."

"They said they'd get here as soon as they could, Mr. Mulvaney. It shouldn't be more than five or ten minutes."

"Call me Scott," he corrected. He tried to smile, but it didn't quite work. "Five more minutes out here, I'll lose my toes. Ten, and they'll have to amputate everything from the neck down."

She knelt beside him, dragging the blanket from her shoulders. "Here," she said, holding it out. "Maybe you should put this on."

"Thanks. Could you do the honors?" He held up his hands. "One of these is broken, I think, and they're both numb to the wrist. I'm not even sure I could find my shoulders right now."

She looked at his hands, which were bare and did look alarmingly pale. She wondered why he had been out here, so late at night, without gloves or a suitable jacket.

She didn't articulate her questions, focusing instead on getting the wrap around his shoulders, which were so broad that her blanket suddenly seemed much smaller. He didn't have to explain himself to her. All that mattered now was getting him into his house, where he could begin to thaw out.

"Your hands are so small." He caught her gloved fingers and squeezed lightly, clearly trying to detect the bones beneath the leather. He eyed her with a frown, as if he'd just noticed how slight she was under the bulky coat. "Do you think you can hold my weight? I need something to grab onto so that I can get my feet under me."

She had been wondering that, too. She was only five-four and just over a hundred pounds, hardly a match for this man, who easily had a good ten inches and eighty pounds of pure muscle on her. If he hadn't been so clearly helpless, with his leg twisted at a dreadful angle, she probably would have found him terrifying.

"I don't know," she said. "But I'm willing to try, if you think it's wise to move."

He laughed again, a harsh sound that exhaled puffs of cold white air. "It's wiser than sitting here. That cracking sound is the blood freezing in my veins."

"Okay, then." She stood, patting her pocket to be sure the monitor hadn't fallen out. "Tell me what to do."

"Put one hand under my arm." He leaned forward. "You'll need leverage. Grab hold all the way up, under my shoulder."

It was an uncomfortable intimacy, tucking her hand under his armpit and letting him grip her by the upper arm. But he was so cold. No warmth made it through her gloves, and in the end it was as impersonal as trying to lift a mannequin.

Unfortunately, it didn't work.

The first time, he came up several inches, but she wasn't strong enough to lift him, and he couldn't get any leverage with his damaged hand. They tried a second time, and a third. Nothing worked. Finally, he dropped back onto the snow with a groan.

"I'm sorry," she said. "Is there someone else I could call? A man might—"

"It's all right." He shook his head, and she saw perspiration glisten on his forehead. He must be in a terrific amount of pain. "The ambulance will be here before anyone else could come."

She felt as if she'd failed him. "Is there anything else I can do? Can I bring you another blanket? Something warm to drink?"

"Just sit with me, if you're warm enough to stand it."

She hesitated. Instinctively, her gaze went back to the small light outside the garage apartment door. The beacon that signaled safety. "I—I don't know—"

"Please. Having someone to talk to will make the time go more quickly."

She felt like a jerk. But, once again, he had no idea how much he was asking.

"All right," she said, failing to sound quite as cheerful as she wanted to. "I can do that."

She tucked the hem of her puffy coat under her bottom, then sat carefully, mindful of the snow, which seemed to have melted, then refrozen, under him, becoming dangerously slick. "Is this okay?"

"It's great," he said, closing his eyes in obvious relief as the wind stopped blowing directly on his face. "You're an angel, Beth, my tenant. Thank you for braving the storm to come help a poor, wounded moron who doesn't even have the sense to wear a coat in the snow."

She wondered when the last time was that she'd heard her own name and "brave" in the same sentence. It felt ridiculous, especially since every muscle in her body was clenched.

"It was the least I could do. You did give me a great rent on the apartment."

She knew she sounded stilted, even kind of gruff. But it was such an unnerving situation, sitting out here in her pajamas, in a snow-storm, with a complete stranger. Fear chased away any social graces she'd ever had.

Tilly had once suggested that Beth might want to try honesty instead of fake bravado, which occasionally could be off-putting. She knew Tilly was right. But she hated sounding pitiful.

Right now, especially, honesty felt dangerous. She couldn't admit how scared she'd been to set even one foot outside the apartment. She didn't want him to think he'd let a lunatic into his life. She'd be out on the street by morning.

"Well, if you'd said no, it would have served me right." He shook his head. "I'm a damn fool, and that's the truth. When Angela finds out what happened, she'll never let me hear the end of it."

"Who is Angela? And...what *did* happen?"

"Angela's my ex-wife. She's says I'm too impulsive. It drives her crazy, since she personally hasn't indulged an impulse in about a decade. We've been divorced for three years, but we have a daughter, and apparently that gives her complaining rights in perpetuity."

He shifted, as if he wanted to edge a little nearer to Beth's warmth, which made her heart knock nervously. She couldn't sit any closer to him. She couldn't...

But abruptly he groaned, freezing in place. "God, I must have smashed that shinbone like an eggshell."

He took a couple of steadying breaths. "As to what happened," he went on, "I'm afraid this time I proved Angela right. I let my temper get the better of me."

"What happened?"

"She came to pick up Jeannie tonight—Jeannie's my daughter—and as usual, Angela was a constant stream of complaints. I was ten minutes late bringing Jeannie back, a violation of our terms. Jeannie shouldn't have had pizza again so soon. The house is a mess. The Douglas fir is going to come down on the roof in the next ice storm. I should have left more lights on in the house. I think she even blamed me because the forecast called for snow."

"Good grief." Beth didn't feel comfortable joining in the criticism of a woman she'd never met, but she could imagine how unpleasant that must have been.

Her father was a lot like that. Nothing pleased him. He seemed to think that his constant disapproval of everything and everyone was a sign of superiority. But it made everyone else feel like dirt.

"I know." Scott shrugged. "I shouldn't have let her get to me. Nothing I've done has pleased her in ten years—and most of the time

I just think it's funny. But tonight I was tired, and out of sorts because Jeannie was leaving. They're going to visit Angela's parents in Chicago. For two weeks. It feels like forever."

He heaved a sigh. "Anyhow, I let her rile me. The last thing she complained about was that I still hadn't brought the Christmas sleigh off the roof. So, like a fool, the minute she left I went up there to dismantle it. Seemed like a good way to work off some steam. No gloves, no jacket, nothing but my temper to keep me warm."

"Oh, dear."

"Yeah. Climbing on a snowy roof when you're ticked off and distracted is just about as dumb as it gets. I missed my footing and came crashing down. When I came to, I was here, with my leg in about four pieces and frostbite gnawing at my fingers."

He sighed. "The sleigh, of course, is still up there, laughing at me."

Beth slanted a covert glance at him. He seemed so...so nice, so open and self-effacing. She hadn't known that men like Scott Mulvaney really existed—men who would admit their own mistakes and even find humor in them. Men who would risk their machismo by admitting to any vulnerability, any flaws.

Out of sorts because Jeannie was leaving, he'd said. That was another thing she'd never known. Men who liked being around their children.

She felt as if she should take him to the shelter and display him to the other battered, abandoned and desperate women, like a unicorn she'd found in this snowy fairyland. Just to give them hope.

But it would probably be false hope, and they'd all had enough of that. She'd only known this man for about three minutes here. Anybody could maintain a nice facade for three minutes.

Suddenly the snow at the north side of the house began to change colors. A hint of red, then white, then red again.

The ambulance had arrived.

"I'll show them where to come," she said. She scrambled to her feet, trying not to reveal how eager she was to turn him over to someone else.

At the last minute, he reached up and caught her hand. This time she felt the warmth of his fingers. She tried not to flinch.

"Thanks, Beth," he said. "I owe you one."

"Don't be silly. I owe you, for giving Daniel and me a place to live. Lots of people would have said no." She heard her voice hardening. "Lots of people *did*."

"Then lots of people are fools. I may be dumb enough to climb up on the roof in a snowstorm, but even I know better than to turn down my very own guardian angel."

WHEN DANIEL GIGGLED, Beth's apartment filled with sunshine, warm enough to melt the snow right off the windows. Her postnatal exercise session, something she'd started at the shelter and had continued since moving in here, was a twenty-minute giggle fest.

She loved it. Daniel's beaming face definitely took the sting out of getting aerobic.

His favorite maneuver was what Beth called the "flying baby." He rode facedown on her shins while she repeatedly tucked her knees in toward her shoulders. Now that he was getting so much bigger, it was quite a workout, and it never failed to amuse him. He seemed to find it excruciatingly funny when, on the last few painful reps, Beth began to grunt and groan.

"You're getting to be as round as a pumpkin, duckie," she said as she lowered him to the floor. He squealed with laughter and rolled onto his stomach, which he'd recently learned to do. He immediately became fascinated by the fringe on his blanket, with that quick turn-around that babies specialized in.

She leaned back, panting, and ran her hand over her stomach, which was finally almost as flat as it had been before the pregnancy. Just five more pounds. Maybe if she didn't have anything but salad for lunch this month...

Unfortunately, she could smell the chicken-and-broccoli casseroles she'd put in the oven an hour ago—clearly they were browning, and almost ready.

She could picture Chrissie Allen, who taught aerobics at the shelter, raising an elegant brow to suggest that those last five pounds of baby fat would come off faster if she didn't indulge in cheesy casseroles, but Beth didn't really care.

"Some people *like* to eat, don't they, duckie?" She did a quick kiss-the-baby push-up, and planted a noisy smack on Daniel's neck, which of course set off another round of giggles. "Let's hope our landlord is one of them."

She scooped him up and arranged him in his carrier, making sure he had his red rattle, which had become his second-favorite toy, right behind his own bare foot.

Then she put the carrier on the small kitchen table, a safe distance away from the bouquet of white roses Scott Mulvaney had sent to her when he got home from the hospital two days ago, with a small note that simply read "Thank you."

He'd called, too, but Beth hadn't answered the phone. She hadn't felt ready to talk to him. She wasn't sure she was ready, even now, but it didn't seem neighborly to ignore his injury—or his flowers.

Daniel stretched wiggling fingers toward the flowers, cooing happily while she set to work pulling the casseroles out of the oven.

It was terrific how well he'd adjusted to the move. Three days here, a brand-new crib, new carrier, new everything…and he seemed to feel right at home.

She wondered if she would ever get to that point herself. Maybe, she thought, scanning the small space. It had a lot going for it. The apartment was seven hundred square feet of silent support, furnished without elegance or uniformity, but with something even better—the constant reminders of all the supportive people who wished them well and had donated so generously.

It provided privacy and independence, both things she feared she'd lost forever. And, in her tiny bedroom, the real magic—a computer into which she entered claim information for a local insurance company and actually earned her own keep.

Yes, she thought, inhaling deeply the comforting scent of bubbling cheese, this apartment might become a safe place. Perhaps the safest place she'd ever found.

Of course, that still didn't mean she could step out on the sidewalk and actually go somewhere. Like across the yard and up those steps to the back door of the main house to deliver the casserole to Scott.

She froze, the glass dish's heat steaming through her oven mitts to warm her tingling fingers. She felt her chest tightening as she pictured herself knocking on the door. Pictured him opening it— filling it with his imposing, muscular body.

No. She set the casserole down with a bang so firm it made Daniel drop his rattle.

"Sorry," she said as he fixed her with an openmouthed stare. She retrieved the rattle from the table, gave it a quick rinse and handed it back. "I forgot Tilly's rule, didn't I, duckie? Don't dither. *Act!*"

She flipped the mitts onto the counter. "Come on, Daniel. We've got to get bundled up. We've got somewhere to go right this minute."

Of course, with an infant you never did anything "right this minute." Daniel thought putting his coat and boots on was a good wriggle-and-giggle game, so it was a full half hour before she was able to get both of them into their winter gear, wrap up the casserole and make her way across the snowy yard to Scott's door.

But she did make it.

The sense of victory flushed through her as she climbed the stone steps toward the kitchen door. Daniel's carrier dangled from her right hand, and she glanced down at him, wanting to share the moment with someone. He smiled, as if he wished he knew how to say, "Way to go, Mom."

Okay. Next step. Knock.

She knocked.

She was certain that Scott was in. His black car was still in the garage beneath her apartment. It hadn't moved since the accident. The ambulance had taken him away immediately that night. When he came back the next morning, he had a cast on his leg and his arm in a sling.

Her computer desk was in front of her bedroom window, so she had seen him drive up with an older man and a woman in a white uniform, who had helped him into the house.

Since then, people had come and gone. She tried not to be nosy, but she couldn't help seeing the activity below. FedEx trucks and businessmen with satchels, and once or twice a florist with huge plants and arrangements. Including the one he'd sent to her.

At least three times in the past two days, a pizza-delivery car had pulled around to the back drive.

That's where she'd gotten the idea that he might be ready for something homemade to eat. She'd always been a pretty good cook. A prompt, well-prepared meal had been one of the few things that would placate her father, so in her house, learning to cook was as important as learning to swim if you lived on a lake.

That, and looking pretty. Her dad had always insisted on that. So had Tony. Putting on makeup and doing her hair had become second nature to Beth. Even when she'd been sleeping in her car, she'd always found somewhere to bathe and fix her hair.

She knocked again, hoping she hadn't wrestled Daniel into the coat for nothing. Surely someone was here. She smelled wood smoke coming from one of the chimneys. On the north side of the house, in the first-floor round tower room, a warm, amber light was glowing.

Finally, she heard footsteps. A tall, brunette man moved slowly by the kitchen window.

"This is it, Danny," she whispered. The butterflies threatened to swarm her stomach again, but she realized that this time it wasn't panic. It was just a fluttery awareness that her landlord was coming, and that he was a very attractive man.

"Beth!" Scott swung open the door, looking pleased to see her. He also looked about ten times as handsome as she remembered. Of course, now he wasn't half frozen and half delirious with pain.

It had been too dark that night for her to see how green his eyes were, or that his cheek dimpled on the left side when he smiled. The snow had left his hair wet and damp, so she hadn't noticed how perfectly its glossy waves framed his face.

He leaned down a little and peered at the carrier. "And this must be your son...Danny, isn't it?" Straightening, he aimed that amazing smile at her. "I'm glad you came," he said. "I've been wanting to thank you in person, but as you can see I'm a little too clumsy on this cast to tackle stairs."

She glanced down at the crutches tucked under his arms. His left leg was in a large cast, with only his toes sticking out from the white plaster. His left hand was no longer in a sling, but she could now see that it, too, had been shrouded, thumb to elbow, in a cast.

"I'm so sorry," she said. "They really were broken, then. It must have been painful."

"Yeah. A big mess. The wrist should heal fine, but the leg took a couple hours of surgery." He patted his leg cast with his good hand. "I was asleep at the time, but I'm picturing lots of superglue and safety pins."

She laughed. "I hope not. Where did you go? Sesame Street General Hospital?"

"More like the Marquis de Sade Memorial Torture Chamber. You should see the size of their hypodermics." He stepped back and held the door open. "Come on in. You must be freezing."

She almost said yes. There was something so easygoing about Scott Mulvaney. He acted as if he'd known her for years, instead of mere minutes.

Best of all, he didn't treat her like a second-rate citizen, just because she had come to him from a homeless shelter. She'd seen that attitude so often. People kept their distance, wouldn't make eye contact, as if you were somehow dirty, as if homelessness were a disease they could catch.

At the last minute, though, she couldn't do it. It wasn't that she was afraid of him personally. With that broken hand and a broken leg, he was probably the least threatening man in the entire state of New Jersey.

No, what stopped her was the same old thing, the same demon she'd been fighting ever since she first left Tony and found herself sleeping in one shelter after another. The fear of strange places. More specifically, the fear of having a panic attack in a strange place.

"Come on in," he repeated. "Actually, you showed up at the perfect time. I could really use another pair of hands. Are you any good with scissors?"

"Scissors?"

"Yeah. Or colored pencils? Glitter? Glue? Papier-mâché? I'll take any help I can get. Can you make giraffes out of clay?"

She tilted her head. "I...I don't know. Why?" She leaned forward. "Are you running a preschool in there?"

"Nope. Just trying to put on the world's best birthday party. As soon as Jeannie gets back from Chicago. She's going to be six on the fifteenth. It's the first party Angela's ever trusted me to handle, so I've got a lot to prove. But one tiny little tumble from the third-story roof and now look. I can't even hold a pair of scissors."

His smile was the most engaging thing she'd ever seen. She wanted to say yes so much it was a physical ache.

She'd love to help him impress his judgmental ex-wife, the insufferable Angela. She'd love to help him thrill his little girl.

But she couldn't. She'd caught a glimpse of the large kitchen behind him, and the shadows of other unknown rooms behind that. The vastness of his house, so strange to her, was too much.

What if she had an attack while she was inside? What if she couldn't breathe? Her lungs were already tightening, threatening to turn to stone.

She'd disgrace herself, crying, or running away, or God only knew what, and then, the next time, he'd look at her differently.

"I can't today," she lied. "I've got a ton of work to do before five. We just came to bring you this."

She extended the casserole, which was covered in shiny aluminum foil that caught the bright winter sun in flashes. "It's chicken and broccoli. I thought you might be sick of pizza."

His eyes widened. "How did you…" He shook his head. "Oh, of course, you can see from the window. Yep, I love pizza. Big, thick, disgustingly unhealthy ones. Pepperoni and hamburger and onion and anchovy. Even up in your apartment, you could probably hear my arteries slamming shut."

"I must have missed that," she said, smiling in spite of herself. "But I wasn't spying on you. It's just that my computer faces the window, and—"

"It's okay," he said, taking the heavy dish out of her hand. "You're my guardian angel. Seems only fitting that you should be watching from on high."

He was so darn nice. She felt like a heel. She shifted Daniel's carrier to her other hand and glanced over her shoulder toward the garage. "Well, I guess I should get to work."

"You sure?" He looked surprised. "We ought to get to know each other, don't you think? And I could really use the help."

He was still balancing the casserole in his one good hand. She suddenly wondered how he was going to maneuver it into the kitchen, with crutches and plaster casts.

She was well aware of how selfish her agoraphobia made her seem. She couldn't just say yes? She couldn't spare five minutes to help the guy put the heavy dish into the fridge? Or a couple of hours, even, to help him salvage the birthday party?

No. That was the sad truth about her life. She had completely forgotten how to say yes.

"I'm sorry," she repeated, the gruff tone again infecting her words, making them prickle. She saw his face change slightly, saw the friendliness drain away.

"But—"

"No. I can't."

CHAPTER THREE

"Oh, Beth," Audra Gilmore squealed. "He's getting so big! And so handsome!"

Beth laughed as she hugged Audra, the high-spirited mother of three who had been one of her favorite roommates at Loving Life. "It's only been two weeks since you saw him, silly. He can't have changed that much."

"Yes, he has! Come on, now. Let me hold him!" Audra extended her arms, and Beth handed Daniel to her without hesitation. No baby could be safer anywhere than in Audra Gilmore's arms.

Instead of moving out when she was ready to "graduate" from Loving Life's program, Audra had taken over the recently installed day care center. She loved everything about babies and children. She believed they were magic—innocence, comfort, laughter and hope bundled together.

"Well, he looks like a mighty happy little boy," Audra said as Daniel cooed up at her. She grinned at Beth. "I told you all those worries were for nothing. Don't know how to be a mother, indeed."

Beth laughed. She had said that one particularly difficult night. She had believed it, at the time. After all, her mothering role model had been pretty crummy.

As Audra scurried around showing Daniel off to the other caretakers, Beth sank into one of the rocking chairs, gratefully absorbing the day care's happy vibes.

About eight or ten children played on the floor, surrounded by brightly colored blocks and balls and picture books. The under-threes were in another room, with cribs and playpens, but out here it was a delightfully controlled chaos. Every toy seemed to beep or squeak or giggle or sing. One little boy sat at a yellow plastic table, pulling a string that made his toy announce, over and over, "The cow says mooooooo!"

One of the workers hurried over and, with a quick wink at Beth, deftly switched the dial on the toy, then headed back to pick up a spilled bowl of dry cereal. The electronic voice now said, "The horse says neigh," which brought a thumbs-up from every adult in the room.

Beth watched the teamwork with a small twinge of envy. This was her first visit to Loving Life since she'd moved out two weeks ago, and she'd missed the communal bustle of shared purpose.

She hoped she hadn't visited too soon. The shelter had been her "safe place" for ten whole months, and Tilly had urged her to resist the urge to come running back right away.

"It takes time to make a home," Tilly had cautioned as she left Beth at the apartment that first day, obviously recognizing the doubt in her eyes. "Settle in. Put your mark on it. Then, when you can come out of love, not fear, come back and tell us all about it."

Beth had thought she was ready, but the contrast between this noisy, vibrant environment, where no one faced a problem alone, and her silent apartment, where she had no counsel but her own, was dramatic.

Last night, Daniel had cried for an hour, for no apparent reason. She'd paced the four moonlit rooms over and over, singing lullabies, patting his back, offering warm formula...but nothing would soothe him. She'd driven herself half mad with anxiety. Was it something serious? Should she call the doctor?

She'd even, in one weak moment, considered calling Scott Mulvaney, but she'd come to her senses. After she'd turned down his request for help the other day, it would be unthinkably selfish to beg him to come to her rescue.

Besides, he probably thought she was an unmitigated shrew, and didn't want anything further to do with her. He hadn't tried to call again, or sent any flowers. She considered herself lucky that he hadn't sent an eviction notice.

Still, it had been hard to tough it out alone. Here at Loving Life, the large apartment units held four roommates. Each mother and child shared a bedroom and bath of their own, but the living room and kitchen were communal.

In such an arrangement, any baby who cried in the night was likely to have a couple of "aunts" stopping by to offer advice or companionship.

But then she remembered the deep glow of pride she'd felt as she laid Daniel back in his crib, finally asleep. She'd weathered the ministorm. All by herself.

True confidence wasn't something other people could give her. It was something she'd have to build for herself, one small victory, one lonely night at a time.

"Beth!" Tilly Argent's warm voice came from the doorway. "I'm so glad you're here, honey!"

Beth rose and hurried over to give Tilly a hug. The silver-haired, steely-eyed woman was wise, hardheaded and practical, but she was also warm and loving, and her hugs had healed a lot of broken hearts.

"I'm glad, too," Beth said. "I hope I didn't come too soon. I remembered what you said, but—"

"No, no, you came at exactly the right moment," Tilly said. She pulled back and took Beth's hands in her own strong, bony ones. "Jo-nell needs a ride to her job interview. Mary was going to take her, but she's gone into labor. And I'm her labor coach, so I can't do it, either. You were *sent,* honey, and just in the nick of time. Can you help us?"

Beth's heart fell. She would do anything for Tilly—all the women in the shelter felt the same way. But...

"Maybe it would be better if I take over for Audra," she suggested. "I could work here with the kids, and she could drive Jo-nell to the interview."

Tilly's all-seeing gaze scanned Beth's face. "You could do that, I suppose," she said. "But Jo-nell is extremely nervous about this interview, and you know she's always looked up to you. She'd be grateful to have you for moral support."

Beth struggled with her rising anxiety. It was true that Jo-nell, who was only eighteen, was especially fond of Beth. They had a lot in common. Both had alcoholic parents, and both had run away from abusive boyfriends. The tragic difference was that, though Tony had let Beth go without a fight, Jo-nell's boyfriend had tracked her down and threatened her here at the shelter.

Beth had just happened to be on the scene. She hadn't done anything, really, except plant herself in front of Jo-nell and order the creep off the property. It was probably the approach of Tilly and her two large Doberman pinschers that had finally sent the boy running, but Jo-nell gave Beth the credit and had worshipped her ever since.

She'd like to help, but… She thought of the bright lights of the office building and imagined her racing heart, the fight to find breath.

She gave Tilly a wry smile. "How much moral support will it be if I break down in front of her?"

"I don't think that will happen," Tilly said calmly. "But if it did, at least it would take Jo-nell's mind off her own worries."

Beth mentally ran through the other women who might be at the shelter right now. Corlie had been clean for three weeks, but Tilly wouldn't want to risk the stress. Virginia was having complications in the last trimester, and spent most of her time in bed. Patrice didn't have a driver's license.

The truth was, everyone had problems—that was why they were here. And most of their problems were even more serious than Beth's.

Maybe she should try. Maybe it was just the new challenge she needed, to take her recovery one more step. Tilly believed that Beth had been "sent" to help deal with the problem. Was that possible?

And was it possible that the challenge had been "sent" to Beth, to help her make progress in this struggle?

She glanced at Tilly's serene, elegantly tough face, with its high cheekbones and sparkling eyes. It was hard to doubt Tilly. This grandmother with a heart of honey and a spine of ice had been running this shelter for more than a decade. She'd been inspired by the Mother/Child shelter in south New Jersey, and had been trained by Sally Hanna-Schaefer, the founder of that wonderful place.

Beth had heard the stories. Through the years Tilly had faced it all—somehow finding a way to help young mothers cope with drug abuse, spousal abuse, sexual abuse, court cases, prison time and even, occasionally, true mental illness.

And of course there was always the perpetual struggle to make ends meet. But no matter what crisis arose, Beth had never seen Tilly lose her cool.

"Something will turn up," she'd say with a calm confidence that had bewildered Beth at first. But then, time and again, Beth had seen it happen. The suite of bedroom furniture donated the night before a graduate moved into a new apartment. The job offer coming the same day the judge ruled that a mother must demonstrate means of support. The volunteer who showed up looking for a way to help, just when it had seemed Tilly would have to close the shelter's thrift-shop doors.

Tilly glanced at her watch. "Beth, I need to get back to Mary. What do you think? For Jo-nell's sake, can you do it?"

Across the room, Beth could see Audra coming toward them with Daniel in her arms. The woman was making silly faces, blowing soft raspberries against his waving hand.

Daniel was giggling, of course, loving the attention. The concept of fear didn't exist for him. Not yet. Beth said a quick prayer that it never would.

But that was up to her. He was growing so fast. And as he grew, he'd be watching her, using her actions to take the measure of his world.

With a smile of thanks to Audra, Beth gathered Daniel back into her arms and held his soft warmth against her racing heart.

She turned to Tilly, who believed in her. Who believed in all of them, even when they didn't believe in themselves.

"I can try," she said.

IT WAS TRUE, WHAT ALL THE therapists and self-help books said. A lot of baby steps equaled a big, grown-up step. One victory led to another.

By the end of the day, after making it through Jo-nell's job interview and riding the bus back to Elmhaven Acres, Beth was so pumped up that she decided to knock on Scott Mulvaney's door and offer her services as party planner.

She was a little self-conscious about showing up unannounced, but in spite of the fancy house and the clearly elegant lifestyle, he was one of the most casual men she'd ever met.

If he seemed busy, or unwelcoming, as if he hadn't forgiven her for the other day, she could always say she had come to collect her casserole dish.

He answered the door more quickly this time—he must be getting used to his crutch. She had hardly framed her opening sentence when the door swung wide.

"Beth!" He looked just as pleased to see her as he had the last time, even though she had no aromatic home-cooked dinner in her hands. "I knew you'd break down and come over sooner or later. What else could you do, when I've been holding your casserole dish for ransom?"

She laughed. The twinkle in his eyes gave him a boyish charm, and that grin was positively infectious.

"Actually, I'm not just here for the dish. I wondered if you still needed someone to help with the party."

His grin broadened. "Do I still need help? Does a drowning man need a life raft?" He backed up, hobbling away from the door as fast as the crutch would allow. "Come in, come in. Quick, before you change your mind!"

He didn't know how strong that possibility was. She didn't allow herself to get too far ahead of herself. She didn't peer into the recesses of the large house, as she had before. She focused only on the kitchen, which was welcoming in a country-farmhouse way, with a pine table in the center and honey-blond cabinets lining the walls. A nice kitchen. Not pretentious, though of course it probably cost a fortune.

Lots of windows. Lots of ways out.

She positioned Daniel's carrier in front of her with both hands, took a deep breath and stepped inside.

After that, everything was much easier. She followed along in Scott's wake like a dinghy being tugged by a yacht. He offered her coffee, or an apple, both of which she refused. He grabbed one of the apples for himself, then led her into the dining room.

Apparently this was alpha base for party planning. The room was large, with high ceilings, but it seemed much smaller, crowded with dozens of overflowing boxes, large cylinders of what appeared to be paper, and bolts of brightly patterned fabric.

The table itself was littered with sketches. She glanced at them. Circus clowns, rose-garlanded horses, and big-top tents with multi-colored stripes...

He reached out and held up one of the sketches—a delightful carousel with fanciful animals. If he'd drawn these, he was a very talented man.

Tilly had told Beth that Scott had inherited Mulvaney Construction, the biggest building company in town. Their signs were on every building site within a hundred miles. In fact, when you were late for an appointment because you'd hit a construction gridlock, you simply reported that you'd run into a Mulvaney, and everyone knew what you meant.

Mulvaney was a name she associated with scaffolding and drain pipes and concrete blocks the size of elephants. It seemed an odd fit for a guy who drew like this.

"I've had a million ideas, as you can see," he said. "But they're all projects for a two-handed guy. I can't even cut out a paper tiger."

She put Daniel's carrier on the table, toward the center, where it couldn't slip off. He'd been exhausted by the big day and had dropped off about an hour ago. When they'd lived at the shelter, he'd learned to sleep through all kinds of noise, so their conversation didn't wake him now.

Now that her hands were free, she looked through the drawings. "These are beautiful. I guess your daughter has asked for a circus theme?"

"Yep. I promised her the coolest circus party in the whole world." He ran his good hand through his hair and sighed. "I'm going to look like a jerk."

"Can't you just hire a party planner?"

"Can't," he said. "That's the tricky part. Apparently Angela made some snide comment to Jeannie about how my idea of putting on a party would be to throw a lot of money at some party company and let them do all the work. Jeannie said she stuck up for me and promised her mom that I was doing every bit by hand."

Beth wrinkled her nose. "Uh-oh."

"Right. Unfortunately, Angela knows me too well. I'd been planning to do exactly that. Now, of course, I can't."

"Hmmm." Beth had to smile at the typical male dilemma. He was terrified of failing at this task. "I see the problem. But they're out of town, aren't they?"

"Yep. But now that I've given her my word…" He shook his head ruefully. "And only seven days left to pull off this miracle."

He tossed the sketch onto the table. "I shouldn't have made such grandiose promises. No Father of the Year award for me."

"Maybe not. But I bet we can pull off something decent. Something that will make your daughter happy." She saw hope dawn on his face, and it made her feel absurdly warm and pleased inside. She hoped she wasn't being just as foolish as Scott, making promises she couldn't keep.

"As you said, you've got some great ideas here," she went on, holding up the carousel sketches. "And while I can't draw a straight line myself, I'm pretty good with scissors. And I do have the one thing you really need."

"What's that?"

She held out her palms and wiggled her fingers.

He took first one wrist, and then the other, with his good hand. He appeared to study them solemnly.

Then he looked up, smiling. "You're right. Just what I've been looking for. A two-handed woman."

He kept hold of her hand, gave her about two seconds to grab Daniel's carrier and led her through the house with awkward excitement, his crutch thumping against the hardwood floor.

They didn't stop until they reached the round tower room at the north end of the house.

He opened the door, revealing a beautiful, spacious sitting room, its round stone walls set with ceiling-to-floor windows. It would be flooded with light on a sunny winter afternoon.

"I'm thinking I'll take the furniture out and make this room the big top," he said. "I'll cover the walls with life-size drawings of carousel animals—horses and swans and elephants. Jeannie loves elephants. I can sketch them on those rolls of newsprint I've ordered, and we can paint them in Jeannie's favorite colors."

Beth nodded. She had no idea what Jeannie's favorite colors were, but she didn't want to interrupt his enthusiasm.

He moved to the center of the room and waved his good hand toward the ceiling. "Streamers all the way across, all different colors, meeting in the center, coming to a point like a tent."

"Perfect," she said. She turned slowly in a circle, checking out the possibilities. "Lots of balloons, too. Caliope music, I think…and maybe a popcorn cart off to the side. A trapeze hanging from the ceiling. And you'll be dressed as the ringmaster, of course."

"Of course! I've already bought a top hat and red silk tails." He shook his head. "You'd be surprised how hard they are to find these days. The salesman at Yuppie Brothers was really quite rude."

They both laughed, the sound echoing like music against the thick stone tower walls. In his carrier at her feet, Daniel stirred. But happy noises didn't trouble his dreams, and he settled right back into sleep.

She looked up to see Scott watching her. "Thank you," he said.

"For what?"

"For agreeing to help me. For being willing to share my vision. For being *able* to. You're going to be much more than a pair of hands to work the scissors. You have such a vivid imagination."

She smiled, trying not to let the compliment matter so much. "Sometimes maybe too vivid. When your imagination works overtime, it's as easy to invent problems as it is to invent carousel horses and tumbling clowns."

His expression sobered.

Darn it. That was too personal. She wished she had bitten her tongue. Like an idiot, she had ruined the mood. If she was going to be such a downer, he'd quickly regret including her in the party.

"You're talking about the agoraphobia, aren't you?" He frowned. "Tilly told me about it. I hope you don't mind."

She lifted her chin. "Of course not. I expected her to tell you. Obviously you had to know everything about me if you were going to let me rent the apartment."

He didn't contradict her. "And as I understand it, the real problem with these panic attacks is the fear. They don't really hurt you by themselves. It's just that, because you're afraid you'll have one, you are uncomfortable going places where you don't feel safe."

She nodded. He must have read up on this. Most people had no idea what agoraphobia was all about. Maybe he'd wanted to be sure it didn't mean she was crazy.

But that wasn't fair, and she knew it. His tone wasn't at all judgmental. It expressed only a normal curiosity, and something that felt like genuine concern.

"Do you feel safe here? Will it bother you to work inside the house? I know the last time you came, you didn't want to—"

"No, it's okay," she said, gruff again in spite of herself. "I'll be all right."

She hoped it was true. She had committed to helping him, and she didn't want to fail. But somehow she didn't think she would. She liked this house.

"Honestly, I'm not quite sure why—ordinarily new places are… difficult. But here…" She looked around, as if the walls could speak and tell her their secrets. "I don't know how to explain it. I don't understand it myself."

"It's a good house," he said. "It's one of the few things I bothered to fight for in the divorce. I'm the fourth-generation Mulvaney to live here. Jeannie will be the fifth. My father always taught me that structures have personalities, and I believe it, no matter what people say. This house has happy vibes."

"Yes, it does. Just wait and see. It will make a marvelous circus."

He nodded slowly. "You really can see it, can't you?"

"Oh, yes," she said. The laughing children danced across her inward vision already…dressed as rainbowed clowns, spangled trapeze artists and bareback ballerinas. They clumsily juggled colored balls, and twisted balloons into animal shapes, and sat very still while a gypsy painted little unicorns on their cheeks.

"Of course I can see it. It will be fantastic, Scott. The party every little girl dreams of."

"Good," he said. He pointed toward the dining room. "Then bring those wonderful hands of yours, and let's get started."

CHAPTER
❧ FOUR ❧

What was that line her mother used to say all the time? Something about excessive pride. Something about a painful fall.

Beth stood at the door of the party store early the next morning, trying to remember the exact words of the quote. It seemed important somehow. She almost believed that if she could remember the quote exactly, she might be able to enter the store.

"Excuse me? Young lady? Are you going in?"

Beth looked over her shoulder. A woman with silvery-blue hair and a strangely unlined, baby-soft face stood right behind her, looking annoyed.

That's when Beth realized she was blocking the doorway. She backed up awkwardly.

"No. No, I'm sorry. You go ahead."

The woman did so, letting out a little sigh, just to be sure Beth understood how inconvenienced she'd been. Beth smelled the woman's perfume as she flounced by. The sweet, powdery scent of *Bal à Versailles.*

Tony had bought Beth a bottle of that perfume one Valentine's Day, back when they still had the occasional happy time interspersed among the bad.

But he'd broken her nose that night—for flirting with the waiter at dinner, he said. She'd never worn the perfume again. The pretty square bottle with its filigreed stopper was probably still at Tony's house, quietly going stale in the medicine cabinet.

Unless he'd given it to his new girlfriend. Beth wondered if she should call his house someday, just to see if a woman answered. If she heard a female voice, what would Beth say? How could she warn the woman?

Tony had probably already laid the groundwork, mentioning casually to his new girlfriend that his old girlfriend, her name was Beth, had been unstable.

That she imagined things.

Things like the odd splintering sound her nose made when it broke, and the bloody stars that exploded behind her eyes...

So what could Beth say? Even if she just whispered one word... just the word *run*...even then the woman would tell Tony, and he'd kiss her neck, and they'd laugh together about poor crazy Beth.

Maybe she *was* crazy. Look at her now, standing outside the party store, having taken two buses and forty minutes to get here but suddenly unable to put out her shaking hand and open that big glass door.

"Honey? Are you all right?"

This time it was a middle-aged woman, a nice woman. A woman with gentle eyes and about twenty extra pounds that said she liked to sit on the sofa at night, watching ball games she didn't care about on TV, just so that she could be with her husband.

Maybe Beth could ask her for help. Maybe the woman would hold Beth's hand and take her inside the store. Maybe, with this kind person beside her, Beth's pulse would stop racing, and her lungs would thaw, and she would be able to breathe again.

But she couldn't tell a perfect stranger her problems. That really *was* the kind of thing crazy people did.

"I'm fine," Beth said. "I'm just feeling a little faint. I just needed to rest for a second."

The woman glanced worriedly down at Daniel's stroller, where Beth had settled his carrier. He was awake, propped up against the blue-checked gingham padding, but tilted slightly to one side, because the ruffle had caught his attention.

"Do you need me to call someone?"

Beth shook her head. "No, honestly, I'll be fine. Don't let me keep you."

The woman squatted down and looked at Daniel more closely. Beth knew what she was thinking. If the mom was a little weird, was the baby okay?

But Daniel was fine, of course. No matter what else happened, Beth never neglected her son. She wanted to tell the woman that, but she knew that it would seem overly defensive, weird in its own right.

She would let Daniel speak for himself, which he did. When he noticed the lady staring at him, he squealed with delight, reaching out his two fat hands to grab her cheeks.

The woman smiled. Of course she did. Everyone smiled at Daniel. She straightened up and gave Beth a sympathetic nod.

"I know it's hard when they're so little," the woman said. "You think you'll never get a good night's sleep again. But you will, honey. He'll be grown up before you know it, so try to enjoy him, okay?"

"Yes, of course. Okay. I will."

Finally, the woman went inside. Beth took two stumbling steps backward and leaned against the shopping center wall, trying to catch her breath.

Through the bright window of the store, she could see giant bouquets of helium balloons that bumped against the ceiling, trailing multicolored ribbons. She saw life-size cutouts of Darth Vadar and Cinderella and the cowboy from *Toy Story*.

And she saw a dozen people or more, all comfortably wheeling carts up and down aisles of blue-flowered birthday plates and pink piñatas and metallic banners that cried "Congratulations!" or "Over the Hill!"

As if protected by some magic spell of normalcy, they wandered those aisles at will, without even the mildest elevation of temperature, without the slightest acceleration of heart rate.

They could do it.

Why couldn't she?

Yesterday, she had felt so strong. Yesterday, she had been the conquering hero, battling any monster that dared to show its face. Fear? Defeated. Panic? Vanquished. Shyness? Annihilated.

She'd been so proud of herself. She and Scott had worked at his dining room table until almost midnight, finishing three of the twelve carousel animals—a flop-eared bunny, a pink-and-silver pony and an elephant that looked just like Dumbo, Jeannie's favorite Disney character.

So, yes, she had been proud. And happy. Almost drunk with it. It wasn't until Daniel finally woke up, demanding a warm bottle and a dry diaper, that she'd even noticed how much time had passed.

Maybe that was the problem—she'd been high on her own successes, blowing them out of proportion, believing they meant she was stronger than she was.

Tilly had always cautioned that moderation was the key to true happiness.

There had been no moderation last night.

She still couldn't remember the whole quote. Something about pride going before a fall. Her mother used to say it when Beth was a teenager, rebelling against her father's alcoholic version of "authority."

Her mother who had no pride, who always bowed down before her father's temper, like a human sacrifice before a ravenous beast.

Beth hadn't ever been able to make her mother see the truth.

The bowing down hadn't made the beast less angry. It only whetted its appetite for more. More submission. More deference. More sacrifice.

Somehow, walking through that door right now would be like proving something to her mother, even after all these years. It would prove that it was better to be brave. It would prove that pride wasn't a bad thing. That standing up for yourself might be dangerous, but it wasn't as dangerous as lying down and being run over.

She wanted to prove those things. But she couldn't.

And so she turned the stroller around and walked back toward the bus stop.

THE COST OF THAT MORNING'S disastrous trip to the party store was still being paid late in the afternoon.

By the time she trudged up to the apartment from the bus stop, she was hungry, discouraged and drained, both physically and emotionally. And way behind on her day's work.

The company that employed her demanded that its work-from-home employees meet a quota each day, a certain number of claims to process, a certain number of diagnosis and procedure codes, patient information and payout amounts to enter.

The workload was serious—about a hundred and twenty-five claims a day—but ordinarily she had no real problem. Luckily, Daniel was an independent baby who was perfectly content to sit in his playpen at her side, playing with his own toys—and his own toes— while Mommy worked.

Not today, though. It was as if he'd caught her malaise, and he fussed all afternoon, until she had to put him in her lap and begin typing one-handed.

By six o'clock, he'd finally fallen asleep over her shoulder, and she was whipped. She clicked her monitor off and rubbed her eyes, which had focused on the computer so long they were stinging.

She ought to put Daniel in his crib and maybe lie down awhile before dinner. But she was too tired to move. She just sat there, staring out the window, soothed by the orderly charm of the winter garden.

The snow had mostly thawed now, but the remaining isolated patches sparkled in the sun like diamond anthills. The brick path that wound from the garage to the main house gleamed wetly, as if washed by the melting runoff.

Suddenly, she heard the dull rumble of approaching cars. She knew that Scott was in Boston for the day on business and wasn't expected back until after dark. She leaned forward to see if she could tell who it was.

It was not just one car, but two. She recognized the first one, the white minivan from the center that Tilly Argent always drove.

But the second…

She knew that car.

It was the cute blue compact sedan she'd seen at the used car lot. The one she'd wanted to buy.

But the loan had fallen through. Her credit history…her brand-new job…her lack of references…

What was that car doing here now?

Both cars came to a stop just outside the garage, just below her window. Tilly jumped out of the minivan with her usual vigor. Audra Gilmore climbed out of the Chevy.

Had Audra bought the car? Beth bit back a twinge of envy. But Audra had put in the time, paid her dues, built good credit. If she owned that car now, it was because she deserved it. Someday Beth would have one, too. She had to cling to that hope, and not let the jealousy monster take over.

Beth waved at the women from the window and motioned them up, glad to see them even if it meant abandoning all hope of a nap. Tilly always made her feel better.

But Tilly shook her head and waved back, clearly indicating that she wanted Beth to come down.

Beth placed Daniel carefully in his crib, slipped the monitor in her pocket, and eased herself out the front door and down the stairs.

They all exchanged hugs, and then, as usual, Tilly got right to the point.

"I can't stay," she said briskly. "But we had a surprise for you, and we couldn't wait to show you." She touched the hood of the Chevy. "Your chariot, my lady?"

"For me?" Beth shook her head. "How? They turned me down. I don't have enough credit, and—"

"You don't," Tilly said, smiling. "But we do."

Beth frowned. "What?"

Audra laughed. "You look like you've been slugged with a brick. It's not that complicated. Tilly co-signed for you."

Beth turned her dazed gaze to Tilly.

"That's right," Tilly said. "I don't have the best credit in the world myself. I'm always spending more than I have. But apparently, between us, we have enough. It's yours, Beth." She patted the hood of the car affectionately. "And so are the payments."

"But—"

"Now, honey," Audra put in with a smile, "haven't you learned yet how pointless it is to argue with the Queen?" She held out her hand. Two silver keys dangled from a ring around her index finger. "Here you go. It drives like a dream."

"No," Beth said automatically. "No, I couldn't possibly—"

"Of course you could," Tilly said. She took the keys from Audra's outstretched hand and pressed them firmly into Beth's numb palm. "You're a good driver. And you're making enough to make the payments, plus gas and insurance, which was a very real consideration. We already talked to Scott, and he said you can keep it in the garage."

She ran her hand across the shiny hood. "Pretty, isn't she? She's about five years old, but she has only fifty thousand miles on her. The mechanic said she's in excellent condition."

Beth just kept shaking her head. "This isn't right. Tilly, you can't take on any risk—"

"There's no risk," Tilly said, her voice clipped. "You'll make the payments. As soon as you get by the lot to sign the new papers, the car is yours."

"But, Tilly…"

She allowed herself to get close enough to look in the window. Blue cloth seat covers, a CD player…and even a baby car seat!

Everything would be so much easier in a car. Getting Daniel to the doctor. Making visits to the clinic.

And it was such a beautiful car. It reminded Beth of her teenage years, when she'd worked at the fast-food hamburger place, saving up to buy her own car. She'd never made it. The last time her father had hurt her, breaking a finger and fracturing her wrist on the night of her eighteenth birthday, she'd packed her clothes and moved in with Tony.

Talk about the frying pan and the fire. She never had another penny to call her own. Tony was ambitious, a time-share salesman who believed appearances were everything. After that, every penny either of them could make went to pay half the rent on a stylish apartment neither of them could afford, and a wardrobe to help Tony keep up with the "big boys" at work.

And Tony's cocaine habit, of course—though she hadn't realized it until it was too late. Not until she'd spent four years having her self-confidence shredded.

Not until she was already pregnant with Daniel.

"Tilly, you know I won't be able to use this car," she said, though every word was agony. "Who knows if I'll ever be able to just drive down the street like a normal person?"

Tilly tilted her head. "Yesterday you drove Jo-nell to her interview just fine."

"That was different. This morning, when I tried to walk into a store, I couldn't do it. I absolutely froze on the sidewalk, like a statue."

Her cheeks felt hot with the memory, though the brisk breeze out here was probably only about forty degrees. "A car would be wasted on me."

Tilly seemed to be considering that. She narrowed her eyes and gazed at Beth for a long minute.

"I hear how frightened you are," she said finally. "But I also know how hard you are on yourself. So you failed today. So what? Tomorrow, you'll try again. And the next day. And the next, until one day you'll walk right through that door and buy everything in the place."

She sounded so sure. In spite of herself, Beth felt hope rising from the ashes. "Tilly…"

The older woman smiled, well aware that she'd won the argument. Nothing new there. Tilly always won. "What?"

Beth squeezed her hand around the keys, her fingertips tingling against the metallic ridges.

"Nothing," she said. "Just…thank you. Thank you for having more faith in me than I have in myself."

"A temporary condition," Tilly said. "One day you're going to wake up and realize what a strong woman you are, Beth. And when you do, I want you to jump in that car and come tell me all about it."

CHAPTER
❧ FIVE ❧

Three days later, just two days before the party, Beth pressed the last carousel animal, a large silver-and-purple swan with a garland of pink roses around its neck, onto the last empty spot on the wall.

And voilà! The tower room was transformed. It was like standing in the center of a magical merry-go-round. As a special, secret surprise for Scott, Beth had ordered a CD of calliope music online, and even sprung for overnight shipping.

She put it on now, in the CD player on the window seat. Daniel laughed and wriggled in his carrier, holding out his hands, asking to be picked up.

"It's awesome, isn't it, duckie?" She scooped him up and held him against her chest, planting a kiss on his hair.

She began to sway to the calliope music, with him in her arms. He giggled, then dropped his head against her breast and babbled something that sounded a little like singing.

She danced in a slow circle, taking in the whimsical animals Scott had created. He'd drawn them carefully, one-handed, on the newsprint while Beth helped hold the paper steady.

Her part had been more mundane. She did the cutting out and much of the painting, while Scott supervised, choosing each color, adding a star or a rainbow here, a rose or a bird or a butterfly there, until each animal sprang to life, as if from a children's gorgeous fantasy book.

They had a dragon, a rabbit, an elephant. Two ponies, a flying pig, a swan, a squirrel, a peacock and a dolphin. All placed on paper "poles" painted in multicolored stripes, one up, one down, as if the carousel had been caught mid-motion. All strung together by garlands of pink roses.

It was messy work. She was splotched all over with silver-and-purple paint, and her blue jeans looked like a Jackson Pollock painting, but she couldn't remember ever having so much fun.

Suddenly the front doorbell rang.

She wondered if Scott had forgotten his key. Or, since he was due home in less than an hour, maybe he'd sent ahead for pizza. He seemed to enjoy any home-cooked dinners she brought over, but the meal that went straight to his heart would always be a pepperoni-and-mushroom pizza.

But the pizza guy knew to go to the kitchen door. Oh, well. Only one way to find out.

Beth switched off the music and hurried to the foyer. She took a swipe at smoothing her hair, but she knew it was hopeless and didn't much care. Scott's friends and coworkers were as informal and friendly as he was, and they all knew about Operation SuperDad.

She opened the door with a smile, but it faded from her face instantly. She didn't know the incredibly beautiful woman standing there, but she'd seen her picture. This was Angela Mulvaney.

The picture hadn't done Angela justice. It was one Scott had taken, about three years ago, just before they finally split up. They'd been out sailing. Scott loved boats, loved the water, but apparently Angela didn't. In the picture, the woman had her arms around little Jeannie, who was probably only about three.

Angela looked miserable, as if she was afraid they were seconds away from drowning.

At first, Beth wondered why Scott kept this picture, but when she studied it she understood. Though Angela looked uncomfortable, little Jeannie was glowing. The wind carried her wispy brown hair out behind her like spun sugar, and her face was full of sweet, energetic life.

"Hi," Beth said finally. The woman on the doorstep looked even more shocked than she was, and someone had to say something.

"Hello." Angela's voice was cordial but held an undercurrent of frost, like one of the last nice fall days before winter. Her disapproval wasn't quite visible, not quite a threat. It was more like an unseen power. Waiting its turn, but inevitable. "I'm sorry. Who are you?"

"I'm Beth Dunnett."

Beth shifted Daniel higher on her shoulder. He was trying to twist around and get a better look at the other woman, who wore a very enticing, sparkly diamond pendant around her neck.

For once, Beth wished her son would not fall in love with every new person he met. Angela wouldn't want baby hands, sticky with applesauce, groping her diamonds. She wouldn't appreciate baby slobber on that handsome, smartly tailored suit.

Announcing her name didn't seem to be enough, so Beth cleared her throat and continued. "This is my son, Daniel. We're renting the garage apartment. I also…I also help Mr. Mulvaney a little around the house."

There. That should satisfy the other woman. People like Angela Mulvaney knew all about maids. She could go home feeling comfortably superior, thinking how typical it was of her foolish ex-husband to hire a maid with messy hair, unkempt clothes and a dirty baby who would obviously make sure she never got any work done.

Angela looked over Beth's shoulder, toward the shadowy foyer. "Is Mr. Mulvaney at home?"

The woman sounded a little unsteady here, as if she didn't feel quite comfortable barging in without permission. Beth knew Scott didn't want her to see the party preparations before everything was ready.

"No, I'm sorry. He had a meeting with a client. I'm sure you could get him on his cell phone."

Score again. Clearly Angela had already tried that. Beth knew, from seeing it happen firsthand, that Scott usually pushed the "ignore" button when Angela's number appeared on his caller ID.

"Well, I'd like to leave a message for him," Angela said. "If that's possible."

"I'll be glad to give him any message," Beth said, though she knew Angela had meant she'd like to come inside and write one out herself. As guardian of the party secrets, Beth did not intend to move an inch from this doorway.

Clearly Angela didn't like that. She licked her full, glossy-pink lips and adjusted the strap of her six-hundred-dollar purse over her shoulder, the way a knight might adjust his baldric before riding to battle.

The effect was intimidating. Beth had never felt so inadequate. Angela was an amazingly beautiful woman. Physical perfection, from her bright blue eyes to her gym-toned calves and elegant, perfectly chosen business heels.

But she was more than beautiful. She was smart. And she sized the situation up quickly. She clearly saw that it would demean her to try to wrestle or bully her way into the home of a man she supposedly no longer cared about. She saw that her only power lay in a dignified retreat.

"Thank you," she said. "Would you tell him to send invitations to

Marlena Simmons and Ally Ross? A note apologizing for the oversight would be a nice touch. They were left off the original list."

"Yes, of course, I'll tell him," Beth said.

At that moment, Daniel took a diving leap, trying to grab Angela's diamond pendant. He loved shiny things. Beth caught him at the last minute, but she nearly tripped over the doorsill in the process. It wasn't her most graceful moment.

To her credit, Angela put out her hand to help without any obvious distaste. She caught Beth's elbow and held it until her balance was restored.

"That's a tricky threshold," Angela said. "I've asked Scott to fix it, but..."

Beth heard the disapproval in the other woman's voice. This was one of those implied criticisms Scott had mentioned. Subtle. You'd really have to listen to hear the annoyance beneath the well-bred concern for Beth's safety. But when you did hear it, you heard the poison.

Beth fought to keep her face impassive. If she defended Scott too hotly, it would just make Angela suspicious. And Scott didn't need that kind of trouble.

"Does he always come with you when you're working?"

"Yes." Beth refused to elaborate, though her instinct was to explain that Daniel was no trouble, he really did help, how he was such a good baby.

But she had no reason to feel defensive. She wasn't really the hired help. Even if she were, she had more right to be here than Angela did. Beth had at least been invited.

With a cool nonchalance, Angela leaned in slightly. "We've been out of town, so I haven't had a chance to check. Has he begun to set things up for the party?"

Her diamond swung against her breastbone, catching the sunlight. Never one to miss a chance, Daniel reached out and got the pendant in his fist, and brought it toward his mouth.

"No, no, honey," Beth murmured, tugging it free. "That's not good for babies. It would taste nasty."

Angela's face was rigid, and two deep furrows had suddenly appeared alongside the corners of her mouth. She plucked the chain between two fingers and held it away from her dress.

"Oh, dear. Applesauce does have an odor, doesn't it?" She gave Beth a tense smile. "I wouldn't mind, ordinarily. But I have a meeting in half an hour."

Beth nodded. She knew what Angela was trying to say. If she were just a little housescrub, a nobody like Beth, getting stained would be no big deal. But a professional woman like Angela...

Here was the judgmental ice queen Scott had described. Beth had thought she was ready for the put-down. She'd faced snobs before. Unwed mothers who spent three months on the street developed a shell that protected them against such people.

But against all reason, Angela's contempt hurt.

Standing next to this cool perfection, looking into those dismissive eyes, Beth felt her courage hissing away like steam from a broken pipe.

And for the first time in months she felt like the person her father had always said she was.

A loser.

THAT NIGHT, SHE SLIPPED the baby monitor in her pocket once again. She pulled thick socks over her feet, then stuffed them into her big fluffy bedroom slippers. Finally she wrapped her wool coat— *the Benson family*—around her flannel pajamas and went down to look at her new car.

The garage was very dark, with only the indirect illumination from the landscaping spotlights to brighten the gloom. It was cold. Within seconds, her fingers began to tingle. She wished she'd brought gloves, too.

Carefully, she made her way around Scott's black car.

In the second slot, over by the built-in workbench and cabinetry, was her own little Chevy, looking more gray than blue in the dim light.

She opened the door quietly and slid into the driver's seat. She'd brought the keys with her, though she had no intention of going anywhere right now. She just wanted to see how it felt to sit here, and insert the key into the ignition.

It felt good. She put her hands on the steering wheel, which was as cold as ice. She let her fingers fit themselves into the grooved plastic, and then twisted the wheel a little, from left to right, imagining herself maneuvering the car on the road.

She used to love to drive. Sometimes, when Tony let her use their car, she would take the longest possible route to her destination—the doctor, usually, or the grocery store—and then the longest route back. She'd wind around other neighborhoods, watching people water their lawns or teach their kids how to ride two-wheelers.

She would wonder…were they happy? Was happiness possible, or did everyone pretend, the way she did? Did that man, kissing his wife goodbye, sometimes slap her around at night? Did that woman, kneeling to pull a weed out of her garden, sometimes cry herself to sleep?

There was no way to find out, of course. Even if she'd stopped the car, walked right over to them and asked, they would have said yes, of course we're happy, what could you possibly mean? She might glimpse the truth, a shadowy specter behind their eyes. But she'd never really know if it was her own ghosts she saw or theirs.

The shelter hadn't answered the question, either, of course. Everyone under that roof had been chased there by ghosts.

Even Tilly. As a young woman, Tilly had been abandoned, with two children and no money. She'd found sanctuary at the Mother/Child shelter run by Sally Hanna-Schaefer, and when she got on her feet she was determined to open a shelter of her own. With Sally's training, she'd been able to do it.

Suddenly the side door of the garage opened, letting in a long parallelogram of light. Into the space stepped a man's shadow.

Funny, she thought. She knew Scott Mulvaney so well already. She could even recognize him by his shadow.

Of course, it helped that his shadow came equipped with a crutch and an oddly shaped, cast-covered leg.

She turned the key to activate the electric windows and brought the passenger window glass down.

"Hey," she called softly. "Over here."

He turned his head toward her voice. "Beth? What are you doing in the garage? It's freezing."

"Just sitting. What are *you* doing here so late?"

He moved to the car and ducked his head to get a better look at her. "There's an alarm on the garage door. When I saw the light blinking, I thought it might be you." He glanced into the empty car seat. "Where's Daniel?"

"Sleeping." She pointed to the monitor, which she'd propped on the dashboard. "If you listen closely, you can hear him snoring."

Scott smiled. "I take it you're just going for an imaginary spin."

"Yeah." She twisted the wheel again and let her bedroom slipper touch the gas pedal. "I love to go on make-believe trips. It's the real thing that gives me trouble."

He dropped his fingers to the door handle. "Feel like picking up a hitchhiker?"

She was embarrassed to realize that she'd actually flipped the locks. As if anyone was going to accost her here, in Scott Mulvaney's garage. She clicked the button to the open position.

"Sure. A poor wounded guy like you? Come on in."

Scott opened the door, and carefully arranged himself in the passenger seat. It was a tight fit. He had to slide the seat all the way back just to make room for the bulky cast on his foot.

He was really too big for a car this size. He dominated it, blocking the light from his window. Immediately, the air in the car was warmer, and she caught a faint whiff of his lemony aftershave.

He turned his face toward her. In the half light she could just make out the sparkle in his eyes and the white gleam of his smile.

"Thanks, lady. Where are we headed? Niagara Falls? Sunset Strip? The Grand Canyon, maybe?"

She squeezed the steering wheel, wishing she had been thinking of such exotic destinations. Even in her dreams, her most daring adventures consisted of actually walking through the glass doors of the party store in downtown Middlefield.

"Sure," she said, trying to enter into the fantasy. "Niagara sounds like fun. But we'll have to be back by morning. I've got a baby who'll want a bottle."

"And a party to put on," he added with a smile. "Otto and I attached the streamers to the ceiling tonight. He did the ladder climbing, but I played foreman and bossed him around. He was a good sport about it."

Beth had met Otto Baum, one of Scott's friends and a VP at Mulvaney Construction. He was a middle-aged father of four who seemed like a great guy.

"Are his kids invited?"

"Sure. Jeannie loves them. She loves everyone, really. She's a born extrovert. I think we've got about fifty kids showing up, at last count. Including the newest two, Marlena and Ally."

"Oh, good. You found my message."

"Yeah. Thanks." He leaned back. "I miss Jeannie like crazy, but in a way I'm glad she doesn't come back until right before the party. I'd have a heck of a time keeping her out. Every time we talk, she asks about how it's coming."

Beth knew that was true. She'd overheard some of those phone conversations when she was at the house. Scott missed Jeannie so much it hurt to see it.

"And thanks for making sure Angela didn't get an advance peek at the decorations. I'm sure she's not expecting much, given my past performances and my current physical condition, so I'm really hoping it'll knock her socks off."

"Daniel and I make a pretty good guard-dog team," Beth said, trying for a light tone. "I don't think Angela dared come close enough for him to touch her with his fingers. We overdid it a bit with the applesauce, I'm afraid."

He chuckled. "I hope he smeared his hand right across her hair. At least I *think* that's still hair under all the spray and mousse and gel and crap."

Beth didn't answer right away. He might talk disdainfully about the perfect Angela, but she knew that impressing his ex-wife was just as important to Scott as impressing his daughter.

"Angela is beautiful," she said. "Amazingly beautiful."

He shrugged. "Yep. She requires perfection of herself, which I guess is her business, but she requires it of everyone else, too. Which isn't."

"It wasn't an easy marriage, was it?"

He shook his head. "Far from it. I drove her insane, because I was so laid back, and she drove me insane, wanting to change me. Eventually, we were fighting all the time. It was a terrible environment for all of us…but especially for Jeannie."

"So you decided to divorce?"

"She decided. As rotten as it was, I probably would have stuck it out, thinking I was protecting Jeannie. But Angela wanted perfection in a marriage, too, so she wasn't willing to settle for that."

Beth shifted on the seat, and bit back her instinctive response. "Settle" for Scott Mulvaney? What kind of woman couldn't see how amazing he was?

But she knew exactly what kind of woman. The mannequin-perfect snob who had come to Scott's door today.

"Anyhow, she agreed to an equitable joint-custody arrangement, and I have to admit she's been a good mother—better, really, now that I'm not around to keep her angry and stirred up."

"That must be a relief."

"It sure is. Luckily, Angela's got one truly warm spot in that cold heart of hers, and it's for Jeannie."

They sat in silence another minute. She couldn't shake the memory of Angela's expression as she pulled away from Daniel's sticky fingers. It shouldn't have stung—what did it matter what Angela Mulvaney thought of her? She'd probably never see the woman again.

And yet…

Scott looked over at her, obviously sensing some melancholy. He touched her shoulder. "She wasn't rude to you, was she?"

Beth shook her head. "No. Not really." She traced the molding of the steering wheel with her finger. "I guess it's just that seeing her… Seeing myself through her eyes… It just made me feel…"

She wasn't sure how to end the sentence without sounding pathetic. Inferior? Inadequate? Those weren't quite right.

"I guess it made me keenly aware of how much work I have left to do. Before I can really feel good about myself, I mean."

She wasn't looking at him, but she could feel him looking at her.

"That's absurd," he said quietly. "Angela is beautiful, yes. But you're—"

"I'm not fishing for a compliment," she broke in before he had to say something flowery just to buck her up. More of that infamous gruffness, she knew, but she couldn't stop herself. "I'm just dealing with reality. She's got it all together. I've made a lot of mistakes in my life, and I almost lost my way. I was lucky enough to find Tilly, and the rest of the people at Loving Life. I can't imagine what would have happened to me if I *hadn't* found them."

"They're wonderful," he agreed. "Mulvaney Construction has been one of their sponsors since the beginning. Tilly is a great lady."

She nodded. "Meeting her changed everything for me. It was the first time I ever saw true courage, I think."

For a moment he didn't say anything.

Then he touched her arm. "How could that be? Hadn't you ever looked in the mirror?"

"Oh, Scott, don't—"

"Beth, I've heard your story. You've endured things no one should have to endure."

"That's just it," she said. "I did endure them, when I should have had the courage to stand up and fight back. Or at least, I should've had the sense to run away."

"Isn't that what you did?"

"Eventually," she said. "But not until I found out I was pregnant. Then I knew I had to go, no matter how scared I was, no matter where I ended up. I wouldn't allow Tony to hurt my baby."

His hand was still on her arm. She was intensely aware of it.

"Exactly," he said. He moved his fingers a little, and a shivery feeling skittered up her arm. "You're extraordinary, Beth. You're very beautiful, and you're very brave. You have no reason to feel inferior to Angela, or to any other woman."

Without question, the atmosphere had changed. It was charged with something now, the same way the winter air was sometimes charged, pulsing with the weight of a snowstorm it wouldn't be able to hold much longer.

Her hands felt frozen on the steering wheel, and she couldn't force herself to turn her head.

"I should go back upstairs," she said stiffly. "Daniel might…might need me."

"Already?"

Finally she looked over at him. He was smiling, but under the smile lay a tension. He wanted more from her. He was attracted to her, and he obviously knew that the feeling was mutual.

And he couldn't understand why she was pulling away.

"Don't go," he said. His fingers tightened slightly against her arm, urging her toward him.

Her heart hitched.

His eyes were intense in the dim light. "We just started our trip, Beth. I don't think we've made it anywhere near Niagara Falls."

She knew she risked making him angry if she left him now. He'd never understand.

But she had no choice.

"No," she said. "We haven't. But I'm sorry, Scott. I think I've gone as far as I can go."

CHAPTER
~SIX~

Right after dinner the next night, disaster struck.

Beth was busy at the computer, trying to get the last of her claims processed before she had her weekly conference call with the managers down at the insurance company's main offices.

She was feeling pressured, because she knew they weren't keen on mothers who worked at home with their children around. Caving as everyone did to Tilly's clever advocacy, they'd agreed to give Beth a chance. But she feared that if she screwed up, or failed to meet her quotas, they would be all too ready to pounce.

Best-case scenario, they'd push her to put Daniel into day care. Worst case, they'd simply fire her, which would be all too easy. She was still in her ninety-day probation period.

So the truth was, she wasn't paying enough attention to Daniel. She didn't realize that the strap of her computer case had dangled over the side of the desk, right into Daniel's playpen.

She certainly didn't realize he could reach it.

But he could, and he must have been batting at it, trying to pull it down.

That would have been okay. The case was soft leather and couldn't hurt him much. But she'd set her training manual on top of the computer case, and it was very heavy, with sharp plastic edges and a large set of metal three-ring jaws.

The jaws were wide open right now, allowing her to remove any sections she needed to read.

The first hint she had of trouble was seeing the binder slip slowly from the desk. Before she could process what was happening, it had fallen into the playpen.

Daniel fell with a thump and instantly began to cry in loud, piercing shrieks.

"Oh, duckie, duckie," she said, jumping up and reaching into the playpen to try to sort out what had happened. When she peeled away the layers of paper, she finally found Daniel underneath.

His face was bright red from screaming, and blood was streaming down the side of his head.

"Oh, my God," she said, and for several minutes that seemed to be the last breath she took. She gathered him to her breast, still screaming, and dashed into the kitchen.

Ice. Ice was the answer to everything. She'd learned that the hard way, as her mother struggled to keep her father's physical violence a secret from the rest of the world.

With shaking hands she filled a plastic freezer bag with every ice cube she had, then pressed it against Daniel's head. He howled even harder. The blood had dripped into his eyes, and it was all over his little fisted, furious hands.

She grabbed her blue blanket she'd been so proud of, wrapped it around him, and somehow made her trembling legs carry the two of them down the stairs and into the garage. She opened the big door, strapped Daniel into his car seat, then slid her keys into the ignition and backed out.

As she passed the front yard, she saw Scott. He waved at her, asking her to stop. At first, she didn't want to. She was entirely focused on getting to the doctor's office, and she didn't want to slow down for anyone or anything.

And she wasn't ready to face him again, not after last night's drama in the garage. He had seemed frustrated when he'd left her and was probably still angry.

But all that was unimportant now. All that mattered was Daniel. And it would help to have someone to keep the ice on the cut. She couldn't do that and drive at the same time.

She braked, and Scott hobbled to the passenger door, pulled it open and arranged his awkward cast in the small space in record time.

"Thank you," she said. "His head. The ice—"

"Got it," Scott replied quickly. He twisted his body to reach Daniel. "Hey, buddy, it's okay. It's okay."

Daniel didn't stop crying, but at least he turned the volume down.

"Thank you," she said again.

"I saw you backing out. I heard Daniel screaming. What happened?"

"A heavy ring binder fell on him," she said, her eyes on the stoplights, trying to time them so that she never had to slow to a stop. "The metal rings were open. It got him just above the eyebrow, I think."

She shivered, suddenly, realizing how close it had come to his eye.

"I'm sure it'll be okay, Beth. Head wounds always look much worse than they are."

"But the blood."

"That's what it's like. It happened to Jeannie once, when she was about three. Even a tiny cut will bleed like crazy. It's scary as hell, but he's going to be fine."

She nodded. They drove the last mile without speaking, just listening to Daniel whimper, which was all he seemed capable of doing now. It was as if he'd worn himself out with crying.

Or with loss of blood? Beth pressed the accelerator harder.

Finally, they were at the doctor's office.

"You go ahead," Scott said. "I'll be too slow. I'll catch up and bring whatever you leave behind."

She nodded, extracted Daniel from his car seat and headed for the door.

Once inside, she made a beeline for the front desk.

"I'm Beth Dunnett. I need to see Dr. Arthur immediately. My son's been hurt."

She was surprised at how calm and coherent she sounded. She was surprised that she wasn't talking gibberish.

The woman looked at her over her reading glasses. "Are you a patient?"

"Yes."

She turned to the computer. "Did you say Dunnett? Do you have an appointment?"

"Please, there's no time to waste. My son needs help. He hit his head, and it's bleeding very badly."

"Just let Beth and Daniel in," Scott said, suddenly standing behind her shoulder. His voice was authoritative. "It's urgent. I'll fill out the forms."

Beth looked at him gratefully. Yes. He could do that. He could fill out the forms. He knew everything about her.

Finally the woman seemed to notice the blood. She stood up, suddenly alarmed, and ushered Beth through immediately.

At the last minute, Beth turned and looked for a split second at Scott, hoping he knew how grateful she was.

His face was dark, worried, tense. He looked almost as bad as she felt. But he nodded and tried to smile.

"I'll be here," he said.

IN THE END, DANIEL'S CUT required only one stitch, just above his left eyebrow. Dr. Arthur was wonderful with babies, and with the help of a tiny bit of local anesthetic, he managed to put the stitch in while Daniel played happily with his stethoscope.

"Good Mommy," Dr. Arthur said when Beth leaned over Daniel and chattered softly, helping to distract him. "You're being very brave, too."

She smiled, looking up from her son. "Stitches are nothing," she said. "I was afraid...all that blood..."

"Oh, that's the way with head cuts. They're a lot of sound and fury, usually signifying nothing."

He stepped back to admire his handiwork. "Not a big deal at all. Very superficial. Small scar, perhaps, but very dashing. Girls can't resist a boy with a scar. You'll have to beat them away with a stick."

Maybe it was the rush of relief, but by the time Dr. Arthur was finished, Beth was half in love with the old man. Impulsively, she hugged him as he handed her the prescription for antibiotic ointment. He grinned, then hugged her back.

"I love this part," he said, winking at his nurse. They all laughed, including Daniel.

The euphoria lasted until she arrived home and got Daniel fed and bathed and put in bed.

Scott insisted on returning to her apartment with her. She'd resisted at first, worried that the stairs might be too much of a struggle. He'd grown much better with his crutch, but still...

He ignored her. He had no intention of letting her handle this alone, and she realized, when he got upstairs, how grateful she was.

Now that the crisis has passed, it was as if she could think clearly for the first time in hours. And the thoughts weren't happy ones. She hadn't made her quota. She'd missed the telephone conference entirely. And she'd spent more than a hundred dollars on doctor bills and medicine, money she didn't have.

Plus, she and Scott had not yet discussed last night. She suspected that he was the kind of guy who always stepped up in a crisis, so the fact that he'd helped Daniel today didn't indicate anything about Scott's feelings toward Beth.

She didn't know how he felt, whether he was annoyed with her, or impatient, or whether he'd decided she was just too much trouble to get involved with.

Worst of all, she'd pulled him away from his last-minute party preparations. Jeannie's birthday was tomorrow, and he still had so much to do.

She should send him home.

But it was so soothing to have a partner in the kitchen, even a one-handed guy. He insisted that she have a sandwich, and had refused to let her do the work alone. He was clumsy and funny, trying to spread mustard with one hand, but it was so great to have someone to share laughter with on a night like this

"Here you go," he said as he limped into the living room, a glass of warm milk in his good hand. She carried the other glass and the sandwiches.

"Get comfortable," he said. "You'll feel better when you eat."

She felt better already, just being with him. But she didn't say that. She kicked off her shoes and pulled her feet up onto the sofa.

He grabbed the woven throw—*Mrs. Pinchot*—and shook it open.

Then he draped it over her, from her chest to her toes. He watched her while she took a sip of milk.

"You did great today," he said.

She shook her head. "I think I was working on pure instinct. And maybe a whopping dose of adrenaline."

"Still. You did it. It certainly should put to rest any question about whether you're strong enough to do what has to be done."

She set down her glass. She should have changed her shirt. It was stained with blood.

"It's strange," she said. "But I always seem to be able to overcome my fears when someone else needs me. Paradoxically, it's the little normal things I can't do. It's the everyday stuff that can bring on an absolutely crippling panic attack."

"Like what?"

"Like anything." She thought of the party store. "An emergency is easy. Getting Daniel to the doctor, or taking a friend to her job interview—that's a snap. But getting myself to the hairdresser, or to the grocery store—those are the things that seem almost impossible."

He leaned back into the secondhand upholstered armchair—which didn't even match the sofa, really. This was the first time he'd been in the apartment since she moved in. She wondered what he thought.

But she didn't have the energy to worry. He wasn't the judgmental type, and he knew her exact financial situation.

Besides, she had nothing to be ashamed of. Maybe she didn't have suites of elegant antiques, as he did, but she was clean and neat, and she loved every stick of this furniture. Each piece reminded her that she had friends, that lots of people in this world were rooting for her success.

He bit into his sandwich and took a minute to chew. He seemed to be mulling over the problem while he waited.

"So," he finally said, "the problem is very specific. There isn't anything you can't do. You've proved that over and over. You can do anything on this earth, no matter how stressful, as long as it's for someone else."

He put down his plate and leaned forward. In the small room, the furniture was close together, and that brought him almost face-to-face with her.

"That's the real problem, then, isn't it? It's how you feel about *yourself*. You just don't believe that you're worth it. Other people, sure. For them, you'll overcome any fear. Just not for yourself."

She looked down at her hands. "You may be right. But I don't see how that helps. By definition, phobias aren't logical. Just being able to name it, to analyze it, doesn't change the facts."

"Someday, it will," he said, his voice somber. He reached out and settled his warm hand over hers. "The negative voice, the one that says you're not worth it. That isn't your voice. It's your father's voice. Or maybe Tony's. They're the ones that took away your joy in yourself. But they're gone now, Beth. You don't have to listen to them anymore."

She shut her eyes. She felt tears forming behind them, and she didn't want him to see. It was just that she was so tired. And she remembered those voices so well. "I'm not sure they'll ever be gone. Not really."

"Yes, they will. It'll just take time. But someday they'll be silent. And maybe, in that silence, you'll be able to hear the truth."

"But is the truth any better? The truth is I have done a lot of dumb things. I've messed up my life."

"No. The truth is that you're a very special woman, Beth. You're a wonderful mother, whose child is happy and healthy. You're a good and generous friend. You're fun and smart."

He lifted his hand to touch lightly the side of her cheek. "And you're beautiful. So beautiful."

She opened her eyes and looked at him. "Scott," she whispered.

He leaned forward another few inches. Perhaps she moved too, tilting her upper body toward him.

"Don't listen to those voices," he said. "Listen to me. I've never known a woman as brave and beautiful as you are."

She knew he was going to kiss her. Her whole body tingled, waiting for him to close the final inch, the last degree of separation.

She knew, and she didn't pull back.

When his mouth touched hers, it was the sweetest kiss she'd ever experienced. It was a kiss of giving. His lips were manly and hard, but he used them with tenderness. Even when he began to move and the heat began to build, the tenderness stayed.

She felt her tension seeping away. She felt her whole body softening. It was like falling into a cloud.

It would be so easy to ask him to stay tonight. To be with her. To fill her with this tenderness.

But it also would be a terrible mistake. She had nothing to offer Scott Mulvaney. They were from different worlds, and a night of touching, of kisses and physical bliss, was all they could ever share.

His world was perfectly ordered, full of big stone houses handed down from father to son. Of beautiful professional women who wore diamonds the size of marbles. Of perfect birthday parties for perfect little girls.

Her world was…completely different. There was no perfection here. Only an uphill climb out of the mess she'd made in the past.

And it was in her world that she'd have to live. It was her world that she'd have to conquer.

Tilly would be glad to know that Beth had finally learned that lesson, at least. She couldn't hand her life over to any man. And she wouldn't hand over her body for a night, or a month, or a year.

She was worth more than that. She was worth forever, and she would wait for it to come.

She shifted on the sofa, breaking the warm connection. Her wet lips felt suddenly cold.

He looked at her, his brows drawing down over his eyes.

"I need you to go now," she said.

He shook his head. "Why are you afraid of me?"

"I'm not." She reached up and touched his face. "Part of me wants very much to do this. But I won't. It would be a mistake, and I'm through making that kind of mistake."

"Isn't it a mistake to keep running away?" His voice was rough-edged. "Isn't it a mistake to wall yourself off from real feelings? From real life?"

She started to say she was sorry but closed her lips against the words. She wasn't sorry. She was glad.

Out of fear, she'd made a lot of stupid decisions in her life. To escape her father, she'd moved in with a man who was just as violent, a man that she knew didn't love her, wasn't ever really going to marry her. She'd sold herself short, over and over.

Being with Scott tonight would be the same thing, the same pattern. It would be an easy way to avoid the painful things, like loneliness and fear.

But those things had to be faced. And she was ready to face them.

"It's the right decision for me, Scott. I hope you understand."

His face looked dark, hollow and grim.

"I'm sorry, Beth," he said. "I just don't."

CHAPTER
SEVEN

At 11:00 a.m. that cold Saturday morning, the party store was a beehive of activity. From the jammed parking lot and the bustling crowd inside, you'd have thought every single person in New Jersey was celebrating something.

Beth stood near the entrance, Daniel's carrier in her hand, watching people come and go. Everyone was laughing, filled with eager anticipation.

Some carried big balloons shaped like spaceships and peace signs and dinosaurs. A brave young couple wrangled long tiki torches and armloads of pastel-colored leis past the other shoppers, clearly planning a party to banish the winter chill.

One smiling father carried a life-size cardboard Harry Potter under his arm, while his little boy trailed behind, zapping everyone with a small wooden stick that obviously was his magic wand.

He pointed it right at Beth and said "Pow!"

"Jim!" The father frowned. "Sorry about that," he said to Beth.

But she just laughed. "It's okay. I could use some magic right now."

Each time the door swung open, she could glimpse the costume section, where teenagers were trying on tricorn hats and eye patches, and slashing the air with plastic swords.

She wondered whether she could make it inside the store this time. Or had she once again overestimated herself?

When she woke up this morning, she'd been filled with a strange new confidence. She'd called her manager at the insurance company and explained the crisis that had made her miss the meeting. To her surprise, the manager had been quite sympathetic.

Then, with that worry behind her, Beth realized that she wanted very much to go to Jeannie's party.

Was she even welcome anymore? She couldn't be sure. When Scott had left last night, he'd been tense, his goodbye clipped and distant. He had clearly been disappointed in her—perhaps even angry.

She had no idea whether he'd want to see her again.

But she wanted to see him. Even if he had decided she was too neurotic and high-maintenance to be interested in romantically, surely they could still be friends.

She hoped so. After he'd left, she'd spent a long, uncomfortable night tossing and turning, rethinking every word, every look…every second of the kiss.

And she had realized that, hard as it had been to turn away from those kisses last night, it would be harder still to give up his friendship.

She'd come to depend on it, maybe more than was wise.

She needed to show him that she was making progress. That she was really trying. She needed to show herself, too.

She didn't have to wear a costume, of course. But everyone else was wearing one. She'd seen Scott in his ringmaster get-up, and he looked both adorable and handsome as sin.

So Beth had rummaged through her clothes, trying to find something that would work. First, she'd considered a clown. Heaven knew she had enough mismatched, baggy hand-me-down clothes to look like a ragamuffin.

But the truth was, she wanted to look pretty. She enjoyed Scott's admiration. She was a smarter woman now, but she was still a woman. And the appreciative glow in a handsome man's eyes felt great.

Trapeze artist, perhaps? But that was going too far. She wasn't confident enough yet for that. And she certainly didn't want to set off alarms in Angela's head. So she ignored the gorgeous spangled leotard and tights hanging right by the door, their sea-green sequins winking under the bright lights.

Someday, maybe. But not yet. She decided to stick with her plan to go dressed as a gypsy fortune-teller. She already owned a peasant blouse that would be perfect, and a colorful skirt. She'd driven here just to buy some of the extras, a scarf for her head, some cheap, dangly earrings, and maybe a jingle belt of gold coins and little gold bells.

The accessories would make the costume more fun. But they weren't strictly necessary.

She didn't *have* to go in.

As she felt her heart begin to race, she backed up a step. She wasn't trapped. She could go home. It wouldn't hurt anything if she turned around now and drove back to the apartment...

Suddenly, she stopped the little, nervous voice inside.

No, it wouldn't really hurt anything to give up now and go home.

But she wasn't going to do it.

She remembered what Tilly and the therapists had always told her, and for the first time it really made sense.

Panic couldn't hurt her, not physically. It might feel as if she couldn't breathe, but in reality she *could*. It might feel as if her lungs were going to turn to stone, but in reality they *wouldn't*.

The only thing to fear, as someone had famously said, was fear itself.

She peered through the window one more time. Wasn't that a belly dancer's hip scarf hanging right there by the hula skirt? Wouldn't it be perfect for her gypsy costume?

"Excuse me." A woman had come up right behind Beth, and she realized that, once again, she was blocking the doorway.

Beth took a deep breath, her heart racing.

The woman made an impatient noise. "Miss? Are you going in?"

"Yes," Beth said with a smile. She wrapped her fingers around the silver door handle and gave it a push. "Yes. I think I am."

SHE GOT TO THE PARTY just in time. Scott was in the tower room, working with Otto Baum, who was dressed like a lion tamer, complete with pith helmet and whip.

"Hey, Beth!" Otto stood on a ladder, fixing a streamer that had come loose from its putty. "You look great. Thank God you're here. I could really use an assistant with two good legs."

Scott, who was standing by the old-fashioned, bright red popcorn cart, getting the first batch started, looked over at her. She couldn't read his expression. She felt her chest tightening. Surely he wasn't so angry that he would refuse to speak to her?

Otto, who apparently wasn't aware of any undercurrents, wiggled his eyebrows salaciously. "And you definitely do have two good legs."

He laughed at his own nonsense, then cursed as the streamer came loose again. "Hell. Can you hand me some more putty, Beth? If I ask him to, it'll be a week before he limps over here."

Beth glanced around and saw the putty lying on the floor, just a couple of feet from the ladder. She retrieved it and handed it up to Otto.

She glanced over at Scott. "I thought maybe I could be helpful," she said carefully. "You did say you could use another pair of hands...."

"Of course," he said, but his voice sounded stiff. "That's great. Thanks."

Polite, cool and definitely distant. But what exactly did that attitude mean? Was he trying to keep Otto from realizing anything had happened between them? Or was that cool courtesy hiding real annoyance?

She turned to Otto. "You two look pretty awesome," she said, making sure to include both men, although Scott was clearly the star. Otto had a middle-aged softness that was cute in a teddy bear way, but Scott was gorgeous. The top hat would have looked foolish on a lesser man, but his height and trimly muscled physique pulled it off…even with his leg in a cast.

She wondered how she'd had the strength to resist him last night.

"Maybe you can read my palm later," Otto said with a smile. "Although I can already tell I'm going to meet a mysterious, dark and beautiful woman."

"Yeah. It'll be your wife." Scott sounded slightly irritable. "Quit flirting and get that streamer up. We're running out of time."

Otto chuckled. "Hey," he said. "I didn't notice Daniel's costume. Cute!"

Smiling, Beth held up the baby carrier. She'd tied a multicolored bandanna around Daniel's head, which had the fringe benefit of covering up his bandage. Then she'd dressed him in a pair of black pants, a black T-shirt, and his best black socks.

"He's my gypsy bodyguard," she said.

Both men laughed, which delighted Daniel. He wriggled madly in his carrier, arching his back as if he wanted to get out and strut his costume.

But suddenly, when his face turned toward the ceiling, he noticed the balloons high above him, and forgot everything else. He stared at the undulating colors, openmouthed, clearly fascinated.

Beth set his carrier on the floor and moved to the far wall, where a unicorn's horn was peeling away. She pressed it into place again. "Is anyone else here yet?"

"Angela just called," Scott answered, speaking loudly over the popping corn. It smelled delicious. Beth had forgotten to eat breakfast, being too focused on conquering the party store. "She and Jeannie are on their way. They should be here any second, actually."

Beth's stomach twisted. She wasn't afraid of Angela anymore. But meeting Scott's daughter…

For some reason, it felt like taking a very hard test, one she hadn't studied for, and wasn't at all sure she could pass.

After a couple of minutes, during which Beth and Otto did most of the talking, Scott hobbled out front to check on the hired magician, who had just arrived with a box of props that needed to be set up. The clown who made balloon-animals drove up just behind him, and then a couple of children dressed as lions and tigers.

The party was clearly under way.

Beth remained in the tower room with Otto, who still needed help reinforcing the streamers, but she watched through the front window, waiting for any sign of Angela and Jeannie.

In a lull, she remembered the calliope music. She rushed over to the window seat, pulled out the boom box and inserted the CD. The happy, lilting whistles filled the room.

Daniel began to make chirping noises, as if he wanted to sing. Beth unhooked him from his seat, put him against her shoulder, and swirled him happily around the room.

"The music is a nice touch," Otto said from his perch high on the ladder. She smiled up at him and noticed that he had a strange expression on his broad face. "But you do know——"

He broke off, his gaze drawn to the front yard. "There she is now. The birthday girl arrives!"

Beth hurried to the window, Daniel still in her arms. She stood to one side, where she could see but, with any kind of luck, wouldn't be spotted.

Her heart was tripping all over itself. This was it—this was the heart of Scott Mulvaney's life. This was what made him tick, what made him get up in the morning.

Beth knew, without ever being told, that Jeannie meant more to him than any woman ever could. She knew that if Jeannie decided she didn't like Beth, there could never be a comfortable friendship between Beth and Scott.

She knew, because that was how she felt about Daniel.

When she got her first glimpse of the little girl, she heard herself inhale sharply. Jeannie looked so much like her mother it was shocking. The child was slender, just like Angela, with long, dark hair that flowed down her back, and a strong, perfect-oval face.

She was also beautiful like her mother, and extremely graceful in her crisp pink tutu and sequined leotard.

But the broad, open smile on her face was pure Scott. She tumbled out of her mother's car, and began to run toward the house. Beth saw Scott come into view, moving as fast as his crutch and cast would allow. His face was beaming. His free arm, the one in the cast, was outstretched toward his daughter.

Jeannie barreled up the front walk, leaving Angela to follow slowly in her wake.

Finally, the little girl reached Scott, and they collided enthusiastically. They both laughed for a second, and then she held out her arms. The hug that followed was so heartfelt, so tender, that Beth felt herself choking up.

This was a kind of fatherhood she'd never seen before.

Beth's gaze flickered to Angela, who was watching with a tender smile. Even a divorced ex-wife couldn't help being glad that her daughter was loved so completely.

Finally, father and daughter pulled apart. Scott bent over his Jeannie, stroking her hair. The little girl gazed adoringly up at him.

And then they both began to move their hands, gesturing gracefully, but very fast. Sometimes separately, sometimes together.

"What…?" Beth exhaled the word under her breath.

They were clearly speaking in sign language.

"I had a feeling you didn't know."

Beth hadn't realized that Otto had climbed down off the ladder and was standing at her shoulder, watching her watch the reunion of father and daughter.

"You didn't know that Jeannie was hearing impaired?"

"No." Beth shook her head, trying to take it in. "No. I had no idea. The way he talks about her… I would never have guessed that she wasn't completely perfect."

Otto smiled. "I guess that's because, in Scott's eyes, she *is* perfect.

That's one of Scott's strong points, don't you think? He takes people as they are."

Beth wondered if Otto was sending her a reassuring message about her own value in Scott's eyes, in spite of her troubled past.

But he probably didn't even know her background. She got the impression Scott had never mentioned her struggles to anyone, just as he'd never mentioned Jeannie's struggles to her. Otto was right. Scott always focused on people's strengths, not their weaknesses.

Scott was one of the lucky people who knew how to be content with reality. He knew how to say yes. Yes to love, yes to happiness. Yes to life itself, with all its challenges and imperfections.

"Jeannie seems happy," she said.

"She is. They've never treated her as disabled. She's great at sign language, and lipreading, too. You couldn't find a more self-confident, normal little girl."

Several other children had joined them now, and some of them clearly knew how to sign. Either they were deaf, as well, or they had learned sign because they wanted to communicate with Jeannie.

Beth didn't understand what they were saying, but the enthusiasm and the sheer innocent energy of the conversation were universally understood.

"You should go meet her," Otto said. "You'll like her. And she'll like you, too."

She wanted to, but there was such a crowd of strangers around the little girl. So much noise. No easy escape, once she'd joined the group.

Beth could feel her heart speeding up already. She could feel the old urge to say no, to give in to fear, to run and hide.

Did she have the courage to quiet that little negative voice?

She had taken some big steps already today. She'd conquered her fear of the party store. She'd said yes to the party itself, in spite of the people and the lights and the chaos.

Maybe, over the past couple of weeks, some of Scott's positive energy had rubbed off on her.

Maybe she had one more leap of faith in her today.

She didn't put Daniel back in his carrier. She kept him against her shoulder, taking courage from his warm, bouncing energy. Her gypsy belt jingling, she made her way through clusters of giggling children and bobbing clouds of big balloons.

Finally, her breath coming shallowly and fast, she reached the front door, just as Scott and Jeannie were coming in.

"Hi," he said quietly. "We were looking for you. Jeannie wanted to meet you."

He turned to the little girl and signed a short sentence. While he moved his hands, he spoke the words out loud, clearly for Beth's sake.

"Jeannie, this is my friend Beth, the one who has been helping with the party. And that's her baby, Daniel."

Jeannie's face lit with excitement. She reached out and shook Beth's hand, then began eagerly to sign again. Her tiara wobbled as she moved. She couldn't seem to get the gestures out fast enough.

Scott watched carefully, his gaze on his daughter, his expression full of protective love. Then he turned to Beth.

"She says she's happy to meet you, she thinks you're very pretty, and she loves your costumes. And she says Daniel is the cutest baby she's ever seen. She wonders if you would be willing to let her hold him."

Jeannie was watching Beth carefully. She had her hands up against her pink-sequined chest, as if she were holding her breath, awaiting the verdict.

Suddenly she tugged on her dad's sleeve. He bent down and she signed a little more. She pointed to his wrist cast and giggled.

Scott smiled. Then he turned his gaze once again toward Beth.

"She says to tell you she'll be very careful. She wants you to know she's not as clumsy as I am."

Beth smiled at Jeannie. Daniel was already leaning forward, dazzled by the rhinestones in her tiara. He wanted to be Jeannie's friend.

She turned to Scott. "What is the sign for *yes?*"

He hesitated a minute, and then he showed her.

She turned to Jeannie, signed "yes," and then held Daniel out close to the little girl's outstretched hands. Jeannie accepted the baby's wriggling weight with somber care. She adjusted him against her shoulder, patted his back, then dropped a kiss on the back of his head. Without her hands free, she couldn't sign any words, but the awed look on her face spoke volumes.

"She loves babies," Scott said. "Funny. It seems like just yesterday she was a baby herself. I know six isn't such a great age, but the time goes so fast."

"I know." Beth was so glad to see Scott so happy. And she was so glad that he was talking to her like this, without the strain she'd seen earlier. "In just the few months I've had Daniel, I can already see how quickly they change. It's exciting. But it's also…scary."

He glanced at her. "Most things are a little of both. Most important things, anyhow. Most of the things that are worth doing."

She wasn't sure what to say. Was she imagining that his comment was a reference to last night? Just because she had been obsessing about it didn't mean he had, too.

A gaggle of little girls swarmed up to them then, and the opportunity to respond was lost. He managed to help get Daniel back to her in one piece, before the children could start to kiss and pat and terrify him. But then Scott was swept away in a wave of dancing and laughter.

Suddenly she noticed Angela standing nearby, watching Scott and Jeannie as they went into the house. She was the only person here who hadn't worn a costume. But perhaps her navy-blue suit was a costume of sorts. She had come as the Perfect Woman, and there was no such thing in the real world. In its way, it was as much an act as Beth's gypsy.

Beth wondered suddenly what insecurities that costume covered up.

Angela seemed to realize she was being watched, and glanced over at Beth. At first she didn't recognize her, but Beth saw the moment awareness dawned. Followed by shock. The frowsy "housekeeper" she'd met the other day, was a costumed guest at the party?

Angela hid her surprise well. She opened her lips with her usual frosty half smile. But Beth was surprised to see that her eyes still held a hint of wistful longing, obviously the result of observing the uninhibited love between her ex-husband and her daughter.

"Your daughter is beautiful," Beth said. Why not make the first move? Even ice queens probably adored their daughters.

"Thank you." Her glance seemed magnetically drawn back to Jeannie, who was now on Scott's shoulders, being carried triumphantly through the front door into the house to view her personal "circus."

"Scott has his flaws," Angela said, half to herself, her long, manicured fingers playing absently with the pearls of her necklace, "but as a parent, he's pretty amazing."

So Beth had been right. An ice queen, yes. But, in the end, just another mother, who feared for her child and prayed that all would be well.

Beth smiled without rancor, suddenly free from intimidation and fear. "Funny," she said. "That's almost exactly the same thing he said about you."

CHAPTER EIGHT

Beth wasn't really sure how it happened, but about halfway through the party, she found herself telling fortunes for the children.

Someone, maybe Otto, draped a purple tablecloth over the kitchen table and brought a big glass bowl out and turned it upside down to create a makeshift crystal ball. The kids thought it was fabulous, and lined up with dimes tightly clutched in their fists, waiting for their turn to cross the gypsy's palm with silver.

At first Beth was self-conscious. When she'd decided to attend the party, she'd hoped to sit quietly in the background, or anonymously circulate with trays of animal crackers and Panther Punch. She'd never dreamed of being this conspicuous.

But it didn't take long for the anxiety to fade away. Six-year-old children weren't exactly very critical audiences. They plopped down on the chair provided, and with wide eyes and open mouths they extended their palms.

Daniel cooperatively slept through most of it, and eventually Beth began to enjoy herself. She discovered she was pretty good at interacting with the children, and it was easy to intuit what they wanted to hear. Mostly, she realized, every human being, big or small, rich or poor, had the same desires. Happiness, love, success.

After that, their costumes gave them away. The ballerinas wanted to be beautiful and admired. The lions and bears wanted to be brave and strong. The unicorns wanted their fantasies to come true. The butterflies craved freedom and grace.

Some of the children were hearing impaired, some weren't. It didn't make much difference in their dreams, though. They all nodded seriously and stared at the creases in their hands, trying to see what the gypsy saw.

Their parents came with them, of course, and signed for the children who couldn't read lips. Beth knew they wanted to be sure the gypsy didn't scare the little ones, or disappoint them. Occasionally, just for fun, the parents would put out their hands, too. The children would giggle as Beth solemnly intoned the same fortune over and over——great joy, great happiness, great love.

Even the parents looked grateful.

Beth smiled at each one, feeling more comfortable than she had in a long time, as if she actually fit in. Out there, in the real world, they all might be pigeon-holed into different slots—doctor, plumber, homeless mom or CEO.

But here, in the gypsy's tent, everyone was part of the same human family.

After about an hour, the line tapered off. Beth leaned back in the chair, sighing contentedly. She pulled off her heavy earrings and massaged her aching ears. Beside her, Daniel still slept.

"So." Scott looked in through the kitchen doorway. "Do you think there's one last prediction lurking in that crystal ball?"

She dropped the earrings on the table. "Madame Beth doesn't use the crystal ball," she said in her best gypsy voice. "Madame Beth sees the future in the palm."

Scott smiled. "Okay. Read mine, then, and tell me what you see."

He made his way clumsily to the chair and collapsed into it with a heavy sigh. She wondered if he was tired, or if the crutch was hurting his arm. He had been pushing his limits for hours, trying to be the perfect host in spite of his injuries.

He held out his hand. For just a moment, she hesitated, but then she took it. It was warm under her fingers.

"Let me see. Yes. It is a good palm. A good life. You will know great happiness, because you bring great happiness to others."

He held his palm still, but he shook his head. "That's not what I want to know."

She glanced up at him. His face was serious, but his eyes were up-tilted, as if he suppressed a smile.

"Of course," she continued smoothly. "I see riches, too. Much success, a shower of gold wherever you go."

He shook his head again, slowly and emphatically. "Nope. Don't care about the money, either."

She tilted her head, smiling slightly. "Madame Beth is not finished. You must stop interrupting her. Yes, here, I see long life. You will live to a great age, surrounded by your children, and their children."

"Sorry," he said. "That's not it, either."

She glared at him. "Do not make Madame Beth angry."

"Then Madame Beth had better tell me what I want to know. What does my hand show her about romance? More specifically, is there any chance that the woman I care about will ever return my feelings?"

Beth felt herself flushing. She let her fingers go slack, as if to drop his hand. But he was too quick for her. He reached out and reversed their positions, so that her palm lay faceup inside his fingers.

"Obviously Madame Beth doesn't see these things clearly. I think I'll have to do the fortune-telling on this one."

Beth didn't speak. She felt the familiar tingle of anxiety at being restrained, but she took a deep breath and told her muscles to relax. To her surprise, with very little resistance, they did.

He began to stroke along her palm, slowly, following one of the lines—though, because she was only a pretend gypsy, she had no idea which one it was.

"Look," he said. "Look at that long line. It shows a long journey, a hard path through sadness and fear. It has taken great courage to get to the end of this path, but you are almost there."

Her blood was still tingling in her palm, but for once it was a pleasurable sensation. She looked at his head, bent over her hand. She looked at his large, gentle fingers holding her trembling palm.

He hadn't given up on her.

Outside the kitchen, she heard the sounds of the party winding down. Children's voices were softer now, their laughter more subdued.

But it all seemed to be happening in some alternate universe. Right now, the four walls of the kitchen seemed like the ends of her earth. And it was all she needed.

"Yes," he said, nodding slowly. "It has been difficult, and you have struggled. But it is time to rest. You are almost there."

She took one more deep breath, for luck. She cleared her throat. "I'm glad to hear it. But where...where does my road end?"

He closed his fingers around her palm.

"Right here, Beth," he said, guiding her hand to his heart. "The road has led you here to me."

For once she didn't hesitate. She felt something warm and blissful spread through her chest, like sunshine moving into a shadowed nook.

She lifted her free hand, curled the fingers in and made the "yes" sign he'd taught her just a few hours ago.

"Yes," she said tremulously, in case she wasn't doing it right. And then with more confidence. *"Yes."*

It must have been the sign he'd been waiting for. With a crow of pleasure, he laughed triumphantly and leaned across the table to catch her lips with his.

Yes, her heart sang. Yes.

And, for a long time, that would be the only word she needed.

Maybe for the rest of her life.

Dear Reader,

At the best of times, being a mother is scary. A helpless child gazes up at you, depending on you for its very survival. You? With no experience, no confidence...no sleep? For too many women, motherhood doesn't come at the best of times. It comes when they're young, poor, homeless. It comes when they've been abused or abandoned.

Sally Hanna-Schaefer doesn't have to imagine how it feels. She's been there. To support her children after her husband abandoned them, she cleaned houses, took in ironing and offered day care to other women's kids. She did whatever it took. For most people, that would be victory enough. But Sally Hanna-Schaefer isn't "most people." When she got her life in order, she decided to help others.

One step at a time, the miracle of Mother/Child Residential Program was born. In 1981 she opened her first shelter for homeless women with children. Since then, more than six hundred women have "graduated" from Sally's program. But even Sally, with all her energy, practicality and sheer determination, can't help everyone. She hopes that her work will inspire others. "There are many ways you could help young women and their babies," she says. "The CFS Mother/Child Program is located in Woodbury, New Jersey. But every area of the country has similar needs, and starting a ministry for this population is possible anywhere!"

Even if you're not ready to start your own program, you can help Sally with hers. Go to http://home.comcast.net/~motherchild/gift.htm1 and see the list of items they need. Or send a contribution to Mother/Child Residential Program, 682 North Broad St., Woodbury, NJ 08096.

With your help, she can realize her dream—"to change the world, one baby at a time."

Kathleen O'Brien